Praise for Shootout

One of the things I quite enjoyed in this novel was the complexity of the interpersonal connections among the characters in each of the sisters' worlds, which reach far beyond sibling and peer dynamics. The characters' personalities are very well developed, with a raw honesty—not only the teens themselves, but the adults as well. We see their struggles portrayed clearly through very real, and changing, lenses. I found the hockey glossary helpful in explaining terminology I didn't always understand. An excellent read!

— **Alison Lohans,** *award winning author of Timefall and Canine Cupid*

Praise for the Jessie Mac Hockey Series!

Maureen knows her characters and the game. I found myself both believing Jessie and believing in her—this despite her terribly human tendency to speak when she shouldn't and not speak when she should. Ultimately, Jessie does choose the truth, and that makes her a hero.

— **Richard Harrison,** *Professor, Mount Royal University*

I enjoy Maureen Ulrich's writing because she explains hockey in a way that makes sense to me. Thrust into the world of girls hockey, Ulrich's reader learns the intricacies of playing on a girls team and being a girl playing on a boys team and the challenges of both.

— **Amy Mathers,** *Amy's Marathon of Books*

The *Jessie Mac Hockey Series* played a huge role in my hockey career; it inspired me to push through tough times and pursue my AAA dream. It also taught me how to be a better teammate and person by not judging people without knowing their stories. This series helped me throughout my schooling, hockey, and personal life. It's more than hockey stories; it's a look into the real world and how situations can be handled. I would highly recommend reading this entertaining and captivating series.

— **Reauna,** *age 17*

Praise for Power Plays (Book One)

Power Plays deals with the important issue of bullying, specifically girl-on-girl violence. I was on the edge of my seat many times with some of the confrontations between Jessie and the other kids. The Jessie Mac Hockey Series is aimed at a YA audience and is obviously ideal for lovers of hockey. But for those of us who don't know our power play from our slapshot, there's a handy "Jessie Mac dictionary" at the back of the book with all the hockey-specific terms one might need. I was so caught up in Jessie's world that I kept turning the pages, desperate to find out what was going to happen next.

— **SaskBooks**

Ulrich demonstrates that there are many ways to succeed in relationships without resorting to any sort of bullying. She stresses the importance of accepting and celebrating the differences between people rather than using them as an excuse for malicious behaviour. This is an excellent novel which provides lots of action, a little romance, and a great deal to think about.

— *CM Magazine*

Maureen Ulrich has grasped many of the key issues young teens are dealing with today and rolled them into one to create a fast-paced novel, like the game of hockey. If in need for a humorous, uplifting read, *Power Plays* is definitely the right choice.

— *What If? Magazine*

Each teammate has a unique personality, and even the meanest characters turn out to be likable. Readers will relate to Jessie: she chats with her friends on the computer, dates, and has struggles with her parents. Some lessons are imparted along the way, mainly about teamwork, forgiveness, and bullying.

— *School Library Journal Review*

The author has managed to insert into the book, without seeming high-handed, a number of other topics, including racism, peer pressure, parental pressure, sexism, and drug and alcohol abuse. I highly recommend this book. With all the underlying themes and topics included in the book, I believe it would be a good one for junior high teachers to include in class discussions.

— *Prairie Fire Review of Books*

Praise for Face Off (Book Two)

Ulrich gives young readers a superb novel with something to pique every interest. Undercurrents of sex and alcohol run through the book along with adolescents learning both about themselves and about their relationships with their peers. Teenage girls will enjoy the sports action of the novel as well as the personal intrigues and will quite likely meet themselves or their friends in its pages.

— *CM Magazine*

So much can be weighed on one wrong moment. While everything seems to go the young hockey player's way in most aspects, she soon finds that one wrong move can shatter her pristine life. *Face Off* is a charming tale that will relate with many teens.

— *Midwest Book Review*

Teen girls who enjoy hockey will like this book. The author includes many other themes of interest to middle teens: teenage problems with alcohol, including binge drinking; self-mutilation (cutting); internet and school bullying; overcontrolling parents; teen violence; and having a parent who is gay.

— *Prairie Fire Review*

This well-paced and detailed book appeals to the reluctant reader. Canadian venues and language make this book appropriate for newer Canadians as well as solid pleasure reading. The author's straightforward character development and theme exploration would support a fun novel study.

— *Resources Links Review*

Praise for Breakaway (Book Three)

Breakaway steers clear of every cliché minefield and offers no simple resolutions. This is a story about a girl growing up, and while dating is a part of it, like friends and like hockey, it isn't central, and nothing ever works out storybook perfect. Jessie's hockey successes are satisfying and allow us to hope for her future, but again there is never a defying-all-odds miraculous victory. The girls win and they lose, and their tangled lives and friendships are part of the game they play. There are some great one-liners, and a lot of wonderful locker-room

— **Catherine Egan,** author of *Julia Vanishes*

Jessie faces uncharted situations with her teammates, coaches, and guys with her usual blend of impulsivity, kindness and soul searching, and Ulrich does a good job of bringing together story events that force Jessie to confront reality and make difficult decisions. Teen readers will recognize many of Jessie's struggles and find encouragement to face their own with honesty and courage.

— **Sharon Plumb,** author of *Kraamlok*

Breakaway has a gritty and realistic tension which will appeal to a variety of young adult female readers. There is hockey action, interpersonal drama, and romance. Jessie Mac not only steps up to lead her team but steps up in her own life to deal with personal issues and set her future course. Like its predecessors, *Breakaway* has all of the attributes of a prize winner and is a "must have" for the shelves of any classroom or library catering to readers in the intermediate young adult age group.

— **CM Magazine**

Ulrich understands the sub-culture of small-town hockey and how it keeps prairie communities alive and connected during the long, cold, winter months. Her many references to familiar Saskatchewan landmarks add a personal touch that make it easy for many readers to connect with the characters and locales described in the book. Breakaway is a fast moving, action packed novel that teenage girls will relate to at many different levels. The author's observations on how teens cope in today's contemporary society is refreshing and realistic.

— *SaskBooks*

SHOOTOUT

Maureen Ulrich

Book Four
in the *Jessie Mac Hockey Series*

A Wood Dragon Book

Typeset by: Christine Lee
Cover photograph by: GetMyPhoto.ca
Cover art by: Callum Jagger

Library and Archives Canada Cataloguing in Publication:
Ulrich, Maureen, 1958-
ISBN: 978-1-989078-64-8 (Paperback)
ISBN: 978-1-989078-65-5 (eBook)
Issued in print and electronic formats

Wood Dragon Books
Post Office 429, Mossbank, Saskatchewan, Canada,
S0H 3G0
www.WoodDragonBooks.com

Maureen Ulrich
Box 53, Lampman, Saskatchewan, Canada,
S0C 1N0
Contact: maureenulrichwrites@gmail.com

To the players, coaches, and support staff of the
2013-2014 University of Saskatchewan Huskies.

Photo by: Keith Minchin - Faces of Fredericton

"We play a game we love for the best school in the country."

Joanie Tulloch, U of S Huskies (2000-2005)

What is a Shootout?

In ice hockey, a shootout is a method of deciding the outcome of a game, which would otherwise end in a tie. A shootout occurs after a sudden death overtime. Each team takes a specified number of penalty shots. The team that scores the most wins the shootout and the game.

University of Saskatchewan Huskies*

No.	Name	Position	Year	Hometown
1	Cassidy Hendricks	G	2	Vancouver, BC
2	Brooke "Mutcher" Mutch	D	3	Nokomis, SK
4	Sara "Gresch" Greschner	F	3	Dodsland, SK
5	Alicia Van Alstyne	D	1	Winnipeg, MB
6	Hanna McGillivray	D	3	Saskatoon, SK
7	Brooke Patron	D	1	Redvers, SK
8	Alyssa Dobler	D	2	Saskatoon, SK
9	Marley "Erv" Ervine	F	3	Kindersley, SK
10	Kori Herner	F	1	Kindersley, SK
11	Paige Anakaer	F	3	Moose Jaw, SK
12	Carlee Hrenkiw	F	2	Melfort, SK
13	Kathy Parker**	F	2	Estevan, SK
14	Julia Flinton	D	3	Williams Lake, BC
15	Alexee Klassen	F	1	Winnipeg, MB
16	Cassandra "Jorgy" Jorgenson	F	1	Winnipeg, MB
17	Chelsey "Chun" Sundby	F	4	Big River, SK
18	Cami Wooster	F	5	Luseland, SK
19	Rachel "Johnny" Johnson	F	2	Edmonton, AB
20	Kira Bannatyne	D	1	Winnipeg, MB
21	Kandace "Cooker" Cook	F	4	Lloydminster, AB
22	Kennedy Harris	F	1	Winnipeg, MB
23	Jessica "Mac" McIntyre**	D	2	Estevan, SK
24	Isabelle "Izzie" Raines**	D	1	Calgary, AB
25	Darian Strosser**	F	4	Saskatoon, SK
26	Hailey Tyndall	F	1	Saskatoon, SK
27	Angela "Angie" Hodgson	F	3	Saskatoon, SK
28	Kaitlyn "Willo" Willoughby	F	1	Prince Albert, SK
35	Karen Lefsrud	G	1	Calgary, AB

Head Coach   Steve Kook

Assistant Coaches   Dan Erlandson (offence), Robin Ulrich (defence), Dean Owen (goalie), Vanessa Frederick (goalie)

Video/Equipment   Dave Westbury

Manager   Diane Glemser

*A comprehensive list for the 2013-14 team can be found at www.canadawest.org.
**Fictional character

Estevan U15 Moose

No.	Name	Position	Year
1	Toby Miller	G	2
2	Michael Carson	D	2
4	Brandon Brown	D	2
6	Josh Thompson	F	2
7	Shane Barber	F	2
8	Austin Hilderman	F	1
10	Jutin Bilku	F	1
12	Courtney McIntyre	F	2

Coach Clint Barber

Manager Abby Barber

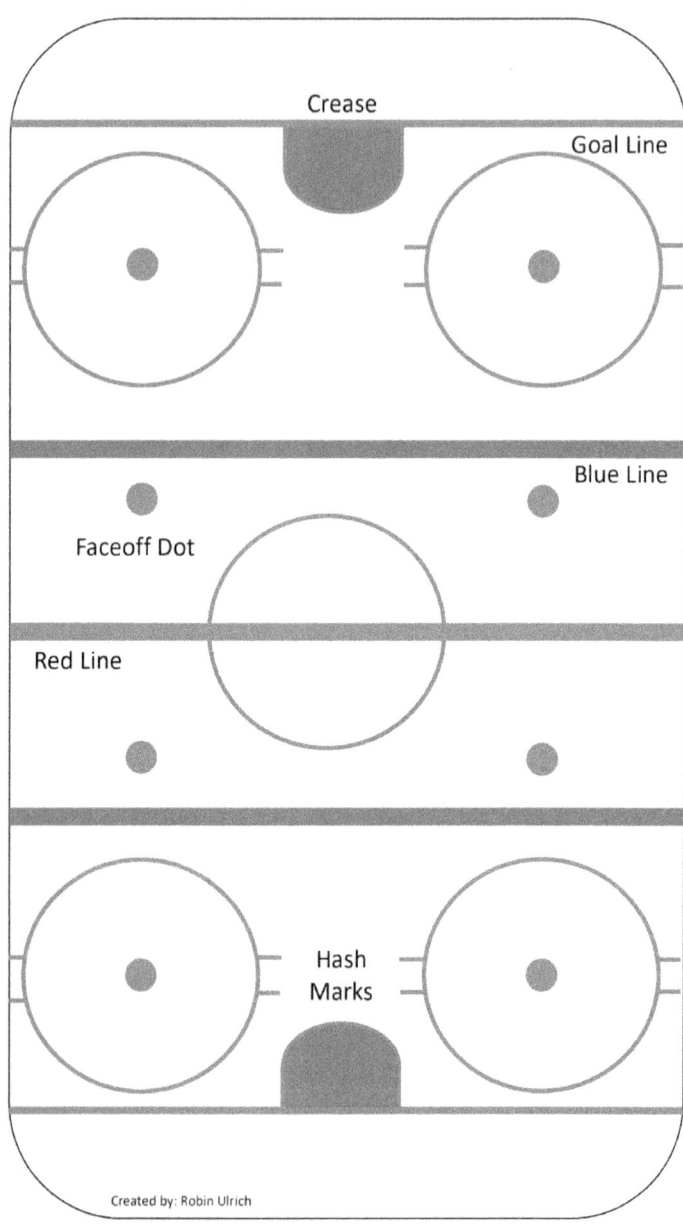

Don't forget to check out the glossary of hockey terms at the back!

1

"IT'S A BAD SPRAIN." Dr. Bilku points at the x-ray on the light board. "No volleyball for ten days, Courtney."

The disappointment is crushing. Her team's home tournament is this weekend.

Mom places a hand on Courtney's knee. "I'm sorry, Court."

Courtney resists the urge to jerk her knee away.

"The good news is you'll be healed up by hockey season," Dr. Bilku says.

"I'm not playing hockey," Courtney says.

"Estevan doesn't have a U15 girls team this year," Mom explains. "We gave Courtney a choice between hockey with Weyburn's team—or volleyball. She picked volleyball."

"You never made Jessie choose between hockey and volleyball," Courtney points out.

"I don't think Dr. Bilku's interested in this conversation," Mom says.

Dr. Bilku perches on the edge of his chair and smiles. "And how is Jessie doing? So exciting for her to be playing on a university team. Traveling all over Western Canada."

Her sister and the University of Saskatchewan Huskies. Everyone's favourite topic. So annoying. Courtney grits her teeth while Mom tells their family doctor about Jessie's hopes as a second-year. How long before Mom suggests they go to Saskatoon for the Huskies' first game?

"I guess Courtney will have to find other ways to keep busy this winter," Mom concludes.

"How about I play with my Barbies?" Courtney suggests.

Mom stands. "Let's go. We've taken enough of Dr. Bilku's time."

"I have two daughters and a son," the doctor says. "Sometimes Jutin and I feel like strangers in our own home. People run to their rooms and cry. Doors slam. It's a mystery."

Courtney isn't sure if he's talking to her or Mom. Either way, she doesn't care. She points to her wrist brace. "How long do I have to wear this?"

"A week," he replies. "When you leave, make an appointment with the receptionist to come see me then."

Courtney restrains the urge to slam the door with her good hand as she follows Mom out of Dr. Bilku's office. She smears away the tear sliding down her cheek and fumes while Mom makes the appointment. Then in the waiting room, Mom runs into someone she knows and stops to chat. Courtney storms out of St. Joseph's Hospital and into the cold October afternoon.

Volleyball season wraps up in a few weeks. After that, there'll be nothing to look forward to all winter. Just once. Can't things go according to plan? She was really looking forward to this weekend's tournament. She's finally figured out her overhand serve and—

Plink! A text from Pam, her best friend.

U ok? What the dr say?

She tries to text a reply, but the brace makes it awkward.

Plink!

This one's from Jessie.

Hey lil sis. What up?

Courtney shoves her phone in her back pocket with the wrong hand, and pain lances up her arm. She leans against the building and cradles her wrist. She closes her eyes and sucks in her breath until the throb subsides to an ache.

A truck rolls up, and a boy her age hops out of the passenger side. The truck roars off. The boy stands on the sidewalk and stares at her.

"Are you okay?" His dark eyes and thin face look familiar.

"Yeah." She wipes her eyes and sniffs. "Do I know you?"

"I'm Shane. I sat beside you at the band recital last June." He gives her a crooked smile.

"Oh yeah," she says. "You pretended to play, even though you didn't know the music. I'm Courtney."

"I know your name." He blushes and points at her wrist brace. "What happened?"

"I dove for a ball during practice," Courtney says. "Sprained it."

"Oh, yeah. You play with the Grade Nine team." He clears his throat. "You should make the junior squad next year. You're already tall enough."

The top of Shane's head scarcely reaches her eyes. She was taller than every boy in her homeroom last year. What guy wants to ask out—never mind dance with—a girl who towers over him? She decides to ignore his compliment. "Why are you here?"

He pulls up the leg of his jeans, revealing some stitches on his calf. "Getting these removed."

"How'd you do that?"

"Got cut trying out for AA." His thin shoulders sag. "Got cut in more ways than one. First my leg. Then me. Looks like house hockey this year."

"Which team?" she asks.

"The Moose. We could use a few more forwards. If you know any guys who'd be interested, they should call my dad. He's coaching."

"Who's on the team right now?" she asks.

When he lists them, she recognizes two names—Austin Hilderman and Dr. Bilku's son Jutin. They're younger brothers of Jessie's former teammates. Would the boys on the Moose mind having a girl on their team?

"Pretty cool that your sister plays with a university team," Shane says.

"Yeah. Super," she replies.

Doesn't he have an appointment to get to?

"So, how do you like high school so far?" he asks.

"It's okay." How could she begin to explain what a relief it is to start all over?

"I really like it," he says. "Especially once I got over being lost all the time."

Mom walks out of the hospital and beckons.

"I have to go," Courtney says.

"See you later. At least, I hope I do." Shane blushes again, steps around Mom, and disappears inside.

"Who was that?" Mom asks as they walk towards the car.

"A boy from school." Should she tell her mom about Shane's hockey team being short of players?

Mom clears her throat. "I'm sorry you feel your dad and I have treated you unfairly. We just figured two sports would be a lot for you to juggle in your first year of high school."

"Right," Courtney says. "Especially when you want to watch Jessie every weekend."

Mom doesn't respond as she unlocks the car doors, and they climb in.

Courtney's mind drifts to her conversation with Shane. Is this how karma works? She hurt her wrist so she could run into him and find out his team needs more players? Would she be taller than the other guys on his team too? Would she be able to handle playing body contact?

"Speaking of Jessie." Mom interrupts her thoughts. "If you can't play volleyball this weekend, would you mind if we all went to the Huskies' home opener? It would mean a lot to Jessie, and to your dad and me."

Courtney buckles her seatbelt and stares out the side window.

Jessie this. Jessie that. Step aside and make way for the superstar.

2

I TAKE A DEEP BREATH, exhale, and knock.

"Who is it?"

"It's Jessie McIntyre." I open the door and lean close to the crack. "I have an appointment. I'm in your Intro to Culture and Psychology class."

"Come in."

Professor Kerr faces her computer screen with her back turned to the door—and me. She clicks her mouse and scrolls through a document on her screen.

I check the wall clock. My stats lab starts in half an hour.

I clear my throat. "Professor Kerr?"

"It's *Dr.* Kerr." Her tone is brittle.

Shit. I know she's sticky about that.

"Sorry. *Dr.* Kerr." I try to emphasize it the same way she did, but it doesn't come out right.

She swivels her chair towards me. Her wire-rimmed glasses are perched on her nose. She has thin lips and perfectly penciled eyebrows. Beats me why she plucks the hairs out and draws them back in.

"I'm sorry to bother you." I sink into the chair across from her. "I'm confused about enculturation. I'm not sure that I understand how it's different from assimilation."

Dr. Kerr's face relaxes. Good sign.

"That confusion is more common than you might imagine," she says. "Also, it's perfectly fine to bother me. However, I could have cleared this up in class. You never ask questions, Ms. McIntyre."

I give her a smile. "I guess I'm shy."

As she launches into an explanation, I focus on her eyes, so she'll think I'm genuinely interested. That I spend every waking hour thinking about this stuff. Which I don't. I'm far too busy staying on top of Intermediate Calculus I, Numerical Analysis I, and Probability Theory.

When she finishes her explanation, I thank her politely.

"Anything else?" she asks.

Get down to business.

"Dr. Kerr, I have a scheduling conflict with your midterm on the 19th."

"Oh?"

"I play on the Huskie women's team, and I'm supposed to be in Edmonton that morning."

"Which team?"

"Hockey."

She sighs and removes her glasses. Her eyes flick over my Huskies windbreaker and toque.

"I'm not looking for special treatment," I assure her, "but for me to write the midterm here, I'd have to miss at least one game against the University of Alberta Pandas. They're our toughest competition."

"Is that so?" She splays her hand on her throat.

Is she making fun of me?

"However, if you let me write the exam in Edmonton on Friday morning under my coach's supervision, I won't have to let down my team."

"That sounds exactly like special treatment," she says.

I don't want to argue with her. Can't she look into my eyes and realize I'm not some jock trying to exploit my status as a university athlete?

Nope. I'm a math honours student who thought this psych class would be an easy A.

"Ms. McIntyre, some students think they can use psychology classes to pad their averages."

Did she just read my mind?

"I would never do that," I tell her. "I have a *passion* for psychology." It's the best word I can think of on short notice.

Dr. Kerr gives me a sideways look before putting on her glasses. She swings her chair back to her computer and resumes clicking.

I've been dismissed, but I can't leave without resolving this. I'm not missing those games because of her stupid midterm.

"Can I ask my coach to call you?" I persist.

"You do that," she says to her monitor.

Who respects a student who needs an adult to plead her case? I might as well have told her my mother would be calling. And I hate to ask Coach to speak up on my behalf. What if he decides he doesn't need me against the Pandas?

As I step in the elevator, I check my phone. I've got time to grab a coffee from the Tim's on the bottom level. While I'm waiting for my order, I spot my boyfriend in the flood of students leaving Place Riel.

I wave at him. "Hey Liam!" When he doesn't hear me, I shout, "Liam McArthur!"

He looks around, sees me at last, and flashes a gap-toothed smile. He slides through the pack of students and puts an arm around my shoulders. "Hey yourself." His dark eyes are warm. "How'd your meeting with Kerr go?"

While I explain, he checks his phone a couple of times. Is he even listening?

"That's too bad," he says when I'm done. He steps aside for the students trying to get around us. "Look. I'd like to talk longer, but I need to get to Bio."

"Okay. Are you coming to our game on Friday?" I ask. "First one ever in Merlis Belsher Place."

"I'll have to take a raincheck. Three midterms next week, hockey girl. See you on the fifth floor after your practice." He takes the stairs—two at a time— to the main level of the Arts Building.

I shove away disappointment. The fifth floor of the university library is one of the few places we meet since Liam moved into that crummy basement suite with two other guys. He's not comfortable coming to my dorm room at Athabasca Hall, and I don't blame him. I've seen the way some of the girls on my floor look at him. His cute smile can't hide the fact his dad's family is from Pheasant Rump First Nation.

"Large double-double for Jessie?" the Tim's employee asks.

"Thanks."

I grab my coffee and take the stairs. No time to waste. I've got a lot to pack in before our home opener—whether Liam comes or not.

3

COURTNEY CRADLES HER WRIST AGAINST her chest while she pedals her bike down Souris Avenue. The traffic makes her nervous. When she reaches the 7-Eleven on the corner of King Street, her best friend Pam waits in the parking lot.

Pam frowns when Courtney pulls up. "You're late."

"I'm sorry," Courtney says.

As Pam leads the way up King Street, Courtney falls behind, and some vehicles cut between them. She doesn't pedal as fast as she normally would. Can't Pam see she can't keep up? Does she even care? Lately Pam seems more worried about what the girls on the volleyball team think than—

Music thumps behind Courtney. A red car pulls up alongside her, and a guy with black curly hair leans out the passenger window.

"Hey!" he shouts overtop the music.

The car is far too close. Courtney pedals faster and tries to ignore him.

"What's the matter? You on the rag or something?" he says.

His friends howl.

Courtney slows and pulls in behind the car. The taillights flash, and she brakes to avoid slamming into the bumper while tires squeal behind her. Somehow, she manages not to dump her bike. The guy who yelled at her pounds the passenger door and cackles like a hyena. The red car squeals away.

Courtney makes a left at the next corner and pulls to the curb. Slows her breathing. Calms herself. A school bus passes her, ferrying children to the nearby K-8 school. Why did she tell Mom and Dad she was getting a ride with Pam's mom?

Pam.

Courtney sets out again, pedaling fast.

A light fog hangs over the dark blue roof of Estevan Comprehensive School. It's the place where she hopes to blend in, make new friends, and have the best four years of her life.

Pam, arms folded over her chest, now waits at the bicycle rack. "Where did you go?"

"I couldn't keep up. You should have waited for me," Courtney says.

Pam gives her a disgusted look. "You shouldn't have ridden your bike with your arm like that, but you wouldn't listen. You're so stubborn all the time."

Courtney bites back a retort. "Will you please help me with my lock?"

After both bikes are secured to the rack, the girls join the stream of students headed up the sidewalk to the school's main entrance. Should she tell Pam about the guys in the car?

But Pam's too busy talking about a cute guy in her science class and two girls on their volleyball team that are so, so smart and popular. Pam's a starter on the Grade Nine squad while Courtney usually warms the bench and waits to get subbed in. The only new friend Courtney's made at ECS is Christina Delgado, who is in her homeroom and English Language Arts class.

"Christina and I are doing a project on *The Wizard of Oz* for ELA. The book, not the movie," Courtney says.

Pam pulls the door open. "Why would you pick a book like *that*?"

Courtney steps inside quickly before the door hits her arm. "It's one of Christina's favourites. I read it over the weekend, and did you know—"

Without saying goodbye, Pam disappears into the crush of students in the foyer.

How rude is that? Courtney shields her arm as she navigates the narrow hallway to her locker, where Christina waits for her.

Christina's dark eyes are concerned. "Are you okay, Courtney? What happened to your arm?"

As Courtney explains, she feels as if her world is imploding. Her wrist. Those jerks in the red car. Plus, Pam is drifting.

"Do you need a ride after school?" Christina offers. "You can come with my dad and me. We can work on the ELA project at my house, and then Dad can take you home."

Christina's dad is a nurse at St. Joseph's Hospital, and her mom is a nail tech. Christina also has two little sisters. The Delgados moved to Canada from the Philippines several years ago.

"I'll let you know," Courtney says. "I better get to class." She fumbles with her lock.

"Let me help you," Christina says.

While Christina dials the combination, Courtney leans against her locker. Her own dad will pick up her and her bike if he has enough notice, but it might be fun to spend some time with Christina, who at least wants to be with her. Unlike Pam.

Four boys walk towards them. One is tall and with dark curly hair. The guy from the red car. Their eyes meet, and he says something to the boy next to him. His friend looks at her and laughs. She turns her back.

So much for blending in.

4

October 4
Canada West Conference Game 1
University of Saskatchewan Huskies vs. Mount Royal University Cougars
Merlis Belsher Place, Saskatoon

FRESH ICE SMELLS LIKE HOPE. All is new. All is possible.
Only 28 games stand between us and playoffs.

Fans pour into MBP. From the Huskie bench, I surf the arena for Mom, Dad, and Courtney, but I can't pick them out.

"Hey, there's your clip, Jessie." Izzie, a rookie and my new defence partner, points at the jumbotron.

The giant screen suspended over centre ice is playing my "hero" video, in which I raise my aviator sunglasses and wink. I'm wearing my new black jersey which has dark green lettering—a departure from the usual Huskie white on green or green on white. The next video is of Darian Strosser, a wiry fourth-year, who ruffles her short, red hair and pretends to kiss her biceps. The woman is *built*.

"I can't believe I'm playing in the first game *ever* in MBP," Izzie says.

Izzie's got that dreamy look that rookies have. She thinks she'll score a pile of goals and set Canada West on fire. Fresh ice does that to the best of us.

"We better get a win, or the men's team will never let us hear the end of it." Kathy Parker shuffles behind us as she joins the forwards at the other end of the bench. "F'ing Mount Royal."

"Was it fun playing minor hockey with Kathy?" Izzie asks me.

"Never a dull moment," I reply.

Cassidy, our second-year goaltender, skates to her crease. The other Huskie starters assemble on our blue line while Mount Royal's lineup skates to theirs. Some officials roll out a red carpet. After the speeches and ceremonial puck drop, Darian's girlfriend Melinda, a slight, pretty music major with long, dark hair, steps onto the carpet. As Melinda raises the microphone to her lips and "O Canada" swells the arena, I face our nation's flag and shift from skate to skate.

Like every young woman on this team, I'm humbled and proud to wear the Huskie logo. Every weekend is a dogfight in Canada West. Every point counts. That's why "work like a dog" is printed on the side of the door we use to step on the ice.

The little hockey players in the crowd go wild as Melinda's voice rises on the final note. The carpet is removed, the starters square off at centre ice, and our new season's underway.

I'm mesmerized by the talent of our starting line. Cami, our team captain and our only fifth-year, is a wizard with the puck. Willo is a rookie with speed to burn, and Erv is a tenacious third-year who will do whatever it takes to win her shift.

But I soon shift my attention as Robbie, the Huskie defence coach, rolls our top D—Flinton, Mutcher, Hanna, and Dobler. I can't wait to show Robbie what I can do.

At last, Robbie taps my shoulder. "You're up, Jessie."

I nod at Izzie.

The faceoff is in Mount Royal's end. When 17 chips the puck past me at the blue line, I chase her and tap her shins with my stick, then try to rub her out along the boards. She goes down in a heap, and I poke the puck away from her.

The referee blows her whistle. "23 Black. Two minutes for body contact."

"I didn't hit her! She *fell*!" I argue as the linesperson escorts me to the penalty box.

My fury fades as I watch our penalty killers Cami, Willo, Flinton, and Mutcher trap Mount Royal's power play unit in their own end. When I return to our bench, Robbie sends Izzie and me on the next shift. We rattle around in our end, allow four shots on Cassidy, and hang our heads as we step off the ice.

"We need to get it together," I tell Izzie as I avoid Robbie's gaze.

Mount Royal takes back-to-back penalties and Izzie and I see no action for the next few minutes while our power play units get a workout. They fail to score and when we're five-on-five again, Robbie gives Izzie and me another chance. A few seconds into our shift, 3 and 10 take advantage of a misread between Izzie and me. After a quick pass up the ice, 2 rips a shot under Cassidy's arm, and Mount Royal jumps ahead 1-0.

Robbie gives me the stink eye as I return to our box.

Our Head Coach, who stands on top of the bench behind us, looks down at me.

"Communicate with your D partner," he says.

Crap.

When Cami earns two minutes for interference, Robbie leans on our top D. Then, in the final minute of the period, she pairs Flinton and Izzie. I'd love to have Flinton for a partner. She's a smart, solid D with a shot like a howitzer. Izzie reads the play well and passes with confidence while I simmer in frustration.

I normally love the way our coaches talk to us between periods, but tonight I feel disconnected. Coach waves his big hands and speaks earnestly while he rolls video of Mount Royal's breakout on the television monitor. Robbie draws up a play for Mutcher and Flinton on her iPad.

Dan, the Huskie offence coach, rakes a hand through his thick, dark hair as he admonishes Hailey and Kori, two of our rookie forwards. "Don't play down to their level. Move your feet. Beat them to the puck."

I'm relieved when I get a shift with Hanna early in the second period. When I try to saucer a pass to her, 27 intercepts and forces Cassidy to make a quick glove save. Izzie taps me on the shoulder and replaces me for the next faceoff.

That's all the time I get?

Later, when Mount Royal takes a roughing penalty, Izzie gets a shift on the power play. Kathy, Carlee, and Johnny—all second-year forwards—set up in Mount Royal's end. Kathy wins the faceoff to Izzie. A few seconds later, Izzie one-times a slapper, and Kathy deflects it in.

Score!

It's the first Huskie goal in our new rink, but I don't look at the jumbotron, where Kathy's hero video will be playing. When Kathy, Izzie, and the rest sweep, screaming, past our bench, I lift my hand for a high-five, but I feel empty inside.

As she wiggles between Flinton and me, Izzie beams. "An assist in my first game!"

"Way to go, Izzie!" Flinton says.

Robbie pats Izzie's helmet, and Coach bends down to congratulate her. Even Dan walks down the bench to slap her shoulder.

I'd kill for that praise.

⋙

We win 3-1.

After the postgame meeting, I strip off my equipment, throw on my shorts and a cool-down top, and head up to the concourse. I'm not looking forward to Q and A with my family. I got more ice-time in the third period, but I played like crap.

Rink rats and girls in minor hockey jerseys scamper around the concourse to gather autographs. Izzie's attracted a crowd. I sign a few programs and ask the youngsters about their own teams and what positions they play.

"Did you get a goal?" one asks.

I reach for her pen. "Not this time."

Not *any* time. I haven't scored even once in my university career.

She pulls the pen back, as if she's afraid I'll contaminate it. "Who did?"

I point at Kathy, and the little twerp darts off, waving her program.

Dad says behind me, "This is some facility, huh? I can't wait to see the rest."

I give him a hug.

"Your coach promised he'd take us parents on a tour," Dad says. "Afterwards, there's drinks and snacks in the alumni lounge."

"I know that, Dad. Where's Mom and Courtney?"

"Your sister's in the washroom. And your mom's over there," he says.

Near the exit to the lower level, Mom's talking to Coach and Basil, the Huskies' Athletic Director. Mom grew up in Saskatoon, and Basil was her high school principal. In fact, she's doing *all* the talking. What's she telling them?

Dad's arm encircles my shoulders. "Don't take your lack of ice-time personally. Your coaches will need you against Manitoba and Alberta."

But I haven't told Coach about my psych midterm yet. I can only hope I'm *going* to Alberta.

"Looks like the tour's starting," Dad says.

He hurries towards the other parents just as my sister exits the washroom. Courtney looks totally unimpressed to be here, and I know better than to try to hug her.

"Hey, little sis." I spread my arms and turn in a slow circle. "Cool barn, huh?"

She shrugs.

"Yeah. Hardly a barn. Did you like our new jerseys?" I prompt.

She shrugs again. "Kinda hard to read the names and numbers. Dad thought so too." She flicks me a look. "I want to talk to you about something later."

"Oh? What?"

"*Later,*" she says.

She turns and walks towards the exit where Coach holds the door open. Mom and Dad and the others have already headed downstairs.

"Watch out for wet paint!" Coach calls to Courtney as she approaches. "Lots of work to be done yet!"

Kathy leans an elbow on my shoulder. "What's up with Little Mac?"

"Not sure."

"Meanwhile, you had a brutal game," she says. "That's gotta sting."

There's no friend like an old friend who tells you exactly how it is.

"Let's go," I say.

The adults oo and ah over our new locker room's high ceiling, grey carpet, black benches, and rows of identical stalls. Dad takes a picture of Courtney and me in front of my stall, and then a closeup of my name bar. Next, I lead Dad into the study lounge, where some of our third- and fourth-year players hang out around a table.

"A big step up from the Rutherford Rink, right everyone?" Dad comments.

"You better believe it," Angie says, "but Old Ruthy had character."

"Also powdered soap dispensers. I bet you won't find *those* anywhere else," Cooker says.

"Is it true you used a construction trailer as a dressing room?" Izzie asks behind me.

"Yeah, and *liked* it," Chun says.

I step aside and let Izzie by. She plops down next to Paige like she's known her all her life.

"Izzie, let me tell you a story." Paige puts a hand on Izzie's shoulder. "Ruthy had a white pole in the middle of the bench. Players on Coach's shit list ended up behind it where he couldn't see them. We called it 'White Pole Syndrome.'"

Maybe it could still happen. Even though MBP has no "white pole." Maybe it's happening already. Like a curse.

Cooker pokes Izzie's arm. "Why aren't you taking notes, rook? This is Huskie *history*."

Right now, I miss Ruthy. The glow of my rookie year there is getting dimmer every minute.

After the parents are done admiring our study area and exercise facilities, we head up to the alumni lounge and get some snacks. I sit next to Courtney at a high table.

"So, what's up?" I ask.

Courtney's latest wild notion pours out. No girls team. Shane Barber. Boys hockey. I can tell she's excited. Oh no.

"That's a big step," I say when she's finished. "Have you talked to Shane's dad?"

"Not yet." She sips her Coke. "Do you know him?"

"I played AAA with his daughter Dayna. Clint's a good guy. He knows hockey."

Kathy pulls up a chair beside me.

"Congrats on the goal," Courtney says.

She hasn't said one nice thing about the way *I* played.

"Thanks." Kathy takes off her toque and stuffs it in her coat pocket. "No matter what happens, your Auntie Kathy will always be the first Huskie to score in this building,"

"Boys hockey," I say, nudging my sister.

"Right." She tucks her long blonde hair behind her ears. "Do you think I should do it?"

This is a revelation. Normally she doesn't want my opinion on anything—least of all her life. I have to consider my words carefully. "You're a fast skater, but you'll be slightly behind in shooting and stickhandling."

Slightly. That's an understatement.

Courtney frowns.

Kathy grabs Courtney's arm. "Little Mac, are you going to play U15 house?"

"Maybe," she says.

"But more importantly, there's the hitting," I continue. "The guys won't rub you out on the boards. They'll *crush* you. You could get hurt." I point a hunk of cauliflower at Courtney. "We're talking broken wrists. Concussions. Busted collar bones."

"Not to mention torn ACLs," Kathy contributes.

"Court, do you know how to give or take a hit?" I ask.

Courtney's brown eyes blink. Am I getting through to her?

"Do you want to be the player some *jerk* decides to launch into next week?" I persist.

"That's why you have teammates," Kathy says to Courtney. "To protect you."

"I can protect myself," Courtney says.

She doesn't have a clue.

"Kathy, you aren't helping," I say.

"Get with the times, Mac. Just because *you* never played with the boys doesn't mean Little Mac can't." Kathy leans back in her chair. "Take it from me. I played. I understand the species. Male hockey players are thirty percent talk. Thirty percent aggression."

"What about the other forty?" Courtney asks.

"You'll find out when you date one," Kathy says.

"Not happening," I interject. "Court, this is a bad idea. Why didn't you just play with the Weyburn girls team?"

Her gaze pins me to my chair. "Mom and Dad would have complained every time they had to drive me for practice. Besides, the Weyburn girls *hate* me. And *you* always say guys are less complicated than girls. No drama. Isn't it time I found that out?"

I hold up my hands. "Okay."

"You *go*, Little Mac," Kathy says. "But I'm warning ya. Boys stink way worse than girls. I'm talking *radioactive*."

"Jessie, will you at least tell Mom and Dad you think it's okay?" Courtney pleads. "They'll listen to you."

What can I say? I'm a sucker for her big, brown eyes.

"All right. If that's what you want," I concede. "But don't make me regret this."

"I won't. I promise." Courtney slides off her chair and gives me a hug. "Thanks, Jessie."

These moments are so rare, I almost let myself enjoy them.

October 5
University of Saskatchewan Huskies vs. Mount Royal Cougars
Merlis Belsher Place, Saskatoon
Huskies 2-1 loss

Izzie parks her jeep on the street where Darian and Melinda live. Darian's hosting the Minute to Win It Olympics the vets have been planning for weeks as a team bonding exercise. Many of their vehicles are already here. Izzie and I are part of "The Swim Team" since cheesy bathing suits are easy to come by at Value Village.

"I can't wait, can you?" Izzie shuts off the jeep's engine and unbuckles her seatbelt. "This is going to be a blast!"

She's already shaken off Mount Royals' crows of victory and our coaches' disappointment. I got more shifts this afternoon, but Izzie and I were on the ice for both Mount Royal goals. I'm not looking forward to next week's one-on-one meeting with Robbie.

As Izzie grabs a duffle bag from the back seat, my phone vibrates. I can guess why Mom's calling. Courtney must have told her and Dad about playing with the U15 boys. I get out of the jeep to take the call.

"Don't be too long." Izzie uses her fob to lock the jeep. Bag bouncing, she sprints down the street towards Darian's house.

I press Accept. "What's up, Mom?"

"You *knew* Courtney wanted to play boys hockey?" Mom sounds tense.

"I'm sorry we didn't talk about it while you and Dad were here." Like I had time to do that. "Is Courtney listening right now?"

"She's inside the gas station, picking up a snack. We have to talk fast," Mom says.

She doesn't interrupt while I outline what Courtney and I discussed.

"We don't want her to play two sports," Mom says when I'm done. "She's not as good a student as you are. She has to work hard to keep her grades up. And we don't want her picking the wrong peer group. She's made one new friend at ECS, but—"

"But volleyball will be done right away," I point out. "What's Courtney going to *do* all winter? You want to keep her busy, don't you?"

Silence.

I lean against the jeep. "Mom, are you overthinking this? Courtney seems really pumped about boys hockey. And I know a few of the guys on the team. They're good kids. Can it hurt to let her try?"

"Getting hurt is exactly what your father and I are worried about." Mom pauses. "She's coming now. I have to go. Are you coming home for Thanksgiving?"

"Plan to. Call me tomorrow and let me know what you decide about Courtney."

As Mom hangs up, a car pulls in behind the jeep. Team Grannie, made up of Kathy and three rookies, gets out. All four are wearing grey wigs, curlers, nightgowns, and cardigans.

Kori waves a cane as she struts past. "You're going down, Mac!" she rasps.

Laughing, Kira and Kennedy follow her.

"Help me, will ya, Mac?" Kathy calls.

She opens her trunk and takes out tubs and laundry baskets while I survey the minefield of empty fast-food containers and plastic bottles in her back seat.

I pick up a tub. "Your car should be declared a disaster area."

Kathy hikes the hem of her nightgown. "You're talking to someone wearing support hose, and she's not enjoying them. I wouldn't push any buttons if I were you."

When we get close to Darian's house, music and laughter leak from the open windows. I hope no one calls the cops.

"So, how's it going with Dr. Kerr?" Kathy asks.

Arms laden with tubs and baskets, we face each other on the driveway while I fill her in on my meeting with my psych prof.

"She's a brick wall, Mac. You can't go around her," Kathy says. "And good luck trying to climb over her."

"Yeah, and my lousy performance against Mount Royal won't help my case when I talk to Coach about it either," I say. "Do you think he'll just leave me behind?"

"Only one way to find out, buttercup," Kathy says.

I trail her up the steps. She sets down her tub and reaches for the handle, but the front door swings open.

"Hurry up!" Izzie says. She's wearing a snorkel set and a leopard print one-piece bathing suit.

"You're a gamer, Izzie," Kathy says as she brushes by.

My phone vibrates again. This time it's Liam.

Izzie makes a disgusted sound and goes in the house.

I still sting from the way Liam brushed me off a few days ago. I stuff my phone in my pocket and step past Izzie into a swarm of sound, energy, and colour.

Maybe tonight, I'll win my shift.

5

"SO, YOU'RE HAVING PAM AND Christina over on Friday night?" Dad asks Courtney as he drives her to U15 boys practice.

"Yes. It's my birthday, remember?"

"Of course. You'll be thirteen."

How can he not remember how old she is?

"Fourteen, Dad."

"Right." Dad turns down the fan on the heater. "Hey, instead of having your mother make you a special supper, how about we order in some pizzas?"

He has a false cheerfulness that makes her wonder where he's going with this.

"I guess." Courtney had hoped Mom would make Chicken Parmesan. She bets Mom will make Jessie's favourite dessert.

"And on Saturday, please send your friends home early so you can help your Mom and me clean the house and do yardwork and get ready for Thanksgiving. Jessie's coming home after her game."

Right. Big Sis is coming home. Roll out the red carpet.

"Pitch in wherever you can. Help out your mom and me." Dad pulls up in front of the rink. "I'll pick you up in an hour. Text me if you need to stay longer.

You're sure you want to play on a boys team?"

"Yes." Courtney opens the passenger door.

"Well, watch the practice closely, so you know what to expect. You can figure out the team pecking order by watching who lines up first for drills. And remember, fake it till you make it."

"Thanks, Dad."

Courtney grabs her backpack and gets out of the SUV. A parent wrestling a hockey bag nearly knocks her over. Inside the rink lobby, a shift change is underway. Parents and hockey players—mostly boys—stream in and out of the ice surface entrance. Where should she go to watch U15 practice? The bench? The stands? The upstairs lobby? While she's debating, a hand taps her arm.

"Courtney McIntyre?"

She turns and looks into kind brown eyes.

"Clint Barber." The U15 coach is younger than she expected. He has light brown hair and a warm smile. "I'm Shane's dad."

She shakes his hand. "Nice to meet you, Mr. Barber."

"Call me Clint. Welcome aboard."

"Thanks. Did you remember I can't practice today?" She holds up her wrist, still wrapped in a tensor. "I'll be good to go next week, I promise."

"That's fine," he says. "Where did you plan to watch?"

"I have homework to do, so maybe I'll go upstairs."

Shane enters the rink, dragging his equipment and staring at his phone. He nearly walks into her.

"Hi Shane," she says.

He starts and drops his phone. They bump heads when they both bend over at the same time. Shane blushes and tucks his phone in his pocket.

"Planning on getting dressed?" his dad asks.

Shane ducks through the doors leading to the ice surface and dressing rooms.

"Can you stick around after practice, Courtney?" Clint asks. "I'd like you to meet the team."

"Sure." Her stomach knots.

She goes upstairs, sets down her stuff, and shoves in her ear buds. She unpacks her math text and starts on her homework. She wishes she'd inherited her dad's math brain, but Jessie seems to have gotten all those smarts.

She struggles through several questions before the U15 team straggles onto the ice. The guys are strong skaters. After they warm up and stretch, they take a knee around Clint. When he's done talking, they toss their sticks in the box and line up along the boards.

What now?

Each boy takes a turn skating between the boards and his teammates while they try to knock him down. The bigger boys are usually successful. She's never seen a drill like this.

The knot in her stomach tightens.

After everyone has a few turns, Clint tosses out the pucks. Most of the boys, including Shane, handle the puck well, and the passing drills are fast. It's both exciting and daunting. She takes out an ear bud.

"Aren't there enough girls sports out there?" a woman says to Courtney's left.

Courtney freezes.

"I wouldn't have a problem if she'd played with boys all along," another woman says. "I hear she figure skated up until a few years ago and then started playing *girls* hockey."

"She's only going to hurt herself," the other one says, "And then look out. It certainly won't be *her* fault." She lowers her voice, as if aware Courtney's listening. "And don't get me started on the dressing room. My son won't be focused on *hockey*."

Courtney wishes the floor would swallow her. She doesn't want to listen, but she doesn't want to draw attention by leaving. Do they know *she's* the girl they're talking about? She looks sideways, but the two women—seated in chairs near the glass—stare at the ice.

"And if she wants to play so badly, why isn't she here?" the blonde woman in the sweater coat says. "Does she think she can just show up for games and get the same ice-time?"

The woman in the leather jacket has short, dark hair. ""Don't get me wrong. This isn't about gender equity. This is about *commitment*."

"Well, at least the Wilson kid finally quit." Mrs. Sweater Coat says. "He was never going to be a hockey player."

Courtney puts in the ear bud and turns up the volume on her phone. She can't hear what the women are saying, but the pitch of their voices stops her from focusing on the practice and her homework. She shoves her stuff in her backpack and leans towards the window, cradling her chin and jamming the buds deeper in her ears.

Clint explains another drill, and the boys listen closely. They seem to respect him. Then the boys line up on either side of the net to execute the drill. The tall one in the green practice jersey is always first. He looks skilled, good enough to be playing AA. Why's he on a house team?

Courtney wishes she knew which players the two moms belong to. Do all the boys' parents feel the same? Maybe she should find out. Music blaring in her ears, she picks up her backpack and walks out.

Downstairs, three dads block the entrance to the ice surface. They stop talking and stare at her. Have they been discussing her too?

She could text Dad to come pick her up. Part of her trembles because of what she overheard upstairs, but there's another part that's fired up. Does she have what it takes to play with the boys? Can getting hit during a game be any worse than the bullying she put up with in elementary school?

She takes out her earbuds, pastes on a smile, and moves towards the men. "Could you please let me through?"

As one of the men opens the door, his smile matches hers. "By all means."

She raises her chin and walks by them.

Fake it till you make it.

"I'm glad you stuck around," Clint says to Courtney after practice. "Any questions about the drills?"

"What was the first one you did?" she asks.

"It's called the Gauntlet. It gets players accustomed to body contact. Would you step into the dressing room for a minute?"

Her stomach lurches into her throat. "Sure."

When they reach Dressing Room #2, Clint knocks, opens the door and peers in, then gestures for her to precede him. Kathy wasn't kidding about the stink. Courtney closes her mouth and takes shallow breaths.

"Guys, this is Courtney McIntyre," Clint says.

The boys hey and hello. They're dressed in street clothes, hockey bags tucked between their feet. Which boy wore the green jersey?

Shane, who sits near the door, gives her a little wave, and she nods at him. She recognizes Austin Hilderman and Dr. Bilku's son Jutin. Jutin and Austin smile at her, and she smiles back.

So far so good.

Shane slides over. "You can sit here, Courtney."

She perches beside him. She still wears her backpack, which prevents her from leaning against the wall. Should she take it off?

A toilet flushes.

"Courtney's a late addition to our roster," Clint continues. "She's a winger, so now we'll have two complete lines. I'll save the introductions till next time. I expect you'll all make her feel welcome.

Someone clears his nasal passage. Long and loud.

A tall boy with collar-length curly black hair stands in the entrance to the showers and toilets. He horks into the garbage can as he walks past.

It's him. The guy who razed her on the way to school. What unbelievable rotten luck.

"That's gross, Michael," Shane says.

At least now she knows his name.

"Should have saved it for you, Shane." Michael sits next to a boy with wavy brown hair, cut short on the sides.

"Enough," Clint says. "Back to Courtney. She won't be dressing with you fellas."

"That's too bad," the brown-haired boy says.

Courtney stares at her sneakers. What has she gotten herself into?

"Listen up while I read the SHA rules for the dressing room," Clint says.

Groans.

Last night her dad showed her the rules on the SHA website. While Clint reads them off his phone, she studies the boys across from her. Michael leans against the wall, arms crossed and eyes closed. His friend, elbows propped on his knees, tilts forward, long-fingered hands hanging loose. Are these boys even listening?

Clint puts his phone back in his pocket. "So now you know."

Michael starts, as if waking from a deep sleep. The brown-haired boy laughs.

Clint glares at them before continuing. "Courtney isn't the first girl to gear up with a boys team, and she won't be the last. She hasn't played as long as most of you, so help her out. Any questions?"

All heads swivel towards Michael.

He stands and stretches. "Sounds good, Coach. Is that it? My mom's waiting."

"That's it," Clint says. "See you guys—I mean—see *you* on Tuesday."

Michael is the first one out of the room. Shane lingers after the other boys are gone.

"That went well, don't you think?" Clint's tone is cheerful.

Is he trying to convince her—or himself?

"Uh huh," Courtney says.

"I'm glad you're on the team," Shane says.

But he looks doubtful too. Does he wish he'd never talked to her outside the hospital?

She walks out of the dressing room. In the hallway, the dark-haired woman in the leather jacket is talking to Michael. Of course. The resemblance is striking.

What will her first real practice bring? Is it too late to quit?

6

"JESSIE, THANKS FOR COMING IN." Robbie gestures to the chair across from her.

I gulp and sit.

Robbie's in her mid-twenties and a former Huskie. Last year, I enjoyed my one-on-ones with her because she was always upbeat and positive. Today, I'm nervous as hell.

Robbie tucks her long, dark brown hair behind her ears. "How do you feel about your performance against Mount Royal?"

I fumble for words. I feel like I'm piling excuse on excuse. By the time I'm done, my heart's thumping so hard I can hardly concentrate on Robbie's own analysis. She takes out her iPad and shows me game tape. Breaks down each of my shifts. All my mistakes are there in glorious colour.

She leans forward, elbows on knees. "Look, Jessie. We have heightened expectations of our second years. Rookies get more leash since they need to learn from their mistakes. You should be one of our top six D, but you didn't make good decisions against Mount Royal."

How can I make good decisions if I don't get chances to make decisions?

"I'll try to do better," I say.

"And how will you do that?" she asks.

"I could show up early for practice."

Although—with my schedule—I have no idea how I'll accomplish that.

She gives me a lecture on organization, time management, and preparation.

Each word smacks me between the eyes. I do plan every minute of my day. I have to because of my class load.

"Is there anything you want to say to me?" she asks.

Is this a good time to bring up the scheduling conflict for my midterm? Maybe ask her to mention it to Coach? No. Not till after the Manitoba series. I'll get my act together first.

"Not really," I say.

Anxiety roars in my ears as I navigate the hallway between the office and exit.

Dave, our video guru and equipment manager, tinkers with the skate sharpener.

He takes off his baseball cap and wipes the sweat from his brow. "Didn't go so well, huh, Jessie."

It's not a question. It's a statement.

Has everyone been talking about how badly I played?

<hr />

October 11

University of Saskatchewan Huskies vs. University of Manitoba Bisons
Merlis Belsher Place, Saskatoon

As I stretch my hip flexors, Kathy turns her back to the boards and leans on her elbows. "Seems like ages since we played with Shauna, huh?"

Shauna's easy to pick out from the other Bisons warming up in their end. She still wears 4, like she did when we played with her in Estevan.

"Did you know she was a Canada West All-star last year?" Kathy whistles. "And she's got an A already."

I still sting from my meeting with Robbie. Yes, Shauna's a born leader, and I'm on my way to becoming a healthy scratch. How humiliating.

Kathy faces the boards and stretches her hamstrings. "So, why's she wearing that ugly brown jersey?"

Kathy loathes all our Canada West rivals. Shauna's decision to play for U of M is high treason. However, Kathy doesn't mind that we have players from other provinces on our own roster.

"I hear you're going back to Estevan after the game tomorrow," Kathy says. "That's too bad. Gonna be a wild dance party at the Scuzz."

I feel a twinge of regret. The Scuzz is always a good time, even though I don't drink. "Sorry to miss."

"Liam going home for Thanksgiving too?"

"Nope."

"And he's not coming tonight either?"

"I don't think so."

"Talk to Coach about Kerr's midterm yet?"

I shake my head.

"We leave in less than week. Better do it soon."

Easy for her to say.

Shauna skates over. A grin splits her face. "Hey you."

I shove aside my black mood and hug her. "Hey yourself."

Kathy hugs her next. "Ready to take a beating?"

Shauna laughs. We talk about our teams and schedules. Kathy presses Shauna for intel on the University of Alberta since Manitoba played them last weekend.

"Good luck today." I take off my glove and hold out my hand.

Shauna takes off her own glove and clasps my fingers. "You too, Jessie."

"Game on!" Kathy says.

We beat Manitoba 3-2 in regulation on Friday night. On Saturday afternoon. Flinton scores the OT winner to cement a 4-3 win in Game Two. I play a regular shift and end up with a Plus-Minus of -3 on the weekend. Brutal. But I think Izzie and I communicated better, and the sweep is exhilarating.

When I shake hands with Shauna after the final game, she says, "We'll get you when it counts."

It's a barely veiled reminder that Manitoba has a history of knocking the Huskies out of playoffs.

After I change, I wait for Robbie outside the coaches' office. I need to know her assessment of me before I head home for the weekend. "How did I do?"

She gives me a tight smile. "We'll talk on Tuesday. Have a nice Thanksgiving."

Not a ringing endorsement.

"Come to the Scuzz," Kathy urges me on our way out of the rink. "You can leave for Estevan in the morning."

I shake my head.

"Girlfriend, we Huskies gotta howl. We just swept the Bisons, remember?"

Right now, I feel disconnected from the rest of the team. I'll do anything to get the old feeling back.

"Okay. You're on."

I'm James Bond, and I'm naked. Izzie, in leopard print, sits cross-legged in a chair. The maniacal villain—is that Dr. *Kerr?*—presses a button on the desk. The metal floor slides open to reveal a snarling pack of junkyard dogs.

Something buzzes. I open my eyes, stare at the ceiling, and fumble on my nightstand for my phone.

"Are you on your way?" a voice asks.

Where am I? My throat feels like the Sahara.

"Jessie, are you there?" It's Mom.

Details come into focus. My desk. Chair. Closet. Hockey posters. I'm in my dorm room.

"I'm here," I croak. I check the time. It's past noon.

"Are you sick?" Mom asks.

Yeah, but not in the way she thinks. I broke my own rule about not drinking last night. Surprising how easy it is to dive into a pitcher of paralyzers.

"Just a minute." I crawl out of bed and take a swig from the water jug I keep in my mini fridge.

"Are you still coming home?" Mom asks.

"Wait a minute." The water tastes heavenly. "I think I'm coming down with something." Yeah, a bad case of dehydration. "Probably not a good idea for me to give you guys what I've got."

"You seemed okay when I talked to you after the game." Mom sounds deflated.

"I thought I was too. Anyway, I'll use the next two days to rest and catch up on homework." I stumble against my desk. Is it possible I'm still drunk?

"It's too bad you'll miss out on the meals we're got planned. Courtney and I are making fruit pizza right now."

My favourite.

"I'm sorry, Mom."

"Here. I'll put your sister on so you can wish her a happy birthday."

Birthday? I haven't talked to Courtney since her first hockey practice. I'm slipping in the Big Sister department.

"Hi Jessie." She sounds miserable.

"Happy cake day, little sis. How was your party?"

"Pam was sick, so only Christina came. We played Xbox." She adds, "Mom and Dad gave me new shoulder pads and a stick."

"Nice. Well, I've got your present up here," I lie. I haven't even figured out what I'm getting her. I can always pick up some athletic wear at the university bookstore.

"Does it have Huskies on it?" She doesn't sound impressed.

Cross out that idea.

"No, it doesn't. I can't wait to see your face when you open it."

I can't wait to see *my* face when I figure out what to buy her.

After I hang up, I text Liam, asking him if he wants to go to Coach's house for Thanksgiving dinner. Mrs. Coach puts on a big feast for the girls who can't go home for the weekend, and we're allowed to bring significant others.

Three little dots blink.

I'm at home.

Like yr place?

No. The farm.

I can't believe my eyes. Why didn't he tell me he was driving back to Estevan? *Since when?*

Got home late last night. Back tomorrow. Thanks for the invite tho.

Thanks for the invite, my ass. The nerve of that guy.

7

BEFORE PAM CAN SET DOWN her cafeteria tray, Christina pounces. "Pam, I saw a picture of you at a party on Friday night. On Instagram. Why did you say you were sick?"

Courtney's hurt, but she tries not to show it. Pam seemed fine when they walked home after volleyball practice on Friday. The sick excuse seems fishy now.

"Whose party?" Courtney asks.

"Just some girls from the volleyball team," Pam says. "Look, I'm sorry I lied to you, but I thought the truth would hurt your feelings."

"Well, it has," Courtney says. "Thanks for that."

"I hear you're playing boys hockey. That's news to me," Pam says.

She's just trying to change the subject.

"When are you playing a game, Courtney? I will come cheer for you," Christina says.

Two boys sit at the next table. Courtney recognizes Michael and his brown-haired sidekick from the dressing room. Michael catches her eye and then says something which makes the other boy cackle.

"Courtney, do you *know* them?" Pam asks.

Why does she look so horrified?

"Not really," Courtney says, "but they're on my hockey team."

Pam's eyes bulge. "You're playing hockey with Michael *Carson?*"

"If that's his full name—yes," Courtney says.

Pam shakes her head. "Michael was in my homeroom last year. He's not someone you mess with."

"I'm not messing with him," Courtney says.

A chair scrapes behind her. From Pam's fearful expression, someone's coming, and Courtney doesn't have to guess who it is.

"Hey, it's Courtney McIntyre." Michael slides into the chair next to her. He's uncomfortably close. "What's happening, Courtney McIntyre?"

Why does he keep repeating her name?

"Not much," Courtney says.

Pam's eyes swivel between her and Michael. Christina, lips pressed tight, stares at Courtney.

"You girls are friends of Courtney's?" Michael asks. "Everybody's gotta have friends. You need them when times get rough."

Pam picks up her tray. "I'll see you later, Court."

What?

"You never ate your lunch," Christina points out.

"I'm not hungry. And I have to—I need to go somewhere." Pam walks away.

"She left in a hurry," Michael says. "Can't imagine why. Say, Courtney. Brandon and I want to welcome you to the team."

"I don't know who Brandon is," Courtney says, although she has a pretty good idea.

Michael waves at the brown-haired boy, who waves back enthusiastically.

"That's Brandon right there." Michael puts one hand on Courtney's forearm and points with the other. "Why don't you come sit with us? We want to get to know you better."

His tone is super creepy. Does he actually think she's fooled by this?

"Please take your hand off me," Courtney says.

"Sorry. Didn't mean to invade your personal space." Michael lifts his hand. "I just wanted to be friendly. It's my job to make new players feel important. I'm going to be your captain."

Captain? Her creep alert is beeping like crazy.

"Please leave me alone," Courtney says.

Michael straightens. "You seem kind of sensitive. But suit yourself. See you at practice."

He walks away.

Fear flutters like the wings of a trapped bird.

Christina reaches across the table and squeezes Courtney's hand. "I can tell he is a bad person. You be careful around him."

Courtney nods. "I absolutely will."

"So, when *is* your first game?" Christina asks.

Courtney tries to remember, but she can't take her eyes off Michael and Brandon. Michael appears to be passing on the details of their encounter, and Brandon seems to find them hilarious.

"Courtney?" Christina asks. "You need to forget about them. Look at me." Her dark eyes are warm and concerned. How can she be so calm?

Courtney takes a deep breath and lets it out slowly. "I play on Friday night at the Power Dodge Ice Centre, but some people call it the Blue Goose."

"I have been there for public skating," Christina says. "And I will be there for you."

"Thanks." Courtney looks for Pam and finally finds her at a table with some of their volleyball teammates. She wonders what the chances are that Pam will eat lunch with her and Christina tomorrow.

Thanks to Michael, she's betting a big, fat zero.

8

AFTER TUESDAY PRACTICE, I STAND outside the half-open door to Coach's office and try to suck up some courage. I've put off this conversation too long. We leave for Edmonton in two days, and my situation with Dr. Kerr's midterm is still unresolved.

"Jessie, I can hear you breathing out there. If you want to talk to me, come in," Coach says.

I push the door open and enter.

Coach sits at his desk, elbows bent, big hands clasped. "What's up?"

I tell him about my problem.

"You want me to call your prof?" he asks when I'm done.

His offer is a good sign. Much better than saying, "We don't actually need you in the Alberta series."

"That'd be great," I say.

"You got her number?"

I dig for my phone.

"What did you say her name was?" Coach asks.

"I didn't, but it's Dr. Kerr."

Coach clears his throat. "How did you end up in one of *her* classes?"

SHOOTOUT • 49

"She wasn't *supposed* to teach it," I explain. "The prof who *was* dropped the class, and Dr. Kerr picked it up. She seemed okay for the first month. I thought the girls were exaggerating."

"Well, she won't budge, Jessie, and I don't want to push her. Can you hop on a plane after your exam? The team can pick up your airfare."

Thank goodness.

"Are you sure, Coach? Won't it be expensive to book something last minute?"

He wakes up his computer screen and checks the airline websites.

I feel like crap for making him throw money away like this, but I *can't* miss any games.

White Pole Syndrome.

"You're not kidding it's expensive," he says. "Would've helped if I'd known this a while ago, Mac."

"I'll talk to my parents," I offer. "They would probably help pay for some—if not all of it."

"That might be a good idea," Coach says.

As soon as I get back to my dorm, I call Mom.

"I'll book the flight," she says when I'm done explaining. But she doesn't sound assertive. She sounds tired—even disinterested.

Relief floods my limbs. "Thanks, Mom."

The logistical side of my brain kicks into gear. I'll pack my equipment after Thursday practice. I'll send it and my suitcase with the team. That way I'll only have my knapsack on the plane.

"Are you still planning to drive to Edmonton with Kathy's mom?" I ask.

"I guess so," Mom says.

She doesn't sound very excited.

"Will you be able to pick me up at the airport?" I ask. "That way I don't have to worry about getting a cab to the rink."

"Yes," Mom says, adding, "So, how are you feeling?"

I'm not sure what she means. "Fine. Why do you ask?"

"On the weekend you told me you were coming down with something." Her tone is suspicious.

"Oh yeah. That." I scramble for an explanation. I'm not used to lying to her. "It was a twenty-four-hour thing."

Long pause.

"Jessie, there's something I need to say to you," she says.

"Okay." Now what?

"Please don't let hockey ruin your university experience," she says.

Holy hell. When did she start thinking like that?

"Is that what you told Coach and Basil after we played Mount Royal?" I ask.

More silence. That's absolutely what she told them. Geez. What *else* did she say?

"Mom, I don't have time to talk to you about this right now, but thanks for paying for the flight—even though you *really* think I shouldn't go to Edmonton."

"You're burning a candle at both ends," Mom says. "I'm worried about you."

"Let *me* worry about me. I have to go. Talk to you later."

I end the call before I say something I'll regret. Besides, I have lots to do to prepare for my midterms. Maybe I should stay here instead of meeting Liam at the library.

I sit at my desk and open my laptop. I'll start with Numerical Analysis I. The entire course is based on MATLAB, a problem-solving software.

My phone vibrates. Damn it. I'm never going to get anything done.

Liam's calling.

"Hey," I say to him.

"Hey yourself," he says. "I'm on my way to the library. Want a coffee or anything?"

"I think I'll study in my room tonight," I say.

"Did you get your psych midterm figured out?" he asks.

I'm surprised he remembers. "Yeah. I talked to Coach, and we worked out a plan for getting to Edmonton." I give Liam a brief explanation.

"That's great your family can afford that," he says when I'm done. "How much is the flight?"

I don't want to tell him the truth, so I lowball.

Still, he whistles at the figure. "Must be nice."

That gets my back up. He's implying my parents have spare cash lying around, while his parents don't. Liam can't afford to do an undergrad degree *and* veterinary medicine. He's determined to get early entry into the program.

"Aren't you happy I could work things out?" I ask. "Hockey's important to me."

"Of course I'm happy," he says.

But he sounds like he could care less. What's happening to us?

"Talk to you later." I press End and shut off my phone.

If only I could use MATLAB to solve *all* my problems.

9

COURTNEY FINISHES LACING HER SKATE, straightens, and leans her head against the wall. She's ready. Physically anyway. Mentally, emotionally—she's not sure. Clint told her someone would knock on her door when the team's ready. What if he forgets?

A knuckle raps. "All set?"

The young woman in the hallway has pretty blue eyes and shoulder-length blonde hair with warm highlights. "I'm Abby Barber. Shane's mom. I'm also team manager. When your husband coaches, you have to get with the program."

"You don't look old enough to have a son in Grade Nine," Courtney observes.

Abby grins. "And a daughter in Grade Twelve, you sweet girl. The boys are ready for you. Let's go."

Clint meets them outside the boys dressing room. "Ready for your first practice, Courtney?"

She wants to correct him—remind him she's played two years already, but she knows what he means. She nods.

The guys, suited up except for helmets, fall silent when she comes in. Shane gives her a shy grin. She avoids looking at Michael and Brandon.

"Have a seat, Courtney, and we'll make some introductions," Clint says. "We'll start with the second years."

She sits between Austin Hilderman and the big blonde boy in goalie pads.

"Shane, you can start," Clint says. "Tell her your name, position, year, and something else about yourself."

Shane blushes. "Courtney knows me already. But here goes. Shane Barber. Winger. Second year." He pauses. "I like chocolate ice cream."

Michael snorts.

"Next," Clint says.

"Josh Thompson. Centre. Second year." Josh has short blonde hair. "I like to hunt and fish. An outdoorsy kinda guy."

"Outdoorsy is right," the goalie says. "Thompson's farts are the worst."

The boys laugh.

"Next," Clint prompts.

Michael heaves a sigh, as if this exercise is beneath him. "Michael Carson. Second year. Defence. I like cats."

Brandon explodes into giggles.

What is *that* supposed to mean?

"Michael's a wise guy," Clint says. "Next."

Brandon stifles his giggles long enough to say, "Brandon Brown. Defence. Second year. I don't get out much."

Michael snickers.

The big goalie stuffs the corner of his sandwich in his mouth. "Toby Miller. Goal. Second year," he says, his mouth full. "My favourite food is pizza."

"Don't choke," Clint says. "Courtney, you're next."

"Courtney McIntyre. Second year. Winger. I play volleyball. My final tournament is this Saturday."

Michael applauds slowly.

Austin says, "Austin Hilderman. Winger. First year. My sister Randi played with Courtney's sister Jessie."

"Fantastic," Michael says.

"Jutin Bilku. Centre. First year. My older sister played with Jessie too."

The other first-years introduce themselves.

"That's it," Clint says when they're done.

"Thank goodness Wilson quit," Michael mutters under his breath.

Clint shoots him a look and folds his arms over his chest. "Let's get down to business. We have our first game tomorrow. Against the Knights. Today we'll try out a few line combinations and see if we can find some chemistry."

"What about the letters?" Michael asks.

"I'll let you fellas—correction—you *players* vote on a captain after a few games. I'll hand out A's tomorrow based on your performance today. Who listens. Who works hard and demonstrates good sportsmanship. Got it?"

The boys mumble agreement.

"I have another question, Coach," Michael says. "Why can't we take off our gear right after the game?"

"The postgame meeting will be fifteen minutes or less," Clint says. "Courtney needs to hear the debriefing. She'll go to her own dressing room after that."

Michael shakes his head and mutters something to Brandon, who listens with his brown head tipped down. Clint made the dressing room protocol sound simple. Why is Michael being such a jerk?

"Let's hit the ice," Clint says.

The boys troop past. Michael walks by without a look or comment, but Josh stops and holds out his hand.

"Welcome to the team, Courtney."

Is Josh mocking her? Maybe trying to prove to Clint that he deserves a letter? His green eyes seem sincere.

She shakes his hand. "Thanks."

Dr. Bilku, Jutin's dad, waits outside the dressing room. "How's your wrist, Courtney?"

She rotates it left to right, up and down. "Wasn't it fine when I saw you a few days ago?"

He studies her movements and manipulates her wrist. "Just wanted to be sure."

Dads are lined up along the boards, but she has no idea if they belong to her team or the younger players on the ice. She watches three girls take part in a shooting drill then gather around their coach with the rest of their teammates. Will she ever fit in like that?

"Courtney McIntyre?" a voice murmurs in her left ear.

She nearly jumps out of her skin.

"I'm Michael's dad." The man smells like he's been drinking. "I wanted to welcome you to the team. If you ever have any problems, please let me know. I'll do whatever I can to help."

In an eerie way, he sounds just like Michael.

"Thanks." She takes off her glove and holds out her hand. "Nice to meet you, Mr. Carson."

He raises an eyebrow. Were his words just for show? He clasps her sweaty fingers.

Yep. She definitely smells booze on him.

The gate opens behind him and the younger team streams off the ice. Their excited voices echo off the metal walls as they jostle and shove. The Zamboni begins the flood.

"I hear you used to figure skate," Mr. Carson says. "Did you have any trouble adjusting to hockey skates?"

"Not really," Courtney says.

"Well, one thing's for sure. That blonde hair of yours is going to be a big distraction for these boys."

Is that supposed to be a compliment?

Thankfully, another dad comes along and strikes up a conversation with him. Shane joins Courtney along the boards.

"Don't pay any attention to Michael and Brandon," Shane says. "They're all right once you get to know them."

Does he know them the way *she* knows them?

When the Zamboni finishes the flood, Courtney's the first one through the gate. She skates a circuit, staying ahead of her teammates. While they goof off and play fight, she lengthens her stride and picks up the pace. Clint signals them to switch to backwards stroking, and she transitions easily. She leans into the corners, knowing the boys' parents will watch every stride and crossover. She wishes she'd asked Dad to stay, instead of telling him to leave. She'd like his opinion on how she looks compared to the boys.

She joins the others as Michael leads the stretches. He acts like he's the team captain already.

"McIntyre, are you ready to run your first Gauntlet?" Clint asks when they're done.

Her legs turn to water. "Sure."

"Remember to keep your weight equally distributed," he says.

She lines up on the boards between Shane and Toby and tries to throw her shoulder into Josh as he skates past. He's solid, and she's the one who falls. Michael alone knocks Josh down, and the others cheer. Austin, Jutin, and Shane are next.

All too soon, it's her turn. Legs shaking, she lines up. Will the boys lay off because she's a girl? Does she want them to?

She bends at the waist and pushes off, trying to keep her weight over her feet, like Clint said. Toby hits her first, and she goes down. She quickens or slows her strides so the other boys miss her. Michael hits her, but she doesn't fall. The

Gauntlet isn't as scary as she thought it would be.

Shane gives her a little nudge when she rejoins him. "Kind of fun, huh?"

"Kind of," she says.

She runs the Gauntlet three more times. Success has a lot to do with timing, and timing is something she understands. On her last turn, she sidesteps Michael before he drills her. When he tumbles hard into the boards, the boys laugh. She's too busy relishing the moment to avoid Josh's hit. She groans and picks herself off the ice.

Clint blows a whistle and tosses out the pucks.

"You can be my partner for the passing drills," Shane says.

She's relieved he's willing to help her.

Her teammates perform the passing and stick handling drills in a higher gear from what she's accustomed. She senses that Shane holds back as they pass cross-ice to one another. She knows she can skate with the faster players, but she can't keep the puck on her blade at that speed, much less give and take clean passes.

Clint blows the whistle again and divides the players for a scrimmage. "No hitting!" he shouts.

She'll play right wing while Shane will play left with Josh as their centre. When they face off, Jutin wins the draw to Michael who passes up to Austin. Courtney steps into Austin's path to poke check. A body hurtles into her, and she slams the boards.

Her lungs clamour for air. Wheezing, she hunches on all fours. A hand strokes her back.

"It's okay. Stay calm," Shane says.

Beautiful air flows in. With Shane's help, she gathers her weak legs under her.

Michael leans on the butt of his stick. "All better now?"

Courtney nods as Shane picks up her stick.

"If you can't handle a hit from a teammate, how will you handle one in a game?" Michael asks. "Or do you think you get special treatment because you're a girl? 'Cause I'm not drinking *that* Kool-Aid."

Her ribs ache.

"Dad said no hitting," Shane says.

"Oh, I get it," Michael says. "I didn't know she was your *girlfriend*. Are you gonna chase down every guy who drills her? Because I'm not. She has to earn her place, like the rest of us." He skates away.

What's his problem?

Clint puts a hand on her shoulder. "I didn't see what happened. Are you okay,

Courtney?"

"I'm fine," she lies. "I caught an edge along the boards. Knocked the wind out of me."

"Dad," Shane says.

"No broken ribs or anything like that? Head okay?" Clint asks.

"Yes. Let's keep going," Courtney says. "I don't want to hold up practice."

"Look at me." Clint performs a quick concussion protocol then takes her arm and leads her back to the bench. "I want you to sit out the rest of the scrimmage."

"I'm okay. Really."

"A person can't be too careful, Courtney."

Would he be this careful if she were Shane or Michael?

She watches while the clock at the end of the arena ticks off the minutes. She takes deep breaths and checks her ribs for discomfort. The rest of the practice passes without incident, even after Clint gives the okay for checking. The boys bump and hit, but they don't run each other, and Michael doesn't crush anybody else along the boards.

"Michael's hit was dirty," Shane says when he steps off the ice at the end of his shift.

She pretends not to hear.

When there's a few minutes left, Clint blows the whistle and tells them to take a knee. Courtney leaves the box and joins them.

Clint unfolds his expectations for tomorrow night's game against the Knights, the other Estevan U15 team.

"We'll cream those guys," Michael promises.

Courtney stays back to help Clint and Shane gather the pucks, then leaves the ice.

Michael talks to his dad outside the entrance to the boys' dressing room. Losers. She steps around them and walks towards to her own room where Dr. Bilku and Abby await her.

"How are you, Courtney?" Dr. Bilku looks worried.

"I'm fine," she says.

"That was a nasty hit," Abby says. "Don't you dare let him get away with it, sweet girl."

"I'm okay," Courtney insists.

Inside her dressing room, she strips off her equipment and tosses it in her bag. The grey walls close in. Is this *fun*? She showers, puts on her street clothes, and sends her dad a quick text.

As soon as she opens the door, she hears an angry voice. Clint's face is red as he confronts Michael, still in his equipment. Abby or Dr. Bilku must have talked to Clint about the hit. Michael listens with a cocky grin while Mr. Carson looks ready to explode. Is he angry with Clint—or his son?

"Courtney, come back in the dressing room," Clint says.

Inside, the guys are showered and changed, but they don't look happy. Oh no. This is getting worse by the minute. She sits between Shane and Toby.

Michael enters, swearing, and smashes the door against the wall. He yanks off his shoulder pads and slams them into his equipment bag.

"Hey, what gives?" Toby asks.

Michael rips off his helmet. "Thanks for squealing, Shane."

"It wasn't me, but I wish it was," Shane says. "You bragged about that hit. Can't you own the consequences?"

"Oh, I'll own them," Michael says. "You wait and see how much." He yanks at the belt holding up his hockey pants.

"Remember the rule," Austin says. "Courtney's here. You can't—"

Michael swears again as Clint storms in.

"I'm only going to say this once." Clint's voice is low but furious. "I won't tolerate head hunting. Michael will sit out tomorrow night because of his flagrant disregard for the safety of one of his teammates. The same thing will happen to *any* player who pulls a similar stunt. Do I make myself clear?"

The answer is total silence, which seems to appease him.

Clint's eyes settle on Courtney. "Don't ever be afraid to talk to me if something like this happens again. Now, are your parents coming to get you?"

"My dad."

She shoulders her hockey bag and crosses the room, eyes down. She pushes the door open. "See you fellas Friday."

The real Gauntlet awaits her in the lobby—a receiving line of parents—some curious, some sympathetic, some angry. Michael's parents are at the end.

His mother's eyes are lasers. "This isn't girls hockey," she says. "If you can't stand the heat, stay out of the kitchen."

Courtney brushes past her and waits for her dad outside the rink. Her ribs still ache, a reminder of Michael's hit. As the other parents and boys leave, she tries to shut out their voices.

Dad pulls up in the SUV, and she throws her equipment in the back.

"How'd it go?" he asks.

"Perfect," she says.

She'll tell him about the hit tomorrow. It's obvious Michael wants her to quit. But she won't give in. No way.

1 0

I SPRINT THROUGH THE EDMONTON TERMINAL, my knapsack banging my ribs. Less than an hour to puck drop. Mom texted me as soon as my plane landed to tell me Mrs. Parker and Kathy's mom are waiting in the cell phone lot.

I lunge through the glass doors and look for the Parkers' big, black SUV. Brake lights flash, and I bolt towards them. I throw open the back passenger door.

Mrs. Parker's round face grins at me in the rearview mirror. "Jessie, glad you made it!"

"How was your psychology exam?" Mom asks.

"Fine. Let's go!"

Kathy's mom wheels into rush hour traffic while I wriggle out of my leggings and into my jill. Mrs. Parker came up with the idea that they could pick up my hockey bag in Saskatoon and lug it to Edmonton, so I could change on the way to the rink.

"We'll get you there in time for the game," Mrs. Parker says, "but you'll probably miss the warm-up."

"Any updates on Courtney's team?" I ask.

Mom stares out her window. What's up with her?

"Estevan Minor Hockey upheld Michael's one-game suspension," Mrs. Parker says. "His dad countered with a formal complaint against Clint Barber."

"For what?" I explode.

"For verbally harassing his son," Mrs. Parker says. "Apparently if you look up #EMHnotfair, you'll find a bunch of opinions and reactions. Not pretty."

I pull off my T-shirt. "How's Courtney doing?"

Mom still says nothing.

"She's a little trooper," Mrs. Parker says. "She refuses to quit. I hope she kicks ass tonight."

Mom shakes her head. She must feel guilty about coming to Edmonton, instead of being home for Courtney's first game.

"You always tell us to do our best. And Courtney's doing that. You should be proud of her, Mom."

"I *am* proud, but I'm also scared." Mom sounds like she's on the verge of tears. "I shouldn't have agreed to let her play boys hockey. What was I thinking?"

"Don't worry. Dad's there," I assure her.

Once we reach the University of Alberta campus, Mrs. Parkers pulls up to the rear entrance to the Clare Drake Arena. A security guard and Trina, one of our trainers, wait by the door.

"Just in time." Trina raps my shoulder. "This way, Mac."

I enter our dressing room to applause. I kick off my street shoes and reach for my skates.

Time for battle.

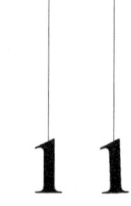

11

October 18

Estevan Moose vs. Estevan Knights

Power Dodge Energy Centre (Blue Goose), Estevan

DAD PULLS UP AT THE RINK entrance, and Courtney drags her equipment out of the back. She's a bundle of nerves, but she's determined to keep them under control. Before she can grab her sticks, Dad hugs her from behind.

"Keep your head up," he says.

Will he ever stop worrying about her?

She wriggles free. "This isn't the NHL."

"Some people think it is," Dad says. "I'll park and come right in."

The Blue Goose is full of hockey parents. Not surprising since both teams are from Estevan.

"I can't believe she showed up." It's the blonde mom with the sweater coat. "She's got a lot of nerve. The only reason Michael got suspended is because she can't handle a hit in practice."

The lobby noise is sucked into a vortex. Little kids stop whining. The other parents stare. Courtney weaves through them, checks the white board for her dressing room number, and opens the arena door.

"Go, Courtney!" Christina holds up a sign decorated with the same words in sparkly letters. Her little sisters, long, black hair floating, twirl beside her.

Courtney lets the door swing shut. "Thanks for coming."

"We can't stay for the whole game," Christina says, "but we will cheer loud!"

Courtney doubts Pam will show up.

In her dressing room, a black and red 12 jersey with a logo of a stick-wielding moose hangs on a hook. New socks are folded neatly on the bench. She dresses quickly.

Abby knocks and sticks her head in. "You have everything you need, sweet girl?"

Courtney nods.

"Let's go then," Abby says.

The boys fall silent when Clint lets Courtney into the team dressing room. She sits next to Shane, who wears an A, as do Brandon and Josh. Most of the boys don't look at her. So much for team chemistry.

"Michael's not coming to the game," Shane whispers. "He's too mad."

She's relieved but still apprehensive.

During warm-up, someone in the stands—is it Mrs. Sweater Coat?—tries to get a "not fair" chant going, but it doesn't catch on.

After puck drop, the Moose struggle to break out of their end, and Toby has to make save after save. The Knights throw punishing hits on the boards. Courtney worries about her first shift.

When it's her line's turn, the faceoff is in the Moose's end. Josh wins the draw back to Brandon, who passes up to Shane. Shane cuts around 10 and throws Courtney a perfect pass in the neutral zone. She manages to keep the puck on her blade. When 6 tries to step into her, she pushes the puck between his skates and jumps around him, scooping it up on the other side. She has a full head of steam when she reaches the Knights' blue line, but she loses the puck and puts herself offside. The linesperson whistles down the play, and she skates to the faceoff dot.

"That was a nice move you made on 6," Josh tells her.

"Thanks," she says.

On the next faceoff, 7 knocks her on her butt, but she catches up to the play in the Moose's end. 13 rips a shot, but it whacks the glass behind Toby's net. 10 smokes Josh in the corner, steals the puck, and winds up to take a shot. Josh lifts 10's stick, and the puck bounces to Courtney. She bangs it off the boards and outmaneuvers 13. Shane steps into view, and she slings the puck to him. He drives at the net, dekes right, and pitches to Josh, who scores on a wraparound.

Heart soaring, Courtney joins the bench run. She's thrilled when her teammates high-five her.

"Nice assist!" Josh says as they step off the ice.

"Go Courtney!" she hears Christina shout in the stands.

Clint taps Courtney on the head, and she takes her place in the middle of the bench. Shane nudges her with his shoulder, and she glows.

On her next shift, she's digging the puck out of the corner when skates scrape behind her. She passes to Shane and leaps aside as a big body hurtles into the boards. Shane battles 5 behind the net. Josh dives in to give support while Courtney goes to the right goal post. She fans on Shane's pass and chases the puck into the corner again. 13 cycles the puck along the boards before he cross-checks her and knocks her down. Arm throbbing, she picks herself up as the referee blows the whistle. She gives 13 a saucy smile as he skates to the penalty box.

"Are you okay?" Clint asks when she returns to the bench.

"Yep, but I'm going to have a big bruise tomorrow," she says.

After an 8-6 victory, the Moose have lots to talk about in the dressing room.

"Where'd you learn those moves, Courtney?" Josh asks.

"I spent a few years perfecting a double axel," she replies.

"Well, whatever that was, it was fantastic," he says. "And I loved it when you stepped aside and let McQuinney take a header into the boards."

"Did anyone even *touch* you the whole game?" Shane wonders.

"Oh yeah." Her arm is still sore from the cross-check.

After Clint's done with them, Courtney heads for her dressing room. She turns the corner, and Dad is there.

"Way to go, kid." His eyes shine. "I was so proud of you. You have no idea."

"Don't get sappy on me," she warns.

"Courtney!"

She turns.

It's Shane—in shower shoes and hockey pants. "Josh's having a party tomorrow night. He wants you to come."

She ignores whatever her father is saying. "What about Michael?"

"He won't be there," Shane says.

She turns to her dad. "Can I go?"

He crosses his arms over his chest. "Won't you be too tired after your volleyball tournament?"

"No, I won't," she says.

Dad stares at her for a moment then looks over her shoulder. "Shane, I'm holding *you* responsible if anything happens. Do I make myself clear?"

"Nothing's going to happen, Mr. McIntyre. I promise," Shane says.

"Hey, everyone, I'm still here," Courtney says.

Dad cocks an eyebrow. "You play by my rules, or you don't play at all."

"Tough guy," she replies, but she smiles as she pushes open the door of her dressing room.

Maybe she's going to fit in after all.

1 2

October 18
University of Saskatchewan Huskies vs. University of Alberta Pandas
Clare Drake Arena, Edmonton

HAS THERE BEEN A MISTAKE?

I busted my butt to get to Edmonton. Poor Mom paid for my flight and rode with Mrs. Parker for ten hours. But I sit like a forgotten doll on the top tier of our players box while my Huskie teammates try to execute the game plan. Coach paces and evaluates. Robbie rolls the D and gives feedback as her defenders come off. Dan juggles the forwards.

My feet are freezing by the end of the second period. As we troop to the dressing room, I'm in a funk.

Izzie falls in beside me. "This is exciting, huh?"

She's my D-partner, and she hasn't noticed I'm not playing?

"Jessie!" Robbie calls behind me.

I turn and wait for her.

"I can tell you're upset," she says. "I didn't have time to talk to you before the game. When you missed the warm-up, I made some changes. Hopefully I can work you in, but that'll depend on how things go."

Robbie's brown ponytail bobs as she walks away.

So, I'll get a shift if a D gets hurt or suspended.

Great.

We lose 3-1 in regulation. I get three shifts in the third period and give up a goal.

"Just call me -1," I mutter to Kathy as we return to the dressing room.

"Quit pouting," she says.

Dan doesn't mince any words. "You ladies played better five-on-five—even four-on-five—than you did on the power play. What's the problem?"

My teammates strap on the ice packs and slouch in defeat.

"I hate these f'ing Pandas," Kathy says.

I change into my cool-down gear and head out to the lobby to look for Mom.

"She wasn't feeling well, so she took a taxi to the hotel at the end of the second period," Mrs. Parker says.

Maybe that's why Mom was so quiet on the way to the rink. I shower and dress, then check my phone. No text from Mom apologizing. No text from Dad asking how it went. No text from Courtney describing her game. And no text from Liam either. Not a "Good luck" or "Hope you made it."

So far, this road trip sucks.

Our bus driver drops us at a restaurant on the U of A campus. As we wait for Diane, our team manager, to arrange our table, I scroll the Estevan Minor Hockey Twitter account for news of Courtney's game. Nothing. I text Dad and Courtney, but they don't respond. Weird.

When our table is ready, I sit between Kathy and Darian.

Izzie plunks on a chair across from me and says cheerfully, "We can still get two points tomorrow."

Typical rookie.

"Anyone hear how Manitoba did against Mount Royal?" Kathy asks.

Darian's grey eyes are glued to her phone. "Won 4-1. No upsets in the other games either." She ruffles her short, red hair, and it stands straight up.

"Hey!" Izzie says.

A large male hand appears beside mine.

"Hey, little sis." The male voice comes from above my head. "Sorry I'm late."

I couldn't find a parking spot."

"Everyone, this is my big brother Scott," Izzie explains.

I look sideways—and up. Scott's a tall drink of water with killer blue eyes.

As Izzie introduces each of us, Scott smiles and shakes hands. I'm last, and his big, warm grip lingers. "Nice to finally meet you, Jessie. Izzie's been raving about you."

Izzie beams at me.

"Too bad you didn't get to play much tonight," Scott continues. "Hopefully, your coaches will rethink that. Izzie says you play solid defence."

"Thanks." Avoiding his intense blue gaze, I withdraw my hand.

"Pull up a chair, Scott," Darian says.

"I'm in Edmonton on business. Not that I follow your hockey team." He grins as he sits next to his sister. "Anyone hear Regina beat UBC 2-0?"

Kathy cheers and pounds the table.

Scott shrugs off his coat. "Your game was very entertaining, despite the loss. You'll take those Pandas tomorrow."

"I like this guy," I say.

Scott's blue eyes swing my way, and I blush. Kathy gives me a nudge. I didn't mean it to sound like *that*.

"Scott, did you go to U of S too?" I ask to cover my embarrassment.

"No. I played with the Golden Bears," he says.

"U of A? Boo!" Kathy says.

"And before that—the Dub," Izzie says proudly. "Scott played with the Hitmen."

"How old *are* you?" I ask.

Another nudge from Kathy.

Scott laughs. "Twenty-seven. But enough about me. I want to learn all about Izzie's teammates."

After we order, we talk about our schedule and our hopes for the season. Our meals arrive, and Scott tells us about his job as an engineer for an oil company in Calgary, and some sponsorship work he's done as a former Hitman.

"Do you know Mark Taylor?" I ask.

"Sure," he says. "How do you know him?"

Heat rises in my cheeks. "He used to live in my hometown. We dated for a while."

He nods. "Too bad about his dad passing away. Hey, did you hear Mark's getting married?"

I'm mildly surprised and pleased this news doesn't arouse any pain or regret.

How nice to be over Mark. "No, I didn't."

"I hope marriage works out for him," Izzie says, adding, "Scott's recently divorced. His ex is a piece of work."

"Hey now," Scott says.

"Do you have kids?" I ask.

He shakes his head. "Probably a good thing."

Kathy elbows me hard. Why do I keep blurting out these stupid questions?

When it's time to get on the team bus, Robbie beckons me to the coaches' table. "Come to the conference room at 8:30 tomorrow, Jessie."

The team meeting's at 9:00, but I decide not to let the early summons bother me. As soon as I'm on the bus, I check my phone. Two missed calls from Liam—and one from Courtney. I still don't know what happened in her game, but my 11:00 curfew looms.

I'll talk to them tomorrow.

"I'm better," Mom says from across the hotel room. Her face is white as death. "You look exhausted. Are *you* feeling okay?"

"I'm perfect," I lie. I hardly slept last night. But she looks terrible, and I don't want her worrying about me.

"How are your feet?" she asks. "They must get cold with you sitting so much. If I feel up to it, I'll go buy you some warm socks."

Her concern is embarrassing.

"I'm going to go use the fitness room. I'll see you later. Take care of yourself, Mom. Get some more sleep."

"I'll try," she says.

I take out all my frustration on the treadmill then return to the room I share with Kathy and jump in the shower.

When I'm dressed, I call Liam and get his voicemail. Rather than leave a message —he never listens to them—I hang up and call my sister.

She doesn't answer until the fifth ring, but she doesn't sound groggy. "Sorry. My first game's about to start. I've only got a sec."

"Game?"

"My league volleyball tournament. Remember?"

"Right," I say, even though I forgot. "I called to ask you about your *hockey* game. How did it go?"

While she gives me a recap, I snack on the boiled egg and orange Kathy left for me.

"Gotta go," Courtney says. "Talk later!"

I check the time. 8:33. I'm late for my meeting with Robbie!

I take the stairs to the bottom floor and sprint to the conference room. Robbie and Coach sit at the end of a long table.

"Morning, Jessie." Robbie gestures to a chair beside her.

If she sees the bags under my eyes, she makes no comment.

"Last night, you made it clear you're disappointed with your ice-time." Coach's face is grim. "Is there anything you'd like to say to us?"

I take a deep breath. "I busted my butt to get to practice early this week. Scrambled to get to the game on time yesterday. And what did I get? Three lousy shifts."

Coach and Robbie exchange glances.

"I want you to think hard about what you just said," Coach says quietly.

Whoa.

"Did you make any mistakes on those shifts?" Robbie asks.

I recall all the times she's leaned over my shoulder. "Get back hard," she'll say. "Give yourself space, so you can make a direct pass to your winger, and not rim the shot along the boards."

Or: "When you're the second D back, go to the boards to give your partner options. Don't hang out in front of the net."

Or: "Stick with a winger if she's got the puck. Don't let her off the hook even if she moves into the high slot."

I close my eyes and visualize my three shifts.

"I did make mistakes," I say after a bit. "But it takes me a while to find my rhythm, and I didn't have a chance to do that."

Man, that sounded weak.

Robbie scrawls something on a notepad and shows it to me. "Would you agree these are our top D?"

I nod.

"Which one should you replace in Game Two?" Robbie asks.

I stare at the names. These players are work horses. Strong and smart. Robbie can load them up, and they'll pull till their hearts break.

"None of them," I mumble.

"Do you notice which players arrive an hour early for practice? Stay fifteen or twenty minutes longer? Work out every chance they get—not just on Mondays? Because we do," she says. "Elite players do the work without being asked and wait for the next shift without complaining. They know that Game

Day begins at 6:00 am with mental preparation, and they hit the ice *running*. Jessie, this team can't afford the time you need to find your rhythm."

I feel like such a fool for opening my big mouth.

October 19
University of Saskatchewan Huskies vs. University of Alberta Pandas
Clare Drake Arena, Edmonton

From the top tier of the Huskies bench, I cheer for my teammates, watch the game closely, and try not to show my frustration when rookies like Izzie, Kira, and Brooke log ice-time on D. I have a perfect view of them during the first period, which ends with no score though the Pandas are outshooting us.

As I climb off my perch, a shopping bag plops at my feet. Mom leans over the glass. I open the bag and discover two new pairs of wool socks. My humiliation is complete.

"Thanks Mom!" I call to her.

She gives me a sad smile.

In the second period, my team jumps ahead of the Pandas 2-1. My teammates are elated, but also banged up, as they file off the ice. No shifts for me, but my feet are warmer.

"Jessie, come here!" Coach calls before I step into the dressing room. He places a big hand on my shoulder. "I need you to play wing."

What? I haven't played on offence in five years.

But there's only one answer. "I'll do anything you want," I say.

During intermission, I pay close attention to the instructions Dan gives the forwards, all the while trying to ignore my butterflies. I understand my new role. First, don't let the Pandas score. Second, get the puck out of our end. Third, earn a faceoff in the Pandas' zone, so our best forwards can take over.

I get my chance early in the third. Dan sends Kathy, Darian, and me to neutralize the Pandas' top line. With Kathy shadowing the Panda centre, I challenge their right D. I block a shot from the point, and the puck squirts over the blue line. Darian picks it up and throws Kathy a pass. The Panda D back pedals, but Kathy gets a shot away, which their goalie freezes. Dan pats my helmet when we return to the bench.

Mission accomplished.

Halfway through the period, I try to chip the puck along the boards. Two passes later, the Pandas tie the score.

Dan scowls at me as I step off the ice. "Always protect the puck, Mac."

The Pandas dominate OT, but when they turn over the puck at their blue line, Willo snaps it up and blasts past their D. She centers a pass to Cami, whose wrist shot soars over the Panda netminder's glove.

Huskies win!

⬦

"Coach wants to talk to you, Mac," Kathy says.

Coach and Robbie stand near the rear entrance. Coach crooks a finger at me.

I swallow my nerves as I walk towards him. "What's up?"

"Just wanted to let you know we noticed an improvement in your attitude on the bench. Also, I don't expect your parents to foot the bill for your flight. I'll talk to Diane about reimbursing them," Coach says.

"Speaking of your mom, there she is," Robbie says.

Mom waves at me from the other end of the hall. I wave back, wishing I could hug her. She leaves with Mrs. Parker while my coaches help Dave wrangle the wheeled bins of equipment out the door and into the parking lot. Our team travels like a small army.

"Too bad about your penalty."

I turn around.

Scott's hands are jammed in the pockets of his pea coat. "But you can hold your head up. Glad your coaches finally realized they need you. Even though it makes no sense to put you on offence."

I'm not sure how I feel about his criticism of my coaches.

"So, the Huskies wind up with two points in the series while Alberta gets three," Scott continues. "That'll shorten the ride home. Have you noticed you don't need as much ice after a win?"

I laugh. "Oh yeah. Those bumps and bruises don't hurt near as much."

"So—Lethbridge next weekend?"

"Yeah. The Pronghorns are tough at home."

"I'm planning to drive down for the games," he says. "Wouldn't mind spending a little time with you if it can be arranged."

What? He's way too old.

"I have a boyfriend," I blurt. "He can't come to many games because he's trying to get into vet med."

"Well, he's a fool if he doesn't watch you every chance he gets," Scott says. "Boyfriend or not, I'd still like to hang out with you and Izzie after your game next Friday. Have a safe trip home."

I mumble a reply then head for the exit. I shoot a glance back at Scott as I push the door open, but he's talking to Izzie. As soon as I'm settled on the bus, I call Liam.

"Hey. How'd it go? Did you win?" he asks.

Halfway through my summary, he yawns.

"You should go to bed," I say.

"No, I gotta study. Maybe we can meet at the library tomorrow night." He yawns again.

"See you then," I say.

He hangs up.

I like Liam a lot. But I don't see him much. What did Scott say?

"He's a fool if he doesn't watch you every chance he gets."

Would I be better off on my own?

13

"GLAD YOU MADE IT." Josh ushers Courtney through his front door.

Courtney watches her dad back out of the driveway. Although he appears to be checking his side mirror, she knows it's Josh he's staring down. She pries off her sneakers.

"Bring your shoes," Josh says. "My stepdad made a bonfire in the back. Can I get you a drink?"

"No thanks. I brought my own water," Courtney says.

Josh's mom and stepdad watch a movie in the den. They don't seem concerned about the assortment of bottles and cans on the kitchen table or the loud voices coming from the backyard.

Josh grabs a beer and leads her through the French doors onto the deck. From there they descend to the lawn, where the rest of the team has gathered around a brick firepit. The fire crackles and snaps. Her stomach lurches when she sees Brandon. Did Shane lie to her about Michael not coming?

Jutin jumps to his feet. "You can sit here, Courtney."

She sinks onto his chair. "Thanks."

"Do you want a blanket?" Shane asks.

Some of the guys laugh. Courtney's glad it's dark, so they can't see her face.

"I'm fine." She unscrews the lid of her water bottle and takes a sip.

All her teammates hold drinks, and most are vaping. Austin pulls up a lawn chair beside her.

"Courtney, you were something else against the Knights," Austin says. "One time, I thought for sure you were gonna get creamed. Do you have eyes in the back of your head or what?"

Courtney laughs.

The rest of the boys chime in with compliments about the way she played. It rings false somehow. What are they up to?

"Look, Courtney. We're sorry about what happened at practice," Josh says. "Aren't we, guys?"

The boys mutter agreement, but Brandon stares into the fire and says nothing.

"We don't agree with the way Michael's acting, but we don't see him backing down," Josh says.

This is the reason he invited her? To talk about Michael?

"So, you want me to quit?" she asks.

"No, no, nothing like that." Josh scratches the back of his blonde head. "Believe it or not, Michael's a good teammate."

"Except when he's being a jerk," Shane says.

"Which is often," Courtney says.

"Yes. Well. Anyway." Josh shoves his hands in his pockets. "This gong show with Minor Sports might go away if you talked to Michael. Butter him up a little. Maybe apologize."

"What exactly would I be apologizing for?" she demands. "He's the one who took a run at me."

"Just say you're sorry things went south," Brandon says. "Say you want to do what's best for the team. That'll appease him—and most of our parents."

Ah, yes. Mrs. Sweater Coat strikes again.

"Do you mean your *mom?*" Courtney asks.

Brandon sucks on his vape and exhales, wreathing his head in a cloud. "Don't take it personally."

"You know the difference between hockey moms and Rottweilers, right?" Toby asks.

"No idea," she says.

"The lipstick," Toby says.

No one laughs.

Courtney screws the lid back on her water bottle. "I'll talk to Michael."

"That's all we're asking," Josh says.

"But I'm not sucking up," she insists.

"No problem. Oh, one more thing. Rookie party next weekend. We would have had it tonight, but we couldn't—because of Michael being suspended."

She gulps. "Rookie party. Yeah. I'll get back to you about that."

Courtney leans into Jessie's old bedroom. "Dad, I'm taking Rufus for a walk." Dad puts down his paint brush. "Will you be back in time to help make supper? I want to have it ready for when your mom gets home. She'll be tired after that long trip."

"Sure thing, Dad," Courtney says.

She's looked up the Carsons' address. They live about a twenty-minute walk away. She hopes Michael will be hanging around his house on this sunny fall afternoon.

As soon as Courtney takes her hoodie and the leash out of the closet, Rufus bounds into the living room. He's a wriggling ball of white fur as she hooks the strap to his collar. She carries him outside and deposits him on the front step. While he trots along, his black nose investigating shrubs, fences, and lamp posts, Courtney calls Jessie.

"Those spineless little creeps expect you to cave to Michael's ego," Jessie says when Courtney's finished telling her about the party at Josh's.

"It makes sense to clear the air before we have another practice or game," Courtney says. "Maybe if I do, his dad will get off Clint's case."

"I hope it's that easy, but don't count on it," Jessie says. "Good luck, and let me know how it goes."

When Courtney reaches the Carsons' house, Michael is washing a white sports car in the driveway. He wears headphones, and he looks angry. She picks up Rufus and tucks him under her arm. When Michael notices them, he shuts off the pressure washer, but he now looks suspicious as well as angry. Her timing is bad.

"Got a sec?" Courtney calls out.

Michael shrugs and takes off his headphones.

As she walks up the driveway, her dog wiggles and barks. "Rufus won't bite," she promises. "He likes everybody."

The anger and suspicion drain from Michael's face. "Cute pup." He rubs Rufus under the chin, and the dog licks his hand. "What breed is he?"

"Coton de Tulear." Bringing Rufus along was a stroke of brilliance. Still, why does he have to like Michael *too*?

"Can I hold him?" Michael asks.

"Sure. Keep a grip on his leash." She places the dog in his arms.

Rufus licks Michael's neck. The little traitor.

"The guys on the team wanted me to talk to you," she says.

Michael raises an eyebrow. He looks exactly like his dad.

"I'm sorry about what's happened," she continues. "But I'm not sorry for anything I did. I didn't do anything wrong."

Michael rolls his eyes.

"Furthermore, I don't have to earn a place on this team. My parents paid my ice fees just like yours did. I've got as much right to play as you do."

Michael shifts his grip on Rufus, who is now licking his arm. "I guess you might have a point."

Is she making progress?

"Do you think your dad could back off the complaint he's made to Minor Sports? Is all this worth Clint getting canned as our coach?"

Michael rubs Rufus' head.

"Too bad you missed our game against the Knights," she says. "It was fast and intense, and most of the guys said I did okay. I'd like to keep playing, and I'd like you to cut me some slack."

Michael sets Rufus on the ground but keeps a grip on the leash.

"That's all I came to say," she says. "I don't want this year to turn into something that has nothing to do with hockey."

"You mean *politics*," he says. "Hockey's full of it." He hands her the end of the leash. "I guess I was kind of a jerk to you."

She bites her tongue before she blurts out—*kind of?*

"I'll talk to my dad," he says. "See if I can get him to lay off."

Wow, this wasn't so hard after all. "That would be awesome."

"As for Clint, is it okay if I tell him we worked things out? He won't let me be captain, even if everyone votes for me. I'd sure like to get that C."

"Okay," she says.

Michael's dad comes out of the house with two beers. "Need a cold one, bud?" he calls.

"See you at practice, Courtney." Michael turns his back and joins his dad on the step.

Mr. Carson glares at her.

Her phone plinks in her pocket. It's her own dad.

Mom's home.

Courtney crosses the street and pretends to fuss with Rufus' collar while she watches Michael and his dad. Mr. Carson's hand rests on Michael's shoulder as he sips his beer.

She better stay on her toes.

14

"DID YOU SEE THE RANKINGS?" Kathy asks while we're lined up for a shooting drill at Tuesday practice.

"Nope," I say.

Every week U Sports coaches vote on the top ten teams across Canada. Last year the Huskies made the list a few times.

"We didn't get ranked. Again. U of A's ninth. Do you think that's fair?"

"Does it matter what I think?"

"Quit being such a diplomat," Kathy says. "I'm wildin' here."

No point in telling her I'm so frustrated about screwing up my playing time I have nothing left for U Sports rankings.

It's my turn.

I drive hard to the net while Flinton shadows me. I catch Erv's slick cross-ice feed and aim top left corner. Cassidy's big shoulder deflects my shot.

Kathy lines up behind me after her turn. "You made quite an impression on Izzie's big bro. She says he's coming to Lethbridge."

"Uh huh."

"Probably going to see him when we play Mount Royal and Calgary too," she persists. "I saw you talking to him after the game on Saturday. Does Liam know?"

"Does Liam know *what*? That I talk to the relatives of my teammates?" I hate it when she takes the moral high ground. "Besides, Scott's way too old for me."

"I don't think *he* thinks he is," Kathy says. "I caught the full episode. Remember?"

"How about we talk about you and Brett?" I counter. "You play U Sports. He refs campus rec. Is that a match made in heaven or what?"

"Leave Brett outta this," Kathy says.

After practice, I walk back to campus, grab a veggie wrap from the food court, and head to the library. The higher the floor, the quieter it is. Liam likes the fifth, which suits me. The sixth floor is so quiet it's creepy.

Liam's already at our usual table, hoodie draped over the chair across from him. He wears headphones while he makes notes from his textbook. He looks tired, and his unruly black hair needs cutting. I pick up his hoodie and push it across the table. He nods at me, tucks the garment behind him, and turns his eyes back to the page.

I take out my veggie wrap and wave it at him.

Liam shakes his head and resumes reading.

Suit yourself. More for me, and I'm starved.

While I eat my supper, I assemble my study materials. I set out my multicoloured highlighters and mechanical pencils and arrange my history notes and texts. I update my planner and colour code the entries.

When I'm done eating and organizing, I review today's lecture notes from *History Matters: The Conquest of America*. I have a paper due next week, and I haven't picked my topic. I could choose just about any chapter from the book *Clearing the Plains*, which presents a detailed history of Indigenous peoples in Western Canada.

I send Liam a text.

Can I ask u a question?

Liam's phone vibrates. He stares at it and then takes off his headphones.

I hold up the book. "Have you read this?" I mouth.

He shakes his head.

"I can't decide on a topic," I whisper, leaning my chin on my palm. "Also, I'm supposed to use two primary sources, and Indigenous ones aren't so easy to find."

"You'll figure it out," he says.

He puts on his headphones and turns the page.

Obviously, this is the end of our discussion. Does the topic make him uncomfortable—or am I wasting his time?

He's not the affectionate, fun, easy going Liam I started dating in Grade Twelve.

Two years ago, he never would've brushed me off like this.

"Will you quit staring at me?" he whispers.

Definitely wasting his time. I stuff my notebook and other study paraphernalia in my knapsack.

"Where are you going?" he asks.

"Back to my dorm. You'll get more done without me. And I'll get more done too." The students at the next table are gawking. "I'll text you tomorrow."

I grab my stuff and head for the stairs. I hear footsteps behind me, but I ignore them. I'm at the third-floor landing before he catches up.

"Hey!" he gasps. "What's wrong?"

"Nothing."

"Sorry I upset you," he says.

But he sounds the exact opposite of sorry. He sounds like I'm being unreasonable and immature. Maybe I am. But I know if I did to him what he just did to me, he wouldn't be impressed.

"I don't want to argue. I'm tired. Let's talk about this another time." I hurry down the steps.

Damn it. I don't need this.

15

October 22
Estevan Moose vs. Lampman-Arcola Imperials
Lampman Community Complex, Lampman

WHEN COURTNEY ENTERS THE LAMPMAN rink lobby, Shane's jaw drops. "Wow! You look nice!" he says.

Tonight, Courtney put on a plaid scarf, taupe blazer, and dress pants. "My girls team always dressed up for games," she explains.

Will the boys think she's stupid for doing it?

Shane looks down at his jeans and sneakers. "I guess we could all do that, huh?"

After Shane disappears into his dressing room, she asks for directions to her own from the woman selling fifty-fifty tickets.

"Hey, Courtney. Come here for a sec," Clint calls.

He's talking to a man she doesn't know. Will Clint think she's silly for dressing up?

Instead, Clint introduces her to the Imperials coach.

"Let me know if any of my guys give you a bad time," the other coach says.

"Also, we have a team rule about female players and body contact. If you hit one of my boys, they'll hit back, but they won't hit you first. You okay with that?"

Courtney nods.

"Everything okay between you and Michael?" Clint asks after the other coach leaves.

"Seems to be," Courtney says.

During the past week, Michael hasn't said anything mean to her at school or at practice. The school gossip machine cooled when Mr. Carson withdrew the complaint about Clint.

"Michael won't wear the C today," Clint says. "I'll let you kids vote on the letters next week. In the meantime, you better get ready. And, Courtney, thanks for dressing like you care."

"You're welcome," she says.

"It was a positive step for Michael to reach out to you over the weekend," Clint says. "I'm proud of him for doing that."

Wow. Should she tell Clint she's the one who did the reaching?

But Clint walks over to talk to another set of parents.

"Dressing to impress?" Someone says behind her.

Her stomach backflips as she turns to face Mr. Carson. Michael smirks at her and ducks into the team dressing room.

"I'm glad you and Michael were able to work things out," Mr. Carson says. "Are you coming to the rookie party? It's at our place."

"I'm thinking about it," Courtney says.

"It'll help you feel like part of the team." Mr. Carson puts a hand on her shoulder. "Can I let you in on a secret? I think Michael has a crush on you." He winks and walks away.

Courtney tries to decide which emotion she should deal with first.

Confusion. Does Mr. Carson seriously think it's possible Michael likes her?

Revulsion. An adult inviting her to a party is just plain creepy.

Fear. Hockey rookie parties have a bad rep for hazing, and hazing is just another word for abuse—from groups of naked players forced into bathrooms on team buses to beatings with broken hockey sticks. Some people even defend initiation rites, saying, "it's part of the game" and "anyone who doesn't play hockey wouldn't understand." No wonder Hockey Canada will ban anyone who participates in or tolerates hazing.

Josh jostles her with his equipment bag, shaking her free of her thoughts. "Nice threads," he says.

"Thanks," she says, but her clothing is now the least of her worries.

The Moose and the Imperials battle in the neutral zone for the first few minutes. After an icing call on the Moose, Courtney skates to the faceoff dot for her first shift.

Josh wins the draw back to Michael, who swings behind their net, dodges the opposing centreman and cuts up the middle. Courtney bangs her stick for a pass, but when Michael rushes, she drops back to cover the blue line. Michael drives at the net and fires. The puck squirts between the goalie's blocker and the net. A beauty.

Josh and the others swarm Michael. He hoots and rockets past their bench. Courtney trails the parade and steps off the ice.

Clint waves at them. "Stay out!"

They line up at centre. This time Josh loses the draw, and she moves to check the winger carrying the puck. She throws her body at him and knocks the puck free. Michael picks it up and passes to Shane, who's wide open. 19 forces Shane wide and crushes him on the boards. Michael pinches, retrieves the puck, and maneuvers into the high slot. Courtney drops back again to cover the blue line. The Imperial goalie deflects Michael's shot, and players from both teams battle in the corner. The puck dribbles to Courtney, and she wrists it back. 28 chops the puck out of the air, blasts past her on a breakaway, and rifles the puck over Toby's glove.

Scores.

Toby slams his stick and digs the puck out of the net. Courtney's cheeks burn with shame.

"You blew it," Michael says as they return to the bench.

She wants to point out that he left his position twice, and she was covering for him. But she squirms between Shane and Josh and says nothing.

The opposition scores twice more before the period ends—once while the Imperials are short-handed and once while Michael is serving a charging penalty. At least she's not on the ice for either of those.

"Demoralizing," Jutin observes as she relieves him on the wing.

With less than a minute left, Josh scores top shelf.

The Moose head to the dressing room down 3-2.

During Clint's analysis, Courtney notices he never mentions Michael's bad habits. Hasn't his selfishness cost them a couple of goals? Then Clint draws up the play where she made a critical error at the blue line. Clint doesn't single her out, but she knows the *guys* know who made the mistake.

"Keep your eyes open out there," Clint says. "Make a read before you throw a blind pass."

She stares at the floor.

She second guesses herself the next period. Her timing is off. She gets knocked down in the corners though none of the hits are hard. The Moose's penalties rack up. Roughing. Elbowing. Interference. By the time the period ends, they trail 5-2.

"Wrong time of the month?" Michael asks as she walks past him into the dressing room.

Should she tell Clint about his nasty remarks?

***

Courtney leans on the counter next to Shane. The Lampman rink cheeseburgers are supposed to be the best in the league, and right now, she needs one. The 7-2 loss stings.

"Hey, Shane, do you ever wish you *hadn't* talked to me that day at St. Joe's?" she asks. "That's when I got the idea to play with you guys."

He jams his thumbs in his belt loops. "I don't regret it for a minute."

"I'm glad," she says.

He turns and leans next to her, his shoulder pressing hers. "Hey, there's something I want to ask you."

"Cheeseburger and fries?" the woman behind the counter says.

"Yes. Thanks." Courtney picks up the foiled wrapped packages. "Where are your condiments?"

The woman points. "Around that corner."

"Are you ready, Courtney?" her dad calls from the rink entrance.

She turns to Shane. "Gotta go."

"Will you come to the rookie party?" he asks.

She thinks about Michael and his dad. Will she let them scare her off?

"Yeah, I'll come," she says. "See you there."

She grabs some ketchup and mustard packs and breezes out the door.

1 6

I'VE WRAPPED MY HEAD AROUND the fact I can't pull off 90s in university as easily as I did in high school. I've convinced myself that 80 is the new 90, and I pull off 80s regularly in my math classes.

I get my psych midterm back on Wednesday.

69%.

So much for Introduction to Culture and Psychology being an easy credit.

I flip through the exam, reading Dr. Kerr's terse comments on my short and long answers. A message is neat script appears on the last page:

Make an appointment to see me.

Unease settles into my lower back. I can't concentrate on her lecture. Blowing this class will mess up my overall average.

I head across campus to the Thorvaldsen Building for calculus. The greystone façade reminds me of a gothic cathedral. Every time I walk through the entrance, I feel like I've gone back in time. I'm early for class, so I linger on the main floor and compose a polite email to Professor Kerr inquiring about her availability later this afternoon.

After I send it, Liam calls.

"Hey, can we get together later?" he asks.

"I have a night class. Remember?"

"What about tomorrow?"

"I'm busy."

"Busy—or pretending to be busy?" he asks. "Look, it's obvious you're still mad at me because I didn't pay enough attention to you at the library."

I start up the stairs to the lecture theatre before I remember its exceptional acoustics. I don't want anyone listening in on this conversation.

"I wasn't mad then. I'm not mad now." The truth is—I'm getting there.

"Glad to hear it," he says. "Can we meet on the weekend?"

"I'm in Lethbridge."

"Jessie, I wanted to talk to you about this in person, but it doesn't look like that's going to happen any time soon." He clears his throat. "I think we should stop trying to see each other."

Shit.

"Let's break this off before we start disliking each other," he says. "We're obviously too busy to make this work."

Even though I've been thinking the same thing for weeks, this feels wrong. Mainly because he's breaking up with me—not the other way around.

"Maybe you're right." I have to say it carefully, so he won't guess how much this hurts.

He talks about bagging up the few items I have at his place and dropping them off at the rink. He'll take care of a few other loose ends—like some concert tickets. How long did he have this mapped out?

"So that's it?" I ask when he's done.

"I guess so," he says. "Good luck this weekend. See you around."

He hangs up.

Guys have dumped me before. But this burns.

Once inside the lecture theatre, I ascend to the top row and slide into a wooden chair. Memories of Liam and the past two summers wash over me. Golfing at Woodlawn. Kayaking in the coolies near his family farm. Football games in Regina with Kathy and Brett. An overnight in a tent on a trail ride. The powwow at Pheasant Rump, where I met Liam's wonderful kooshie and metagoosh.

I resurface in the present when Professor Hale begins the lecture. In our first class, he told us that World War II pilots in training started the practice of tossing weighted paper planes at the ceiling. I stare up at the dozens—thrown there by fellow U of S students—hanging over my head.

Why do I feel like my own happiness hangs by a thread?

Dr. Kerr sits, back rigid, hands folded on her desk.

"You wanted to see me?"

"No need to sit, Ms. McIntyre. This won't take long."

Oh, this is going to be bad.

"I want you to know I was not fooled by your veiled reference to our last encounter," she says.

What is she talking about?

She opens a file folder on her desk and removes a piece of paper. "Do you recognize this?"

It's a photocopy of a page from my midterm.

"Yes."

She narrows her eyes. "Read the underlined sentence in your answer to E7."

I look at the page. The question relates to a recent chapter in our textbook on culturally defined ways of regulating emotions.

"In terms of an example from my own experience, I had a recent encounter with an adult who—" The words—my words—swim.

"Why did you stop, Ms. McIntyre?"

Anxiety hammers in my ears.

"I wasn't referring to you, Dr. Kerr." My voice is barely a whisper.

"Really. You're certain I wasn't having an emotional experience that—" She snatches the paper from my hand—"distorted my view of actual events and created a potentially harmful situation?'"

"No," I say firmly. "I was referring to someone else."

How would giving Dr. Kerr specifics about my mom unburdening herself to the Huskies Athletic Director and my head coach help my case?

"So, this isn't about your dissatisfaction with staying behind to write my midterm? You didn't twist the content of this class to send me a snide and hateful message?"

"No, I didn't."

What can I say? I can't think of anything else, and I doubt she'd believe me even if I did.

"You may go." Dr. Kerr flicks her long fingers. "I'm sure you have more pressing concerns."

Any hope I had of getting any slack from her for the rest of the semester has been dashed.

It's been a shitty day.

1 7

THE NIGHT AND THE SHADOWS of the trees close in around Courtney as Michael smacks the ping pong paddle against his palm. She looks hopefully at the lights on in the Carsons' house. Should she scream?

"Okay, Courtney McIntyre. Either you're one of us—or you're not. Simple choice. This is what we do to rookies," Michael says.

Why does he insist on using her full name all the time?

"Nobody did anything to us last year," Toby points out.

"I'm not a rookie. I'm a second year." Courtney's voice shakes when Michael smacks the paddle again.

Austin and the others stand with their hands in their pockets.

Are they as scared as she is?

"Courtney's right," Josh says.

Michael bumps Josh with his chest. "Who asked your opinion?"

"You know hazing's not allowed. I don't want to get suspended," Josh says.

"Neither do I," Shane says.

"Come on, Michael," Brandon says. "You'll never get away with it. McIntyre will squeal for sure."

"And so will I," Jutin says indignantly.

Michael shakes his head. "What a bunch of wusses." He tucks the paddle in his back pocket. "Well, there has to be *some* kind of initiation. How about we pour the rookies some drinks?"

"I'm not getting wasted for your entertainment," Courtney says.

"Then go home," Michael says.

"Michael, stop being a prick," Josh says.

"You're such a bleeding-heart snowflake," Michael mutters. "Gender equity bullshit." He walks into the garage and slams the door.

Courtney reaches for her phone. "I'm calling my dad to come get me."

"Please don't leave," Shane says. "Michael will have a couple of drinks and play Xbox and forget you're here."

"Yeah. Hang out for a while," Brandon says. "Come on, Toby."

Brandon and Toby disappear inside the garage.

Courtney realizes that she's cold. She rubs her arms.

"Let's go inside, and I'll get you a Coke," Shane says.

Someone cranks the tunes as she walks through the door. The overhead LED lights in the garage are dim, and she can tell no vehicle has ever been parked inside. It has a built-in sound system, beer lights and boxed hockey jerseys, a wet bar, and leather furniture. Some of her teammates are gathered on the sectional in front of a huge television while others play table hockey or darts. Clutching her water bottle, Courtney sits on a couch near the ping pong table. She wishes some adults were here.

Shane slips behind the bar while Josh leans over the back of the couch. Beer fumes wash over her. "I'm glad you decided to stay."

She unscrews the cap of her water bottle and takes a long drink.

Brandon and Toby belly up to the bar. Michael comes out of the washroom and grabs beers from the fridge while Shane pours Coke and ice into two glasses. The boys laugh and joke with one another. Michael drifts over to the boys playing video games.

"What's Michael's deal anyway?" she asks. "Everybody tells me what a great guy he is when he's not being a jerk. Will you let me know when he stops?"

Josh laughs. "A beer will help loosen you up."

"I don't need to loosen up."

"Aw, come on," he urges.

"One of my sister's friends ended up with a brain injury because of alcohol and a bad decision. It changed her life." Courtney taps her forehead. "I'd like to keep this."

Josh pushes off the couch. "Have it your way. I gotta take a leak. Talk to you later."

Courtney sighs and takes another drink. Did she sound like Jessie just now? Maybe she *should* loosen up.

Shane returns with two red plastic cups and perches on the arm of the couch.

She takes the cup he offers her. Sips. Tastes booze. "What did you put in here?"

"Coke," he says. "Hey, have you seen the new Avengers movie?"

"No." She sets the cup on the floor. Not loosening up *that* way.

Shane slides off the arm so he's sitting beside her. He spills a little of his drink. "We should go see it. Together."

He's too close. She can smell booze on his breath. Obviously, that's what's giving him the courage to ask her out.

She leans away from him. "That's not a good idea. We play on the same line. How would it look to the other guys?"

He sighs.

"Could we just go as friends?" she asks.

He drinks. "You mean—I'd pay my way, and you'd pay yours."

"Cheaper for you," she says.

He looks depressed. "Not what I had in mind."

"We could share popcorn," she offers.

"And a pack of licorice?" he asks.

He's kind of cute, but no way. It'd be like dating her cousin. "Sure," she says.

They talk about the league for a while. The Moose play in a division with the Estevan Knights, two Weyburn teams, Oxbow, and Lampman-Arcola, but they will have a few crossover games with the teams in the other two divisions. While Shane talks and sips, he sinks lower and lower. His words and ideas ramble.

Brandon and Toby stand with their backs to the bar. They guzzle their beer and glance at her and Shane. Did they spike her drink?

She nudges Shane. "You any good at ping pong?"

"Sure!" He pushes off the couch and staggers to the ping pong table.

She learned from Jessie's boyfriend Liam that a little competition perks a guy up every time.

She pours her cup in the bar sink and refills her water bottle at the refrigerator.

"How'd you know?" Brandon asks.

"I could taste it," she replies.

Brandon and Toby look at each other.

Shane taps his paddle on the table. "I'm waiting!"

She leaves the boys at the bar and joins Shane.

"Do you want to rally for a while—to get a feel for it?" Shane asks.

"No, let's have a game." Anything to get her mind off the losers who tried to spike her drink. "We'll play to 11."

Shane's eye-hand coordination is terrible, and Courtney easily wins the first game.

He laughs and leans on the edge of the table. "You're pretty good."

"I'm sober, and you're not," she says.

Halfway through the next set, Shane stumbles and nearly falls as he flails at the ball. He straightens and sips his drink, spilling some on his shirt.

"I think you've had enough," Courtney says.

Shane laughs, takes a few steps, and falls into her arms. She staggers beneath his weight, which forces her to her knees. "Help me out here!" She eases Shane to the ground. His eyes are rolled back in his head.

"What's happening back there?" Michael shouts.

"Shane passed out! Help me please!" she calls.

The boys gather round her.

Josh kneels and pats Shane's cheek. "Wake up, buddy."

"Be careful!" Courtney swats Josh's hand away. She puts her head on Shane's chest and listens to the rapid thump of his heart. "We should call 911."

"No way," Michael says.

"He might have alcohol poisoning," she reasons.

"No, he doesn't," Toby says.

Michael pushes him. "Shut up!"

"He got *your* drink," Toby says to Courtney. "There wasn't any booze in it. Just cannabis oil."

The earth shifts under Courtney's knees.

Brandon stares at Michael and scratches his head. Michael swears.

What in the hell?

1 8

October 25
University of Saskatchewan Huskies vs. University of Lethbridge Pronghorns
ATB Centre, Lethbridge

SO FAR, WE'VE OUTSHOT AND outworked the Pronghorns. Their netminder is playing lights out, but so is Karen, our rookie goaltender. We're tied 1-1.

"Mac. Parker. Darian. Hustle," Dan says.

I've jumped out of Robbie's frying pan and into Dan's fiery furnace. Dan is a tough taskmaster who sets the bar high for his Huskie forwards, and he has no problem telling us when we haven't reached it.

We face off against the Pronghorns' first line. When Kathy wins the draw, we move the puck to Lethbridge's end and keep it there for the next two minutes. Dan switches us out, player by player, to maintain pressure.

"Good reads, Mac," he says when I come off.

I get more shifts with Kathy and Darian in the second and third periods. Our objective is to shut down the Pronghorns' top lines. When we do, Dan can unleash Cami, Erv, and Willo—then Gresch, Johnny, and Cooker—on

Lethbridge's third and fourth lines.

"I like this," I say to Kathy and Darian as we come off the ice late in the third. "Do you?"

"Hell yes," Kathy says.

"What's not to like?" Darian says.

With seventeen seconds left, it looks like overtime. We'll face off in our end, and Dan sends out my line again. The Lethbridge centre wins the draw back to her left D. The D shifts to the middle of the ice and fires a shot. It deflects off the glass and into the corner. I sprint after it and pin the puck against the boards while two Pronghorns slash my skates.

Time runs off the clock.

We get a two-minute rest before the ten-minute overtime. I guzzle water while Coach draws up our next play.

When OT begins, our top two lines battle the Horns in the neutral zone. 6 fires the puck down to our end, and the linesperson waves off icing. We howl in protest. When the play comes back up the ice, Cassidy opens the gate for Darian and me while Kathy hurdles the boards.

I ride 18 into the corner and try to wrench the puck away from her. She goes down and takes me with her. I scramble to my feet and flail at the puck.

The whistle blasts.

"23 Green. Two minutes for body contact."

Not again!

After the Pronghorns' trainer attends to her, 18 skates on wobbly knees to her players box. Dan taps Cami and Willo while Robbie sends Mutcher and Izzie to kill my penalty. Meanwhile, I hang my head and dread what Dan will have to say about being short-handed during sudden death.

There's a scramble in front of our net, and 13 deflects the puck over Karen's stick. The Pronghorns celebrate their victory while I skate, shamefaced, to join my teammates.

As we line up to shake hands with our grinning opponents, I feel a hand on my shoulder.

"Tough break," Darian says. Her red bangs drip with sweat.

In the dressing room, I suffer Coach's postgame analysis in silence. Dan doesn't mince any words about the consequences of stupid penalties.

I don't have family waiting for me in the lobby, so I cool down, shower, and change. In the hallway, I take out my phone to check on the other Canada West scores. Two missed calls from Mom. I don't feel like talking, but I call her back.

She picks up immediately. "Jessie. Thanks for calling. I wanted you to tell you before you hear it someplace else." She sounds out of breath.

Oh no. "What happened?"

"Someone put cannabis oil in Courtney's drink at the rookie party."

I lean against the wall.

"She's fine. She never got it. Shane Barber did."

"Do you know who's responsible?"

"No one's owned up to it," Mom says.

"The cops can start with that Michael kid," I say. "He's been such an asshole." The voices and phones in the background register. "Are you at the police station, Mom?"

"Yes. Courtney just finished giving her statement. I have to go now, but please call her in the morning."

"I will for sure. Thanks for letting me know."

"Hey, Jessie!" Izzie beckons to me. She's with her brother Scott.

I walk over, hands shoved in my pockets. This is the last thing I need right now.

"Good game," Scott says. "Tough way to end it."

"Yeah. Always great to watch the game winner from the penalty box." My mind reels with images of Courtney. Why did I back her decision to play with the boys?

"You'll get them tomorrow," Scott assures me. "In the meantime, I'm starved. Want to grab some food?"

"The team's going to the Cheesecake Factory," Izzie says. "Dobler says they make the *best* desserts."

More pictures of Courtney spin and tumble. Although I'm starved, I don't feel like eating.

"Everything okay?" Scott asks.

"I've got some stuff going at home. I don't feel like socializing. I'd like to grab some food at the hotel and go to bed."

"I could give you a ride." His blue eyes are sympathetic.

"That'd be great. Thanks."

"I'll go shower," Izzie says.

As soon as she's gone, Scott takes out his phone. "Did you have a chance to look at the other scores?"

"Not yet."

He steps close so I can see the screen. He's a lot taller than Liam, who only has an inch on me. While Scott scrolls and talks, I try to concentrate on the scores and visualize how they affect the standings. But my eyes are drawn to the big hand cradling his phone.

"Hey Jessie," Kathy says behind me. "You forgot this in the dressing room."

I turn around. She holds my Huskie scarf.

"Thanks." My blush deepens as I take it from her and drape it around my neck.

The view from behind couldn't be great. Me snuggled up to Scott, his free hand on my right shoulder. Will she tell Liam what she just saw? Should I care?

Kathy's pale blue eyes are icy as she turns and walks out.

"Do you want to go back to the hotel now?" Scott asks.

"Please."

We don't talk much on the drive across the river. I pray he doesn't ask about my family. I don't want to talk about what happened to Courtney.

Scott pulls up in front of the hotel. "So, your boyfriend isn't here again."

"I told you he's a student." I avoid his gaze. "But he's not my boyfriend anymore."

"Oh? Well, I have to say—the guy can't be very bright," Scott says.

My cheeks feel hot as I open my door and get out.

"Get a good night's rest, Jessie," he says. "Hope I can see you tomorrow."

I step back and watch him drive away. He really is gorgeous but far too old. And right now, the only thing on my mind is my baby sister.

19

COURTNEY'S PHONE BUZZES ON HER nightstand. She opens her eyes and fumbles for it.

Reads Jessie's text.

U awake yet?

There're a bazillion other texts. The whole team wants to cover their ignorant asses.

Courtney wipes the sleep from her eyes and sends a reply to her sister.

Give me a sec.

She crawls out of bed and uses the bathroom across the hall. The mirror reflects a girl with pouches under her eyes and hair like a rat's nest. Did she even sleep after she got home from the police station? All night four words haunted her.

"Boys will be boys."

Mr. Carson said that to Constable Dufferin as the paramedics loaded Shane in the ambulance.

What would have happened if she'd gotten the cannabis oil instead of Shane? What did Michael and the others have planned?

She remembers what Toby said before she dialed 911.

"He got your drink. There wasn't any booze in it. Just cannabis oil."

"Tell me from the beginning," Jessie says when Courtney calls her.

"I told Constable Dufferin everything when I gave my statement. I'm not supposed to talk about it," Courtney says. "Do you know anything about cannabis oil?"

"Fortunately, not much," Jessie says. "How's Shane doing?"

"I haven't heard anything since last night. I hope he's okay. I just feel so bad for him." She wipes away a tear.

"Mom says nobody owned up to it," Jessie says. "Do you know who did it?"

"I told you. I can't talk about that."

"Sis, are you going to keep on playing?" Jessie asks.

Courtney pushes down a sob. "I don't know."

"I don't blame you. But don't do anything hasty. Give it a week. Maybe it wasn't the whole team. Maybe Shane gave it to himself on purpose—or by accident."

"That's not what happened." Courtney's phone buzzes. "I gotta go, Jessie. Clint's calling."

"Let's talk later. Take care of yourself." Jessie hangs up.

Clint's voice fills Courtney's ears. "Morning, Courtney. How are you feeling?"

"A little rough, but I'll be okay. How's Shane?"

"He's all right. He spent the night at St. Joe's, but I expect they'll release him later today."

She's relieved. "That's good news."

"Courtney, I'm sorry to make you go over this again, but I'd like you to tell me what happened. This is my team, and I need to know."

Clint interrupts constantly to ask questions, get more details. Plus, he gets angrier by the second.

"I can't believe these guys tried a stunt like that," he says when she's done. "I've coached most of them since initiation. I'm having a tough time with it."

"Me too," Courtney says.

There's a long pause. "It might sound strange, but I'm glad Shane screwed up the drinks. I don't want to think about what might have happened to you."

Courtney's hands shake.

"I've cancelled Tuesday practice. There won't be any hockey until we get to the bottom of this. I've already talked to SHA and Estevan Minor Hockey. Everyone is taking this seriously, Courtney."

"Do you think it would be all right if I came to see Shane tomorrow?" she asks.

"I'm sure he'd like that," Clint says.

When Clint hangs up, Courtney shuts off her phone and crawls under the covers.

Great. A tornado about her team, and where is she?

Spinning right in the middle.

Wrapped in a blanket, Shane sits in a recliner in his family room. He looks awful.

"I'm way better than yesterday." He points to the sectional. "Have a seat. Stay a while. I'm not going anywhere."

Courtney sits and shrugs off her hoodie.

"Do you want something to drink? It's safe. I promise." He smiles wryly at his joke. When she doesn't reply, he says, "Sorry. I shouldn't have said that."

Abby enters and hovers over him. She brushes his hair back from his face, and he jerks his head.

"Mom!"

"Sorry." Abby puts her hands behind her back. "I'll get you a glass of water, Courtney. And you too, Shane." She picks up his empty glass. "Remember what Dr. Bilku said about fluids."

Shane rolls his eyes. "It's so embarrassing," he says after Abby leaves. "Is your mom like that?"

"Pretty much."

"How'd the Huskies do this weekend?" he asks. "I never heard their scores."

"They lost in OT on Friday and won on Saturday."

"Not terrible then," Shane says. "You talk to Jessie since then?"

"A couple of times." Courtney tucks her hair behind her ears. "You don't look very good, Shane. Are you sure you're going to be okay?"

He shifts his position. "I'm just tired and dizzy. Yesterday I slept the day away. I felt like I was going to throw up, but I never did. I gave my statement to the cops, but I don't remember much about what happened."

"What *do* you remember?"

He reclines his chair further. "I remember getting to Michael's place. Talking to you on the couch." He shrugs. "And then I woke up in a hospital bed."

"You don't remember playing ping pong with me?"

He thinks. "I got nothing," he says at last. "That's scary, huh?"

"Yes, it is. So, you don't know whose idea it was to put stuff in my drink?"

"No," he says.

"Would you protect guys who thought they could get away with it?" she asks.

"Courtney, if I knew, I'd tell. I swear."

"I know what guys you talked to before it happened," she says. "I've told the cops who they were, so the truth is going to come out."

"It's going to get ugly," Abby says.

Courtney never heard her come back into the living room.

"Mom," Shane says.

"There's no way it won't," Abby says. "Not with the cops and SHA involved." She places one glass on the end table next to Shane's chair then hands Courtney the other.

"Thanks." Courtney sips the water though she isn't thirsty. "Pretty sure people will blame me for what happened."

"Why would they do that" Shane asks.

"It's a parent's first instinct to protect and make excuses for their kids," Abby says. "And kids will say anything to get themselves off the hook." She sits beside Courtney. "Besides being a sweet girl, you're a smart one, and you just turned fourteen. How do you know so much?"

Courtney takes another sip. "My sister went through a lot of stuff when she was in school, but she had a bunch of friends on her hockey team to help her." The tears come. "I wish I had that."

Abby puts an arm around her shoulders. "No matter what happens, the Barbers have your back. Okay?"

Courtney's phone plinks, and Abby releases her. It's Dad.

I'm outside.

"I gotta go." Courtney hands the glass to Abby. As she walks by Shane, she squeezes his shoulder. "Get well soon. Long way from the heart, bud."

He smiles weakly. "You better believe it."

2 0

I LEAN ON THE BOARDS next to Darian as former NHL goalie Pete Myers models balance and footwork for Cassidy and Karen. Masks flipped up, hands resting on their sticks, our goaltenders watch his every move. Dean and Vanessa, our goalie coaches, observe from our players box.

"Where does Pete live?" I ask Darian.

"Montreal," Darian says. "You want to know his stats?"

"No thanks. Did you see there's a reporter from Global News up there?" I point to the concourse where a camera is set up. "Trust Coach to use this skill session for team promotion."

"Not every day an ex-NHLer drops in to help out the female Huskies," Darian says. "I hear the men's team is choked."

"Oh, don't worry. They'll score a session with him too," I predict. "How did Coach swing it?"

Darian points to the stands facing us. "See the old guy sitting below Melinda?"

I wave to Darian's girlfriend, and she waves back. She's such a sweetheart. The old guy waves too, and I acknowledge him.

"That's Pete's dad. He's turning seventy this weekend, and Pete came home to help celebrate. Somehow, Coach got wind of it," Darian says.

"Thanks for taking the time to do this for me, ladies," Coach says.

I jump. I never heard him walk up behind us.

"Ask and you shall receive, Coach," Darian says.

I'll do anything to improve my chances of earning a regular shift, even if it means skipping my stats class to be a shooter for this special session.

"Hey, Coach, did you see we made the Top Ten?" Darian asks. "Number nine with a bullet."

They use Coach's phone to go over the U Sports rankings. Then Pete beckons to us.

"Let's go, Darian." I bend over and pick up a bucket of pucks.

As Darian skates away with her bucket, Coach says, "Hey Mac, what's this about SHA suspending some guys in your home town?"

Yikes. News travels fast in the hockey pipeline.

I pretend to watch Darian set pucks along the blue line so Coach can't see my face. "What have you heard?"

"Three U15 guys tried to drug one of their teammates." He leans closer. "Didn't you tell me your *sister's* playing U15? Come on. I won't tell anybody."

Pete motions at me again, and I back away from the boards. "Gotta go, Coach."

Darian and I take turns firing clapper after clapper at Cassidy. It's what Pete wants. Does he know we don't use the slapshot much—unless as a one-timer?

Darian and I take a breather while Karen replaces Cassidy in the crease.

"Look who's here," Darian says. "She must have cut her last class. Now hopefully we can do some passing plays."

Kathy steps on the ice, and for once, I'm not glad to see her. She's given me the cold shoulder ever since she saw me with Scott in the lobby of the Lethbridge rink. She glowers at me as she skates towards us.

Here we go.

After practice, Pete and his dad stand outside MBP's rear entrance when I come out.

"Thanks for helping today, Jessie," Pete says. "This is my dad Walter."

The old guy's got a firm grip, and his eyes shine. "You can bet I'm coming to your game on Friday."

"I hope we put on a good show for you," I say.

Darian comes out next, arm slung around Melinda's slender shoulders.

More introductions. Walter looks very uncomfortable, even angry. What's wrong?

"We better get going, Pete." Walter turns and walks away.

Pete looks embarrassed. "Nice to meet you all. I'm back for another session tomorrow if you ladies can manage it."

"Sure thing," Darian says.

"I wish I could, but I can't," I say.

"Well, I'll see you Friday night," Pete says. "I want to see how your goalies handle a game situation. See you later."

I watch the Myers climb into a truck and drive away. Did Walter's sudden change of mood have something to do with Darian and Melinda showing up together? Darian's parents haven't spoken to her since she told them she's gay. Good thing Melinda's parents are completely supportive. It's a shame if Walter doesn't—

Kathy walks out of the rink and heads straight for us.

Great.

"You doing anything special for Halloween, Jessie?" Melinda asks, breaking in on my thoughts.

"I think I have a date with MATLAB," I say.

Last Halloween, Liam and I dressed up as Captain America and Wonder Woman and went to a party with Kathy and her boyfriend Brett. The memory is a knife in my gut.

"Want to come to our place and hand out treats?" Darian asks.

Kathy scowls at her.

"I'd love to get out of my dorm, but I can't stay long," I say.

"Come for supper after practice," Melinda says.

"Sounds good."

Darian and Melinda walk away.

I face Kathy. "Are you going to talk to me *now?*"

She tucks some blonde strands under her Huskie toque. "What do we have to talk about?"

"We could start with why you're mad at me."

Her pale blue eyes narrow. "I saw you with Izzie's brother. Mac, you just met him. And he's so old. What are you *thinking?* Besides, Liam deserves better."

It hurts to talk about it, but I'm determined to set her straight.

"Did you know Liam broke up with me last week?" I ask.

Her blue eyes spring wide. "What? How come?"

I wipe away a tear with the cuff of my hoodie. "Because Liam says he's too busy. With our class loads and my hockey, are you surprised?"

She wraps her arms around me. "I'm sorry, Mac. I shouldn't have jumped to conclusions."

There's nothing like an old friend who's there for you when you need her most.

"You've always shaded towards impulsivity," I reply.

"True." She gives me one last squeeze before letting go. "Now, maybe you can tell me what's going on with Little Mac. Is she okay?"

I wipe my eyes. "Shit. Does the whole world know? How did you hear about it?"

"Dad told me. And if by the world, you mean Estevan, then the whole world knows," Kathy says. "Did the cops figure out where those kids got the stuff? I'm guessing the Carsons. The old man's a boozer, and his wife—"

"Can we not talk about it?" I beg. "I need to get back to my dorm and hit the books."

"Want a ride?" she asks.

"Thanks, but no thanks. I can use the fresh air."

"Are we still friends?" Kathy looks remorseful.

"Always," I assure her.

Night closes in as I jog across the overpass that connects the rink to the U of S campus. I stop for a sec to watch the headlights rush beneath me. Why does life have to go so fast? This university hockey will be over before I know it. And then what?

Picking up the pace, I think about what nearly happened to Courtney on the weekend. Why did I tell Courtney it was okay to play with those boneheads?

I have a bye-weekend coming up on November 7th—the same weekend as my sister's U15 tournament—and I'm spending it at home.

21

COURTNEY OPENS THE BACK DOOR and pushes Rufus outside. He does his business and sniffs the orange leaf bags piled against the fence. The black faces on the bags make them look like huge pumpkins. When she gets home from school, she'll drag them to the front step and hang some Halloween decorations from the eave over the porch. Normally Mom does all this, but she hasn't gotten around to it yet. Courtney's pretty sure all the crap going down with Michael has a lot to do with it.

Michael has cast himself as the victim—again. His parents insist he confessed "under duress." Though he admitted "borrowing" the cannabis oil from them, he says he has no idea what it would do. He claims no one in particular was supposed to get it. Estevan Minor Hockey has suspended him until January 1st. Brandon and Toby are each suspended for thirty days. Clint cancelled the Kipling game.

"You've been staring out the window for two minutes," Mom says. "What are you thinking about?"

"Nothing." Courtney turns around. Her mom's still in her bathrobe. "Aren't you going to work today?"

"I don't think so," Mom says.

Courtney frowns. Mom has called in sick a lot lately, but she never ends up with a cold or the flu. What's going on?

Rufus scratches at the door. Courtney opens it and grabs Rufus before he can dart past her. She uses a rag to wipe off his dirty paws, but he still smears mud on her white T-shirt, leggings, and shorts.

"I know the man from SHA told you not to do anything hasty, but—"

"I'm not quitting hockey," Courtney says.

"Will you at least consider playing with the Knights?" Mom asks.

"I'm not switching teams. No one's going to say I ran from this fight," Courtney says. "And why haven't you said anything about my costume yet?"

"Costume?" Mom says.

Courtney spreads her arms and turns slowly. "I'm Harley Quinn. The Joker's girlfriend?"

"I wondered why you put your hair in pigtails," Mom says listlessly. "You haven't done that in ages."

"You haven't said anything about how short my shorts are," Courtney says. "What's going on with you?"

"I'm just tired," Mom says. "I didn't sleep well last night."

There's got to be a way to cheer her up. "Hey, when I come home from school, we can make popcorn balls and figure out a costume for Rufus," Courtney suggests. "And let Dad and me figure out supper."

"That'd be nice." Mom's blue eyes are dull.

Courtney slips on her hockey jacket and backpack. "See you later." She gives her Mom a hug, but Mom hardly hugs her back.

What's with her?

At lunch Courtney carries her tray past Pam and her friends. They're dressed as angels—wings, haloes, and white robes. Pam—the coward—avoids eye contact.

Christina sits at their usual table. She wears one of Courtney's practice jerseys and an old helmet. She's painted a black circle around her left eye and drawn neat stitches on her cheek.

Meanwhile Courtney's the one who feels beaten up. Nasty remarks have shadowed her all morning. Hunted her in the hallway. Whispered to her from neighbouring bathroom stalls. Lurked in the back row of her classes. Her teachers seem oblivious.

She's an attention-seeker. That drink was never intended for her. She's making it all about herself again.

Why does she think she had the right to play with the boys in the first place? She's just a troublemaker.

I heard the Weyburn girls didn't want her because she's a cancer in the dressing room.

"Do you want a chocolate cupcake? Ma and I made them," Christina says.

The cupcakes are decorated with black witch's hats and swirly green hair.

Courtney sits and takes one of the cupcakes. "Thanks, but I'll save it for later. I'm not that hungry right now."

As she picks at her salad, Courtney surveys the cafeteria. Michael, too cool to wear a costume, is eating lunch with some older students. The controversy seems to have increased his popularity. Shane, Josh, and Toby, dressed as ECS cheerleaders, are at another table. Shane avoids her gaze. So much for the *all* the Barbers "having her back." In fact, her teammates have been avoiding her all week. If only everyone wasn't so afraid of Michael.

Speaking of Michael. She realizes he's making his way over to her table and everyone in the cafeteria seems to be watching him. Why does he insist on embarrassing her in public?

"Fight or flight," Christina says.

"What?" Courtney's gaze is glued to Michael's cruel smile.

"Those are your choices," Christina says. "I am here for you either way. But I think you should choose 'fight.'"

"What's new?" Michael asks.

"Not much," Courtney replies.

"Come on," Michael says. "Everyone knows you've got the SHA on speed dial. This could ruin my hockey career."

"Career?" Courtney repeats. "You play *house* hockey. Correction. You *were* playing house hockey. *Now* you're playing video games—at least until after Christmas."

"No, Courtney McIntyre. I'm doing community service," Michael says. "Yardwork at one of the nursing homes. Can you believe it?" He leans towards her. "*You* could make it all go away."

"It's out of my hands," Courtney says.

"But you weren't supposed to get the stuff. It was an *accident*," he insists.

"Please stop." Christina waves her cupcake in front of Michael's nose. "You are breaking my heart. Take this, and go away."

Michael looks at the cupcake. Confusion clouds his face.

"You can have mine too if you want," Courtney says.

Michael blinks at her, straightens, and walks back to his table.

"That was a big win," Christina says. "Am I right?"

Courtney takes a deep breath to calm her racing pulse. "I think so."

"Still, I am glad he didn't take the cupcake." Christina holds hers up. "A toast to inseparable companions. Like Dorothy and her little dog Toto."

Courtney raises hers as well. "Which one of us is *Toto?*

Christina winks. "You have to ask, *Toto?*"

It's the nicest thing Courtney's been called all day.

22

November 1

University of Saskatchewan Huskies vs. University of Calgary Dinos
Merlis Belsher Place, Saskatoon

AFTER MELINDA ROCKS THE ANTHEM, we're set for battle with the Dinos. It feels great to play in front of a hometown crowd—and my family.

Cami scores on her first shift, and Gresch scores five minutes later. 4 takes a tripping penalty near the halfway mark, and our power play keeps the opposition on their heels. Dan puts Darian, Kathy, and me out when we're five-on-five again. We maintain pressure and finish our shift with a faceoff in Calgary's end.

"Good job, ladies," Dan says when we return to the bench.

However, 6 slips a shot past Cassidy with less than two minutes left. We're up 2-1 at the end of the first. In the dressing room, Coach tells us to keep forechecking.

"I'm not supposed to tell you, but Scott's coming to the game tomorrow," Izzie tells me on our way back out for the second period. "I don't think he's driving six hours to see *me*."

Scott's a distraction I don't need. Apart from supper at Darian and Melinda's place, this week I've focused on my classes, practices, and workouts. I haven't had a chance to think about Liam. I'm too busy having nightmares about Dr. Kerr.

Calgary receives another tripping penalty four minutes into the period and then gets called for interference. On a shot from the point, Izzie scores a beauty—her first ever U Sports goal—and puts us ahead 3-1. Cami retrieves the puck from the referee. As Izzie leads the bench run, she yanks up her jersey. She's wearing her leopard print bathing suit underneath.

"Atta girl!" Kathy screams.

Cami hands the puck to Robbie, who slips it in her pocket. She'll present it to Izzie after the game.

And here I am grasping for ice-time.

"I can read your mind, Mac," Kathy says.

"Oh?"

"A rookie D just scored on the power play. Is that hard to take when you've never bagged a U Sports goal?"

"Kinda," I reply.

"Well, a two-goal lead means more ice-time for us," Darian says.

"Have you ladies got your heads in the game?" Dan growls behind us.

We keep pressure on the Dinos while the clock ticks away. Dan calls up Kathy, Darian, and me with less than a minute left.

"Don't let me down," he says.

The faceoff is to Cassidy's right. Kathy wins the draw to Dobler, and she throws the puck my way. I chip it past the Dino D and break up the ice. Someone's breathing down my neck, and I accelerate, passing cross-ice to Darian before we hit the blue line. We're three on one. Darian passes to Kathy in the slot. Kathy blazes a shot over the Dino goalie's right shoulder and throws up her arms.

"Our checking line just became a *scoring* line!" she screams when we hug her.

We're howling as we fly past our bench.

I start to step off the ice, but Dan waves us back. "Stay out! And Mac, don't take another penalty!"

I manage not to.

We beat Calgary 5-1.

After I change into my cool-down clothes, I head up to the concourse where minor hockey players beg autographs from our top lines. Izzie and Kathy have a crowd around them too. Not one little twerp gives me a second glance, but Pete and Walter Myers do.

"I never realized women's university hockey would be so entertaining," Pete says. "You can bet I'll try to get to more games." He holds out his hand. "And if the Huskies make it to Nationals, I'll be there."

"Deal." I shake his hand.

"Where is Nationals this year?" he asks.

"Fredericton," I reply. "As in New Brunswick."

"Step aside, Pete." Walter grips my shoulders. "I loved the way your line played, Jessie."

"Does this mean you'll be back?" I ask.

Walter winks. "Of course! Though I hope you'll understand I can't come tomorrow."

"Dad has a few candles to blow out," Pete says.

"Yes, I do," Walter admits. "Still, I'm not too old to learn something new." He looks over at Darian, who is talking to Melinda and Melinda's parents. "If your line keeps working hard, you'll take your team a long ways."

"You should tell Darian that," I say. "It would mean a lot to her."

"I'll do that," he says.

I feel like the world just became a better place.

"Pete, can I get your autograph?" a little hockey player holds up her program and a pen.

Soon, he's surrounded by young fans. Walter looks pleased by the attention too.

Long arms slip around my neck from behind. "Nice assist."

"Thanks, little sis." I turn and hug Courtney. "How are you?"

She sighs. "Sure glad you're coming home next weekend."

She seems like she might mean it. Dad doesn't have to tell me how proud he is. I can see it in his eyes. But Mom just looks tired.

"Do you want to go to Boston Pizza, Mom?" I ask.

She gives me a faint smile. I've got to find the time to get her alone and talk to her. She just doesn't seem right.

I'm heading towards the exit to the lower level when I notice Kathy and her boyfriend Brett talking to Liam.

He's here? Did he change his mind about me? Decide I'm worth the time and effort?

I'm a hot mess. Hair stiff with sweat. No makeup. Stained pits. Shower sandals. I'm not even wearing nice socks. But I throw back my shoulders, paste on a smile, and walk over.

"Good game, Jessie," Liam says. "Not often you Huskies get a runaway win.

Glad I came."

"I'm glad too," I say.

Is his heart hammering the way mine is?

A girl with long blonde hair walks up and slips her arm through his.

What?

The blonde flashes perfect, white teeth. "You used to play goal, didn't you, sweetness?"

"Sweetness?" I blurt.

Who *is* she?

Kathy grabs my hand. Brett's round face looks mortified. Even Liam looks uncomfortable.

"Yeah, but only till I was fifteen," Liam says. "Hey, Jessie, I heard some stuff about Courtney's team. Is she all right?"

"She's okay," I say.

I'm the one who's not doing so well at the moment. Could he have been seeing this girl *before* he broke up with me? I feel like someone's standing on my chest.

Liam's dark eyes are worried. "Does Courtney want to talk about it?"

"She might talk to *you*," I say. A little pang. Liam and Courtney always got along.

"I'll go check on her." Liam frees himself from the blonde girl's grip. "I'll be right back, Lee."

Lee. The blonde born to wear a cowboy hat. I met her two years ago.

Lee wrinkles her pert nose at me. She remembers me too. We stare each other down for what seems like a long time. We're like gunslingers in an old Western movie. Then she turns and walks away, as if she knows her butt in those Wranglers is a hundred times nicer than mine.

"How long has *that* been going on?" I ask.

"No idea," Brett says.

"I'm going to go shower," I say.

"Good idea," Kathy says. "You should cool off."

※

"Michael's latest excuse is that they were playing Russian Roulette with cannabis oil," Courtney says.

I put down my forkful of pasta. "Do you believe that?"

"Not for a minute," she scoffs.

"But he's still suspended," I say.

"Yes," Dad affirms. "Meanwhile, Michael's dad says the incident was not hockey related so the SHA has no authority."

"But the whole hockey team was there," Courtney says. "No one else."

"Can we stop talking about it?" Mom says. "I was looking forward to getting away from this for a while."

"So why was Liam there with that other girl?" Dad asks.

Like that's a great subject right now.

Courtney glares at me. "He told me you broke up."

"Really?" Mom doesn't sound upset, just deflated. "When did that happen?"

"A while ago. It's not a big deal, Mom."

Scott walks into the restaurant. Didn't Izzie say he wouldn't get here till *tomorrow?*

"Liam was really good to talk to," Courtney says. "He said I can call him anytime." She gives me a strange look. "I can't believe you broke up with him."

"Actually, it was the other way around," I say.

Courtney frowns. "What did you do to make him do *that?*"

"He was at my game with someone else. Do you really think *I'm* the one at fault?" I point out.

Scott walks over to Izzie, who sits with rookies Brooke, Kennedy, and Kira at the next table. Izzie squeals and hugs her brother. I try to focus on what Courtney is saying, but when Scott swings over to our booth, my mind's a jumble. Why does he keep showing up?

"Hey, Jessie. I'm guessing this is the rest of the McIntyre clan." Scott holds out a hand to my dad. "I'm Scott. Izzie's brother."

I make the rest of the introductions.

"I just got here. Sorry I missed the game," Scott says. "Jessie, can I talk to you alone for a minute?"

I don't want to, but since I'm not enjoying the inquisition about Liam, I let Scott guide me to the narrow hall leading to the restrooms.

"I was hoping we could grab a coffee tomorrow before your game," he says.

"That would be nice, but I'll be with my family. Between that and homework and game day prep, I won't have time for coffee," I explain.

His blue gaze intensifies. "But I drove all the way from Calgary."

"I didn't ask you to do that," I say. "Now if you'll excuse me, we're having a family meeting. My sister has some stuff going on."

"I'm sorry," he says. "I had no idea. We'll talk some other time." He squeezes my forearm. "It's nice to see you again. Even for a few minutes. Good luck tomorrow night."

As I walk back to our table, Izzie winks and signs that I should call her later. Scott sits next to her.

Mom asks, "Who was that again?"

"Just a fan," I say dismissively. "Now where were we?"

"Talking about Liam." Courtney's gaze is direct.

Here we go.

23

November 5
Estevan Moose vs. Carlyle Cougars
Power Dodge Ice Centre (Blue Goose), Estevan

DAD TURNS INTO THE PARKING LOT but instead of pulling up to the rink entrance, he backs into an empty spot. It's Courtney's first practice since the rookie party, and her nerves are frazzled.

Dad opens the rear hatch, and she reaches for her hockey bag.

"Let me," he says.

"Dad, I have to carry it," she says.

"You're a tough cookie," he says.

Her somersaulting stomach says otherwise.

Dad holds the door for her. She recognizes the parents by the pop machine—although she still isn't sure which parent belongs to which teammate. Some look surprised to see her; some look angry. A few dads look impressed.

She checks the white board for her dressing room, straightens her shoulders and plots a course through the sea of faces. No one says a word, but they give way. It feels good to know her dad is right behind her. A man opens the door for her.

"Glad you're back," he says.

She nods and smiles.

As the door swings shut behind her, she realizes she's been holding her breath. She lets it out in a rush. Maybe she's been making a big deal out of all this. Maybe Michael exaggerated the community reaction. Maybe—

"There she is," Mrs. Sweater Coat says. Michael's parents are right beside her.

Courtney stares straight ahead.

Clint pulls up beside her. "How are you doing? You need anything, let me know."

A nod is all she can manage. She drops her bag and unpacks her gear in her dressing room. Her phone plinks. It's Jessie.

We got ranked 8th.

Whatever. Still, Courtney sends a smiley emoji.

How's yr world?

She sends a confused emoji.

Call me after practice.

Courtney shuts off her phone. There's not much to look at since she suspended all her social media accounts. She's not worried about her teammates since they're abiding by the SHA policy regarding online criticism, but the kids and parents beyond the reach of Minor Sports and SHA have ramped up an online campaign.

Someone knocks.

Expecting Abby, Courtney calls out, "It's open!"

A girl with short brown hair breezes in. She looks seventeen-ish. "Hi, Courtney. I'm Dayna, Shane's sister."

"Hello," Courtney says. Why is *she* here?

"Dad asked me to hang out with you while you change. Is that okay?"

"I wouldn't mind the company," Courtney says.

"Awesome." Dayna sets her backpack on the bench.

Courtney already knows Dayna's in Grade Twelve and plays AAA in Weyburn. "Don't you have your own practice?"

"I'm already done," Dayna says. "I drove down after. I'll spend the night with Mom and Dad and go back to Weyburn in the morning." She takes out a textbook, pen, and notebook.

Courtney steps into her hockey pants. "You ever play boys hockey?"

Dayna nods. "I played in Redvers before we moved to Estevan—from initiation up to U15. I switched to girls hockey after that. I played AAA with your sister."

"You used to wear your hair long," Courtney says.

Dayna tucks a few loose strands behind her ears. "Jessie used to razz me because I didn't style it. I learned a lot from her." She turns her head and listens when someone walks by the door.

"Are you my security detail?" Courtney asks.

"I'm supposed to make sure no one bothers you," Dayna says.

"Did your dad ask you to do this?"

"Jessie did actually, but Dad thought it was a good idea."

Wow. Jessie did that?

Courtney straps on the rest of her equipment while Dayna fills her in on the Weyburn team.

When Courtney's dressed, Dayna says, "Do you know why Michael and Brandon aren't playing AA this year?"

Courtney shakes her head.

"The coach didn't want to deal with them. They're talented, but they're impossible to coach, and they're poison in the dressing room. My dad said he'd give them a fresh start. Try to turn them around. All I can say is, he's got his work cut out." Dayna doodles on her notepad. "My billet has a son who plays U15 house. He wanted me to tell you something."

"I'm not supposed to talk about it," Courtney says.

"I get it. You probably feel like the world's caved in. Anyway, he said, 'You tell that girl to stick to her guns. Tell her to keep her head up and don't be scared.'"

Courtney swallows. If only her own teammates would say something like that.

"You ready?" Dayna asks.

"Uh huh."

Courtney's gut clenches. She grabs her sticks and follows Dayna to the team dressing room, where Clint leans against the wall. He slips his phone in his pocket as soon as he sees them.

"So far so good, Dad," Dayna says.

Clint knocks on the door and opens it. Courtney walks in.

The breath, words, and testosterone are sucked from the room, but it's a relief not to see Michael, Brandon, or even Toby. Courtney sits near the door.

"The fellas have something to say to you, Courtney. We'll start with Josh," Clint says.

"We didn't know what Michael was planning. Honest," Josh says.

"What else?" Clint rasps.

"We hung you out to dry at school," Shane says. "We're sorry about that too." He sniffs. "I promised your dad I'd look out for you, and I didn't do a very good job."

"We'll do better from now on," Jutin says.

"We won't let you down again," Austin says.

The others chime in with apologies and promises that gradually peter out.

Courtney stares at a spot on the wall. Are the boys sincere? Will she ever be able to trust them? Why doesn't Clint say something to end the silence?

"That's good enough for now," Clint says. "Let's hit the ice."

2 4

November 8
Estevan Moose vs. Oxbow Huskies
Affinity Place, Estevan

IT'S 7:50 WHEN I PARK SUNNY, my green Sunfire, in front of Affinity Place. When I'm inside the foyer, I run into one of my former high school teachers. He wants to hear about the Huskies and maybe score some inside information on what happened at the U15 rookie party. I manage to escape just as the Moose finish their warm-up. I find my parents in the stands near centre ice.

"How's it going?" I ask.

"So far, so good," Dad says. "I'm worried about your sister though. Besides all this other crap going on, she's about to play four games in three days."

"She's tough, Dad. She can do it," I say.

Mom scrolls on her phone. "Have you seen what people are saying about us on social media?"

"Mom, put your phone away. And promise me you'll stay off your accounts for a few days."

"I'll try," she says, adding, "I hope Michael and his family don't show up."

"They just walked in," Dad says. "I'd love to tell them what's on my mind."

"Please don't," Mom says.

"That's so not like you. Where's the momma bear who marched through the doors of Estevan Junior High to defend me?" I ask.

She bites her lower lip as she tucks her phone into her purse.

I feel terrible. "Sorry, Mom. Which kid is Michael?"

Dad points him out. "See that tall kid in the black jacket on the rail? Dark, curly hair?"

"I see him," I say. "He's got a lot of friends."

"Players from the Knights," Dad says. "I hope he plays with them after Christmas."

"He's supposed to apologize to Courtney," Mom says, "but he hasn't done it so far."

"Toby came to the house last night," Dad says. "Not a bad kid, but he's not the brightest bulb in the box. And Brandon called soon after. For someone with a lot of potential, he's a weak little bugger."

"So, Michael won't see the ice until the new year?" I ask.

"Yes. That should be enough time for the excitement to die," Mom says. "There were two letters to the editor in the *Mercury* on Wednesday."

My phone bings.

Kathy snapchats a picture of her and her boyfriend Brett holding a cardboard cutout of my head on a mini stick.

U cant dump us! Takin u out!

The Huskie veterans will party hard all weekend. It was a good idea for me to come home. I'll get more homework done if I'm not in Saskatoon.

Bing.

This time Kathy and Brett share a fishbowl while Brett holds a straw to my cutout's lips.

"Something wrong?" Mom asks.

"Not a thing."

The Moose jump out early when the centreman on Courtney's line scores on a saucer pass from my baby sister.

Impressive.

"Where did she learn how to do that?" I ask.

"Probably our garage," Dad says. "You should see the dents in the walls."

"Can I have the program?" I ask.

Dad hands it to me. "Josh Thompson scored the goal. I don't like that boy."

"Dad, you don't like *any* boys," I remind him as I study the Moose roster. "I see Clint picked up a few U13 kids for the weekend. Smart. Oh, and Jutin Bilku's in net? He's not a goalie."

"He is now that Toby's suspended," Mom says.

I set aside the program and try to concentrate on the game. The Moose play their positions well though the hitting is reckless. Courtney jumps back when a big Oxbow kid tries to crush her in the corner.

Mom sighs. "Oh goodness."

"Courtney's doing great out there. She's light on her feet." I pat Mom's knee.

"Glad the figure skating was useful for something." Mom sighs. "All those private lessons."

I slip an arm around her waist. "Let it go, Mom."

I shift my gaze to Michael and his entourage. The kid's popular, but I can't imagine why.

⸺

"That was a hell of a game your sister played." Josh's stepdad shakes his head. "One hell of a game."

I know he wants to compliment Courtney, but the fact he's so amazed is an insult.

"And one hell of a person, considering all she's gone through this past week," he concludes.

Obviously, I didn't give him enough credit.

Dr. Bilku gives me a wink. "She reminds me of you, Jessie."

While the other dads congratulate my parents, my phone bings like a pinball machine. I ignore the snapchats flying in from Saskatoon.

When we reach the foyer, Mom and Dad run into some friends I don't know. I keep an eye out for Michael—I have a few words for him—but he must have left before the end of the game.

Toting her hockey bag and sticks, Courtney trudges up the stairs from the lower level. Her face is red, and her hair is wet from her shower.

"Hi, Jessie." She dumps her equipment at my feet.

Am I supposed to carry it for her?

"Hey!" I hold up my palm. "Great game!"

She ignores my hand. "Yeah, well we still lost."

"10-7," I point out. "You didn't get blown out."

Two boys, also carrying equipment, come up the stairs behind her. The one with the thin face and dark hair is Shane Barber. I don't know the other boy.

"Hey, Shane," I say. "How's Dayna doing?"

"She's good." He ducks his head and blushes.

Shy as ever.

I hold out my hand to the boy with the short blonde hair. "I'm Jessie. Courtney's sister."

His green eyes rove over me as he shakes my hand. "Josh Thompson. We meet at last."

Is this fourteen-year-old hitting on me?

Josh slings an arm around Courtney's shoulders. "Did you see your sister's assist? She was chuckin' sauce."

I hope she's not going out with him.

When Mom and Dad show up, Josh jumps away from Courtney while Dad grabs Courtney's equipment and glares at Josh. "Let's go."

"Who do you play next?" Mom asks.

Josh makes a mournful sound, like a cow calling its calf.

"Regina Buffaloes," Shane says. He looks miserable.

Do *both* these boys like Courtney?

As we leave the arena, I grab Courtney's arm. "Is Josh wheeling you?"

She yanks free. "Quit being so noisy."

Bing.

My teammates pose with the Short Twig's house band, and the lead guitarist is kissing my cutout.

25

November 9
Estevan Moose vs. Regina Buffaloes
Power Dodge Ice Centre (Blue Goose), Estevan

COURTNEY CHECKS THE WHITE BOARD. Dressing Room #3.

Clint waits for her on the other side of the double doors to the ice surface. "Courtney, I need to talk to you." He looks stressed out.

"What's up, Coach?"

He leads her down the hall and stops beside #3. "You're going to be sharing a dressing room with a girl from Regina."

Courtney shrugs. She knew this would happen eventually.

"The thing is—" Clint runs his hand through his hair. "Aiden is trans. Are you okay about changing with her? I told her parents I needed to ask you first."

Wow.

"It's okay, Coach."

Clint looks relieved. "You're a good kid. You've been through a lot the past two weeks. I appreciate you doing this."

"Don't make a big deal out of it," Courtney says. "Is she in the dressing room already?"

Clint nods. "Before you go in, you need to give me your phone. Her mom insisted."

Courtney fishes it out of her pocket and hands it over.

"Do you know much about this trans stuff?" Clint asks.

"A little," Courtney says. "I met a trans girl at a youth conference last year. Didn't you cover some of this in your SHA coaching clinic?"

"Yeah, but that was a while ago, and I didn't think it would ever happen." He heaves a sigh. "I've been so busy getting stuff organized for this tournament, I kinda got blindsided. I don't want to mess things up for her."

"Neither do I." Courtney knocks on the door. Just make small talk, she thinks. At the conference, she was paired with the trans girl for an icebreaker activity, and she made the mistake of asking some questions that were way too personal.

"Come in," a low voice says.

Aiden is short and stocky with light brown hair. She wears all her gear apart from her helmet.

Courtney wrestles her equipment inside and lets the door swing shut. "Hey, Aiden. I'm Courtney. Guess we're sharing this space today." She takes off her jacket and hangs it on a hook. "Is this your first game of the tournament?"

Aiden nods.

"We lost last night," Courtney says.

"That's too bad," Aiden says.

Courtney unpacks her gear. "This is my third year playing hockey. What about you?"

"I started playing when I was four," Aiden says.

When Aiden doesn't volunteer any more information, Courtney kicks off her jeans and pulls on her jill and hockey pants. What should she talk about next? The weather? No. That would be unbelievably lame.

The silence is oppressive. A leaky faucet drips.

"How are the guys on your team treating you?" Courtney asks.

"How are the guys on *your* team treating you?" Aiden replies.

Courtney gives herself a mental smack on the forehead. She should know better.

"Have you got an hour?" She tries to keep her voice light. "It'll take that long to explain."

Another drip from the faucet.

Courtney decides silence is preferrable to asking stupid questions. Still, she tries to speed up the pace of getting ready.

"I think the guys on my team are scared of me," Aiden says at last. "They don't talk to me much."

"It's early in the season. They'll get over it," Courtney says.

"You sure about that?" Aiden asks.

"No, I'm not," Courtney replies. "The guys on my team don't know what to make of me either. It's a bit of a process."

"You can say that again," Aiden says.

"It's a bit of a process," Courtney says.

Aiden gives her a weird look.

"I'm not trying to make light of your situation. Or mine," Courtney adds quickly. "I seem to be making a mess of things. Can we just start over?"

Aiden picks up her helmet. "I should go."

"If you're worried that I'll say something to my teammates, I promise I won't," Courtney says.

"I don't care what you do with your team," Aiden says. "Anything you do will say a lot more about *you* than it does about me."

Courtney jams her arm through her elbow pad and sucks in the strap. "Don't worry. What happens in here is none of their ..."

Aiden walks out.

"Business," Courtney says to an empty dressing room.

Whatever she just tried to do, she didn't do a very good job of it.

When she joins the rest of the Moose, Josh asks, "So, what's it like?"

"What is what like?"

Across the room, Austin watches her like a coyote circling its kill.

Josh grins. "The *she*-male."

Courtney's face feels hot. "You shouldn't say things like that."

Austin snickers and nudges Shane. Shane looks uncomfortable.

She wonders how her teammates found out about Aiden so fast. Then again—the hockey world isn't big.

"She—I mean *It*—is playing *our* game. In *our* rink. That means I can say whatever I want," Josh says.

"What do you mean 'your game?'" Courtney shoots back. "Did you *invent* it?"

"Climb off your soapbox," Josh retorts.

Clint walks in. The argument ends, but Josh glares at Courtney throughout Clint's pre-game remarks.

Why does she feel like she's been swept up inside a giant tornado again?

Josh doesn't say a word to Courtney when they leave the dressing room. Instead, he and Austin stare and whisper while Aiden and her teammates warm up at the other end of the ice.

Still, when the game starts, the boys on the Moose give Aiden a wide berth. Obviously, they know better than to target her—or else they're afraid of her. Courtney's line plays terrible. Josh won't communicate with her or Shane. He doesn't pass. It's like he's playing in his own world, a world where he tries to crush every Buffalo but Aiden every chance he gets.

Courtney's relieved when the ref gives Josh a charging penalty.

"Maybe he'll cool down now," she says to Shane on the way back to the bench.

"Hopefully," Shane replies.

Austin's line gets trapped in the Moose's end for the entire penalty kill. Clint calls a time out as soon as Josh leaves the penalty box.

"Thompson, you're playing like a hammerhead." Clint throws up his hands in exasperation. "What's wrong with you?"

"It's not fair!" Josh yells.

Courtney and Shane exchange glances. Apparently two minutes wasn't long enough.

"They ruin everything," Josh continues. "They show up everywhere. Now they want to take our game away from us."

"That's enough." Clint's eyes drill into Josh. "When you're ready to drop the lousy attitude and play hockey, let me know. Until then, you can watch the game from here."

Josh sulks while Clint gives them all a lecture with the usual catch phrases. Be a good sport. You're representing your city. Keep your head up and your stick on the ice.

"Why are you being such a jerk?" Courtney whispers to Josh when Clint's done. "Get over it."

"You get over it!" Josh snaps.

Later, Shane nudges Courtney and whispers. "Josh shouldn't have said that stuff."

"I'm glad you think so," Courtney says. "But if you don't stand up to him, he'll think you agree with him. Am I the only one who's prepared to call him out?"

Shane's cheeks redden. "My dad told him to stop. Isn't that enough? This is our *home* tournament. We're supposed to be having *fun*. Stop preaching at us."

"We're *all* supposed to have *fun*," Courtney says. "Aiden included."

When play resumes, Courtney chases the puck into the corner and arrives at the same time as Aiden. Aiden checks her hard. Courtney picks herself up and watches Aiden throw a pass to her captain, who rips a shot over Jutin's glove. She also notices that Aiden doesn't get a congratulatory head rub or shoulder smack from her teammates.

When Courtney returns to the bench, she plops next to Josh and gives him a poke. "Aiden had a nice assist. Did you notice?"

"She got lucky," Josh says.

"Maybe you're lucky," Courtney says. "When you woke up this morning, you didn't have to worry about other people questioning the way you want them to see you."

"Whatever you say." Josh's green eyes are stormy. "You know everything, don't cha?"

Courtney looks at the clock. There's over ten minutes left in the period, and she's not looking forward to more wrangling in the dressing room when it's over.

It's going to be a long game.

Midway through the second period, Josh finally sets aside whatever's bothering him and tells Clint he's ready to play.

At first Courtney's afraid Josh won't even try, but he proves her wrong and settles into the rhythm of the game.

Courtney's digging the puck out of the corner when she hears someone coming. She leaps out of the way, and Aiden crashes into the boards.

"Nice try!" Courtney says as she scoops up the puck.

Aiden flails her stick at Courtney's feet, dragging her down, and earns herself a tripping penalty.

As the linesman escorts Aiden to the penalty box, Josh says, "'Bout time."

But Josh passes to Courtney the next time she's open. She tries to one-time the puck but whiffs on her swing. She steals the puck back from the Buffalo defenceman and stuffs it between the goalie's skates.

Red light! Her first goal! On a power play!

She turns to her linemates, but they skate away. When she asks the referee for the puck, he gives her a strange look but hands it over. She hurries to catch up to Josh and Shane.

"Thanks for the great pass, Josh," she says.

"Kind of a greasy goal," Josh says to Shane.

"Kinda," Shane says.

They step into the box.

No bench run to celebrate her goal?

The rest of her teammates ignore her as she takes her place on the bench. Clint taps her arm, and she cranes her neck to meet his brown gaze.

"Way to not give up," he says.

She has a feeling he's not just talking about the goal.

"Thanks," she says.

"Give me the puck," he says. "I'll keep it for you until the end of the game."

The Moose beat Regina 8-6, but apart from the rosy moment of her goal, Courtney feels defeated. What fun is hockey when her linemates hardly talk to her? After the postgame meeting, she trudges to #3 where Aiden's already in her street clothes and slamming her shoulder pads into her bag.

"Are you okay?" Courtney asks. "Did one of my teammates say something rude?"

"No. One of *mine* did. He's mad because I never got hit enough. He said I get special treatment." Aiden stuffs in an elbow pad. "I'm sick of this!"

"Aiden, I've dealt with SHA about some stuff with my own team," Courtney says. "The man who handles suspensions is really nice, and—"

"You think I haven't *already* spent hours on the phone with SHA?" Aiden explodes.

Courtney senses this is a time to listen though she'd like to tell Aiden how courageous she is.

"Why does this have to be so hard! It's like I start over every game! And don't you dare tell me how courageous I'm being! I don't want to be courageous! I just want to play!" Aiden zips her bag shut and hoists it on her back, wearing it like a backpack. She grabs her sticks.

"I'm sorry," Courtney says.

Aiden stops in front of the door and takes a deep breath.

"I wish I could help you, but I don't know how," Courtney says.

Aiden wipes her eyes and nose on her sleeve. "Thanks for wanting to." She sounds calmer. "Good luck in your next game."

"You too," Courtney says.

Aiden pulls on the door and props it open with her foot. "I got a question for you. Were you ever a figure skater?"

Courtney grins. "Yup."

"Thought so. Pretty slick how you got out of the way when I lined you up."

"Thanks," Courtney says.

After Aiden's gone, Courtney leans forward and runs her hands through her hair, massaging her scalp. As complicated as her life might seem, she knows she's fortunate her heart, head, and body align. And also, lucky that hockey gives her the chance to meet so many different people.

In the end, maybe that's the whole point of playing.

2 6

I WAIT OUTSIDE THE RINK for Courtney and Mom and Dad.

Michael walks across the parking lot ahead of two people I assume are his parents. I step into his path, so he has to walk around me. "Hey, Michael."

He stops and narrows his gaze. He doesn't know who I am.

Mr. and Mrs. Carson catch up. Glorious. I've got all three to myself.

"Just wanted to tell you how badly I feel about what happened. You sure got a raw deal. You're obviously the real victim."

"Who are you?" Mr. Carson asks.

"I'm Jessie McIntyre. Courtney's sister. Michael, you could apologize to her. You know, clear the air? It might help your case."

Michael gives me a sharp look.

Mrs. Carson inhales. "Michael has nothing to apologize to her for."

"It's a huge misunderstanding," Mr. Carson says. "Everything's been blown out of proportion. Michael has apologized to *Shane*, and that should be the end of it."

"Exactly," Mrs. Carson concurs.

Michael shuffles uncomfortably.

The rest of my family walk out of the rink. If I don't wrap this up, it'll turn into a shootout in front of Affinity Place.

"Michael, you might have sucked in some people with the 'I didn't mean for her to get it' act, but I'm on to you." I lower my voice. "What did you plan to do to my sister?"

Michael crooks a forefinger. I lean ahead, so he can whisper in my ear. "She's not my type. In fact, she's not my entire *team's* type. I just figured—if she got stoned, there's no *way* Mommy and Daddy would let her keep playing. Surprised you haven't figured that out. I thought you college athletes were supposed to be smart."

The jerk turns his back and walks away. The Carsons look daggers at me, then follow.

Dad whips past me. His stride is purposeful, his neck rigid.

Courtney grabs his arm. "Dad! No!"

"I want to have a word with them." The veins in his neck are so tight they look like they'll snap.

"Leave it, Dad!" Courtney pleads. "You'll just make it worse!"

"Please, John," Mom says.

"Courtney's right," I say. "Nothing good's going to come from a yelling match in the parking lot."

Dad takes a deep breath, lets it out, slumps. He looks defeated.

I know the feeling.

"Jessie, what in the world were you talking to them about?" Mom looks upset.

"It's not important." I put an arm around her shoulders. "Let's grab some pizza."

Michael won this game, but he's not going to win the series.

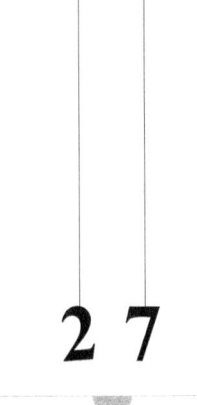

27

November 9
Estevan Moose vs. Indian Head
Affinity Place, Estevan

"JUTIN, THERE'S SOMETHING UNDER YOUR nose. Is your face dirty?" Courtney asks.

Jutin finishes tying his lace. "It's my stache."

"Moustache? You're *thirteen*," she reminds him.

"It's Movember," Austin says. "The season to celebrate testosteroni."

"It's not testosteroni," Courtney corrects. "It's *testosterone*."

"Don't expect her to understand. She's a *girl*," Josh's voice drips with sarcasm. He's been referring to her in the third person ever since she stood up to him about Aiden. "She can't get prostrate cancer."

Before she can correct him, Jutin pounds his thigh with his water bottle. "That's *prostate*, Thompson! Not *prostrate*. How can you be so ignorant about your own junk?"

Courtney points at the red smudge under Austin's nose. "And you're growing lip lettuce too?"

"You bet," Austin says.

She looks closer at the rest of the boys. It's an epidemic. But at least *some* of the boys are talking to her again. Maybe they can move past this stuff about Aiden.

"I'm open for Movember donations," Jutin says. "No amount will be considered too small."

"Hey, I was going to hit her up!" Austin says. "You got any cash, Courtney?"

"I can't sponsor all of you," she says. "But I'll gladly shave your moustaches at the end of the month. If there's anything worth shaving."

"Hey, we're supposed to collect donations?" Shane asks.

"That's the whole point," she says. "Not just growing a *greasy* stache. And speaking of shaving—how about I quit shaving my legs in recognition of your cause?"

"You don't need to do that," Shane says.

"But I *want* to," she replies.

"Courtney, you're okay," Austin says.

Josh makes a disgusted sound.

"Come on, Thompson," Austin says. "Admit it. She's trying to be one of us."

The others murmur in agreement.

"So, you think I'm 'one of the guys?'" Courtney makes little quotation marks with her fingers.

"You are right now," Austin says.

"But I'm *not* a guy, and I don't want to *be* a guy. The only label I want is *player*."

Josh rolls his eyes. "Women are so worried about what we call everything."

"And you're not?" Courtney counters.

"Here we go," he spouts. "Anything I say will be wrong because I'm a white male. We're always under attack."

Things were headed in the right direction. Why did she stir them up again?

"I'm sorry you feel that way," Courtney says.

"What's the big deal about Aiden anyway?" Shane says. "Live and let live and all that."

Courtney stares at Shane in wonder.

"You were right," he mouths.

Wow.

"Why can't things be like they used to be?" Josh says. "The good old days."

"Every generation is supposed to make things better than they were," Shane counters. "We need to do that."

Josh makes a disgusted sound.

"Okay. Let's pretend we do," Austin says. "Aiden's still risking her hockey career by being trans."

"Yeah! Where's Aiden gonna play one day?" Josh demands.

Shane looks uncertain.

"She can play university hockey—or any university sport in Canada," Courtney says.

"No way," Josh says.

"Did your *sister* tell you that?" Austin asks.

"Look it up," Courtney says. "It's on the U Sports website."

"You mean Aiden could try out for a *women's* team?" Josh asks.

"As long as she passes the drug tests," Courtney says. "She can't take steroids or hormones."

Austin grabs Josh's shoulder. "Looks like *you* could get a university scholarship after all."

"What do ya mean?" Josh demands.

"Well, you're sure as hell never gonna get one playing with *guys*," Austin asserts.

Josh jerks free and takes a swing. Austin ducks. Pretty soon the two of them are wrestling on the floor. At least they're mad at each other, and not her.

Courtney leans against the wall and makes eye contact with Shane.

"Thank you," she mouths.

His smile makes her heart proud.

November 10
Estevan Moose vs. Estevan Knights
Bienfait Memorial Arena, Bienfait

Courtney stares at the scoreboard as the Knights' sixth goal is tallied. Michael, who stands directly across from their bench, raises his arms and hoots.

"What the hell is *he* doing up so early?" Shane mutters.

Thank goodness Austin scored in the first minute of play, or there'd be a goose egg under Visitor. They've been shut down ever since—with only ten minutes remaining in the third period.

"I hate playing here," Josh complains. "You could freeze your nuts off in the dressing room." He looks at Courtney sideways. "If you had 'em, that is."

"Why isn't your sister here today, Courtney?" Shane asks.

"She's headed back to Saskatoon."

"Sucks we lost to Indian Head," Josh gripes. "Why does it always end up like this? Us against the Knights. I hate these guys."

"I thought you liked the way things used to be," she says.

His green gaze narrows. "You sure know to twist someone's words."

"I'm not twisting them. I'm giving them back to you. If you don't like it, don't give me ammunition."

The Knights score again.

"Way to go, Knights!" Michael shouts, pounding the boards.

"If he wants to play with you guys in January, he has a funny way of showing it," Courtney says.

Josh stares at her and grins.

"What?" she says.

"You *guys*?" Josh repeats.

What did she do now?

"Won't he be playing with *you* too? Aren't you a *player*?"

He's turned her own words on her. She takes a sip from her water bottle while Josh jumps up and performs some hip-hop dance moves.

"Quit clowning around and get on the ice!" Clint shouts.

"Let's roll," Josh says.

Josh loses the draw. Courtney drives at 14 who's trying to find open ice. She throws her shoulder at his chest, but it's like hitting a wall. She goes down, and 14 still has the puck. She pops back up and tries to get in his passing lane. His shot strikes her just above her pants, where there's no padding. It stings like hell. She throws the puck to Shane, who heads up the ice. Josh matches him stride for stride.

Courtney hurries after them, catching up to the play when Shane crosses the Knights' blue line. Josh drives at the net. Courtney bangs her stick and Shane saucers the puck to her. She takes a hit along the boards but keeps her feet under her. She drags the puck into the corner and behind the net. Another hit. She goes down on her knees and swipes the puck up to Josh, who one-times a shot past the goalie.

Red light!

Courtney screams and hugs Josh while he pounds her back.

"Way to play!" he shouts.

The pain in her side is an afterthought as she soars past her bench. She looks over at Michael, who leans, expressionless, on the boards.

When she enters the box, Clint bends over her. "Way to go, but are you okay? You took a few hits *and* blocked a shot. You want to sit out for a while?"

"Hell no," she says.

The Moose lose 6-5 to the Knights and watch in silence as their archrivals receive tiny C-side Winner trophies.

"Big deal," Josh says. "I've got a box of that crap under my bed."

Courtney laughs, but she wishes they'd been able to pull off a win. She would have made a special place for that trophy on her shelf next to her first-goal-with-the-Moose puck.

"We ran out of time," Shane says. "We dominated the third."

"They have some good players," Josh says. "But they never would have beaten us if Michael, Brandon, and Toby were playing. In fact, we'd be in the A final."

Courtney joy deflates. Does Josh think it's *her* fault they lost?

She doesn't listen to Clint's postgame talk, even though he's pleased with the Moose's performance. She's not sure when the "hammerheads" turned into "grinders" and "beauties." Side throbbing, she heads to her dressing room where she finds Aiden strapping on her hockey pants.

"You lost, huh?" Aiden asks. "That's too bad."

She sounds like she means it. Courtney slumps on the bench, cradling her side.

Aiden frowns. "What's wrong?"

Courtney pulls up the hem of her jersey. There's a big red mark on her belly.

Aiden's eyes widen. "Should you see a doctor or something?"

"I don't think I hurt anything important," Courtney says though she knows Dr. Bilku will want to talk to her just to be sure.

"Well, you're going to be black and blue," Aiden says.

"Uh huh." Courtney unlaces her skates. "How's the tournament going for you?"

"We're in the B final, so that's pretty good," Aiden says.

"Is everyone treating you okay?" Courtney asks.

"Everyone's been acting pretty weird," Aiden says. "My coach is doing his best, but . . ." She leaves the sentence unfinished and stares at the floor.

"Have you ever thought about switching to girls hockey?" Courtney asks.

Aiden laughs—a harsh sound. "Oh yeah. That'll go over well. I'm not sure I'm ever gonna fit in anywhere."

"Give it time," Courtney says. "People can change."

"Let's hope they do." Aiden picks up her stick and helmet. "Maybe I'll see you around. Are you going to any Regina tournaments?"

"I hope so," Courtney says. "Good luck in the B. And with everything else."

Aiden smiles. "Thanks." She opens the door. "Look me up on Instagram."

"I'll do that," Courtney says.

Maybe the weekend turned out okay after all.

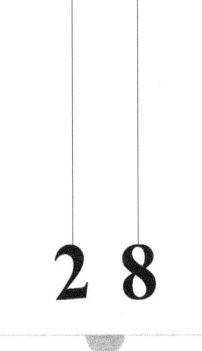

2 8

I RUN A FINAL SPELLING and grammar check on the psych paper I've been working on all week. I'll overthrow Dr. Kerr's Reign of Doom. I'll prove she's got the wrong impression by submitting this assignment six hours before the midnight deadline. I check my phone. 6:40. I attach the document and click Submit.

A backpack plunks on the table in front of me. I look up.

"Hey Liam," I whisper.

"Hey Jessie." His dark eyebrows are raised. "I didn't think you'd be here."

"The fifth floor was already full," I say. "I'm taking off right away for my night class."

He looks relieved.

I stare at my laptop, willing for the document to upload. It's at 25%.

Liam sits across from me. "Where are you playing this weekend?"

"Vancouver. We fly out early tomorrow." I watch the little bar creep across the bottom of my screen. Hurry up.

"I'm glad I ran into you," he says. "I wanted to tell you I learned something from what happened. With us."

My turn to raise an eyebrow.

"I need to take some time off once in a while. Have some fun," he says.

"I gathered that when I saw you at my game with Lee," I say.

Do I sound jealous?

"I hear you're seeing someone else too," he says.

Is he talking about Scott?

"I'm not *seeing* him," I say. "I barely know him."

"Whatever. Anyway, I wanted you to know it wasn't all your fault things fell apart," Liam says.

"Funny. I never felt like it was. You're the one who called it off," I say.

"I don't want to argue with you," he says.

"Good because I don't have time for that either." I shut my laptop and tuck it in my knapsack. "I have to go."

"Good luck in Vancouver," he says.

As I hurry down the library steps, I flick a tear from the corner of my eye.

Kori and Brooke, the rookies sitting behind Izzie and me, bubble with excitement. Some of my teammates have never flown before. Besides that, the UBC double-header is the only road trip where we get to overnight after the second game. The vets are already planning what bars and clubs to hit on Saturday night.

"Scott asked me for your phone number, and I gave it to him. I hope that's all right," Izzie says.

Is she for real?

"Well, you're single now, right?" Izzie points out.

"I sure am, but that doesn't mean I'm *looking*," I reply. "Besides, when Scott graduated from high school, I was in Brownies."

"He's not that much older, and you don't have to get serious," Izzie says. "Just have fun."

Fun. Right. Sometimes, she seems so naïve.

After takeoff, I wait for the seatbelt light to extinguish and dig out my laptop. The first thing I see is the icon for my psych paper.

Did it finish uploading before I left the library last night?

"Something wrong?" Izzie asks.

I feel like throwing up in my air sickness bag. "How do I get on the internet?"

"Did you download the airline app?" Izzie shows me her phone.

"No. Can I borrow yours to log into my Blackboard account?" I ask.

In a few minutes, my fears come true. My psych paper never loaded.

"Got your toonies?" Dave, our equipment manager, asks Izzie and me at the baggage carousel.

"What for?" Izzie asks.

"First bag off takes the pot." Dave turns his baseball cap so the brim faces the back and rubs his hands together. "If you don't play, you don't win."

Izzie digs a coin out of her purse.

"What about you, Mac?" Dave asks.

I wave him off and sit on a bench so I can connect my computer to the airport WIFI. While I wait for my psych assignment to upload, my teammates cluster around the conveyor belt like it's a craps table in Vegas. Johnny, a second-year, is videoing the event. Next, I find Dr. Kerr's phone number at the bottom of an email. When I get her voicemail, I leave what I hope is a polite explanation and ask her to call me.

Izzie squeals.

"Looks like Izzie won the luggage pool," Dave says. "Rotten rookie luck."

A charter bus picks us up in front of the terminal. After we check into our hotel, Robbie takes us on a walking tour of Granville Island. The weather is cool and damp, but not inclement. The rookies chatter, point, and take photos of everything that moves.

My phone rings. I recognize Dr. Kerr's clipped voice as soon as I answer.

"I got your message and your submission. I'll keep this brief, as I know you have more important things to do. The assignment was late. You know my policy. You'll take a zero."

Shit.

"Is there a way I can make it up?" I ask.

"Start by holding yourself accountable. Strive to attain the same standards as the rest of your peers, instead of investing the bare minimum." Dr. Kerr pauses for a moment. "Good luck."

She hangs up.

I tuck my phone in my pocket and meet Dave's gaze.

"You look like you just got bad news," he says.

"I took a zero for a paper." I swipe at the snot threatening to drip on the sidewalk. "The worst thing is—the prof has me all wrong. I'm the *good* kid. I've never asked for favours or special treatment."

"You could drop the class," Dave says. "I think there's still time."

"I never quit anything in my life, and I'm not starting with my university education. I'll go see Dr. Kerr as soon as I get back to Saskatoon. I'll do whatever I have to do."

Robbie spots a Vancouver Canuck at a coffee kiosk. She approaches him for a photo with our team, and he agrees. A woman walking her golden retriever agrees to snap the picture on a dozen cell phones.

Pretty sure I forget to smile.

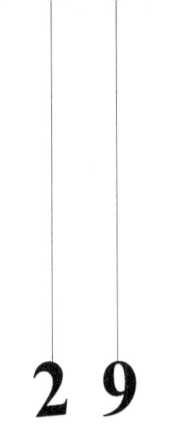

29

November 14
Estevan Moose vs. Weyburn Knight Dodge
Tom Zandee Sports Arena, Weyburn

"ARE YOU THE GIRL WHO GOT Michael Carson suspended?" Weyburn 16 asks as he lines up beside her at the faceoff.

Courtney shrugs. "Maybe."

"You did *us* a big favour," he says.

When the referee drops the puck, 16 slew foots her, and she goes down hard. By the time she rejoins the play, the Weyburn captain has a shot on net. Jutin freezes the puck.

As Courtney lines up for the next faceoff, she says to 16, "Keep your feet to yourself."

"You got it, blondie."

After play resumes, she tries to nail 16 on the boards, but he sidesteps. When his centre feeds him the puck, she tries to knock it free. She's way out of position, but she can't help it. In frustration, she raps 16's forearm with her stick, and he howls.

Whistle.

"12 White. Slashing," the referee says.

Her first penalty. She darts a glance at the bench as the linesman accompanies her to the sin bin. Clint's arms are folded in displeasure, but her teammates look impressed.

The Weyburn captain scores a few seconds into the power play, and it's the Skate of Shame back to Clint.

"Sorry, Coach," she says.

"Don't start acting like the rest of these boneheads," Clint grumbles.

"16 deserved that slash," Josh says.

"I lost my cool, and I shouldn't have." Courtney turns to Shane, who's reading a paperback. "What are you *doing?*"

He flips the page with a gloved thumb. "I have to finish this by tomorrow."

She looks back at Clint.

"I promised Abby that hockey wouldn't affect his marks," he says. "He got a 65 in ELA on his last report card."

"No wonder Clint's in a lousy mood," Courtney says to Josh.

"Was it 16 that slew footed you?" he asks.

"You don't need to look out for me," she says.

"Are you a player on this team?" Josh asks.

"Yes." What's he getting at?

"Then it's my job to look out for you. Not because you're a girl. Because you're my teammate."

She doesn't like the notion of Josh picking a fight with 16 on her account, but she does like what he just said. It makes her feel ordinary.

On Courtney's next shift, 16 is receiving a cross-ice pass when Josh lays him flat. The Moose bench explodes with cheers and whistles. The referee blows down the play. Josh bends over 16, who slowly picks himself up.

What's he saying to him?

Josh skates to the penalty box, and 16 limps to his bench.

Courtney settles into the rhythm of the game, and the rest of the first period passes without incident. As she steps off the ice to go to the dressing room, someone calls her name.

It's Dayna, Clint's daughter.

Courtney hoped Dayna would be here. Has she played okay so far?

"Great first period," Dayna says. "Also, gold star for not letting 16 push you around. My coach said so too."

"He did?"

"*She* did," Dayna corrects. "I hear you've got an overnight trip in a few weeks."

"Yep. Moose Jaw and Notre Dame," Courtney says.

"You better get going. Dad's giving you the eye," Dayna says.

Clint stands at the arena entrance, holding the door. "Move your butt, McIntyre!"

As Courtney hurries towards him, she thinks about the AAA Gold Wings. Would *she* be able to make that team next year if she tried out? It would mean going to a new high school and billeting with a family. She decides she'll play even harder—to make a good impression on Dayna and the Gold Wings coach.

The possibilities that hockey presents are endless.

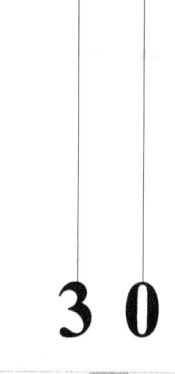

3 0

November 15
University of Saskatchewan Huskies vs. University of British Columbia Thunderbirds
Doug Mitchell Thunderbird Sports Centre, Vancouver
Huskie 3-2 loss

November 16
University of Saskatchewan Huskies vs. University of British Columbia Thunderbirds
Doug Mitchell Thunderbird Sports Centre, Vancouver
Huskie 2-1 OT loss

"Sorry your games didn't go well," Mom says.

"We traveled all this way for *one* point," I tell her. "And my line didn't shut down the Thunderbirds' top two lines. In fact, I was on the ice for two UBC goals."

"Oh dear," she says.

"And the UBC football team sat behind our bench for Game Two, and one loser—probably an offensive linesman—yelled at us the whole time. He called us quitters." I heave a sigh. "I tried to ignore him, but between shifts, his insults got to me. It's like he tapped into all my inner doubts."

"Jessie, I can't hear you that well. Where are you?" Mom asks.

"A club."

Music and lights pulse while my teammates dominate the dance floor. Cassidy brushes by me, carrying Kathy on her broad shoulders.

"Cassidy, we're gonna ride you to Nationals!" Kathy shouts, pumping her fist.

Clearly, she's already forgotten about our one-point weekend.

"I'll call you tomorrow, Mom." I press End.

Bing. A text with a 403 area code.

Too bad about the OT loss. Loads of coaching errors. You still awake? Call me.

It has to be Scott.

I take my phone and sweater outside. We're not allowed to wear Huskie gear when we're out on the town. There's a team legend about a player rolling Dukes of Hazard-style across the hood of a cop car while running from two bouncers. Coach doesn't like to talk about it.

Scott picks up. "You're in a club."

"The Roxy. The house band is fantastic. And you should see the bartenders flip bottles and do handstands."

"Sounds like a cheesy act to pick up girls," he says. "Speaking of cheesy, your coaches definitely let you girls down. Totally incompetent."

I don't like the way he rags on them all the time.

"We didn't execute the game plan," I say.

"Whatever that was. And you're home against Regina next weekend?"

"Uh huh."

"I'll get to see you when you play Mount Royal at the end of the month. Looking forward to that."

"Me too," I say.

That didn't come out the way I meant it.

"Then nothing till the first week of January," he continues "That's a long break."

"It's because of December exams," I explain. "Good for school. Bad for hockey. It's like we play two seasons. We get momentum, and then we start all over in the new year. It sucks." Why am I telling him this? He played university hockey.

"You sound a little down," he says.

"Our line didn't play well this weekend."

"You looked fine to me," he says. "Maybe a little pixelated."

I laugh.

"So, what are your plans for Christmas holidays?" he asks.

No Liam to hang out with.

"Nothing except watching World Junior games on TV," I say.

"How about skiing at Lake Louise?"

The offer blindsides me. "With you?"

"Of course with me. It's a great way to spend your break."

I hardly know this guy.

"I'm a student. I can't afford a holiday like that," I say.

"Let me worry about it. I'll fly you out. Look after your expenses. What do you say?"

What *do* I say? I'm nineteen, but I still have to ask my mom and dad?

"I haven't skied much. Never in the mountains. If I got hurt, I'd mess up my season," I explain.

"Good point," Scott says. "So, we better stick to snowshoeing."

He's backing me into a corner. "We'll talk about it when I come to Calgary," I say.

"You bet," he says. "Will you call me again next weekend? After each game?"

"Sure thing," I lie.

"Have a safe flight tomorrow." He hangs up.

Kathy is the first one I see when I come back inside the club. She drags me onto the dance floor, breathing beer fumes in my face. She hugs me and then starts a Conga line. I join in with the rest of the Huskies trailing behind us. I try to shake the feeling Scott is railroading me.

On Monday, Coach asks me to come to his office before dryland.

He leans back in his chair, heels propped on his desk. "Jessie, thanks for coming in. I won't keep you long." He looks benign—almost fatherly.

I tuck my hands under my yoga pants and stare at the floor. Where is this headed?

"I want to talk to you about something other than hockey."

A bell clangs in my head. A big steel one with a clapper.

"I just got off the phone with Dr. Kerr. She said you never handed in a major assignment, which will have a serious impact on your final grade. What happened?"

I bite my lip. Liam aside, it's absolutely my fault for not making sure that assignment uploaded. "I talked to her today after class—to try to get her to at least look at the paper. She refused. It's not fair. I'm doing the required readings. I ask questions in class. But nothing is good enough. When she looks at me, all she sees is a Huskies logo."

"You'll have to eat that zero, Jessie." Coach presses his palms together and places his fingertips against his mouth, considering. "How are your other classes?"

"They're fine. I promise."

I feel like I'm back in junior high with my homeroom teacher trying to figure out what's wrong with me. Does Coach micromanage all his players like this? Or has he singled me out for special attention? It sure feels like it.

"What did you think of the way I played this weekend?" I'm literally begging him to throw me a bone.

"Remember, we're not talking about hockey." He swings down his legs and leans across his desk. "Jessie, in the world of university athletics, there are three things you can dedicate time to: hockey, school, or your social life. But only two matter. Do you know which?"

I nod. Damn my leaking eyes and runny nose. I don't want to cry in front of him.

He yanks a tissue out of the box on his desk and hands it to me. "I think the third one might be a problem for you right now."

I blow my nose. Is he kidding? I don't party near as hard as some of my teammates.

"You should square up your classes. Put your education first. Your mom thinks you've bitten off a lot this year in terms of your course load, and she's worried you'll burn out."

Thanks for that, Mom.

He places his big hands on the desk, spreading his fingers and studying them for a moment. "The vets know how much time to assign to letting off steam. They don't let it get in the way of their fitness or education. They also allocate time every week to volunteering. I don't imagine you could consider working with Special Olympians or cooking meals at Ronald McDonald House?"

Not a chance I'd have time. I shake my head.

"Jessie, that's what comes with being a veteran on this squad. You need to figure out how to do the same."

He doesn't say "or else" but there is definitely an "or else" in his tone.

I toss the tissue in the garbage can beside his desk. "I could have dropped the class, but it would have interfered with my honours status."

"I'm going to check with Dr. Kerr in a few weeks," Coach says. "I hope she'll give me a good report. I don't think you should miss any more classes. For that reason, you should consider staying behind when we go to Calgary."

There goes my toehold on the third line.

"You better get ready for dryland," he says.

Dismissed.

After I change, I go to the arena to run the stairs. The men's team is on the ice. Panting and sweating, I stop and watch one of their drills. The players look big and confident. If only I could be more like them, and less like me.

When I'm done my run, I head back to the lower level. In the weight room, Cami bench presses while Gresch and Willo spot her. Robbie, Coach, and Dan watch video in the coaches' room while the soundtrack for "Top Gun" blares from the television mounted over Dave's skate sharpener. As I walk past, Dave applies a skate blade to the wheel and sparks fly. The skate's partner—battered, laces busted and retied—awaits its turn. There's an 18 on the heel flap. These are my captain's skates, and those puppies were brand new when the season started.

I look into the long barrel of three and a half years, and I know what I need to do.

3 1

"HEY COURTNEY! OVER HERE!" Toby stands and waves half a grilled cheese sandwich.

"You can sit with them if you want," Christina says. "They are your team, right?"

"*You're* my team," Courtney says. "Come on."

Courtney takes the long route through the cafeteria, avoiding the table where Michael hangs out with some older guys. Josh, Toby, and Brandon look at her expectantly as she sets down her tray.

Courtney doesn't trust Brandon with herself—much less with Christina. What do the boys want? She slides into the chair next to Josh while Christina sits across from her.

"This is my friend Christina Delgado," Courtney says.

"Nice." Brandon gazes at Christina like she's an exotic creature. "Which boat did you come in on?"

Why, oh why, did she set up Christina for this?

Christina's dark eyes snap. "I didn't come on a boat. I flew on a *plane*. From the Philippines. Should I show you on a map?"

Brandon's jaw drops.

"No point in that. Brandon couldn't find his ass with both hands," Josh says.

"Take a hike," Brandon says.

"Don't be a prick, Brandon," Toby says. "Remember what we're supposed to do."

What's Toby talking about?

Brandon leans back in his chair and folds his arms over his chest. "Whatever."

"What's that under your nose?" Christina asks him.

Brandon touches his upper lip. "My moustache."

"Really?" Christina snorts. "You fooled me."

Toby laughs.

Brandon brushes his brown hair away from his face. "Look, Christina. I shouldn't have made that crack about the boat."

"You are forgiven," Christina says, "but you are still a prick with dirt under your nose."

Josh cuffs Brandon's shoulder. Brandon gives Christina a little smile, like he knows he's met his match.

Relieved, Courtney dips her spoon in her soup. It's lukewarm. She isn't hungry anyway.

"See, Courtney?" Josh says. "All better. We may be boneheads, but we're not racist boneheads."

Courtney turns to Toby. "Why did you ask me to sit with you?"

Toby looks sideways at Josh. Is Josh pulling invisible strings? "Our suspension ends November 28th," Toby says. "How do you feel about Brandon and me coming back?"

"Are you asking me because you want to—or because you have to?" Courtney asks.

Toby takes a bite of his sandwich. "Making restitution is part of our Return to Play."

Whoa. Big words.

"You should not talk with your mouth full," Christina says.

"I want to put this behind us," Courtney says.

Brandon leans forward and smiles. "That's good news."

"But those dimples won't suck me in," Courtney says. "I know what you guys did. I know you did it on purpose. I don't trust you, and I won't *ever* trust you."

"That's not good," Josh says. "Teammates need to trust one another."

"Right on, man," Toby says.

"I'll be polite. I'll take your hockey advice. I'll even laugh at your jokes," Courtney continues. "But if you ever try *anything* like that again, I know who to talk to."

Brandon raises his eyebrows.

Toby pauses with the last bite of his sandwich halfway to his mouth.

"Fair enough," Josh says. "I'm supposed to let Clint know how this went. Do you all trust me to present it exactly as it happened?"

"Sure," Toby says.

Brandon nods.

"Okay." Courtney makes a mental note to ask Clint about it before their next practice.

Brandon's eyes flick at Christina. "Are we good too?"

"I am good. You not so much," she says.

Toby swats Brandon on the back. "She throws serious shade."

"What about when Michael comes back?" Courtney asks.

Toby looks uncertain.

Brandon shrugs.

"I guess we'll find out in January." Josh wraps his arms around the back of his chair. "In the meantime, why don't we talk about the rest of the schedule?"

Relieved, Courtney pushes aside her soup and eats her salad while the boys review the Moose's upcoming matchups.

She looks at Christina and mouths, "Toto."

Christina winks and points at Courtney. "Toto," she mouths back.

3 2

November 22
University of Saskatchewan Huskies vs. University of Regina Cougars
Merlis Belsher Place, Saskatoon
Huskie 4-0 win

November 23
University of Saskatchewan Huskies vs. University of Regina Cougars
Merlis Belsher Place, Saskatoon

KATHY, DARIAN, AND I GET a regular shift in Game 2, which remains tied 0-0 at the end of regulation and OT.

"I hate shootouts," I say to Kathy.

"You wouldn't say that if you ever got picked to shoot," Kathy says.

My teammates gather round Dan, our offence coach, as he lists our order for the shootout: Cami, Gresch, and Jorgy.

Cami skates to centre ice and waits, poised over the puck. When the referee blows the whistle, she drives at the Cougar goalie and scores five-hole on her backhand. We cheer and pound the boards as Cami returns to our bench.

Cassidy skates to our net. She stretches, loosening the muscles in her back and shoulders.

"She's such a *beast*," I say to Kathy.

"No f'ing Cougar is getting past *those* pads," Kathy says.

"Hang on, ladies," Darian says.

Regina 23 tries to deke Cassidy but loses the puck before she gets a shot away. No goal.

The shootout continues.

Gresch. No goal.

Regina 6. No goal.

Jorgy. No goal.

"Come on, Cassidy," Kathy murmurs beside me. "One more save gives us the win."

My heart is in my throat as Regina 17 comes in hard on Cassidy, pulls the puck to the left, then tries to jam it past Cassidy's left skate. Our goaltender pushes the puck wide, and we mob Cassidy in her crease.

I don't go up to the concourse afterwards. My family didn't come to Saskatoon for the weekend, and that leaves me with a hollow feeling. I shower, dress, and try to slip out the back door of the rink.

"Jessie, wait up," a voice says behind me.

Dan walks down the hall towards me. He's got a young family, and he doesn't hang around long after home games. Players aren't the only ones juggling responsibilities.

"How does second place in Canada West feel?" he asks.

"Feels pretty good," I say.

"You're not going out to celebrate?" Dan asks.

"Not this time," I say.

"Well, I want to reiterate what we talked about in the dressing room," he says. "Your line outworked Regina's top players consistently. Looked like you were having fun doing it too."

"Yeah. We absolutely were."

"So, you've bought into playing on a checking line?" Dan asks.

"Completely," I say.

"Good to hear." Dan smooths his dark hair. "What was the difference maker this weekend?"

"I scored some tape from Dave," I say. "Fair to say, I've been dreaming about

Regina's top lines all week."

"Well, I'll be watching some tape too, but I'm pretty confident about what I'll see," Dan says. "I'm really proud of you, Jessie."

My phone vibrates in my pocket. Half of me wants to see who it is. Half of me wants to hear what else Dan has to say. He doesn't hand out praise easily.

"Are you going to get that?" Dan asks, pointing at my pocket.

"Maybe. But first—are you going to tell Coach you need me in Calgary?"

Dan scratches behind one ear. "Your education comes first, Jessie."

"I'm looking after that, I promise."

Dan smiles. "Wouldn't think of leaving you behind." He pushes the door open and disappears into the night.

I look at my phone, expecting to see Mom or Dad's caller ID.

It's Scott.

I never called him last night, hoping he'd forget this notion of me connecting with him after every game. Every week, he sends pics of people skating on Lake Louise or snowshoeing in the mountains.

I let his call go to voicemail and dial Mom.

"Hi, Jessie," Dad says.

"Hey," I say, "is Mom still up?"

"She's sleeping," Dad says.

"Is she okay? I mean—what's going on with her?"

"She's going through a rough patch, but she's going to be okay, Jessie. Don't worry about her. I've got to go, but let's talk tomorrow, okay?"

"Okay."

I stare at my phone after he hangs up. How can I not be worried about her?

I make my way to the front of the classroom where Dr. Kerr is packing up her laptop. She flicks a glance in my direction and zips her satchel closed.

"What can I do for you, Ms. McIntyre?" she asks.

"I'm wondering if you had time to read my proposal," I ask nervously.

"I did." She slips the satchel strap over her shoulder.

"And what did you think?" I step aside so the students bottlenecked in the aisle behind me can get past.

Dr. Kerr furrows her penciled eyebrows.

I'm about to get shut down again. She *is* a brick wall.

"I thought I might like to see what you have in mind," she says.

I let out the breath I've been holding. "I'm glad to hear it."

"I don't normally do this sort of thing, but your premise interests me. Can you walk with me while we talk about it? I need to get back to my office." She rolls her eyes. "I have an appointment with a first-year psych major—and her mother."

As we negotiate the busy hallway of the Arts Building, I notice that students step aside for Dr. Kerr. As I walk beside her, I pitch my plan to interview Pheasant Rump elders about the changes they've seen within their lifetimes.

When we reach the Tower elevators, Dr. Kerr presses the Up button and turns towards me, "I think you've turned a corner, Ms. McIntyre, but with finals coming up in a few weeks, I'm pressed for time. You need to submit that paper no later than December 16th. Can you do that—and complete all the required research? That's a lot of interviews."

The elevator light pings, and the doors slide open. Dr. Kerr steps inside and stares at me, penciled eyebrows raised.

"I've got no alternative," I say.

"Then, to coin an expression from *your* world, you'd best 'work like a dog.'" The doors close on her smile.

I fist pump. Yes!

But the adrenalin rush is brief. I have my work cut out for me.

33

November 28

Estevan Moose vs. Redvers Rockets
Redvers Recreation Centre, Redvers

MOM HOLDS THE DOOR TO THE RINK open so Courtney can maneuver her equipment through the gap. "It feels strange to be here for hockey instead of figure skating. You won a gold here, didn't you? With that pirate number."

"Yep." Courtney's relieved the lobby is nearly deserted. She wanted to get here ahead of Toby and Brandon—even though they promised there'd be no drama.

At least their first time back isn't a home game. She wonders if Clint planned it that way.

A woman working in the concession gives Courtney directions to her dressing room. "You'll be sharing with Jade," she says with a broad smile. "We are so proud of that girl."

Courtney has heard about Jade from her teammates. She's a D who doesn't need to take a back seat to any guy in the league.

Shane and Josh walk into the lobby. Underneath their toques and hockey jackets, they're wearing suits and ties.

"You guys clean up pretty good," Courtney says.

Shane blushes, and Josh rolls his eyes, but she can tell he's pleased she noticed.

When Courtney gets to her dressing room, Jade is lacing her skates. Her waist-length blonde hair hides her face. "How's it going, Courtney?"

Courtney's flattered Jade knows her name. They're like members of a special club. "Good. You?"

"I'm always good." Jade straightens, and her smile is wide. "I hear this is your first year with the sausage fest."

Courtney unzips her bag. "Sausage fest?"

"You play with guys. Guys have sausages," Jade says. "Should I draw a picture?"

Courtney blushes. "No."

"And speaking of sausages, that Michael Carson is some dick," Jade says.

To change the subject, Courtney asks, "How long have you been playing with a boys team?"

"Since initiation," Jade says. "I've known these guys all my life. I go to school with them. Went to their birthday parties. And now real parties. The guys have my back, and I have theirs."

Courtney wishes she felt the same.

They talk about the obvious things. Their teams. Their league. Jessie and the Huskies. Blah. Blah Blah.

"Can I give you some advice, Courtney?" Jade says as she tugs her jersey over her head.

"Sure," Courtney says.

"If you don't agree with something a teammate says or does, tell him. Half the time guys don't have a clue what they're doing. And they're brutal at reading your mind."

"Yeah, I've tried telling them," Courtney says. "It doesn't always work out."

"Well, it doesn't mean you should stop doing it. Eventually you'll get through to them. And one more thing. My mom told me this. Don't date your teammates—at least not for a long time. It's the best way to keep the peace."

"I don't *want* to date any of them," Courtney says. "Have you seen their moustaches?"

Jade laughs. "My team's the same." She grabs her helmet and stick. "Thanks for the chitchat. But for the next sixty minutes, you're the enemy." She winks. "Don't take the hits personally."

"Good to have Toby back in net," Josh says as they wait for the Zamboni to leave the ice.

"Hey, didn't I do all right?" Jutin asks.

"You sucked," Josh says. "Let in beachballs my grandma would have stopped. Do you want me to roll out the stats?"

Courtney releases the latch and opens the gate. "Let's go."

"Hey, 6 is hot," Austin says as the Redvers team pours onto the ice.

"Serious heat," Brandon says.

"I'm in love," Jutin says. "Look at her hair."

"You meet her, Courtney?" Austin asks.

"Briefly," Courtney says.

Austin bats his eyelashes. "Put in a good word for me, huh?"

Courtney laughs, positions herself on their blue line, and takes off her helmet. When the concession lady belts out the anthem like an opera singer, Courtney exchanges wide-eyed looks with Josh and Shane.

Josh wins the draw, and a few passes later her line is headed for the Redvers zone with Shane carrying the puck. Jade pushes him wide. When Courtney dives into the corner to battle for the puck, Jade crushes her. Courtney recovers and scoops the puck along the boards then turns and fires a wrist shot on net. The Redvers goalie deflects the puck into the other corner where Shane chases it down and chips it over to Josh. Josh shoots blocker side, and the puck squeaks in.

When Courtney joins the bench run, she feels like part of the team. If only Michael would go play for the Knights.

"Jade can *hit*," Brandon says in the dressing room between periods. "When she rode me into the boards, I wanted to thank her."

"Knock it off. I staked my claim," Jutin says.

"Good luck with that," Brandon says.

"Courtney, did you get a chance to see her naked?" Austin leers.

"That's an awful thing to say." Courtney says.

She can't believe her teammates are talking like this.

When the conversation grows even more X-rated, she smacks her gloves together. "Hello! You can't talk like that in front of me!"

"Why not?" Toby asks.

"Because you're objectifying her."

"Objecti-what?" Austin wonders. "Speak English."

"How would you like it if I talked about you guys like that?" she demands.

"Wouldn't bother me," Brandon says.

"Me neither," Austin concurs.

"Go ahead," Jutin says. "You won't say anything we haven't heard a hundred times."

"You look up to my sister, but you don't talk about *her* that way," Courtney says.

"Who says we don't?" Josh says.

Courtney takes a deep breath. "How would you like it if someone in here talked about your sisters like that?"

"Hey, leave them out of this," Jutin says.

"And my mom," Shane says. "I'm sick of the Hot Mom jokes."

"Seriously, Abby is the best part of being on this team," Josh says.

"You're talking about our coach's *wife*," Courtney says. "Our team manager. Show some respect. She busts her butt for you guys."

"And what a butt," Josh says.

"Thompson, you're a butt-*hole*," Shane says.

Josh rises. "Bring it, clown."

Shane jumps up. "Drop your mittens."

Josh flicks off his gloves. Shane tackles Josh and drives him towards the wall. Laughing, Jutin and Austin scramble out of the way. Josh pulls Shane's jersey over his head, and the two of them grunt insults as they tussle. Josh slams Shane against the other wall.

Courtney is horrified. "Why doesn't somebody stop them?"

Brandon gives her a bored look. "Come on, Courtney. This is a team standard."

Shane wrestles Josh to the mat. The two of them groan and pant like a pair of bear cubs. Shane lands a punch. The smack of flesh on flesh sickens Courtney.

"That the best you can do, Barber?" Josh taunts.

Courtney smells rotten eggs. Eyes watering, she tugs her jersey over her nose.

"Thompson!" everyone shouts.

The door bangs open. Clint walks in.

"What in the hell—get up you guys." Clint isn't angry, just disgusted.

Josh and Shane peel themselves off the floor and sit next to each other, rearranging pads and jerseys.

"While you dickheads were taking a round out of one another—" Clint stops midsentence and covers his nose and mouth with his hand. "Geez, Thompson. What did you eat before the game?"

Josh chuckles.

Austin fans the door to dissipate the stink.

Clint continues, voice muffled. "I was just talking to the Redvers coach. They're hosting a three-on-three tournament over Christmas. Might be a good way to stay in shape over the holidays. Anybody interested?"

A chorus of howls and hand slaps provides the answer.

"What do you say, Shane?" Josh asks.

"Count me in," Shane says.

Courtney stares in disbelief. "But you were just trying to kill each another!"

"Naw, we were having fun," Shane says. "How's your cheek, Josh?"

Josh rubs the red mark. "Pussy hit. You in or not, Courtney?"

"In on what?"

"The three-on-three tourney," Shane states the obvious. "You're on our line, aren't you?"

"It'd be a good chance for you to learn how to play a little defence," Josh says.

Courtney shakes her head. "You guys are unbelievable."

⬥

"How was the game?" Mom asks as she turns the SUV onto the highway.

The sky is dark blue and stretches to the horizon. It's a beautiful winter night on the prairies.

Courtney wonders if she should tell Mom about all the dressing room shenanigans, then decides against it. Mom probably wouldn't find the stories funny—or reassuring. "It was great," she says. "I'm having fun."

"In the end, that's all that matters," Mom says.

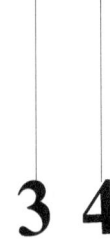

3 4

THE BUS BATTLES A HEADWIND as we blow through Drumheller.

Coach plops in the seat beside me. "Next stop—Calgary. Hey, what are you working on?"

His casual tone does not fool me. He's checking on me.

I show him my computer screen. "Psych. I've got a makeup assignment to do." I tell him about my special paper for Dr. Kerr.

"I'm proud of you, Mac," he says when I'm finished. "If you need to miss a practice or two—"

"I'm not missing any practices. I'll figure it out."

"Glad to hear it." He gets up.

"Coach?"

He looks down at me and sways with the rhythm of the bus.

"I'll be better. I'm committed to two things—school and hockey. I promise."

He raises an eyebrow. "Not Izzie's brother?"

He knows about Scott? Is *that* what he and Dan and Robbie talk about in their meetings?

"For sure not him."

"That's good news. I never doubted you for a minute, Mac."

Oh, he did, but not nearly as much as I doubted myself.

＊

We pull into Calgary around 4:00 pm. We check into our rooms and head to the restaurant across the parking lot for supper. I'm not surprised to see Scott's Audi in front.

Inside, Scott stands near the long table reserved for the team. He hugs Izzie, then me. "I thought the three of us could sit over here." He gestures at an empty booth.

"I think we're supposed to sit with the team," I say.

"I don't think it matters," Izzie says.

As I slide in next to Izzie, my pulse quickens. I need Scott to understand that my focus this weekend—and every weekend—is hockey.

Once we've ordered our meals and drinks, Izzie says, "Hey, I need to use the washroom. Can you let me out, Jessie?"

She slides out of the booth and heads for the exit. I sit and pretend to look for something in my purse. Anything but make eye contact with Scott.

"So, Jessie, what's new?" he asks.

"Not much," I say.

"Not much," he repeats. "Only a whole new role on a checking line. How do you feel about the transition from defence to offence?"

"Less decisions to make, that's for sure." I take a drink of water. "You should ask Kathy how she feels. After years of being a loose cannon, she's learned to play the systems properly and check tightly—without taking penalties."

Scott laughs. "Typical Jessie. Always deflecting attention. Speaking of attention. Mount Royal's only got two wins so far. Might be a chance to pad your stats."

"What stats? I'm not a sniper."

He frowns at me. "Everything okay?"

"Yep."

"I can tell you're not happy," he says.

"No, everything's good. I'm just tired from the bus trip."

He reaches across the table and takes my hand. "Let's have a drink after supper. Just you and me. I promise to get you back to your room before curfew."

"I can't drink before or between games, and besides, I've got homework."

He releases my hand. "I'm disappointed, but I understand. We'll try to carve out a little time later this weekend. I want to bring you up to speed on our trip to Lake Louise."

What?

"I told you I couldn't commit to anything like that," I say.

"I know, but I had to get on it, or we'd miss out. Have you ever stayed at the Chateau? It's one of the most beautiful places on earth. I booked us a room overlooking the lake."

Room. The singular rings in my ears. "I'm not going."

His face hardens. "I thought we'd sorted out your concerns."

My timing is terrible. Izzie will be back any minute, and here I am making things awkward with her brother.

I meet Scott's gaze. "If I did anything to make you think I'm looking for a relationship, I'm sorry."

"This doesn't have to be a relationship," he says. "You're not a kid. And neither am I."

But right now, I feel a lot like a kid.

"Scott, why are you interested in me? Can't you find someone your own age?"

"What's that supposed to mean?" he asks.

"I think you know exactly what I mean. And another thing," I say. "I *like* my coaches. I might not agree with everything they say or do, but I know they have my best interests at heart. Every time you ran them down, you ran down our program, and I didn't like it."

Scott stares at me.

"I'm going to sit with the team, so you and Izzie can spend time together." I slide out of the booth and pick up my purse. "Enjoy your time with her. Have a great night. And please stop calling and texting. I don't have time for you."

I'm trembling from head to foot. I walk to the team table and pull up a chair next to Kathy.

Her pale blue eyes are quizzical.

"Don't ask," I warn her.

November 29

University of Saskatchewan Huskies vs. Mount Royal University Cougars
Flames Community Arena, Calgary
Huskies 1-0 win

November 30
University of Saskatchewan Huskies vs. Mount Royal University Cougars
Flames Community Arena, Calgary
Huskies 5-4 OT win

Kathy yawns and stretches and tries to rub the frost off the bus window. "Where are we?"

"Just went through Irricana," I say.

"Since when is Erv's first name Melanie?" Darian says behind me.

"Where'd you see that?" I peer between our seats.

"In the game report." Darian scrolls on her phone.

"Happens all the time." Kathy leans on top of her seat. "You'd think they'd have no trouble with Parker. But no."

Darian scrolls further. "The sportswriter gives Cassidy most of the credit."

"Well, I'll bet there's no mention of our line." Kathy stretches her arms over her head. "No credit for the grinders."

"Dan noticed," I say. "And that's all that matters."

Izzie walks by without saying a word to any of us. She hasn't spoken to me since Thursday night.

"Did you feel a chill just now?" Kathy asks.

I'm not going to tell them how rocky the last two days have been—avoiding Scott in the rink lobby and Izzie in the dressing room and at the hotel. She used to look up to me. Now she hates me.

I can't wait to get back to my dorm room.

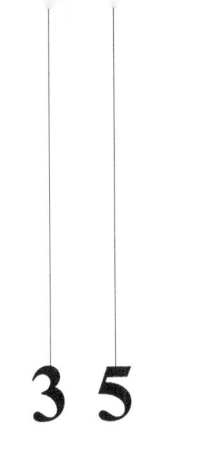

3 5

December I
Estevan Moose vs. Milestone Flyers
Affinity Place, Estevan

"HAVE YOU USED ONE OF THOSE before today?" Shane asks nervously.

Courtney presses the power button on the electric razor. "My dad let me practice on him last night. I know what I'm doing."

"Tilt your head back," Christina says.

Eyes wide, Shane obeys. He doesn't have much of a moustache, just a dusting of dark hair with some coarse stragglers framing the corners of his mouth.

"Can you lean to the left?" Abby holds her phone close.

"Mom," Shane moans.

"Quit complaining, buddy. Your grandparents want video."

Parents and fans swarm the Affinity lobby. The rest of the second-years have lined up behind Courtney, waiting their turns. Courtney has already shaved all the first-years.

"Do you know how much we've raised so far?" Courtney shouts to Abby over the razor's buzz.

"Just shy of a thousand!" Abby shouts back.

"Can I take a picture for the *Mercury?*" the man hovering beside Shane asks.

"I guess so," Courtney says.

"Then look this way," he says.

She looks into his camera lens and smiles.

Click.

"Let me see," Christina says.

The reporter holds his camera so Christina can see the screen.

"It's a good picture, Courtney," Christina says.

Courtney gives Shane's lip one more pass. What will the rest of the Moose say if *her* face ends up on the front page instead of one of theirs?

"What are you raising money for?" the reporter asks.

"The family centre," Shane says proudly.

Courtney focuses her attention on the razor. "Stop talking."

"Why are you so shy?" Abby asks after the reporter leaves.

"This isn't about me," Courtney says.

"This is about the *team*," Abby murmurs in her ear, "which you are a part of. And don't forget. Your turn's coming."

Courtney laughs and straightens. "You're done, Shane."

Shane rubs his upper lip as he gets up. Josh slides into the chair, twirling the ends of his blonde moustache. His green eyes dance.

"Get this thing off my face, McIntyre."

Courtney pops the end off the razor. "You definitely got the biggest head of lettuce."

His smile and the green glint vanishes. "What are you doing?"

"Just changing the head. Wouldn't want to tug out any hair by the roots."

Josh laughs nervously.

She places a palm on his forehead and steps close, applying the razor. He opens his mouth. "Zip it, Thompson."

The small of Courtney's back, her upper arms, and her shoulders ache by the time she gets to Brandon, the last of the second years.

Mrs. Sweater Coat leans in, phone turned on its side. "So great to have something positive about the team in the newspaper for a change."

Courtney meets her steely gaze. Will Brandon's mom ever cut her some slack?

"Now it's your turn," Brandon says when Courtney's done shaving him.

She sinks onto the chair and rolls up the hems of her leggings.

"You were supposed to grow the hair on your legs," Austin says, disgusted.

"A deal's a deal."

"I did!" she protests. "I never said you'd be able to see it!"

Toby and Brandon examine the light blonde hair on her shins.

"Hardly worth the effort," Brandon says.

"Let's get it over with," Courtney says.

"You first," Brandon says to Toby.

"Step aside," Josh says. "This isn't a job for *boys*."

"Who are you calling a boy?" Toby says.

"If the jockstrap fits," Josh says. "Where's that razor?"

"You're not using the electric one," Courtney says. "It gives me a rash." She snaps her fingers. "Toto! My makeup kit."

Christina produces a can of foam and a pink razor. "Here you are, Toto."

"Why do you call each other Toto all the time?" Brandon asks.

"Inside joke," Christina says.

"No, seriously," Brandon says.

Christina shrugs. "We both like *The Wizard of Oz*. The book, not the movie."

Courtney finishes spraying her calves and shins then holds out the razor to Josh.

"Ah. No thanks," Josh says.

As if by agreement, the rest of her teammates—with the exception of Jutin—take a step backwards.

"Me?" Jutin says.

"Your dad's a *doctor*," Josh points out. "Didn't you inherit the hands of a surgeon?"

Jutin takes the razor from Christina and holds it daintily between thumb and forefinger. "I shaved my own legs once for Halloween. I was a sexy French maid."

Dark brows furrowed, he applies the razor to Courtney's left calf. The boys shuffle closer. Courtney lets Jutin take a few tentative strokes before shouting, "Ow!"

Jutin and the others jump.

"Just kidding," she says.

"Hurry up!" Clint calls from the top of the stairs. "Anybody remember we got a game today?"

In homeroom period on Monday morning, Mr. G greets Courtney at the door. "Saw your picture on the front page of the *Mercury*. You're quite the celebrity." He scrolls on his phone and shows her the article. "See?"

Courtney's face stares back. It's a flattering picture.

"Way to go, kid," Mr. G says. "So, how's your sister's team doing?"

"They just swept Mount Royal," she says. "They've been ranked Number Eight in the country for several weeks."

"You don't say," he says. "I was a big fan of Jessie's AAA team. She played great defence."

"Yeah, so you've told me," Courtney says. "Anyway, she's not playing defence anymore. She's on a checking line."

"Good for her," Mr. G says.

Whatever.

Courtney walks into the band room. Lately, everyone seems to eye her with new interest. All because of a silly newspaper article? She ignores the whispers and curious stares as she makes her way to the carpeted tiers and sits next to Christina.

Mr. G reads through the day's announcements and then adds, "We're still looking for parent chaperones for the Santa's Sleigh Dance in a few weeks. What about you, Mr. Smith?" he says to a Grade Twelve boy leaning against the wall.

"No way," the boy says. "Mine did the last one."

Mr. G grumbles. His gaze sweeps the room.

"Courtney," Mr. G says. "Your mom has taken a turn in the past."

"Maybe," Courtney says. "I don't remember."

She's lying. Mom chaperoned some dances when Jessie was in high school, but Courtney's pretty sure Mom would say no. She naps as soon as she gets home from work. Dad's doing the heavy lifting in the supper department.

Christina pulls her knees against her chest. "If I go to the dance, will you come with me, Courtney?"

The buzzer rings.

Saved by the bell, Courtney thinks as she heads to her next class. She grew another inch since the beginning of hockey season, and she has no intention of going to that dance.

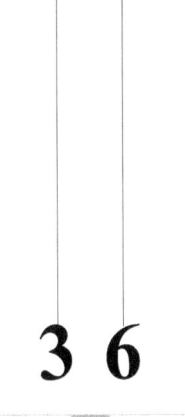

3 6

December 14
University of Saskatchewan Huskies vs. University of Saskatchewan Huskies
Arena #2, Merlis Belsher Place, Saskatoon

AN ICY WIND BUFFETS ME as I jog across the overpass. Winter creeps through the seams of my down jacket and my yoga pants. I've got two days to complete my paper on cultural and social behaviour for Dr. Kerr. The interviews with Liam's grandparents and other Pheasant Rump elders have been fascinating, time-consuming, and heart-rending. I need a break from it, and our annual hockey game against the men's volleyball squad will be just the thing.

When I get to the rink, Darian and Kathy are already in the dressing room.

"How was your history final?" Kathy asks.

"Pretty good." I hold up my right hand. "Still suffering from writer's cramp though."

Kira, a rookie D, walks in.

"Is Melinda coming tonight?" I ask Darian.

"Nope. Choir practice." Darian kicks off her flip-flops.

"It's colder than hell out there, and you wear those?" Kathy points out.

Darian shrugs.

"Will the men's volleyball team be any good?" Kira asks.

"Good? Most of them grew up in little towns playing volleyball *and* hockey," Kathy says. "They beat us last year."

Kira looks confused. "And we play them because . . .?"

". . . we don't have any games till January," Kathy says patiently. "Some healthy competition helps keep us sharp."

"Is Brett reffing?" I ask.

Kathy nods.

"He missed a lot of holding and hooking calls last year," I point out.

Kathy looks miffed.

"We need more than Brett to win," Darian says. "Trina's strapping on the pillows."

"Trina the *Trainer*?" Kathy demands. "What happened to Cassidy and Karen?"

"They've both got exams tomorrow. And don't worry about Trina. She used to play net," Darian says.

"When?" Kathy demands.

"U11, I think," Darian says.

"That was ten years ago," Kathy says. "There's been a bit of water under the bridge. Does she remember how?"

"Which bridge?" Kira asks.

"Never mind, Kira. And lighten up, Kathy. This is for fun," I say.

"Anytime we suit up against guys, there's no such thing as fun," Kathy says.

The men's volleyball team makes their end of the ice look small. Besides being long and lean, they're smooth skaters, and their wrist shots ricochet off the glass like cannon fire. Their goalie, who's shorter than his teammates, is the last one on the ice.

"Who's playing net for them?" I ask Brett.

"Liam," he says.

While I get over the shock, Liam scrapes his blades from side to side in his crease.

"He looks pretty relaxed for someone who hasn't played goal since forever," Kathy says.

"Should be able to sneak a few by him. Time to shame, ladies," Darian says.

Darian, Kathy, and I take the first shift.

Kathy taps Brett's butt with her stick as he crouches for the faceoff.

"No playing favourites, ref," 17 says.

Brett snaps the puck, and 17 wins the draw. Our opposition spreads out, passes around us, and talks to each other the whole time. They pin us in our end and rip slappers at Trina. She moves well, even makes a few glove saves. Darian clears the puck, and we go for a change.

"Do they seem better than they were last year?" I ask Kathy.

"Uh huh," she says.

The men hammer in two goals when Kori, Kennedy, and Carlee's line is out. Trina's armour has some chinks.

"Not much action in our end," 26 heckles me when it's our turn again. "Why is that?"

"We'll get there," I mutter.

Kathy wins the faceoff. I throw a shoulder into 26 as I go by and set him on his ass. His two D laugh their own asses off, so I have no trouble getting around them. I catch Kathy's pass, drive at Liam, and wind up to shoot. He poke-checks, but my momentum carries me into the net. I'm sprawled on top of him when we slam into the boards.

"Whoa, hockey girl," he says. "So aggressive."

I'm all elbows and knees as I crawl off him.

Brett helps me untangle myself from the net. "Hey, Jessie, cool down."

"McArthur, why did you have to show up for this?" I demand as Liam gets to his feet. "You're a schmuck!"

"Take a pill," Liam says.

"I'd rather choke." I skate away.

"You're doing a good job of that!" he shouts.

Kathy, Darian, and the other Huskies are doubled over on the bench.

"What're you laughing at?" I growl.

"You," Kathy says. "I thought this game was 'just for fun.'"

"Fun's over," I say.

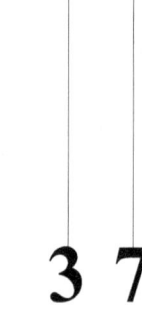

37

COURTNEY SLIPS ON PAJAMA PANTS and a loose-fitting T-shirt and climbs under the covers. The hotel pillows are super comfy.

"Are you going to bed already?" Mom asks, scrolling on her phone.

"I nearly froze on the bus," Courtney says.

"I told you to dress warmer," Mom says.

"I wore a jean jacket." Courtney snuggles under the duvet. "What's the WIFI password?"

Once her phone's connected, Courtney puts in her ear buds and tags Aiden in a TikTok video she made with Josh and Shane on the bus.

Plink!

A text from Shane.

Come to 331.

Abby booked an extra hotel room, which the team uses during the day and the parents at night for socializing.

Courtney throws off the duvet. "I'm gonna check on the guys." She pulls on a hoodie and sneakers. "What time's supper?"

"5:30," Mom says.

"I'll be back before that."

Courtney takes the stairs down to the third floor. She sees Toby in the hallway.

"Wait up," she says.

Toby faces her, but he looks uncomfortable. What's he up to?

"Am I not invited?" she asks.

"Sure." Toby raps on Room 331.

The door opens a crack, and Jutin's eye appears. "Password?"

"This is like a bad spy movie," Courtney says.

"Just kidding." Jutin throws the door open. "But get in quick."

Three smells confront her: coffee, hair dye, and vape.

"Want a cup of java?" Jutin holds up a mug. "It's fresh, but it's decaf. Brandon drank all the dark roast."

"No thanks." She looks past Jutin.

The vets are sprawled, vapes in hand, on the two queen beds, while the rookies sit on the floor.

Shane perches on a chair in the corner. "You guys shouldn't vape in here."

They shouldn't vape. Period. It's not even legal.

Josh emerges from the bathroom, white towel draped around his neck. His blonde hair is dyed black.

"What did you do?" she gasps.

He gives her a brilliant smile. "Relax. It'll wash out."

"Remember the time we stayed at the hotel that had those bathrobes, and we wore them to 7-Eleven?" Jutin asks.

Austin waves his vape. "Was that the same time we got kicked out of the pool for making a train on the water slide?"

A loud beeping comes from the hallway.

"What's that?"

Josh opens the door and looks out.

Brandon leaps off the bed, hurdles the rookies, and pushes past Courtney. "That's the fire alarm!"

"They're probably just testing it," Austin says.

"I *told* you guys not to vape in here," Shane says.

Austin gets a funny look on his face. Jutin squirms between the door and the wall. The action pushes Josh and Brandon into the hallway.

"What are you doing, Bilku?" Brandon demands.

"Trying to read the hotel evacuation plan," Jutin says.

"Maybe we better go downstairs," Courtney says.

The boys pocket their vapes and stream past her. Other hotel patrons crowd the hallway. Red lights blink, the alarm shrieks, and Courtney covers her ears. The hallway pulses with excitement, consternation, and curiosity—but no smoke.

Toby stops in front of the elevator doors.

"Shouldn't you take the stairs?" a man calls.

The line reverses. Courtney follows her teammates to the ground floor. When they go outside, wet, heavy snowflakes blanket the parking lot. She shivers and wishes she had her jean jacket.

Brandon shoves his hands up his own sleeves. "Where's the bus?"

"Probably went to fill up," Josh says.

More hotel patrons and staff pour out the exits. Some of the hockey parents, like Dr. Bilku, look confused. Others, like Mrs. Sweater Coat, are angry. Sirens whir in the distance. Abby and a woman that Courtney assumes is the hotel manager move from adult to adult.

"Everybody split up. Look innocent," Josh says.

The boys, apart from Shane, drift—heads down, hands in pockets—over to their families. They couldn't look guiltier if they tried.

"This is bad," Shane says. "Real bad. Dad's gonna blow a gasket."

Courtney searches the parking lot for her own mom. Her phone plinks.

You outside?

Yup.

Coming. I've got your jacket.

Courtney studies the roofline of the hotel.

"I don't see smoke," she says to Shane. "I didn't smell any in the hallway either."

Clint prowls from family to family. His investigation has begun.

She feels the weight of her jacket on her shoulders. "Thanks Mom."

Mom looks worried. "Do you know why the alarm went off, Courtney?"

Oh no. Clint is coming their way.

Shane tugs on Courtney's sleeve. "Don't tell anyone," he mouths.

Clint's brown eyes are furious. "This is your chance to come clean, Courtney. Your only chance. Why did the alarm go off?"

"I don't know anything," she lies.

Clint frowns.

A firetruck, siren blaring and lights flashing, wheels into the parking lot. An ambulance and two police cruisers are right behind. Firefighters run into the hotel.

Courtney has serious doubts they'll be playing Notre Dame tomorrow.

3 8

WE LOSE 7-6 TO THE men's volleyball team.

Liam's waiting for me when I come out of the dressing room. His hair is soaked and sticks to his forehead.

"Do you play like that against the Pandas?" he asks.

I shrug and concentrate on beating down these old feelings for him.

"Maybe you should kick it up a notch. You'd crush them." He tucks his dark hair behind his ears. "What are you doing right now?"

"The girls are going to Whiskey Jack's for karaoke. I'm going back to the dorm. I've got two exams left—and a major assignment to finish."

Kathy slings an arm over my shoulder. "Hey, Liam, can you give Darian and me a ride?"

"Sure. Can I drop you off too, Jessie?"

His gap-toothed grin is irresistible.

We cram into Liam's truck—an antique with no back seat. The passenger door doesn't open, so Darian ducks in through the driver's side. Kathy leverages her legs around the steering wheel and slides onto Darian's lap so there's room for me next to Liam. I narrow my eyes at Kathy as I climb in.

"What?" she says.

As the truck coughs and jerks out of the lot, all I can think about is Liam's thigh pressed against mine. Instead of taking me to my dorm first, he heads for Whiskey Jack's.

Kathy quizzes him about his vet med application. I can only pray he doesn't sense what I'm feeling. I can't focus on the conversation around me, much less participate.

Liam wheels up outside the bar. All four of us climb out, and Kathy nudges me. "Be nice," she warns.

I get back in the truck and climb across the seat, pressing my body against the cold metal of the passenger door. Liam jumps in, and we're off with a sputter and a lurch. He doesn't say anything all the way back to campus. I don't know what to say either, and the tension is killing me.

He parks in the loop between the College Building and my dorm and shuts off the engine. I can't get out until he does, and I don't want to move closer.

He drapes both arms on the steering wheel. "I miss you."

I close my eyes and try not to panic.

"I said some stupid stuff a few months ago. I don't even remember what. Or why. But I'm sorry we're not together anymore." He takes a deep breath. "And I'm going to be honest with you here. I think I pushed you away because I was jealous."

"Of what?" I ask.

"You've found a way to play hockey *and* go to school," he says. "Maybe I didn't like the fact you picked your team over me most of the time."

"I did?" I shake my head. "Shocker. I had no idea you felt that way."

"Okay, then you'll find this even more surprising." He turns so he's looking at me. "Will you come home with me tonight?"

Damn.

"I can't. Psych assignment."

"Then let me take you for a *real* supper tomorrow. No Tim's."

"Liam, I really need to focus on school," I plead.

"I made a big mistake when I pushed you out of my life. I haven't been able to concentrate on anything the past few weeks."

Righteous anger sizzles. "But you made time for Lee."

As soon as the words spill out, I want to pull them back. Here he is trying to make up, and I'm throwing Lee at him like a pail of slop water.

"I only went out with her that one time. The night you saw us at the rink. She's not *you*, Jessie." He wipes a hand across his jaw. "Besides, is it fair to accuse me of something you're doing yourself?" His tone is sharp. "Are you turning me down because you're seeing some old guy from Calgary?"

Old guy? He makes it sound like Scott's ancient.

"What if I am. He's been nice to me, and he's interested in my team, unlike some people I know."

Why am I even saying this? I haven't had anything to do with Scott since Calgary. Sometimes, I say the stupidest things.

"That's not fair, Jessie," Liam says.

I smooth my jeans across my thighs. "We made the right choice a few months ago. If all we're going to do is argue, then—"

"I want to work things out," Liam says.

I can't do this. I just got my life back on track. I can't afford to blow it again. "Please get out, so I can leave," I plead. "I've got hours of homework."

Liam opens the door and climbs out. I slide across the seat. My body brushes his as I exit the truck. He grips my forearms and pulls me close.

"No." I tug free.

"At least let me walk you to the door," he says. "I want to make sure you get inside the building okay."

"I can look after myself."

"Then I'll wait here till I see the light go on in your room."

As I walk away from him, a car pulls up and two girls get out.

"If you ever need anything, just ask," Liam says behind me.

I quicken my pace.

"Should he be here?" one of the girls calls out to me.

"Of course he should!" I call back.

When I get to my room, Liam leans against his truck, arms folded over his chest. I like him so much, but I can't afford to do this right now. I turn on the light beside my bed and then watch him drive away.

3 9

"I DON'T BELIEVE IT." Josh sits on the edge of the bed, hands dangling between his knees. "We finally get a road trip, and I have to spend the night in my room with my *mom?*"

"You're lucky the hotel manager and the fire chief were understanding," Clint says.

Courtney lifts her head. At least Clint's not yelling anymore.

"Go to your rooms," he says. 'I don't want to see your faces until breakfast."

"Are you going to bench us in Notre Dame?" Austin asks.

"I haven't decided what I'm doing," Clint says, "but I can guarantee you won't like it."

"That sounds ominous," Jutin says.

Clint opens the door and eyeballs the Moose as they slink from the room. When Courtney moves to follow, Clint says, "Not you, McIntyre."

Clint steps outside the room and gestures at Courtney. When she joins him, he closes the door and pockets the room card. Josh walks backwards down the hallway, staring at her. What does he think she's about to do?

"I'm disappointed," Clint says when the hallway is clear. "I asked if you knew what was going on, and you lied to me."

"You wanted me to narc on my teammates," she says. "They've just started to treat me like I belong. Are you saying that because I'm the only girl on the team, I have to tattle on them when they screw up?"

Clint leans his head against the wall and closes his eyes.

"I'm sorry I lied, but if this happened again, I'd do exactly the same thing," she says.

"I get it. Though I don't agree with it. But ask yourself how far you'll go to protect these clowns."

"I don't know," she says. "But they keep giving me chances to find out."

He sighs. "I'm having a tough time deciding on how I'll allocate consequences. There're kids who vaped and owned up to it. Kids who vaped and didn't. Kids like you who were in the wrong place at the wrong time."

"I don't look at it that way," Courtney says. "I'm glad I was there. If you decide to bench me tomorrow because I lied, I'm okay with that. All I want is for the guys to talk to me in the dressing room and at school on Monday."

December 15
Notre Dame Tournament
Estevan Moose vs. Athol Murray College Prep Hounds
Duncan MacNeill Arena, Wilcox

Courtney's lungs are on fire as she staggers off the ice and flops on the bench. The Olympic-sized ice in Wilcox takes a toll.

"Getting enough ice-time?" Clint asks.

She gasps and sucks on her water bottle.

The players who were vaping are lined up along the boards. Clint won't let them sit on the back of the bench.

Wheezing, Jutin throws himself beside her.

"How's it going?" Josh asks.

"Shut up! If you guys ever pull a stunt like this again, I'll . . ."

Courtney's jaw drops as Jutin finishes the threat.

She's exhausted. How much longer can their skeleton squad skate with the Hounds? So far, Toby has stymied the ND offence, but he gets up slower each time he flops or butterflies. His equipment must be soaked.

"Coach, are we going to have to double shift the *whole* game?" she asks Clint.

"I haven't decided." Arms folded, Clint stares at the ice. "You're up, McIntyre."

Courtney skates to the faceoff dot.

The linesman towers over her. "Has your coach got something against half your team?"

"Long story," she replies.

"You can tell it to me in instalments. One per shift," he says. "Looks like you'll have a lot of them."

Funny guy.

The linesman drops the puck, and Shane loses the draw. Courtney ties up 24 then chases the puck into the corner. She sidesteps to avoid the check, slides the puck behind Notre Dame's net and tries to tuck it in between the goalie's skate and the goalpost. Someone rams her against the post, and pain lances her right shoulder.

The ref whistles down the play and gives 24 a penalty for charging while she slumps against the boards, her shoulder throbbing.

The linesman drops on one knee. "You okay?"

She shakes her head and blinks back tears.

Dr. Bilku hovers over her. "Where does it hurt, Courtney?"

"Shoulder," she says.

The doctor performs a quick exam. "Hold still now." He grabs her wrist and jerks her arm.

She sucks in her breath at the sharp pain—and the relief.

"We need to immobilize the arm," Dr. Bilku says.

"Use my scarf," Mom says.

Courtney didn't know she was here. "Mom?"

"Courtney, hold your arm like this," Dr. Bilku instructs. He fastens the scarf so that her arm is bent across her chest. "Help me lift her."

"Careful," Mom says.

The doctor, Clint, and the lineman ease Courtney to her feet. The pain has subsided to a dull ache.

"Don't worry. We'll get you to a hospital," Clint says. "The closest one is Moose Jaw."

"Weyburn would be better," Mom says. "My husband can meet us there."

Notre Dame 24 skates beside her. "I'm sorry I hurt you."

"You're a dick, 24," the tall linesman says. "Go to the penalty box." He swings the gate open for Courtney. "Sorry about your shoulder."

Her discomfort makes it impossible for her to care that he cares.

One of the teachers from Athol Murray College offers to drive Courtney and Mom to Weyburn Hospital.

"I feel responsible," she says as she helps Courtney with her seatbelt. "My younger son Levi is the player who hit you."

As they drive away from the rink, Mrs. Bonokoski points out important locations on campus, including the statues of Pere Athol Murray, the founder of the College, and Our Lady of Notre Dame—one hand withered and one raised in blessing. Courtney wishes the Lady could reach out and heal her shoulder.

Her phone plinks. It's Dad.

Hang tight. On my way.

Mrs. Bonokoski turns out to be the linesman's mom too.

"Reid plays with the AAA team, but he likes to officiate our minor hockey games. As for Levi, he's a great kid, but a little impulsive," she says.

As they turn onto the highway, Courtney cradles her arm and focuses on the conversation in the front seat to take her mind off the pain. Mrs. Bonokoski took a teaching job at Notre Dame so her three children could play sports there. Her daughter plays AAA with the female Hounds.

"My kids love it here. Pere Murray's legacy. Mind. Body. Spirit." Mrs. Bonokoski clears her throat. "Courtney, did you ever think about playing AAA?"

How can she ask that while they're on their way to emergency?

"The good news is that although your shoulder was dislocated, it's back in place," the ER doctor tells Courtney. "The bad news is you've got a hairline fracture that's going to take a while to heal."

"How long?" Courtney asks.

"You'll be good as new in six weeks," the doctor says.

In the meantime, she has to wear this stupid sling. And there'll be no three-on-three tourney with Shane and Josh during Christmas break. No hockey until the end of January. Michael's suspension ends after the holidays. What will the Moose be like when she returns? She tries to ignore the ache in her shoulder and her heart.

"Still leaves you a few months to play," Mom says brightly. "Not the end of the world."

Is Mom *happy* she can't play right now?

Mrs. Bonokoski waits for them in the hospital lobby.

"Thanks for your help," Mom tells her. "My husband will be here soon. I can't believe you waited this long. You're too kind."

"Not a problem," Mrs. Bonokoski says. "It's the least I could do. Courtney, please give me your phone number. Levi is going to call you and apologize."

The last thing Courtney wants to do is talk to him.

"He already apologized," she says.

"Then he'll do it again," Mrs. Bonokoski says.

It's dark by the time Dad gets there. Courtney tries to make herself comfortable in the back of their SUV. The painkiller the doctor prescribed barely takes the edge off, and she is miserable.

Her phone plinks. It's Josh.

how bad is it

Out for 6 wks. Did we win?

lost 6-1

She calls him. Maybe his postgame analysis will take her mind off the pain.

"Did you get a few shifts at least?" she asks.

"Oh yeah." Josh laughs. "Clint was a real hard ass. Wouldn't let us off the ice. He kept asking, 'How are your lungs now?'"

Plink! It's Jessie.

How u doin? Dad says u got a separated shldr? Sad face emoji.

"Look, I'll let you go," Courtney says to Josh. "Talk to you at school on Monday."

"See you, McIntyre. Take care of yourself."

She can't imagine sitting through a day of classes, much less catching a ride to school with Mom or Dad. She presses End and stares at Jessie's text for a minute, then turns off her phone and closes her eyes.

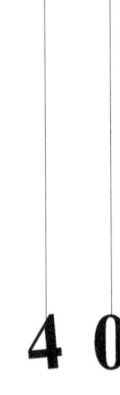

4 0

I CHECK OVER THE EXAM one more time, erasing the penciled asterisks I use to mark the questions for review. I'm one of the few psych students left writing, and I only have ten minutes left to finish up. It's my last chance to get a decent mark in this class.

I scan one more time for asterisks and make my way to the front of the auditorium, where a psych postgraduate student waits. Dr. Kerr isn't even here so I can say a proper goodbye. I hand in the exam and grab my knapsack on the way out.

The white hoarfrost on the campus trees and the bright blue sky lift my spirits. I'm free of hockey and school for ten whole days. I'll celebrate with fast food on my way to Estevan. I throw my knapsack in Sunny's back seat and let her warm up while I check my messages. There's one from Liam.

U left for home yet? Need a ride.

He's attached a gif of a truck engine blowing up.

Five hours alone with him will be awkward. Maybe even dangerous. I'd like to tell him I'm on the road already, but if our roles were reversed, I wouldn't appreciate being brushed off.

Pick u up in 10. Want coffee?

He replies with a thumbs up.

While I wait in the Tim's drive-through, I try to clean up the front seat. When I hand the cashier a shopping bag full of garbage, she gives me a strange look. Why do I care about making a good impression on Liam? He knows I'm a car slob. Not as bad as Kathy obviously—no one else could possibly be that bad—but bad none the less. I dig an air freshener out of my console to combat the smell of my hockey bag. Besides using our backyard rink for shooting practice, I hope to squeeze in a game or two with my dad's rec team.

Liam waits on the sidewalk in front of the house where he lives.

"Thanks for picking me up," he says as he tosses his duffle bag in the back seat and climbs in. "I knew that truck would crap out one of these days."

"Battery?" I ask.

"Alternator, I think. I didn't have time to mess around with it. It's my kooshie's birthday, and my family's having a party for her tonight. Do you mind dropping me off at the Nation? I know it's out of your way, but—"

"Not that far," I tell him. "We can take 33 from Regina. Traffic will be lighter."

"You got anything up tonight?" he asks. "Maybe you could join us. Kooshie says you interviewed her and Metagoosh and some other elders for a psych paper. Want to tell me about it?"

I do so as we tie into the breakfast sandwiches and coffee. He never looks at his phone once. It's like old times. But I can tell he's tired. When we near the hill at Hanley, Liam folds his hoodie into a pillow, tucks it under his head, and closes his eyes.

He doesn't wake up till I stop for gas at Davidson. Yawning, he insists on paying and fuels up while I grab us more coffee inside. While I'm waiting to pay, I notice a display rack of tin coffee mugs. There's one with his name on it. I could always pretend I bought it before we broke up. I pay for it and slip it in my purse.

"Want me to drive for a bit?" Liam asks when I come back to the car.

A few sips later, I'm snuggled against my pillow. I wake up with a loud snort when he slows down at Chamberlain.

"Was I snoring?" I wipe a dribble of spit from the corner of my mouth. My pillow has a wet stain. How humiliating.

"Loud and proud," he says.

I look in the mirror on the visor and straighten my hair. "When did the wind pick up?"

"Storm's coming," he says. "Didn't you know?"

I stifle a yawn. "I didn't pay attention to the forecast."

When we take the Regina bypass and turn onto 33, snow gusts and ripples.

It's not thick or sticky yet, but the flurries hide the lines on the pavement. Finger drifts appear. Darkness falls, and my nerves kick in. After I drop Liam off at Pheasant Rump, I'll still have a long drive to Estevan in the dark.

As if reading my mind, Liam says, "I'm sorry I took you out of the way. You should spend the night at Kooshie's."

"I want to get home to *my* family," I say.

"You can leave first thing in the morning. It's always better driving in daylight."

When we arrive at Pheasant Rump, his grandparents' lane is plugged with snow, and we get stuck. Liam pushes Sunny free while his metagoosh waves a big flashlight to show him where to park. We grab our stuff and hurry to the house as the wind whips my hair and clothing.

Inside, Christmas ornaments hang in the windows and from the branches of a real pine tree. Warm bannock fresh from the oven is laid out on the kitchen table, but Liam and I and his grandparents are the only people here.

"Your mom and dad decided not to come when the weather turned." Liam's kooshie gives him a hug. "Looks like you get all the bannock you want."

My mouth waters.

Metagoosh pours me a glass of dark liquid. "Chokecherry juice," he explains. "My brother dropped it off."

From my interviews, I've learned that berries aren't plentiful anymore, so that makes the gift more special.

"The darker the berry, the better the juice," Metagoosh says. "What do you think?"

I take a sip. "It's very good."

He leads me to chair by the wood stove. "Chokecherries are medicine for our people. We use crushed ones in ceremony. Did my grandson ever tell you that?"

I look over at Liam, but he's talking to Kooshie.

"So, how did you do on your paper?" Metagoosh asks.

"I don't have my mark back yet. I'll let you know when I do."

"I'd like that," he says. "Everyone enjoyed talking to you."

Kooshie brings me a plate of bannock. "How are your parents?"

I realize I didn't let them know we arrived safely at Pheasant Rump—that I'll be spending the night. "They're fine, although they're probably worried about me." I dig out my phone. "I'll call them."

I slip into the kitchen to talk in private. Mom is relieved. I promise her I'll get away in the morning as soon as the roads are clear.

"Liam's grandfather has a snowblower. He'll get me out," I assure Mom. "I'll be home by noon."

I plug in my phone on the kitchen counter and enter the living room. Liam speaks in a low voice to his grandparents. Kooshie gives me a strange look. I wonder if they were discussing sleeping arrangements. Last time we stayed here, Liam and I used the spare room. I hope Liam's explained we won't share a bed this time.

"Look what Liam gave me," Kooshie says, as if to dispel the awkwardness. She holds up a brightly flowered, rectangular scarf.

"It's beautiful," I say.

"Liam shouldn't waste his money on gifts. What do I need?" She beams as she arranges the scarf on her head and shoulders.

We all compliment her.

"Liam will sleep down here on the couch," she announces. "Jessie gets the guest room. But first we'll play cards. It's my birthday, so I get to pick the game."

Liam groans. "Not euchre."

"Yes, Small Boy." She often calls him that. She digs in the drawer for a deck of cards.

"I'll be your partner," I tell Kooshie. "I barely remember the rules, so it'll be easier."

She looks at me sideways. "You better catch on quick."

Metagoosh refills my glass, and the next few hours at the kitchen table fly by. We laugh at the tricks I should have taken, and the harder I try, the worse I play.

After we put the cards aside, Metagoosh tells stories. He's the best storyteller I know, and the woodsmoke from the fire and the wind tearing at the roof and walls provide the perfect atmosphere.

"Where did the McArthur name come from?" I ask.

"A long time ago a retired RCMP officer moved here," Metagoosh says. "He was the first McArthur. He married Sitting with a Stone and had a son with her and adopted another. Then he left. I don't think he was a nice man. But his sons had many children, and that was the beginning of the McArthurs."

It's a pleasant story compared to some of the ones he, Kooshie, and the other elders have told me. Stories of disease, starvation, and lost lives and years. Stories that make me feel angry, helpless, and privileged.

When it's time for bed, I use the upstairs washroom then change into shorts and a T-shirt, keeping my socks on. The double bed is piled high with quilts and pillows. I climb in and listen to the blizzard howl outside my window. Frost has built up on the inside of the glass. Though the day hasn't turned out the way I expected, it's been a good one.

I realize I left my phone downstairs. When I wake up in the morning, I'll have no idea what time it is. Kooshie and Metagoosh's voices murmur next door, and water trickles through the pipes in the walls. I slip out of bed and sneak down the stairs where the fire crackles and snaps in the wood stove. I dig through my purse at the front door, then remember I left the phone in the kitchen.

The bathroom door opens, and Liam emerges in a damp cloud. A towel is wrapped around his hips. His black hair glistens and hangs in his face.

I gawk at him.

"What's up?" he asks.

"I forgot my phone."

He raises an eyebrow. Does he think I came down here to find *him*?

"I must have left it in the kitchen." I try to step around him, but he steps with me, like we're dancing.

"Jessie, we should talk."

"And you should put on some clothes."

His gap-toothed smile glitters. He places his hands on my hips and pulls me against him. His mouth swoops down, and I forget everything for a while.

"This is a bad idea," I tell him when he pulls away to bury his face in my neck.

"What are you going to do about it?" he murmurs.

I wrap my arms around his waist. His flesh warms my hands. "There wasn't anything wrong with your truck, was there?"

"Not a thing."

⚓

I awaken to sun streaming through the window, coffee brewing, and bacon sizzling. I stretch on the couch and wonder where I am. Then I remember. Blushing, I wriggle into my clothing under the quilt and try to sneak upstairs. I meet Kooshie on the way down.

She grins. "Sleep okay?"

I nod and try to slip past her.

She taps my cheek. "Hope you worked up a hunger."

I feel better after a quick shower and a change of clothes. When I enter the kitchen, Metagoosh hands me a cup of coffee. His cheeks are red. "I dug your car out of a snowbank. Still, you might need Liam to give you a push."

"Thanks. And thanks for letting me stay last night."

Kooshie laughs out loud, and Liam says something to her I don't understand.

Cheeks burning, I sit at the table. Liam sets a plate of bacon, eggs, and bannock in front of me. I mumble a thank you and dig into my breakfast, refusing to meet his eyes.

"What are your plans for the holidays, Jessie?" Metagoosh asks.

While I swallow a mouthful of eggs and start to explain, Liam sits across from me. Our eyes meet, and I lose my train of thought. He looks so calm. Sure, his hair is a disaster, but his features are content, the way I wish I felt.

I gulp down the rest of my food, wrap the bannock in my napkin, and push back from the table. "I should get going."

"Have some more coffee," Metagoosh says. "I'll get the snow blower and tackle the lane."

"I'll help you," Liam says.

When they've gone outside, Kooshie says, "I have something for you, Jessie."

She gives me a pair of black mukluks that reach to my knees. The black, green, white, and charcoal beadwork on the top of the foot and around the calf is gorgeous.

Tears film my eyes. "Huskie colours."

"I had these made for you last summer," Kooshie says.

"Thank you, but I don't have anything for you."

"You don't give gifts because you expect something in return," she says. "You give because it fills your heart."

"I'll wear these with pride," I tell her.

Her eyes shine. "We want to get to one of your games sometime. Maybe when you come to Regina."

"I'd like that. Whether Liam and I are together or not."

"Don't be too hard on him," she says. "He likes you."

"I like him too, but between hockey and school, I don't have time for him. Not the time that he deserves. And I don't want to interfere with his plans to get into vet med."

She waves a hand. "You kids worry too much. Let things take care of themselves. It'll work out between you two, or it won't. But the thaw will come in the spring, the geese will return, and the earth will start over."

It's an hour before the lane is clear. When I'm packed up and ready to roll, I hug Kooshie and step outside.

A sparkling, white shroud covers the yard, and the reflection of the sun off the snow burns my eyes. Sunny, engine running, awaits, and I throw my stuff in the back. When I straighten, Liam pulls me against him.

"I'll call you in a few days," he says. "In the meantime, enjoy your holiday. I see Kooshie gave you the mukluks. You make them look good."

His breath on my skin makes my knees weak. Remembering the mug I bought at the gas station at Davidson, I step out of his embrace and dig in my purse. "Merry Christmas."

His eyes light up. Kooshie was right. It doesn't matter that he never got me anything. His reaction makes the giving worthwhile.

41

"COURTNEY, ARE YOU SURE YOU want to go to this dance?" Mom asks. "Aren't you afraid someone will jostle your arm?"

"I don't want to go, remember?" Courtney explains. "*Christina* wants to go. I'll work our shift at the bake table, and then Jessie can come get me."

"Will you be much help as a one-winged salesperson?" Jessie rakes Courtney's hair into a high pony and wraps a silver scrunchie around it.

"If I can't lift a plate of six cookies, I might as well stay home." Courtney stands and totters on her red velvet pumps. "Maybe I should wear my Vans."

"At least until you get to the dance," Jessie says. "Here. I'll help you with your coat." She zips the Moose jacket over top of the sling.

Mom holds up a tissue. "Don't forget to blot your lipstick."

"Will you two quit fussing over me?" Courtney fumes.

"It isn't every day that my little sister—correction—my little sister who's officially one inch taller than me—goes to her first high school dance," Jessie says. "It seems like only yesterday that I went to *mine*."

The doorbell rings.

"That'll be Christina," Courtney says.

Mrs. Delgado whisks Courtney and Christina off to the school in her van, a mobile nail salon with bright red bubble letters on the side that say "Camela's Studio." Christina and Mrs. Delgado chatter the whole way, while Courtney struggles to maintain her balance on one of the salon chairs. When the girls exit the van, Mrs. Delgado hands Christina a large plastic container.

"I did some extra baking," she says. "Sugar cookies. Some cupcakes."

"Thanks, Ma," Christina says.

"If you run out, just call!" Mrs. Delgado shouts as they make their way up the sidewalk. "I've got more in the freezer!"

When the two girls get inside the school, Josh, Brandon, and Shane are at the back of the line for the Breathalyzer.

"I thought you weren't coming," Courtney says.

Brandon rolls his eyes. "Mom *made* me. She says it's a 'healthy activity.'"

The walls of the gym are hung with banners of cartoon Santas. Courtney unzips her jacket and hangs it on the back of one of the chairs behind the bake table.

"Whoa. Sexy!" Christina says.

Courtney's red dress clings to her bust and hips. "It's Jessie's. She made me wear it, but I never would have got out of the house if Dad had seen it."

Christina wears black pumps, black leggings and a long, white blouse bordered with lace. Large silver hoops dangle from her dainty earlobes. She pops a set of felt reindeer antlers on her head and asks, "How is this?"

"Looks smashing," Courtney says.

Christina unpacks the boxes of baking while Courtney arranges them on the table. Each item is priced at two dollars.

As the gym fills, the DJ plays Christmas tunes. Pam and her friends are working at the mocktail table, and Toby's hanging around Pam. Is he *interested* in her? Toby catches Courtney staring, and he waves. Courtney waves back. Pam raises her hand and then says something to Toby about her. This is so weird.

Courtney and Christina do a brisk business at the bake table for an hour. When her sore feet and shoulder get the best of her, Courtney pulls up a chair. Once the DJ abandons the Christmas music and plays requests, the dance floor hums while red, blue, and green LED lights flash.

Courtney checks her phone and sees that Aiden liked one of her selfies on Instagram. They've connected a few times since they shared a dressing room at the Estevan U15 tournament. She snapchats Aiden a pic of the bake table with the hashtags #Christmascalories and #doIhavetoeatwhatIdontsell.

Aiden snapchats her latest Xbox score.

Holy.

"Feel like dancing?" a voice rasps in Courtney's ear.

She nearly drops her phone. Josh leans over her, and his breath is boozy. How did he smuggle alcohol past the teachers stationed at the main entrance?

Courtney puts her phone away and rearranges the plates of cookies. "I can't dance. I'm working." She's glad the sling conceals most of her chest.

Jade's words ring in her ears.

"Don't date a teammate."

Josh grabs her hand. "Come on, Courtney. We're linemates. Friends even."

"All right," she says, though his green eyes are hardly friend-like. "Just one dance."

He slides an arm around her waist and steers her towards the crowd.

Her heels make her slightly taller than him. The fast tune ends as they reach the dance floor and fades into a number that starts slow. Josh reaches for her hips and tugs her close. With her sling between them, she rests a hand on his shoulder and tries to ignore his sweaty palm on her spine, his eyes on her mouth. He says something, but she can't hear him over the music.

She leans closer, and he murmurs in her ear, "You're beautiful."

"It's the booze talking," she says.

His embrace tightens. "Want a drink?"

She shakes her head. Yeah, the doofus snuck some booze in.

Josh stumbles against her, making her stumble into whoever's behind her.

"Sorry." She looks over her shoulder.

It's Shane. He's dancing with a girl she doesn't know, and he looks angry. Is he jealous because she's dancing with Josh? Why does life have to be complicated?

When the song ends, she heads straight for the bake table. Josh catches up to her and tries to put his arm around her again, but she lengthens her stride.

"Please have a drink with me," he says.

She faces him. "Go hit on someone else."

His face clouds. "You don't trust me. You think I'll try to pull something stupid."

How could he possibly guess?

"I want to be your teammate, Josh. Nothing more," she says.

"This is your last chance." He thrusts out his lower lip in a pout.

She smiles. "Do you promise?"

"I'm walking away now." He turns his body but not his head. "I'm going to ask another girl, and then it'll be too late."

"Hurry," she says.

He wanders away.

When Courtney sits in her chair, Christina eyes her reproachfully. "When is it my turn to dance?"

"You can go anytime. I'm done," Courtney says.

Christina straightens her antlers. "I am going to ask a boy. Wish me luck."

"Luck," Courtney says.

Christina disappears into the press of bodies. For the next few minutes, Courtney tries to pinpoint her white blouse. Then she sees Pam dancing with Toby.

Hm.

Mr. G wanders over and leans on the table. "How're sales?"

Courtney shows him the contents of the cash box.

"Nice work," he says. "What are you raising money for again?"

"The food bank."

"Beautiful. Where's your sidekick?"

"She's out there." Courtney catches a glimpse of Christina. Who is she dancing with?

Mr. G purses his lips. "Notice anything suspicious?"

Courtney swallows. "Like what?"

"I saw you with Thompson. Whatever's fired him up isn't a naturally occurring male hormone."

A loud hoot draws Courtney's attention to the dance floor, where a circle has formed around Josh. He's stripped off his shirt, and he swings it around his head like a lasso.

"Sometimes he gets a little wild," Courtney says.

"Smell anything on his breath?" Mr. G. persists.

"I'd rather not say," she replies.

"He your boyfriend?"

"No, but I don't want to get him into trouble."

"You smell alcohol on anyone else?"

She shakes her head, then realizes he just trapped her into tattling.

Mr. G fishes a toonie out of his pocket. "Score me some of those sugar cookies. They're screaming my name."

He walks away, munching a cookie, and talks to a female staff member near the mocktail bar. He offers her a cookie before the conversation turns serious. Courtney senses the wheels of justice are turning.

Christina marches back to the table with Brandon behind her. His dress shirt is rumpled, and his thin tie is askew. She was dancing with *him*?

"Is it okay if we dance another?" Christina gasps.

Brandon sways and leans on the table.

Courtney doesn't trust Brandon as far as she can throw him. And what if Christina gets scooped up in Mr. G's net?

"Okay, but just one," Courtney says. "There's something I need to tell you."

Christina scowls. "It will have to wait."

Brandon's hand slips and knocks a plate of cookies to the floor. "Oops."

Courtney grabs his tie and tugs him close, so Christina can't hear. "If you get her in trouble, you're going to be sorry."

Brandon grins and hiccups. He stinks like booze.

"Where did you guys hide the alcohol?" she whispers.

He blinks.

"Don't pretend you don't have any. Mr. G knows it too." She jerks her head at the mocktail table. "Tell me where it is, so I can get rid of it."

"*You* can't get rid of it," Brandon says. "It's in the guys' john. In the back of a toilet."

"Courtney, we want to *dance*," Christina insists.

Courtney releases the tie and watches, helpless, while Christina drags Brandon back to the dance floor. Shane staggers towards the washroom exit. Courtney slips off her shoes, tucks the cashbox under her coat, and follows Shane to the boys' bathroom.

Once he's inside, she knocks on the door, then places her ear against it and listens. Someone is puking his guts out. Violently. She tries the handle, but the door is locked.

"Shane! It's Courtney! Let me in!"

After a long moment, the latch turns, and Shane opens the door. He has puke breath.

"I'll let you in, but nobody else," he slurs.

Courtney steps inside and locks the door behind her. There's vomit on the floor, and here she is in bare feet. Shane hiccups and staggers into the closest stall. His heaves sound painful.

Courtney avoids the puke and crumpled paper towels on the floor. The stench of the urinals is overwhelming. Boys are pigs.

She hopes there's at least soap in the dispenser so she can wash her hands after she checks the toilet tanks. She has no luck with the first two tanks, but half a bottle of rye whiskey in a plastic bag bobs inside the third. She pours the rye into the toilet and flushes it. What should she do with the bottle?

Shane moans.

Courtney peers in his stall. He's sprawled over the toilet, arms wrapped around the bowl. His cheek rests on the seat. "Go away and let me be sick with dignity."

She hears a knock. Now what?

She listens at the door but hears only the throb of music and shouts from the dance floor. The next knock startles her, but it's not a loud, authoritative knock—like Mr. G would make. She unlatches the door and opens it.

Josh leans a hand on the door jamb. "Hey, what gives?"

"I'm trying to save your sorry asses," she says. "I got rid of the booze."

More heaves and a gut-wrenching groan.

"Who else is in here?" Josh asks.

"Shane," Courtney says. "He's not in a good way. How much did he drink?"

Josh slips through the gap and locks the door behind him. He slides through the puke and leans into Shane's stall. "How's it going, bud?"

Shane's spine arches, and he spits phlegm.

"What do I do with the bottle?" Courtney demands.

Josh takes the bottle and goes to the sink. He fills it with water, caps it, and thrusts it in a tank. "Nobody was gonna look for it. You flushed away good booze." He closes the stall door in her face.

"Are you going to leave it there forever?" she asks while he's peeing.

"I'll come get it later," he says.

A fist hammers on the door. "Open up!"

"That's Mr. G! What do we do?" Courtney says.

Josh opens his stall door. "Got a stick of gum?"

42

"MR. G FOUND YOUR SISTER in the washroom with two male students whom we know were drinking," Ms. Merril, the ECS vice principal, says. Behind me, Mr. G grunts.

"And you think Courtney was too?" I ask.

"No," Ms. Merril says, "but she helped with the coverup."

I look through the window of Ms. Merril's office into the school admin area, where Courtney sits, ponytail drooping, and Josh and Brandon slouch, arms folded. Shane, who looks like crap, has a wastebasket between his legs. The door to the principal's office is closed. Christina's parents are losing their minds in there. Poor kid.

"You should be talking to my mom or dad," I reply. "Courtney shouldn't have texted *me* to pick her up."

"I told her to call home," Ms. Merril says. "She put off facing them by dragging *you* over here. Tell her to come see me at 8:00 am tomorrow—with at least one of your parents."

"Sure." I'm relieved Courtney's not looking at more serious consequences.

"As for those other clowns, I'm sick of their attitude," Mr. G says. "I'm supposed to take them along on a band trip to Colorado during February break.

This is a stupid stunt to pull before the holidays. Don't you think I'd rather be at home with my *own* family tonight, instead of arguing with parents about why it's not okay for boys to be boys?"

When I leave Ms. Merril's office, Courtney grabs her backpack and follows me. The boys' heads swivel towards me. I'd like to knock them together.

"Hey, Jessie, are you still going out with Liam?" Mr. G calls across the room.

How am I supposed to answer that?

"Sort of. Maybe." I take a breath. "It's complicated."

"Well, tell him I said 'hi,'" Mr. G says. "I always liked that kid."

I open the door for Courtney. As soon as we're in the hallway, I mutter, "What the hell?"

She tosses her pony, and the scrunchie slips further. "Don't start with me. I've had a rough night."

Love that attitude.

"You better tell me *everything* before you talk to Mom and Dad."

"Can we at least wait until we're in the vehicle?" she begs.

In the foyer, we meet a blonde woman in a sweater coat who look daggers at Courtney.

"Who does *she* belong to?" I ask when we're outside.

"Brandon. His mom hates me. This whole thing will be my fault." Courtney sniffs and wipes her nose with the back of her good hand. "Here I am with one arm in a sling, and I still manage to take down the team. Why didn't I play hockey in Weyburn? There's no way it could be any worse than this. Maybe I should quit altogether."

I slip an arm around her waist. "McIntyres don't quit. Now tell me what happened."

<hr />

"Go to bed, Courtney. The world will look different in the morning." Mom sips her cocoa.

I can't believe she's so calm. This is my *mother*?

Courtney heaves a sigh and trudges up the stairs.

"So, which one of you is meeting with the vice principal tomorrow?" I ask.

Mom and Dad look at one another.

"You go ahead," Dad says. "I know you like to stay on top of this sort of thing."

"I'm okay if you'd rather do it," Mom says.

I turn to follow my sister.

"Oh, Jessie. Liam stopped here while you were gone," Dad says.

"What?" My pulse quickens.

Dad points to our Christmas tree. "He dropped off gifts for you, your mother, and Courtney, and a bottle of Scotch for me. Are you sure you're not going out with him anymore?"

I root through the presents. "Which bag is for me?"

"The big blue one," Mom says. "I thought the mukluks were enough."

"Those are from his grandparents." I read the gift tag.

To: Hockey Girl.

From: The Schmuck.

I'm dying of curiosity, but I tuck the present behind the tree. I don't want to open it until Christmas morning. My feelings are confused enough. When I turn around, Mom wears a serene expression.

"Jessie, thanks for making our job so easy," she says. "You're a great role model for your sister. Tonight, she screwed up trying to look out for her teammates, but she didn't get dragged down by their stupidity. She's going to be punished for it, but those boys will have more respect for her, even if their parents don't."

"She's going to win this thing. You wait and see," Dad says, aiming the remote at the television. "Now, if you'll excuse us. We want to finish this episode."

Where were these people when I was fourteen?

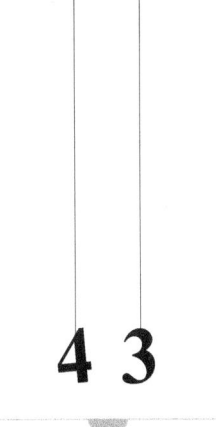

43

"Hey, Courtney. Can I talk to you for a sec?"

Courtney looks up from her science text. Pam stands on the other side of the table.

Her voice disturbs the quiet of the ECS library. The educational assistant behind the circulation desk puts a finger to her lips. At the next table, two older girls, tall enough to be senior basketball players, lift disdainful eyes. Christina sulks at a table across the room.

Courtney hasn't talked to Pam in weeks. Funny that after spending so much time together at figure skating practice, test days, and competitions, Courtney feels like she never knew Pam at all.

"Have a chair," Courtney says, keeping her voice low.

Pam sits. "How long are you suspended?" she whispers.

"I have to stay here all morning," Courtney whispers back. "I can't go to the talent show if that makes you feel any better."

"I'm sorry you got into trouble," Pam says.

"So am I," Courtney says.

Did Pam come here to apologize? Or does she want something else?

Who Brought the Booze is the question of the day. Josh, Shane, and Brandon are suspended from class and all extra-curricular activities until one of them fesses up. Brandon's mom is on a rampage. As for Christina—

"I want you to know that Toby and I didn't have anything to drink at the dance," Pam says. "Toby's a good guy, and I really like him."

"Good for you."

The comment earns Courtney a shush from the library assistant. Across the room, Christina peers around her textbook.

Pam takes a deep breath and lets it out slowly. "Toby really respects you."

As angry as she is with Pam, Courtney is glad to hear this.

"I want to be friends again," Pam says.

"Does your change of heart have anything to do with Toby?" Courtney asks.

Pam blushes. "Maybe. But I'm sorry for the way we drifted apart."

"We didn't drift," Courtney asserts. "You *dumped* me."

"I was scared," Pam whispers. "Michael is . . . you know. He's *Michael*."

Courtney nods. Yeah, is there even a word to describe him? She hasn't seen him all day, but she knows it's only a matter of time.

"Maybe we could hang out sometime. I miss Rufus," Pam says.

Is she for real?

"You miss my *dog*?"

Another shush.

The older girls pack up their stuff. Christina ducks behind her textbook. Pam looks like she's going to cry.

"Pam, I'll hang out with you anywhere. You name the place," Courtney says.

Pam blinks. "Thanks Courtney. That means a lot." She stands. "I'll talk to you soon."

As Pam walks away, Courtney forces her eyes back to her textbook. The repair of this rift won't go well with Christina. Then again, she's not sure Christina's talking to her anyway.

The older girls approach Courtney's table. They wear ECS Elecs jackets, and they have legs that go on forever. Definitely basketball players.

"Hey, Courtney," one says. "Just wanted to say we think Michael Carson's a certified jackass. We don't like the way he's treated you."

"You got guts," the other one says.

"Thanks," Courtney says.

The girls turn and walk out of the library.

Courtney has no idea what just happened, but she thinks there's a good chance it might be earth-shattering.

Ms. Merril's voice booms through the public address system. "Would

Courtney McIntyre and Christina Delgado please come to the office?"

Courtney gathers her stuff and waits for Christina outside the library. When Christina comes out, she sweeps past, arms loaded with books.

"Hey, Toto!" Courtney calls.

Christina throws a middle finger salute over her right shoulder. A binder slips from under her arm and bounces on the floor, spewing handouts. "Go away!" she says as she kneels.

Courtney wishes she could help Christina, but she has her books in one arm and a sling around the other. "Christina, I know you're upset about getting suspended."

"Maybe it is not a big deal to you, but it is to me!" Christina says.

Is she crying?

"It's a big deal to me too."

Christina stuffs handouts in her binder. "What did Pam say to you just now?"

"She wants to hang out some time," Courtney says.

"You should not let her do that." Christina sits on her heels and glares up at Courtney. "She *betrayed* you. She is not your friend."

"I think she's sorry for what she did. And *I'm* sorry one of my teammates dragged you into this mess."

A tear slides down Christina's round cheek. "Brandon did not drag me. He had a flask, and I had a taste. Maybe more than one."

"You didn't," Courtney says.

"Ma is furious. Pa is too. I am grounded for a whole month—including Christmas holidays."

A buzzer sounds to announce the end of the period as Courtney trails Christina down the stairs. At least Christina doesn't blame *her* for what happened.

"Brandon asked me to a movie, and now I cannot go," Christina says mournfully.

Maybe the grounding is a good idea if it keeps Brandon away from her.

When Courtney and Christina enter the office, Brandon and Josh sit a few chairs apart. They look hungover.

"Don't even think about talking to them," one of the admin assistants says. "Christina, you can sit over there. Courtney, Ms. Merril is waiting for you."

Courtney talks a deep breath and enters the vice principal's office.

"Close the door behind you," Ms. Merril says.

Courtney obeys and slides into a chair.

"So. Some things have changed since I talked to you earlier. Josh owned up to bringing the alcohol. He also said he's the one who tried to hide the empty bottle. He claims you did nothing wrong. You tried to help Shane when he got sick. And you poured out the rest of the booze to stop them from drinking. We're lifting your suspension. As for the discipline form I wrote up last night . . ." She removes a paper from a file folder and tears it in half. "You're cleared to return to class."

The bell for next period rings.

"What about Josh's punishment? And the others?" Courtney asks.

"That's for them to tell you," Ms. Merril says. "I understand you're all friends?"

"Yes."

"You could pick better ones. They've managed to drag you and poor Christina into their dark web of deceit." The vice principal feeds the pieces of Courtney's discipline report into a shredder. "If I don't see you again today—and I hope I won't—have a nice holiday."

Courtney walks out of Ms. Merril's office in time to see the principal close the door to his. Courtney mouths a thank you to Josh. He nods. Brandon gives her a wry smile.

Michael and some older guys are waiting in the hallway. Courtney tries to slip past them, but Michael steps in front of her.

"Hey, don't rush off," he says.

Students on their way to class swim around them. Others stop to stare. Michael's friends look super interested.

"I heard Josh, Brandon, Shane, and that Filipino chick are suspended," Michael says.

His reference to Christina makes Courtney bristle. She steps to one side, and he moves with her.

"Come on. Tell us what happened." He rests his hand on her bad shoulder.

"Don't touch me," she says.

Michael raises his eyebrows. His hand drops.

"This is a game for you," she says. "But I'm serious. I'll be back on that team as soon as my shoulder heals. Merry Christmas."

One of the boys tugs Michael back so she can get around him.

Michael can say or do whatever he wants, but she's pretty sure his days of swaying public opinion against her are over.

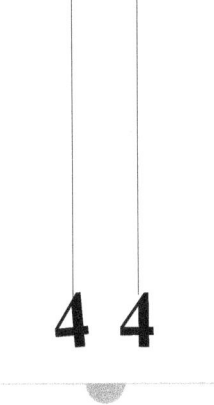

44

CHRISTMAS MORNING IS CRISP AND clean, and the sky blushes pink. The snow crunches and squeaks under my runners as I make my way to our backyard rink. I grab a snow shovel and start scraping the thin layer of fluff. The ice surface isn't as wide as I'd like, but it's long enough for a decent game of shinny, and it's perfect for practising my shooting.

I sit on the garden bench and put on my skates. I pick up my stick, step onto the ice, and skate a few circuits. I stretch along the fence, which acts as the boards on the west side and fire a shot on net, striking one of the plastic targets Liam gave me. His present also included stick tape and a sock of hockey pucks. You have to appreciate a guy who knows exactly what a girl needs.

I've worked up a sweat by the time I realize I'm not alone. Mom, wrapped in a quilt, sits on the bench. She wears her robe underneath, but she's donned a toque, boots, and scarf, and her mitts hold a to-go mug.

I take a drink from my water bottle. "Merry Christmas, Mom."

"Merry Christmas to you too," she says.

I dig the pucks out of the net, fill the pail, and skate to the other end of the rink, where I line them up. I take a dozen shots then lean on the boards.

"Whenever you want to open presents, I'll come inside. I know we're on a tight schedule."

"Not that tight," Mom says. "I've got a hashbrown casserole and a ham in the oven, and I don't have to put in the turkey for a few hours." She takes a sip from her mug. "Everything okay?"

"Sure. Everything's cool." I take a deep breath. "I checked my PAWS account this morning. I aced my psych exam and the make-up project. My honours status is intact."

Mom nods and screws up her mouth. I love it when she does that. It makes her look like a kid. "I knew you could do it. What's your next semester look like?"

"Intermediate Calculus II, Intro to Differential Equations, Intro to Indigenous Literature—"

"That's interesting," Mom says.

"—sociology and another stats class."

"You can handle all that plus hockey?" Mom asks.

"Uh huh."

I don't mind the inquisition. Mom feels it's her job to "check in." But how often have I wondered if something's up with *her* and been afraid to ask?

"How are *you?*" I ask.

Her pensive look makes my heart skip a beat.

"Better, now that I'm taking anti-anxiety medication. Did your father tell you?"

"No." I lean my stick against the boards and let the gate bang shut behind me. I sit next to Mom, shaking with relief.

"He probably didn't think it was his job to tell you," she says. "But I'm not ashamed. I don't want it to be a secret. At least not anymore."

"Does Courtney know?"

She shakes her head. "Not yet."

"Are you going to tell her?"

"Soon. She's been dealing with a lot of stuff. Dealing well. I didn't want to burden her." She laughs nervously. "Heck of a Christmas present."

"So, the medication's helping?" I ask.

She nods. "Yes. It took a while for Dr. Bilku to figure out the right type and dosage. But now I have more energy, and I'm sleeping better."

I'm wracking my brain trying to recall anything I've said or done that's made things worse for her. Then I remember her calm reaction to Courtney's latest scrape at school. Why didn't I clue in?

"What made you decide you needed it?"

"I was making decisions that impacted Courtney and you and your dad," she says. "I was thinking about quitting my job. Thinking I needed a glass of wine or two every night to decompress and shut off the voices in my head." I must look alarmed because she adds, "Not those kinds of voices, hon. I was tired of second guessing every decision. Worrying all the time."

Pieces fall into place.

"That time in Edmonton—when you said you had the flu—you didn't, did you?"

"No, I didn't." She clears her throat. "That was a low point for me. I knew you were struggling with the team, and I didn't know how to help you. I couldn't even help *myself*. I'm sorry I let you down."

"You didn't let me down," I assure her. "I should have known. All this stupid stuff Courtney's gone through has only added to your stress, hasn't it?"

"This isn't about you or Courtney," she says. "It's about me. But I'm fine. I wanted you to know, so we can talk about it." She takes a sip. "Now. You and Liam. It's not over, is it?"

"Doesn't appear to be."

She heaves a sigh. "I'm glad. I like him a lot, but whatever happens, you need to make a decision about what's right for *you*." She stands. "I'm going to check on brunch. But a word of warning. Liam called yesterday to ask if he could come over this afternoon. He's not staying for supper or anything, but he wanted to spend part of the day with you, and I told him he could. Is that all right?"

"Sure." I can't believe how happy and nervous this news makes me.

"Good, because he's bringing his goalie equipment."

"Don't be afraid to reef on those straps. I'll let you know if they're too tight," Liam says.

Courtney straddles each of Liam's legs and fastens the pads with one hand. Rufus, spiffy in his green and white Saskatchewan Roughrider sweater, bounds over and licks Liam's face. Laughing, he pushes my dog away.

The winter sun is bright on this warm afternoon. Water drips from the icicles on the eavestroughs. Dad reflooded the rink after my morning skate, and the ice glistens.

Mom waves at me from the deck, and I wave back. I feel better about her morning revelation. When I turn around, Dad leans against the boards. He gives a litle nod, and I nod back. So, he knows that *I* know about Mom. I imagine we'll talk about that eventually. In the meantime, I have a score to settle.

Liam stands and brushes the snow off a damp patch on his chest.

"McArthur, you are going down," I tell him.

"Bring it, hockey girl," he says.

Courtney positions herself along the boards with a whiteout board and marker.

A whistle dangles from Dad's neck. Liam settles in the crease while I hinge at the waist behind the puck, legs spread.

Dad blows the whistle.

I push the puck straight at Liam, shift left, direct it right. Liam drops and robs me with the toe of his left skate.

"One for Liam!" Courtney announces, marking her whiteboard.

Liam pops back on his skates and calls to me, "That the best you can do, McIntyre?"

"Not even close, McArthur!"

Dad tosses me another puck and backs away. When he blows the whistle, I weave towards the net while Liam's shoulders mirror my movements. When I reach him, I ease up, pull the puck back and fire top corner, gloveside. Liam snaps the puck out of the air and plops on his butt.

Mom cheers.

"Liam—two! Jessie—zero!" Courtney shouts.

On my next attempt, I turn my body at the last minute and fire—backhand—between his legs.

Courtney whoops.

"Nasty five-hole, cowboy," I point out.

He rewards me with a gap-toothed grin.

My strategy is to keep firing shots that make him drop, so he'll tire out. But after a dozen, he's ahead, and though he's sweating buckets, he isn't giving up.

"Can I interest anyone in shortbread?" Mom calls.

Liam wipes his damp face with a towel. "Let's take a break."

"Go get us some cookies, Court," I say.

"Want a beer, Liam?" Dad asks.

"No, thanks. I'm leaving soon anyhow."

"But you just got here," I say.

When Dad opens the gate, Rufus bounds onto the ice.

"I don't want to wear out my welcome." Liam scoops up Rufus, who licks his neck.

Dad, Mom, and Courtney go into the house.

"All right. Enough." Liam pushes Rufus's nose away.

An impulse strikes me. "Hey. We're making a big spread for tomorrow for the Team Canada/Russia game. Appetizers. Charcuterie. The whole shebang. Want to join us?"

Liam's dark eyes are serious. "Don't ask me unless you mean it."

"I'd like to hang out. No strings or anything."

He nods. "What time?"

"2:00. The Massey twins are planning a road hockey match with the kids on our block before the Team Canada game—one team is Team Russia and the other Team Canada."

"Are we kids?" Liam asks.

"Apparently. And I hear Team Russia needs a goaltender."

Mav and Beau, the sixteen-year-old twins who live next door, play AAA in other cities, but they're home for the holidays.

"Can I be captain?" the girl in a pink Team Canada jersey asks Beau.

He tapes a C to her chest while Mav divides up the teams.

Liam and I—the goalies—are outfitted with ball gloves and shin pads. Courtney, who's borrowed a striped jersey and some over-sized, sparkle-framed glasses, is the referee.

When she announces that only goals scored by children under ten count, the older ones whine and gripe. But once the game is underway, the bigger kids work their butts off to throw passes to the little ones.

The pavement is icy from last night's gift of freezing rain—perfect road hockey conditions. Our street is busy, but drivers don't seem to mind slowing down to creep around our nets. The action is fast and furious for the first period. No one wants to stop for hot chocolate and marshmallows, but Mrs. Massey insists.

The afternoon ends all too soon. Team Canada wins. Beau and Mav pick the Players of the Game, and Mrs. Massey pins a crocheted medal to each child's chest. The children drag their sticks homeward while Courtney, cheeks flushed, talks to Beau and Mav. The sun drops low in the sky, and the chill cuts through my jersey as Liam and I manhandle the hockey nets through our side gate.

"Good workout, huh?" Liam asks as we reposition the nets on our backyard rink. "Are you cold? Your lips are turning blue."

I curl up my frozen fingers inside my mitts and nod.

He tugs me close. "I can help with that." He bends his head, and I surrender to the kiss. "I've been wanting to do that all day," he says as he wraps me in his arms.

I tuck my head against his neck. If only it could always be like this. Over Liam's shoulder, I lock eyes with Dad in the kitchen window. He waves and lowers the blind.

"When are you heading back to Saskatoon?" Liam asks.

"The 30th. Do you want to drive back with me?" I ask.

"Thanks, but no. I want to work at the vet clinic as many days as I can. I'll catch a ride."

"I was hoping we'd spend New Year's together," I say.

He steps back and smooths my hair away from my face. "I want to make this work, Jessie."

"I do too. But when classes start, I need to focus on school and hockey. I don't have a bye week for the homestretch. Could we press pause until after playoffs and your vet med interview? Whichever comes last?"

Liam smiles. "That's the smartest thing you've ever said."

I cup my mittens around his cheeks. "You are so important that I'm not going to let you get in the way of my hockey or my classes. And if you get into vet med, then—"

"We'll figure it out," he interrupts. "Let's not think too far ahead."

"I'm only looking as far as March," I say. "I need this time, Liam. I really do."

He gives me a funny look. "Something's up with you. Something different. What is it?"

"Nothing you need to know yet," I tell him. "Come on inside. The game's starting."

"Go Canada go," he says.

45

PAM OPENS HER FRONT DOOR. "Hey, Courtney. Oo! What did you bring?"

"Asparagus wrapped in cream cheese and bacon," Courtney says.

"Looks yummy! I'll put them in the oven and then we can go downstairs. Let me take your coat."

Courtney shrugs hers off, revealing her sparkly silver cami and short black skirt.

"That is so cute," Pam coos as she hangs the coat in the entry way closet.

Pam's enthusiasm seems phony, if not forced. Maybe it's nerves. Pam's parents are strict, and for her to host a New Year's Eve party is a big deal. Courtney wishes Christina could come, but she's under house arrest for at least two more weeks.

Pam's mom and dad are seated at the island in the kitchen.

"So, Courtney, what did you bring to drink tonight?" Pam's dad asks. "Some of those hard seltzers that are the rage these days?"

"Just some soft drinks." Courtney holds up her cooler tote.

He looks uncomfortable. "Well, the only place we let Pam drink is in our own home. Under our supervision."

"How're your mom and dad?" Pam's mom asks.

"They're both fine."

Her response is automatic. Things are different now. Courtney's a little frightened that Mom was on anti-anxiety meds for weeks before she told anyone—apart from Dad—and that one side effect could be suicidal thoughts.

"Let's go downstairs," Pam says. "Nearly everyone's here."

In the basement, Pam introduces Courtney to two girls from her homeroom plus their boyfriends. Did she miss the text about bringing a date? Not that she has one to bring.

Toby's behind the wet bar inspecting the hard liquor. He and Courtney exchange awkward smiles. She's not surprised to see him since Pam's been going with him since the school dance.

Courtney tugs down the hem of her skirt and sets her cooler on the counter. "Can you put these in the fridge for me?" she asks Toby as she extracts a can and her metal straw.

He ties a towel around his waist and rolls up his sleeves. "Can I offer you a glass? Slice of lime? Some ice?"

"Check. Check. Check." She pushes the can towards him.

He makes a big show of yoyoing the can and dropping in a pink umbrella. "Your shoulder must be better. You're not wearing a sling."

"Yeah, it's better," she says. "Not good enough for hockey though."

"That was quite the gong show at the dance," Toby says. "Glad I managed to avoid it." He leans closer. "And I'm really sorry for what happened at the rookie party too."

"You already apologized," Courtney says.

"Yeah, but I know you better now. You're a good person, Courtney. I shouldn't have been so stupid."

Wow.

Pam walks behind the bar and puts an arm around Toby's waist. "Will you mix my drink, babe?"

Babe.

While Toby mixes a Vodka special, Pam chatters about who's doing what with whom for New Year's. Courtney wishes Pam would find something else to do so she and Toby can talk about the Moose.

"Hey Toby. The Swiss just scored to go ahead 1-0," the guy on the coach says.

Toby drops his ice tongs in the sink.

"You think the Swiss can knock off the Americans?" the guy on the sectional says.

"The Swiss have got six guys that play in the NCAA," Courtney says.

It's a tidbit she picked up from Beau and Mav. She never paid much attention to the World Juniors until the Massey twins ignited the Team Canada fire.

Pam glares at her. "Hockey is forbidden."

"You can't ban us from talking about it," Courtney says.

Soon, she and the guys are in deep regarding playoff scenarios and MVPs.

"The problem is—every team hates Canada," Courtney says. "We're the team to beat."

"Naw, they hate the US more," Toby says.

"Enough!" Pam claps her hands like she's disciplining small dogs. "We're going to play 'Never Have I Ever.'"

"I vote no," Sectional Guy says.

"Hey, why don't we watch the US-Swiss game?" Courtney suggests. "You guys can have a drink every time one of the analysts says 'grinder.'"

"Please, babe, can we watch it?" Toby asks.

"Babe, you promised," Pam says.

"But the World Juniors only happen once a year," Toby begs.

"All right," she concedes.

Courtney holds up her hand for a high-five, and Toby smacks it.

Midway through the second period, Courtney's phone plinks.

HAPPY NEW YEAR!!! shoulder ok?

She doesn't recognize the number, and the prefix isn't local.

Pam shrieks. The girls are playing Cups on a folding table.

Courtney texts a reply.

Who is this?

She waits. Three little dots blink. Disappear. Reappear.

Reid Bonokoski mom gave me ur # that ok?

The linesman from Notre Dame? The guy whose boneheaded brother separated her shoulder?

Yes.

Call u sometime?

Wow.

The boys erupt as the Swiss score and go ahead 2-1.

Courtney closes her eyes and tries to visualize Reid's face. She recalls a crooked nose and a goofy smile. A funny guy. Maybe a guy with insight on her teammates. Boys might complain about girls being hard to figure out, but guys are no picnic.

She sends a thumbs up.

He replies with a smiley face.

Maybe she *will* have a date in the new year.

4 6

January 3
University of Saskatchewan Huskies vs. University of Manitoba Bisons
Wayne Fleming Arena - Max Bell Centre, Winnipeg
Huskies 2-1 OT loss

January 4
University of Saskatchewan Huskies vs. University of Manitoba Bisons
Wayne Fleming Arena - Max Bell Centre, Winnipeg
Huskies 3-2 loss

A WINTER SQUALL PUMMELS OUR BUS as we retreat westward
on the TransCanada Highway. I rearrange my pillow to stifle the draft sneaking
down my neck. Kathy snores, head snuggled against my shoulder. Across the
aisle from me, Darian huddles under a fleece blanket. This road trip is the
longest one of the year, and tonight it's made worse by our team's pathetic
performance in Winnipeg. I remember what Shauna told me when we played

the Bisons in Saskatoon.

"We'll get you when it counts."

Is the Manitoba curse going to get us in the end?

"One measly point," I say.

"F'ing Winterpeg," Kathy murmurs in her sleep.

Darian leans across the aisle and whispers, "You didn't get much playing time, Jessie. How are you doing?"

I fake a yawn. "I'm okay."

But I'm not. Coach and Dan tweaked our forward lines and being left out of the new strategy hurt.

"You show the coaches how wrong they were when you come to practice this week," Darian says.

"I'll try," I say. "Can we not talk about it?"

She squeezes my forearm. "The highs can't be too high, and the lows can't be too low, Jessie."

As she huddles back under her blanket, I try to remember where I've heard that before. It's good advice. Still, I don't sleep a wink the whole way home.

The prairie sky is pale when our bus rolls up behind MBP. Like the walking dead, we help Dave unpack our equipment and haul it in the rink. When we're done, Coach offers me a lift back to Athabasca Hall. I'm grateful because I don't feel like wheeling my suitcase across the overpass. Coach's vehicle is warm when I climb in the shotgun seat.

"The joys of command start," he says.

My eyelids are heavy.

The next thing I know he's shaking my shoulder. "Wake up, Mac. You're home."

The bulk of my dorm building looms through the windshield. I finger the drool at the corner of my mouth. Did he notice?

"Look, this could've waited till Monday, but I'll tell you now," Coach says.

Oh great.

"I'll be the first to admit Dan and I made some mistakes this weekend," he says. "We had a checking line with great promise, and we shouldn't have changed it. Get some rest and prepare for some hard work next week. Remember to bring your A game."

January 9
Estevan Moose vs. Kipling Royals
Power Dodge Ice Centre (Blue Goose), Estevan

Plink!
coming to Weyburn to watch my sister's game on the 22nd?
I'll try.
want you to meet my sis u already know little bro.
My shldr remembers.
"Who are you texting?" Pam asks.
"My mom," Courtney lies.

Reid Bonokoski has texted her all week. One time they threw memes and emojis back and forth for an hour. But if she tells Pam, Pam will tell Toby, and Toby will tell the team.

The horn blows, announcing another Kipling goal. Josh's stepdad, the goal judge, flips on the red light.

Toby digs the puck out of his net and fires it down the ice.

Pam stands and waves at him. "It's okay, babe!"

"Four-goal deficit," Mrs. Sweater Coat says. "Hard to come back from that. Too bad Brandon was in the penalty box. He barely touched that kid."

Pam and Courtney exchange long looks. Brandon's mom is quite the cheerleader.

"Too many penalties," Michael's mom says. "Ridiculous. Clint doesn't have any control."

"You know what these boys need?" Michael's dad says. "An old-fashioned bag skate. Clint should come unglued. Shake them up."

Pam rolls her eyes at Courtney, and Courtney rolls hers right back.

Like the Carsons would tolerate Clint criticizing *their* son.

"Our boys are the best players out there," Mrs. Sweater Coat says, "but Minor Hockey is out to get them. When something goes wrong, it's always Michael or Brandon's fault. Let's hope they play AAA next year and put this forgettable year of *house* hockey behind them."

Courtney remembers what Dayna told her.

"They're talented, but they're impossible to coach, and they're poison in the dressing room."

What AAA coach will want them after all that's happened?

On the ice, Michael leans against the boards while Clint rattles off a lecture. The rest of the players look frustrated. Courtney knows that if they can't win on the scoreboard, her teammates will collect more penalties and pick fights.

Josh's mom climbs into the stands next to her. "How's your shoulder, Courtney?"

"Getting better," Courtney says.

She feels Dr. Bilku's hand on her arm. "If you take care of your body, it will take care of you."

"Too bad you won't be back till the end of the month," Austin's dad says behind her. "The team needs you."

Mrs. Sweater Coat and the Carsons turn and stare at him. Their looks of disgust are almost comical.

"Thanks for saying that," she says to Austin's dad.

Three sets of eyes swing towards her, but she rivets her gaze to the Moose bench. Michael or not, she can't wait to rejoin her teammates.

4 8

January 10
University of Saskatchewan Huskies vs. University of Alberta Pandas
Merlis Belsher Place, Saskatoon
Huskies 3-2 OT loss

ICE PACKS TAPED TO SHOULDERS and hips. Heads bowed. My teammates look like they've been thrashed.

At least Liam came to watch. He got to the game late, but he stayed long enough to give me a hug and tell me our line played great. And we did. Alberta's top lines never scored on us, and Kathy managed to squeak one by their star goalie.

"F'ing Pandas," Kathy says.

January 11
University of Saskatchewan Huskies vs. University of Alberta Pandas
Merlis Belsher Place, Saskatoon
Huskies 2-1 OT win

Three points for us, and three for the Pandas in the series. A straight up draw.

"You ladies really stepped it up," Coach tells us in the dressing room afterwards. "Way to rebound. Keep working hard, and you'll be rewarded."

My line is +2 on the weekend. That's reward enough for me.

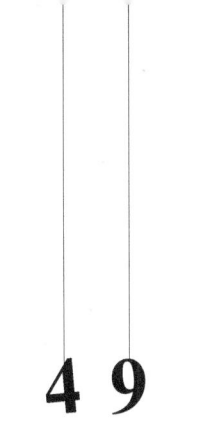

4 9

January 12
Estevan Moose vs. Lampman-Arcola Imperials
Affinity Place, Estevan

"So, who is this Reid?" Christina asks.

"A guy I met before Christmas." Courtney looks back at Mr. Delgado, who stands at the rail, and whispers, "Your dad is still staring at us."

Christina glances over her shoulder. "He watches me like I am a criminal." She angrily digs her fork in her taco-in-a-bag.

"How much longer?" Courtney asks.

"One week. But I still have a 9:30 pm curfew. 9:30!" Christina waves her fork. "*That* is criminal!"

Pam stands up and squeals. "There's Toby!"

Courtney tugs the hem of Pam's coat. "Don't embarrass him. Okay?"

"Courtney, I think your coach wants to talk to you," Christina says.

Clint leans on the glass behind the players box. Courtney makes eye contact with him as she walks down the aisle.

"Want to join us?" he asks. "The guys play better when you're in the box."

"Thanks a lot, but I'd just be in the way. Besides, somebody might bump me when they jump over the boards." Somebody like Michael, she'd like to add. She holds up her clipboard with her good hand. "I'll keep track of shots like you wanted."

"Make sure you come to the dressing room after the game," Clint says. "Even if you're hurt, you're still a Moose."

Brandon steps onto the bench and waves at someone behind Courtney. Courtney turns. Christina checks to make sure her father isn't looking and then beaming, waves at Brandon.

Oh no. Apparently Christina's curfew hasn't cooled the flames of young romance.

The stench of sweaty equipment and a 6-2 loss permeates the hallway. When Courtney turns the corner, Michael, already wearing his street clothes, talks on his phone outside the Moose dressing room. When he notices her, he holds up his forefinger.

"Just a minute," he mouths.

She's supposed to stand here till he's done talking? Oh well. She has to wait for Clint to let her into the dressing room.

"No, babe, I didn't mean that," Michael says. An angry female voice reaches through the phone. "Babe, I gotta go. I'll get there as soon as I can, I promise. Bye." He tucks the phone in his pocket. "Got a sec?"

"Sure."

"I'd like to talk to you about Miss Philippines. Apparently, Brandon has the hots for her."

"Her name's Christina, and I wouldn't put it that way," Courtney says.

Michael crosses his arms and leans against the wall. "Then how would you put it?"

"I think he respects her because she stands up for herself," she says.

"Right. Just like you," Michael says. "Sure would hate for you to come back too soon. Get hurt again. Stuff can happen. Even in practice."

"Is that a threat?" The question is out before she can stop it.

He puts up his palms. "Hey, it's my job as a vet to look out for my teammates. Don't get pissy and sensitive."

"Can I go in the dressing room?" she asks.

Michael opens the door a crack and peers in. "Coast is clear." He steps away from the door.

Courtney yanks on the handle with her good hand. When she rounds the privacy wall, a second wall of flesh greets her. Flesh everywhere. Far too many bits that she shouldn't see at once. Shane, wearing nothing but his jock, stands in the middle of the room and blinks at her. Jutin squeals and dives in the shower. On the bench, Brandon doubles over and howls.

Michael has played her. Again. Cheeks flaming, she backs out of the room.

Michael's shoulders shake. "You should see your face!"

Courtney storms down the hallway. At the bottom of the steps, she meets Clint and the Imperials coach. She veers around them.

"Courtney, what's wrong?" Clint asks.

"Ask Michael!" she shouts over her shoulder.

That prick. That absolute prick.

***

"I can't *unsee* it," Courtney says. "I couldn't sleep last night. My brain kept looping."

"Lighten up," Jessie says. "It's kind of funny. And no harm done."

"It's *not* funny. I didn't dare go to the cafeteria for lunch. When I saw Shane today at school, he ran the other way. I feel like a pervert."

"You're not a pervert."

"I'll never live it down."

"Shake it off. Don't let Michael know he got to you. How's your shoulder?"

Courtney gives it a few rolls to ease the ache. "Don't tell Mom or Dad, but I tried shooting in the garage after school today." She takes a deep breath. "And don't tell them this either. A guy from Notre Dame has been messaging me."

"Notre Dame?" Jessie repeats. "Sis, girls from Estevan do *not* date Hounds. How old is he?"

"I looked him up on the AAA website. He just turned seventeen."

Courtney also knows from the team photos that Reid *does* have a crooked nose and a goofy smile. Also, friendly blue eyes and reddish blonde hair.

"Too old."

"He seems really nice. I commented on one of his TikTok videos, and he commented on one I did of Rufus," Courtney says. "He's a goalie."

"Courtney, no. A *goalie*?"

"But he's funny."

"Funny guys are the worst. Their clever parlay is just a disguise for raging hormones. I've seen them wheel girls at hockey parties. You're too young," Jessie says.

"How old were *you* when you started going with Mark?" Courtney counters.

Jessie clears her throat. "Things with Mark were different. Furthermore, half the Notre Dame guys aren't even from Saskatchewan. That guy will break your heart or worse. And Mom and Dad will freak when they find out."

"I'll tell them when the time's right," Courtney says. "I know what I'm doing."

At least she hopes she does.

5 0

January 17
University of Saskatchewan Huskies vs. University of Lethbridge Pronghorns
Merlis Belsher Place, Saskatoon

WE'RE MIDWAY THROUGH THE THIRD PERIOD, and the Pronghorns are up 2-0. Kathy throws me a pass in the high slot, and I ring a shot off the right post. Darian bangs in the puck to bring us within one goal.

"Way to persist, ladies," Dan tells us when we come off.

Late in the period, we're still down by one goal. When the Pronghorns take a tripping penalty, Dan taps Cami and Erv and then raps my helmet.

I swing around to look at him. He jerks his head at the open gate. I shuffle down the line while my teammates smack my shoulders and back.

"You go, Mac!" Willo says.

But she's the one who should be out there. Not me.

Cami talks to me all the way to the faceoff dot. I nod like I play wing on the power play all the time. I hope I don't humiliate myself.

Cami wins the faceoff back to Flinton, who passes to Mutcher. The four Pronghorns back in as Mutcher looks for an opening. She fires the puck to Erv in the corner, who passes to Cami. Cami shoots, and the goaltender gives me a juicy rebound. I aim top corner.

And score my first ever U Sports goal!

Screaming, my linemates mob me. Faces are blurred as I lead the bench run. We're tied 2-2!

OT is an adrenalin rush each time I hit the ice, but time runs off the clock with no decision.

When we go to the shootout, Jorgy, Johnny, Cami, Gresch, and Flinton fail to score, but the Pronghorns don't get past Karen either. In the next round, Cooker scores twice. So does Lethbridge 11. When Cooker doesn't score on her next try, and 11 does, Coach and Dan look at me.

Oh no.

"You're up, Mac," Coach says.

"It's what you always dreamed of," Kathy says as I shuffle past her.

"You can do it, Jessie," Darian says.

Pulse hammering, I take my place at centre ice, bend at the waist, and wait for the referee's whistle. I pretend I'm in my backyard. That Liam's the netminder. That keeping the hope of a Huskie win doesn't depend on—

Tweet!

I push the puck ahead of me and skate straight at the Lethbridge goaltender. I deke right and then pull the puck to the left. Shoot at the sweet spot above her left shoulder.

She snaps the puck out of the air.

Damn.

Lethbridge wins 3-2.

"I hate pronghorns," Kathy says. "Such stupid animals."

Darian tries to console me on the way to the dressing room. "You did your best. Don't take it too hard."

Dan pats my head when he walks in. "You just played your best game ever, Mac. You rocked the OT." He hands me a puck. "And congrats on your first goal."

I'm still holding that puck when I go up to the concourse. When Dad hugs me, I slip it in his pocket. "For you. For all those times you believed in me."

"I couldn't be prouder," Dad replies.

"Jessie, I know you're disappointed you didn't score in the shootout, but you played so well," Mom says.

Courtney gives me a little hug. "Way to go, Jessie."

How is it possible to feel so sad and so happy at the same time?

January 18
"Play for the Cure" Game
University of Saskatchewan Huskies vs. University of Lethbridge Pronghorns
Merlis Belsher Place, Saskatoon

In recognition of breast cancer victims and survivors, our team dons special jerseys. The Huskie dog on our logo wears a little pink collar. We wear pink socks and laces and wrap our sticks with pink tape.

Early in the first period, Cooker scores from Johnny and Flinton on the power play—the only goal of the game. It's a shutout for Cassidy.

"We should have beaten Lethbridge by more," Dan says in the dressing room. "You girls let them hang around till the end."

"Maybe we did," Darian whispers, throwing an arm around Kathy's shoulders and mine, "but we're in the hunt for a Canada West title. Right, ladies?"

"Oh yes we are," I reply.

51

January 19
Estevan Moose vs. Oxbow Huskies
Power Dodge Ice Centre (Blue Goose), Estevan

COURTNEY'S PHONE RINGS AS SHE ENTERS the swarm of parents and hockey players leaving the rink. "Give me a sec," she says to Christina.

Courtney steps to the side. Reid is trying to FaceTime. Wow! She presses Accept and resists the urge to yank off her Moose toque by one of its stuffed felt antlers. How silly does she look?

Reid's goalie helmet perches on top of his head. "Going on the ice right away," he says. "Told Coach I had to take a leak. What's with the toque?"

Courtney adjusts the brightness of her screen. "It was our manager's idea."

"It makes you look sassy," he says.

Her cheeks burn. "Is sassy good?"

"Always," he says. "Hey, are you playing tonight?"

"Not yet. Just watching my team."

"So. Wednesday. You coming to my sister's AAA game in Weyburn?" he asks.

"I want to, but one of my parents has to get me there. And my dad lives in the 1880s."

"Bonokoski, what are you *doing?!*" a man shouts in the background.

"Is that your coach?" Courtney asks.

"School president," Reid whispers. "Talk to you later."

The call ends.

Jessie warned her about the funny ones, but Reid doesn't seem dangerous. When Courtney enters the rink, she notices Christina and Brandon tucked in the space between the wall and the pop machine.

Whoa.

Now *that* guy is dangerous.

"Hey, Courtney," Brandon says. "After you caught us *showering* the other day, Shane came up with an idea for another fundraiser. How about a team calendar?"

And this is the guy Christina likes?

"Like the firemen do." Austin strikes a Superman pose, pretending to bare his chest.

"Courtney, for the record, this is *not* my idea," Shane says.

"Courtney could decide which of us goes in," Michael says. "Seeing as how she's seen all of us." He starts. "Well, not all of us." He stands and grasps the belt holding up his hockey pants.

Brandon snickers.

"Stop it," Courtney says.

"This isn't funny," Shane says.

"I'll decide what's funny." Michael unfastens the belt, and his pants sag.

"If you go one step further, I'm taking this to SHA," Courtney says.

Michael glares at her. "You planning to hold *that* over our heads for the entire year?"

"That would be *your* head, Carson," Josh says.

Michael swears at Josh, and Josh swears back. A staring contest ensues. Courtney hopes they won't fight.

Michael hikes his pants in place and tightens the belt. He raises his hands and shows Courtney his palms. "All right. All right. I was just kidding. Are we good?"

Hardly. Still, she nods to keep the peace.

"I'm sorry, Courtney," Toby says. "We shouldn't give you a rough time about what happened the other night."

"And nobody wants to do a sleezy calendar," Josh says.

Michael sits. "You guys coming to my place after the game? Win or lose, let's get wasted."

What's with him always trying to round up his teammates and run them off a cliff?

"Who gets wasted on a Sunday?" Toby asks.

"I do," Michael says. "You gotta come. Otherwise, I have to drink with my old man. Go over every play. Sucks to be me sometimes."

"I'll come," Brandon says.

Courtney recalls the two beer in Mr. Carson's hands that day she walked Rufus over to Michael's house. Does Michael drink with his dad all the time?

January 22
SFU I 8AAA Weyburn Gold Wings vs. Notre Dame Hounds
Crescent Point Place, Weyburn

The SUV's headlights gleam on the snowy ditches on either side of Highway 39.

"So, explain to me again why we're going to Weyburn to watch a Gold Wings game?" Mom asks. "Are you thinking you want to play AAA next year?"

"Maybe." Courtney takes a deep breath. "But there's another reason. I've been texting and stuff with Mrs. Bonokoski's son, and he's going to meet me at the rink."

Mom taps a finger on the steering wheel. "You're talking about the boy who hit you? I thought you said his apology was lame?"

"No. The older one. But not that much older. He only just turned seventeen and—"

"Courtney Jean McIntyre."

It's a bad sign when Mom uses middle names like swear words.

"He's in Grade Eleven," Courtney says quickly. "And so was Mark when you let Jessie date him. And Reid plays AAA with the Hounds, so he's super busy, and this probably isn't going anywhere anyway."

Mom stares out the windshield for a long time.

What's she thinking?

"Does your father know about this?" Mom asks at last.

"No, and I'd appreciate it if you didn't tell him. I don't want him to know until

I decide if I like Reid enough to go out with him."

"Like that's your decision," Mom says.

"Mom, haven't I made some pretty good decisions this year? Don't I deserve some trust to make another one?" Courtney crosses both fingers.

Mom sighs. "Well, while you're hanging out with . . . "

"Reid," Courtney says.

". . . I could sit with the Barbers, I suppose. Dayna's playing, right?"

"Yes." Courtney clenches her fists. Yes! "Thanks Mom."

"And promise me that no matter what, you won't get serious," Mom says. "Your sister . . ."

Courtney shuts her ears for the next five minutes. Yes, Jessie was gaga over Mark far too long. She won't make the same mistake with Reid.

Still, she's nervous as a cat when they walk into the arena, and she spots Reid and his mother. Reid comes right over and shakes Mom's hand. "Nice to meet you, Mrs. McIntyre. Thanks for driving Courtney. You remember my mom?"

More greetings.

"Can I get you a hot chocolate or something?" Reid offers.

"Hot chocolate would be nice," Mom says.

"How's your shoulder, Courtney?" Mrs. Bonokoski asks.

As she explains, Courtney looks forward to the time when people will stop asking about it. Then they talk about Reid's younger sister Shannon, who plays wing on the Notre Dame squad. Courtney's almost as excited to watch a girls AAA game as she is to hang out with Reid.

Reid returns with a tray of drinks and hands them out. "Inside or outside?" he asks Courtney.

"Outside," Courtney says.

They sit in the bleachers where a dozen students in red and white toques, scarves, and mitts are already assembled.

"My mom loaded a cheese wagon with fans and drove us here," Reid explains. "She doesn't like to miss Shannon's games."

"What about your dad?"

His expression changes, and Courtney's sorry she asked.

"He passed away last year," he says. "Colon cancer."

She slips her hand around Reid's and squeezes. He clings to it long after the first period starts. Through the Notre Dame chants and songs. Through Shannon outworking Dayna in the corner and feeding a pass to 15. Right up to the moment Shannon stuffs 15's rebound between the Weyburn goaltender's left skate and the post.

Reid throws his arms over his head as Shannon and her linemates wheel past their bench. He wipes his eyes. "I'm glad I got to see that."

She pulls his head down so she can whisper in his ear, "Your dad saw it too."

5 2

January 24
University of Saskatchewan Huskies vs. University of Regina Cougars
Cooperators Centre, Regina
Huskies 4-3 shootout loss

January 25
University of Saskatchewan Huskies vs. University of Regina Cougars
Cooperators Centre, Regina.
Huskies 1-0 win

"ARE WE STOPPING TO GET some grub?" Kathy calls to Coach.

He steps aside to let some of the rookies on the bus. "We'll pick up subs on the way."

"Awesometown," Kathy says.

Kennedy, one of the rookies, drops in the seat across the aisle from me and Kathy. "Only two more weeks of regular season. I can't believe my first year is

232 • *Maureen Ulrich*

nearly over."

"What do you mean—*over*?" Erv reaches between the seats and tugs Kennedy's toque over her eyes. "Ever heard of *playoffs*?"

"Nice that Liam's grandparents came to the game." Darian says behind me.

My fingertips brush the beads around the top of my right mukluk. Kooshie couldn't hide her delight when she saw I was wearing them. I was thrilled to introduce her and Metagoosh to my own parents.

"Didn't know Liam's grandparents were such big hockey fans," Kathy says.

"I think they're *Jessie* fans," Darian says. "Just like the rest of us."

I don't deserve a linemate like her.

"Third line really clicked tonight," Johnny, a second-year, says as she walks by.

"Thanks, Johnny," I reply.

Izzie is next down the aisle. She meets my gaze and walks past. She's polite when we have to interact, and on the ice, she treats me like any other player. But the warmth has vanished. It's worse than her being cold or rude. And all because of her horny brother.

Kathy gives me a nudge. "So much for clicking with the defence."

"You never miss a thing," I say.

"You should tell her how much pressure Scott put on you," she whispers.

I drag my stats text out of my knapsack. "Like I'm going to make it worse."

If only life had one right answer—like math.

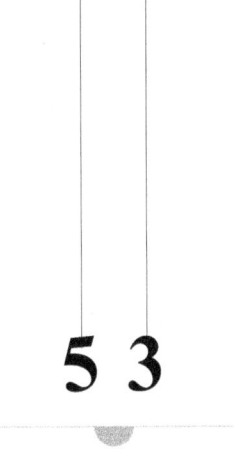

53

January 30
Estevan Moose vs. Estevan Knights
Power Dodge Ice Centre (Blue Goose), Estevan

"You're sure your shoulder's okay?" Clint asks when Courtney walks in the team dressing room.

Courtney raises her elbow and rotates it forward and back. "Good as new."

"Well, keep your shifts short, and stay out of the corners," Clint warns.

"Don't worry, Courtney. We got you," Shane says as they make their way to the ice surface.

Courtney isn't nervous about the Knights. It's the *Moose* she's worried about. Michael hasn't spoken a word to her since she returned to practice last week. Maybe her threat about complaining to SHA has done the trick, or maybe he's awaiting another opportunity to drive a wedge between her and her teammates.

"There's Christina. I can't believe Brandon dumped her," Shane whispers.

Christina and Pam sit together in the stands behind the Moose's net. Courtney knows how hard it is for Christina to be here. On Monday, Brandon

234 • Maureen Ulrich

walked into the cafeteria wrapped around a popular Grade Nine girl.

"Christina is crushed," Courtney whispers back, "and Brandon is a loser."

There's a short delay while the maintenance guy repairs the ice in front of Toby's crease. Courtney looks down the bench at Brandon, who's smirking while Michael tells him a story. When she gets a chance, she'll tell Brandon what she—

"Courtney, what are you thinking about?" Josh says. "I bet it isn't hockey. I can see the gears turning."

Shane winks at her.

"Sorry, guys," Courtney says.

When the repair is finished, Austin's line, with Michael and Brandon as D, line up for the faceoff. The referee snaps the puck, and the game is underway.

At the first stoppage in play, Courtney follows Josh and Shane to the faceoff dot in the Moose's end. Josh loses the draw, and Courtney steps up to cover 12. She pokes the puck free, and Josh picks it up and heads up the ice. 12 hooks her stick and yanks it out of her hands. Her shoulder zings. By the time she retrieves her stick, three Knights descend on her. Caught flatfooted, she misses her chance to check the guy with the puck. He stickhandles around her and snipes a shot under Toby's arm.

Red light.

What a humiliating start to the second half of her season.

Michael meets her halfway to the bench. "Quit worrying about getting hurt." He slaps Josh's helmet. "Tough one, buddy."

He's so predictable.

"Shake it off, Courtney," Clint says to her as she steps off the ice.

She sucks down some water and leans on the boards. "Let's go, Moose!"

She feels a hand on her shoulder.

"Atta girl," Clint says.

Courtney stretches out on her bed and holds up her phone with her good hand.

Reid wears a skater toque. In the background, his mom and brother argue over homework.

"So, how is it?" Reid asks.

It. The shoulder again.

She repositions the bag of frozen peas. "Fine during the game. Kinda sore now. But I'm not missing any more hockey because of it. Did *you* win?"

"5-4."

"Nice."

He lifts the edge of his toque and smooths his reddish blonde hair. "Something's bothering you. What's up?"

Should she tell him about Michael? It's early in their relationship. Or is that what this is?

"I know your team had some trouble at a rookie party last fall," he says. "The school president used it as a 'teaching moment' at one of our morning assemblies."

"Wow. Bad news really does travel." Courtney takes a deep breath and lets it out. "Do you know the book *The Wizard of Oz?*"

Reid raises his eyebrows. "I saw the movie once at my babysitter's. Like when I four years old. Those flying monkeys scared the—" He rubs his crooked nose. "Never mind."

"Well, then you know there's good witches and bad witches in the story. I like to think of myself as Glinda the Good Witch. But if there was a Wicked Witch of the West on our hockey team, it would be Michael."

Reid looks like he's thinking hard about something.

Probably about what a baby she is. She shouldn't have said anything. Here she is complaining about Michael and—

"I like hanging out with you," Reid says. "Same time tomorrow?"

"Sounds good," Courtney says.

5 4

January 31
University of Saskatchewan Huskies vs. University of Calgary Dinos
Father David Bauer Arena, Calgary
Huskies 5-1 win

February 1
University of Saskatchewan Huskies vs. University of Calgary Dinos
Father David Bauer Arena, Calgary
Huskies 3-2 win

"So—DEPENDING ON WHAT HAPPENS with the Pandas, you could clinch first or second next weekend against the Thunderbirds," Kathy's mom says to us in the lobby.

"Yep. It's all on the line," Kathy says. "Sure love to get a bye for the first round and host a semifinal."

"Well, I know someone who's had fun this weekend." Mrs. Parker waves at

Dan's two-year-old daughter.

Calla, brown curls bouncing, waves back, and Mrs. Parker goes over to talk to her. The healthy scratches have fallen over each other to babysit Calla during our games. She's cute, but I'm glad I've got a regular shift on the third line.

Behind Calla and Mrs. Parker, I notice Scott talking to a pair of my teammates. He tried wheeling one of our vets after last night's game.

"He's gonna crash and burn," Kathy says.

"No doubt about that," I reply.

The players he's talking to already have significant others. Their girlfriends.

"Maybe Scott doesn't care about the Huskies as much as he cares about cruising his sister's teammates," Kathy says. "And for once, you managed to avoid a debacle. Proud of you, Mac."

"Thanks."

"Now let's go see if Calla's got any stories about her daddy. Never hurts to have a little ammunition in the dressing room."

Laughing, I follow her. But I'm not worried about ammunition. Dan loves the way our line is playing, and with any luck, we'll peak at the right time.

Playoffs.

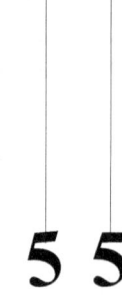

55

February 6
Estevan Moose vs. Weyburn Co-op Wings
Power Dodge Ice Centre (Blue Goose), Estevan
Moose 7-1 loss

"YOU KNOW WHAT YOUR PROBLEM IS, Courtney McIntyre? You don't have heart," Michael says.

"I may not have as hard a shot as the rest of you, and I may not be able to stickhandle as well, but don't ever say I don't have heart." The words pour out of Courtney. "You of all people have no right to say that. *You're* the one without one."

The loss hurts, but not near as much as Michael's comments when Clint isn't around.

Her teammates say nothing. Do they agree with Michael or are they too bummed out about the game to care? This losing skid is depressing.

Michael places a hand on his chest, as if mortally wounded. "Ouch," he says sarcastically.

Is he hoping she'll storm out of the dressing room and skip the postgame meeting? Make Clint angry?

"You've had it in for me ever since my first practice," Courtney says.

"Enough of your whining," Michael says.

"I'm not whining, and I'm sick of you running me down because it makes you feel better about yourself," she says.

"Isn't that the truth," Josh says. "You tell him, Courtney."

His words give her courage. "I'm just trying to do my best. I'm not quitting, Michael."

"Who cares?" Michael says. "I'm sick of you too, Courtney McIntyre. You cost us games, and then you expect us all to feel sorry for you."

"You know we didn't lose because of her," Josh says. "I played like crap today." He turns to Brandon. "How many goals were you on the ice for?"

Brandon shrugs. "A few."

"Okay. Okay." Michael waves his hands. "Sorry I freaked. I'm just an intense guy who wants to break this losing streak. Am I wrong for trying to motivate my teammates?"

Courtney hopes someone will say, "Bullshit," but no one does.

"Let's put this behind us and focus on beating Moose Jaw tomorrow. It's our last chance to earn a playoff berth," Michael says.

Courtney sips her water bottle. She isn't fooled, but at least he's not targeting her.

"So, Courtney," Jutin says. "Shane said you're going out with some Notre Dame dude."

She sputters and coughs.

Josh scowls. "How long has that been going on?"

"I wouldn't say we're going out," she says.

"Shane, didn't you say she was holding hands with him at a Gold Wings game?" Jutin asks.

Shane blushes.

"And you say *girls* like to gossip." Courtney screws the lid back on her bottle. "Don't you have anyone else to talk about?"

Austin shakes his head. "So, it *is* true. I can't believe you're going out with a *Hound*."

"Who is it?" Josh asks.

"It's none of your business who I go out with," she argues.

"Shouldn't that be *whom*?" Jutin says.

Toby belches. "Pam would've told me if she knew. Why's it such a big secret, Courtney?"

Michael watches her, arms folded. She doesn't want to say anything about Reid in front of him.

"It's not a secret. And I'm not going out with him—at least not yet," she admits. "It's too early to tell."

"Then why were you holding hands?" Brandon asks.

She explains about Reid's dad, and the boys nod. Drop their gazes. Even Michael looks away.

"Yeah, that's brutal," Jutin says. "Sorry for bugging you, Courtney."

"You don't have to apologize," she replies. "But don't make a big deal out of it."

"No problem," Michael says. "Now tell us about the Huskies and UBC."

Every head swings in his direction.

What?

"Yeah. Tell him what the head coach said about your sister's line," Shane urges. "I heard your mom telling my mom about it."

Courtney shakes her head.

"Come on," Josh says. "Aren't you proud of your sister? If you aren't, why not?"

Maybe there're a few things she can learn from these fellas—besides how to shoot and stickhandle better.

"Yeah, I guess I am," Courtney says. "He says the Huskies have the best third line in Canada West, maybe the whole country."

"Nice," Brandon says.

Clint walks back in, and Michael acts like a model of sportsmanship. Like he's changed his mind about how to treat his teammates. Like she should be able to relax and let down her guard around him.

Not a chance.

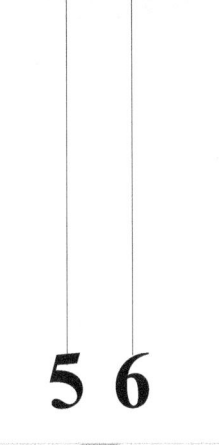

5 6

February 7
Canada West Conference Game 27
University of Saskatchewan Huskies vs. University of British Columbia Thunderbirds
Merlis Belsher Place, Saskatoon
Huskies 2-1 OT win

February 8
Canada West Conference Game 28
University of Saskatchewan Huskies vs. University of British Columbia Thunderbirds
Merlis Belsher Place, Saskatoon

AS WE LEAVE THE ICE after the second period, the Thunderbirds have a 3-2 lead, and I can't shake the feeling that my left skate is sloppy. As soon as I get to my stall, I start unknotting my lace.

My teammates are quiet. The atmosphere is tense.

"So, what do we have to do to get first place?" Kathy asks at last.

"We can't get first," Darian says. "U of A is beating Regina 3-0. The Pandas will finish Number One." She holds up her phone. "Best we can do is second place."

"Put the phone away, Darian," Dan says. "Not much point in talking about second place if we don't win *this* game."

Coach runs through the plan for the third period. Robbie gives some insight on defence, and Dan rags on us forwards. I now feel like my skate's too tight and cutting off my circulation.

"It's time," Coach says. "Do us proud, ladies."

I yank on my lace, and it snaps. I dig for the spare in my stall while the rest of the team files out.

"So, we were three points behind UBC heading into the weekend," Robbie says. "Even if we win, we're tied in overall points with 42."

I sneak a look. Our three coaches are gathered in the centre of the room. I've never seen them look this serious.

"The second tie-breaker is head-to-head," Dan says. "We'd be tied there as well."

"Where does goals-for-and-against fit in?" Coach asks. "We might need three more goals, not just two."

My head reels. Maybe there's a reason they don't talk about this in front of my teammates.

Robbie scrolls on her phone. "According to the Canada West website, the third tie-breaker is how we did against a team that placed higher. That'd be Alberta. We got five points against them while UBC got four."

Crap. This is complicated.

"Sock that information away because we might need it later," Coach says.

"UBC's going to argue they had more wins in regulation, so *they* should get second." Dan clears his throat. "Jessie, why are you still here? Aren't you ready to go yet?"

"Just about." I tie the knot and reach for my helmet.

"I'll get hold of Basil and ask him to check with Canada West," Robbie says as I leave the dressing room.

Twenty more minutes. The suspense is killing me. Where will we finish this season?

Midway through the third period, Cami toe drags past the D and scores to tie us up. When UBC 16 takes a bodychecking penalty a minute later, Dan sends Erv, Willo, and Cami on the power play. Erv scores with seconds remaining in the UBC penalty.

We're up 4-3. I recall the coaches' discussion in the dressing room. Do we need another goal to clinch second place? While Kathy's on PK, I tell Darian about what I overheard.

"Seriously?" she says. "It's *that* close?"

We slog it out as time ticks off the clock. UBC 10 takes a tripping penalty, but we don't capitalize on the power play. We push hard, playing on the edge. With seven seconds left, Gresch heads to the sin bin on an interference call. We're short-handed, and Coach calls a time out.

"What's he worried about? We're seconds from a bye and a home playoff berth," Kathy says.

Do I tell her a win might not be enough?

Coach speaks earnestly to Cassidy while she drains her water bottle. Is he going to pull her so five attackers can go for *another* goal? Dan paces and looks frustrated. Robbie stares into the stands.

"Are we killing time or something?" Kathy asks.

"Probably," Darian says, giving me a sideways look.

Basil jogs down the aisle and leans on top of the glass. "You're good!" he puffs. "You don't need another goal!"

"Basil to the rescue!" I hold up a glove for a high-five.

Kathy taps my glove, but she looks confused. "I don't get it."

"Go grind down that clock, ladies," Dan says.

Kathy, Darian, and I hop over the boards and hustle to the faceoff dot.

When the buzzer sounds to end the game, we squeal, hug, and pile on Cassidy. As we shake hands with the despondent Thunderbirds, their coach and the referee are locked in a serious debate.

In spite of what Basil said, maybe we don't have second place.

57

WHEN IT COMES TO THE Huskies, Jessie is *so* dramatic.

"UBC insisted more wins in regulation give *them* second place. Our coaches hung around for two hours after the game waiting for another ruling," Jessie says.

Courtney yawns and puts Jessie on Speaker. "And what did *you* do?" She props up her phone with her pillow and runs a brush through her hair.

"I searched the Canada West website to try and figure out if we had a chance. I fell asleep with my laptop open. I woke up when Coach texted to say we got second for sure."

Courtney gathers her hair into a ponytail and secures it with a band. "Well, would it have been the end of the world if you got third?"

"Listen," Jessie says. "That would mean another round of playoffs. And maybe running into Alberta or Manitoba."

Courtney sighs. "So, who do you play in the first round?"

"No one, Courtney." Jessie sounds annoyed. "We get a bye, remember? We'll host the winner of the UBC and Calgary series."

Time to change the subject.

"We'll probably have to play Weyburn for *our* playoffs," Courtney says.

"But you made it. That's the important thing." Jessie seems more relaxed. "How are things with Michael?"

"Better," Courtney says. "At least he doesn't rag on me all the time. And he passes to me now."

"That's good. Maybe he's learned his lesson," Jessie says.

Is Jessie serious? This playoff thing has affected her brain.

"So, do you see much of that Notre Dame guy?" Jessie asks. "Have you told Dad yet?"

"No and no," Courtney replies. She wonders if FaceTime qualifies as "seeing."

"How's Mom doing?"

"She's really good," Courtney says. "I think the medication helps. Are you coming home this weekend?"

"I'm going to stay here and get caught up on classes," Jessie says. "I've got two midterms next week. Looking forward to February break. What have you got planned?"

"Not much," Courtney says. "There's no hockey. Half my team will be in Mexico. Hey, do you ever see Liam?"

"He phones a few times a week. That's the best we can do right now." Jessie sounds sad. "Gotta go, sis."

Courtney stares at her bedroom ceiling. With any luck, she'll be able to see Reid over the break. Even once would be an accomplishment. And keeping Dad in the dark a few weeks longer would be an even bigger one.

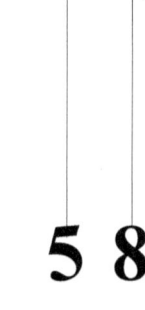

5 8

February 21
Canada West Semi-Final (Game 1/Best of Three)
University of Saskatchewan vs. University of British Columbia Thunderbirds
Merlis Belsher Place, Saskatoon
Huskies 2-0 win

February 22
Canada West Semi-Final (Game 2/Best of Three)
University of Saskatchewan vs. University of British Columbia Thunderbirds
Merlis Belsher Place, Saskatoon
Huskies 4-2 loss

I REWIND THE VIDEO ON Dave's phone. Erv cuts hard around the UBC net and hooks the goalie's skate. The goalie spills and flails her limbs like a beetle on its back.

"UBC claims Erv slew footed her," Dave says. "They want Erv suspended.

Canada West officials are reviewing it."

"But the ref never gave Erv a penalty," I point out. "Besides, UBC won the game. A suspension won't change the outcome."

"No, but it'll keep Erv off our top line tonight." Dave picks up a skate and fires up his sharpener.

As I head for the weight room, I can't get that video clip out of my mind. What if Erv can't play?

Sunday, February 23
Canada West Semi-Final (Game 3/Best of Three)
University of Saskatchewan vs. University of British Columbia Thunderbirds
Merlis Belsher Place, Saskatoon

Erv doesn't join us for the pre-game warm-up. When we return to the dressing room, she sits, head bowed like a condemned prisoner.

I feel so bad for her. "No word yet?" I whisper.

Erv shakes her head.

"I have a good feeling about this," Cami says.

"Better than the feeling I have," Erv replies. "I'm gonna throw up."

Coach's phone vibrates, and he digs it out of his pocket. "It's Basil. Let's hope he's got good news."

Will Erv get a pardon?

Coach answers, listens, and gives Erv a thumbs up. She heaves a huge sigh and slumps against the wall. We look at one another and grin.

"F'ing right!" Kathy shouts, then covers her mouth when Coach glowers at her.

He ends the call with a flourish and fist pumps while we cheer.

"We are so going to pluck those Thunderbirds," Kathy says.

We win 3-2 in regulation.

"I knew the black jerseys were lucky!" I scream in Darian's ear as we celebrate.

"In other news, the Cougars upset Alberta," Coach tells us in the dressing room after our excitement has calmed to periodic explosions. "We're not just playing in a Canada West final. We're *hosting* it."

"F'ing A," Kathy says. "U of A that is. Have I mentioned lately how much I love them Cougars?"

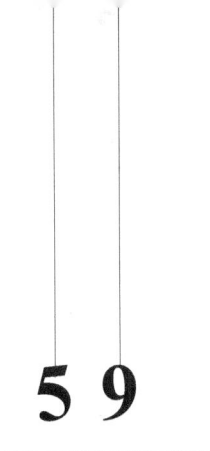

59

February 25
Moose Mountain U15 League Quarter Final (Game 1/Best of Three)
Estevan Moose vs. Weyburn Co-op Wings
Tom Zandee Sports Arena, Weyburn
Moose 5-4 win

"JUST BECAUSE WE WON TONIGHT, doesn't mean we've got this wrapped up," Clint says to the Moose in the dressing room. "There are two more games to play. Skate them into the ice like you did tonight, and we've got a chance to move on to the next round. Understand?"

Courtney's teammates murmur in agreement.

"You all played like a team for a change," Clint says. "It was nice to see."

Tonight, Michael fed Courtney a pass on the power play, sending her on a breakaway—though she fanned on the shot. If only she'd scored.

"Hey, McIntyre, how's that shoulder?" Clint asks.

She ungrits her teeth. "Fine."

"Liar. I'll tell Abby to get you some ice," Clint says.

"When's Game Two?" Austin asks.

"Saturday night at the Blue Goose. Game Three on Monday in Weyburn. That work for everyone?" Clint asks.

More murmurs of agreement.

"Aren't the Canada West finals this weekend?" Shane whispers to Courtney. "Don't you want to watch?"

"I'm not watching my *sister's* playoffs and missing my own," she whispers back. "But don't worry. My mom and dad will fight over who gets to go, and who has to stay behind."

"That's harsh," Shane says. "You should give them a little credit."

"Whatever," Courtney mutters as she leaves the dressing room to go change in her own.

"Hey, Courtney, wait up."

She turns to face Brandon. Now what?

"I want to talk to you about Christina," Brandon says. "I know she's mad at me."

"Mad? What would you expect? You *hurt* her, Brandon. She absolutely did not deserve that."

"I know, and I'm sorry." He wipes his nose with the back of his hand. "I still like her."

He seems upset. She's never seen him like this.

"Then why did you dump her?" she asks.

"Michael gave me such a bad time. You wouldn't believe the stuff he said. I thought he would make her life miserable. Will you talk to her?" Brandon pleads. "Tell her I'll make it up to her as soon as hockey season's over. She won't respond to my texts or snapchats."

"Well, I'm not going to set her up for you to break her heart again." Courtney leans against the wall and folds her arms over her chest. "If you want her to know something, you have to tell her *yourself*. You might even try talking to her at *school*."

Brandon looks doubtful.

"But you're not going to do that, are you?" Courtney says. "You already made that mistake once—at the dance. Why are you so afraid of that guy?"

Brandon stares at her for a moment before ducking back inside the team dressing room.

Yeah, she knows why.

February 26
Notre Dame AAA Hounds vs. Estevan AAA Bears
Affinity Place, Estevan
Hounds 6-3 win

Water drips from Reid's hair as he sucks on a bottle of Gatorade. "I normally lose five pounds a game." He smiles at Courtney. "You were my good luck charm today, Crash."

"Crash?" Christina pounces on the word.

"I hear your friend's accident prone," Reid says.

"Yes, she is." Christina laughs and winks at Courtney. "I am going to the washroom now."

It's all part of the plan. This is the first time Courtney's been able to see Reid in person since the AAA game in Weyburn. They won't have much time together—since Reid will have to get on the bus soon.

Once Christina is gone, the conversation with Reid is awkward. They start sentences at the same time. You go. No, you go. Why is it easier to FaceTime than talk with the *real* person?

Reid loosens the knot of his red tie. "This isn't what I meant when I said I'd like to see you again."

"I've got nothing else for you," she says. "We're both tied up with hockey."

"We'll figure something out," he says.

A hand grips Courtney's shoulder.

"Who's your friend?" Josh asks.

It's a possessive grip—a "she belongs to us" grip. So much for "alone time." While she makes the introductions, Michael and Brandon show up too. Terrific.

"Nice game, man." Michael holds out his hand. "Michael Carson."

Reid's eyes flicker, but he shakes Michael's hand.

Michael winces.

Is Reid applying pressure?

"You've got a bit of a rep, *man*," Reid says.

Michael laughs. "Rep is all a man can hope for."

Reid and Michael talk about some mutual friends, but it goes over Courtney's head. Are the two of them talking for the sole purpose of gathering information about one another? Meanwhile, she's missing out on time with Reid. How long before he has to leave? So frustrating.

Christina emerges from the washroom and leans against the wall, studying her phone. Brandon walks towards her.

What's he going to do?

"Hey Brandon, where are you going?" Michael calls. "Time to blow."

Brandon freezes and unfreezes. His shoulders slump. He slinks back to Michael like a dog who knows his master's voice. The two of them leave while Christina, oblivious, scrolls on her phone. Is it better she doesn't know Brandon still likes her?

"So, are you coming or not, Courtney?" Josh asks.

Josh and Reid are staring at her. What did she miss?

"Coming where?" she asks.

"Ice fishing at Mainprize on Sunday afternoon," Josh says. "Shane's going. And Reid is too."

Reid smiles his goofy smile.

"You're gonna love my stepdad's shack," Josh continues. "Great place to hang out on a winter afternoon."

And just like that, she's got another date—with her linemates as fifth wheels.

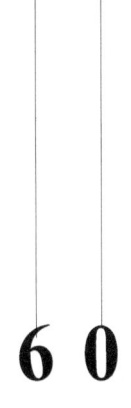

6 0

February 28
Canada West Final
University of Saskatchewan vs. University of Regina Cougars (Game 1/Best of Three)
Merlis Belsher Place, Saskatoon
Huskies 1-0 OT2 Win

March 1
Canada West Final (Game 2/Best of Three)
University of Saskatchewan vs. University of Regina Cougars
Merlis Belsher Place, Saskatoon
Huskies 2-1 OT4 Loss

I DRAG MY BUTT OUT of the rink after midnight. I can't believe we just played *seven* periods—and *lost*. Even though Diane, our team manager, had chicken and pasta delivered to our dressing room after the second OT, I'm weak as a newborn kitten.

Izzie pulls up in her Jeep and rolls down the passenger window. "Hop in,

Jessie. I'll give you a ride."

It's more of an order than an offer, and I'm too exhausted to stumble back to my dorm. I climb in.

Izzie dissects our game on the way to Athabasca Hall. The scoring opportunities missed. The Cougar mistakes on which we failed to capitalize. She's become quite the defensive analyst. She pulls over to the curb, parks, and shuts off the engine.

"I want to talk to you about something," she says.

Oh no. I don't have the energy to have it out with her about Scott.

"You made a big transition moving to the third line," Izzie says. "I wanted you to know that the defence appreciates your sacrifice."

When did Izzie start sounding so grown-up? Of course, we've hardly spoken in months.

"Sacrifice," I repeat. "Did they also notice I was drowning and grabbed the first life preserver Dan tossed my way?"

"Whatever. Anyway. About Scott." Izzie pauses to clear her throat. "I'm a typical little sister. Always taking her brother's side."

"We all get a little weird when it comes to our families," I offer.

"I did the same thing when Scott got divorced. It's a bad habit, and I'm sorry," Izzie says.

"It's okay," I tell her.

I wonder if the veterans on defence have informed her that since I told him to take a hike, Scott's tried to pick up just about everyone on our team.

Izzie looks relieved. "Now, more importantly. Sleep fast tonight. Just sixty minutes between us and Nationals."

I open the passenger door. "Let's hope it's only sixty."

61

"You'll have her back in Estevan by 5:00? She wants to watch her sister's game. Puck drop is 7:00 pm," Dad says.

"I plan to watch the game too, sir," Reid says. "Courtney and I will watch it together and then I'll drive back to Wilcox."

"I'm standing right here," Courtney says.

Right here at the Midale Quik Stop between her dad's SUV and Reid's truck. She and Reid should be at Josh's cabin already.

Dad's gaze targets Courtney. "And you're spending the night at Pam's?"

"Yes!"

Is Dad worried she and Reid will be up to something besides streaming the Canada West feed of Jessie's game?

He swings back to Reid. "The whole point of Courtney staying behind is for her to get a proper night's sleep for her game on Monday night."

"You can trust me," Reid says.

Dad hugs Courtney hard before he leaves. "You grew up too fast."

Reid's truck is a dark green, two-door Mazda with bucket seats in the front, jump seats in the back, and a manual transmission.

"It was my dad's," Reid explains, pressing the clutch and shifting.

His barrage of details about the engine and wheelbase zooms over her head. But the light grey interior and carpeted floor are immaculate, which tells her this guy takes care of his stuff.

"It's old school. Kinda like me," Reid concludes.

Courtney watches him shift. She's never seen anyone drive a stick before.

"What's that other knob?" she asks.

"That's the four-wheel drive." He presses the clutch and shifts again. "Can I let you in on a secret? I've never been ice fishing, and I've no idea what to expect."

"That makes two of us. I've never even been *regular* fishing," she says.

"But this means I can spend more of the day with you." Reid shifts down as they near a yield sign. "Won't be doing much of that for the next few weeks. Not with playoffs, officiating, and exams." He sighs. "Here I am blabbing. And you've got a big game tomorrow night. Are you nervous?"

"A little," she says. "Clint says if we play like we did in Game One, we can knock off Weyburn. But if we play like we did in Game Two, we're toast."

"And if you advance, who would you play next?"

"Redvers, I think."

She's excited about that possibility of another matchup with Jade and her teammates. Plus, she wants to keep playing as long as she can. Things have been pretty good lately, and she doesn't want hockey to end.

"That was some game of your sister's last night. Four overtime periods? Man, that's incredible. Did you watch it?"

Courtney nods. "Yeah. After I got home from losing to Weyburn. I fell asleep a few times, but every time I woke up, the Huskies were still playing." She looks sideways at Reid. Will he understand what she's about to say? "I've been a little touchy about Jessie and university hockey. Everyone talks about her. Asks about her. And I hated it. But last night, I finally understood what the hype was about. And I was a little in awe of her."

When Reid reaches over and puts his warm hand over hers, her pulse begins to race.

To cover up her emotions, she studies the heavy, grey sky to the west, and her thoughts move in a new direction. "Do you think it's going to storm?"

"Hope not, but I'll make sure we leave well before dark." Reid removes his hand so he can shift down. He slows and turns off the highway at the Mainprize

Park exit.

Courtney checks the GPS on her phone. Josh sent them a pin for his stepdad's cabin. "Keep driving around the inlet."

The cabin turns out to be a huge A-frame house with a wraparound deck. Josh and Shane lean on the rail and watch as Reid pulls onto the driveway in front of the double garage.

"More like a mansion," Courtney says.

One of the French doors opens, and Michael steps onto the deck.

Crap.

"I didn't know he was coming," she says. "Did you?"

Reid shakes his head.

Michael and Shane load a cooler in the back of the truck. Courtney gets out so the three boys can pile in behind her. Shane crouches on the floor between Josh and Michael.

After manly greetings are exchanged, Josh thumps the roof with his fist. "Let's go, Bonokoski. The fish are waiting."

"Cold beer too," Michael says.

A tab snaps, and the beer fizzes.

Reid glares at Michael in his rearview mirror. "Hey, throw that out. I'm not paying a fine because of you."

"I'll drink fast," Michael says.

"Toss it. Now," Reid says.

"Okay. Okay." Michael rolls down his window and flings the beer can on the lawn.

Their journey begins in silence.

Courtney should never have agreed to come along. Her gaze flicks to the clock on the dash. Puck drop is six hours away. They can leave in four.

She can't wait.

The sky is dark grey—the same colour as the ice. A village of fishing shacks populate the lake. Many shacks have a half-ton parked nearby.

"Welcome to Dead Lake," Josh says.

"There must be forty shacks out here," Courtney says.

"Probably closer to sixty," Josh replies. "You should be here at the beginning of the season when everybody's trying to get their rig out. I saw a fistfight once."

Reid eases the truck onto the ice. "Where am I headed?"

Josh points south. "That way. In the meantime, roll down your windows and unbuckle your seatbelts."

"How come?" Courtney asks.

"Electronics don't work well in water," Josh says. "You need an escape hatch if we break through the ice."

Nervous, she reaches for the switch, and cold air bites her skin. "How thick *is* the ice?"

"Quit worrying," Michael says.

"We're good, but anytime you're on water, you gotta be careful," Josh says.

Michael pulls a silver flask out of his pocket, takes a sip, and passes it to Shane. Shane takes a pull and wheezes before handing it to Josh.

Reid looks angry.

Josh offers the flask to Courtney, but she shakes her head.

Michael clucks like a chicken.

Whatever.

Michael takes the flask back and leans between the seats. "Fuel for the driver?"

Reid doesn't say anything, and his jaw is tense. Definitely angry.

The flask makes a few more rounds while Josh gives Reid directions to his fishing shack.

"This is it," he says at last.

Reid circles the small log shack and parks facing the shoreline.

"Is there room inside that place for all of us?" Courtney asks.

"It'll be a tight squeeze." Josh unlocks the door. "Grab the cooler, Shane."

The chairs in each corner are draped with fake furs and blankets. Tackle boxes and fishing gear are stacked against the walls. There's a small fridge, propane stove, and mounted deer antlers.

"No television?" Michael asks.

Josh makes a disgusted sound. "My stepdad and I come out here to get away from it all. No radio or sound system either. But there's a generator I can fire up. Make yourselves at home."

Courtney sits on one of the chairs and shivers.

Michael uses a drill to open one of the ice holes. He hands the drill to Shane, who does the same. Meanwhile Michael sets up a wire rig on the edge of the hole he drilled.

"What's that?" Courtney asks.

"A jigger. Works better than a rod. It uses a battery, see?" Michael says.

"It's not legal," Josh says.

Michael frowns. "So?"

Shane holds the drill out to Courtney.

"Um. No thanks." She watches while Reid drills out his hole. "What exactly are we trying to catch?"

"Perch if we're lucky," Josh says. "But we'll probably end up with walleye or jack." He pulls a cast iron frying pan from the cupboard.

"Are we eating here too?" she asks.

Michael laughs. "Haven't you heard of a fish fry?"

She leans forward. Water laps at the edge of the hole.

"Crack me a beer, Shane," Josh says.

Shane opens the cooler and tosses him a can. Reid shakes his head, and Courtney declines. Michael refills his flask from a spiced rum bottle in the cabinet.

"How about some hot chocolate instead?" Josh asks.

"Sounds good," Reid says.

"I don't need anything," Courtney says. Although a hot drink would warm her, she's not sure what will happen if she has to go to the bathroom, and she doesn't want to ask.

"I'll have some too," Michael says. "Let me make it."

Josh is the first one to pull a fish through the hole. It's the length of Courtney's forearm and yellowy green. "Too small." He unhooks it and eases it back into the water.

"Looked big enough to me," Courtney says.

"Want to give it a try?" Reid asks. "Maybe you'll have more luck." He hands her the rod, and she leans closer to the hole.

"The water's so clear," she marvels. "Will I see the fish take the bait?"

Michael laughs. "Why don't you stick your face in?"

She resists the impulse to snap back. The conversation drifts from fishing to local hockey to the Huskies to the NHL and back to fishing. Reid sips his hot chocolate and listens without comment.

Courtney's line jerks, and she nearly drops the rod.

Reid comes to life. "Reel him in!"

The fish she draws through the hole is the biggest one she's ever seen and the closest she's ever been to a live one—apart from Pam's goldfish.

"That's a big assed walleye." Josh stretches the writhing fish on top of a

260 • Maureen Ulrich

measuring stick. "Twenty-one inches! You got us a fish to fry!"

"But I want to let him go," Courtney says. "He's too pretty to eat."

Josh shakes his head and laughs.

"Dumb blondes," Michael mutters.

"Shane, can you take the hook out of his mouth?" Courtney asks.

Shane uses a pair of pliers to free the walleye before he tosses the fish back into the hole.

Courtney watches her prize wriggle away. "I like fishing."

"You want to try again?" Shane asks.

"I'll quit while I'm ahead." Courtney notices that Reid is hunched over, eyes winced. "Are you okay?"

"Is there a chemical toilet in here?" Reid asks.

"Just pee in the hole," Michael says.

"You fish and pee in the same hole? Gross," Shane says.

Reid slowly stands. "My guts aren't so good."

"Then pull up the five-gallon pail with the toilet seat," Josh says. "Don't be shy."

Michael snickers. "Got a gas mask in here?"

Reid makes his way to the pail. His discomfort is obvious. Courtney turns her head as he unzips his jeans. Poor guy. He must be mortified. She would be.

After his second bout passes, Reid takes the pail outside. He alternates between curling up in the back of his truck and crawling out to crouch over the pail.

"We should leave," Courtney says. "You're really sick."

"It's just stomach flu. Or food poisoning," Reid says. "It'll pass. The last thing I need is to get behind the wheel."

"Try to keep hydrated." She hands him a new water bottle. "I'll check on you in half an hour."

"This is the shits. Literally." He sighs. "You better go. I have to use the pail again."

She closes the passenger door. The wind stings her cheeks and sweeps swirls of snow across the reservoir. She checks the time. At this rate, they'll never get back to Estevan before dark. She unlatches the door of the fishing shack, but Shane's angry voice stops her from opening it.

"Michael, you're an idiot!"

"Relax. It's a joke."

"To you maybe. Everything's funny to you. That was a crappy thing to do."

"Crappy is right!" Michael laughs. "It's a miracle he hasn't crapped his pants."

Of course, *he's* responsible. But how did he manage it? Besides water, the only thing Reid's had to drink all afternoon was—

She jerks the door open. Shane gives her a guilty look, though she can't imagine why. He had nothing to do with it. Josh is half passed out in his chair. He must have drunk six beer already.

"How's Bonokoski doing?" Michael asks.

"What did you put in his hot chocolate?" she demands.

Josh starts and drops his pole.

"Hey now," Michael says.

Courtney flings open the cabinet doors and scans the shelves full of dishes, spices, and to-go mugs.

"Is this what you're looking for?"

She turns as Michael lobs a pill bottle at her. She catches it and reads the label. It's a fast-acting laxative.

"You're supposed to add it to a hot drink," Michael says. "Didn't I follow the directions?"

She hurls the bottle at him. Misses. It ricochets off the wall and rolls into the corner.

"Easy," Michael says.

"How could you do that? He's never done anything to you!"

"Courtney, I had nothing to do with this. Honest," Shane says.

Michael shrugs. "Big, tough Notre Dame *man*. Not so tough now, is he?"

Speechless with horror, she retreats outside. Honestly, the guy is such an asshole. She can't tell Reid what Michael did. He'll never want to see her again.

She surveys the frozen lake. There are only a handful of trucks left. Everyone has headed home to hunker down before the storm. They need to leave as soon as Reid is well enough to drive.

⟶

"We should go," Courtney urges. "The weather's bad. I think we're the last ones on the lake, and it's going to be dark soon."

The whole afternoon has been a disaster. Poor Reid.

While Michael packs up the cooler, Courtney pulls Josh aside, "Did you know about the laxative?"

"What are you talking about?" He's so drunk, he's totally out of it.

It's dusk, and snow gusts across the ice. The temperature has dropped. Reid sits in one of the jump seats in the back of his truck. He looks pale and weak.

"Are you up to driving?" she asks.

"Not really," Reid says. "But I'm the only one with a licence. My vote is that we stay here and wait out the storm."

"It's only ten minutes to our cabin," Josh says, swaying. "I can drive that far."

"But you're drunk," Courtney says.

"Then let me do it," Michael offers. "Dad lets me drive him all the time when he's wasted."

"Courtney, you're sober. You should drive," Shane says.

Her stomach flips. "I don't know how to drive a stick."

"Neither do I," Shane says.

"It's easy," Josh says.

"Have *you* ever done it?" she asks.

He shakes his head.

She looks at Reid. "It's your truck."

"Better you than the others. Hopefully, we won't run into any cops," he says.

Courtney climbs in the driver's seat and steps on the clutch—like she saw Reid do—and turns the key in the ignition. Shane and Josh get in the back with Reid. Michael takes the passenger seat. Reid coaches her on the gear positions.

"Roll down your windows," she says.

She stalls a few times. Michael laughs while she tries to get the knack of releasing the clutch and pressing the gas pedal. Then—success. The truck eases ahead. She accelerates and grinds gears as she shifts to second.

"Give it gas," Reid says, "or you'll stall again."

The back end fishtails. Michael howls and pounds the roof. Snow slants across the windshield. What if she drives into a fishing shack?

"Turn on the wipers," Josh slurs.

She fumbles for the knob. "I can't see very well."

"Drive slow then," Reid says. "No rush. Keep heading east."

She hopes they're headed east.

They crawl along. No one gets out to check the thickness of the ice. What if the truck breaks through?

Reid groans.

"Do you need me to stop?" Courtney asks.

"No. I got nothing left. My guts just hurt."

The truck lurches and bounces as they leave the ice.

"We're back on shore," Michael says.

Courtney closes her window. "Buckle up."

"Bossy," Josh murmurs.

Courtney drives slowly, praying she stays on the grid road. The truck is climbing—a good sign. She breathes a sigh of relief when she sees the barbed wire fences on either side of the road. Once they get to the intersection, they can stop at a farm and ask for help. The flat light and swirling flakes make her feel disoriented. What if she drives in a ditch? She eases off the gas, and the truck sputters.

"Step on it," Michael says. "I wanna get to the cabin. I gotta take a leak."

He leans across her, blocking her view. His foot presses on hers, and the truck accelerates.

"Stop it!" she says. "We're going way too fast!"

"What's going on up there?" Reid demands.

Michael's left elbow spears her ribs. He swats at the knobs on the left side of the dash. Snowflakes swoop at the windshield.

They hit a finger drift, the truck shudders, and Reid grunts when Josh lands on top of him.

"What did we hit?" Shane asks.

Courtney tries to wiggle her foot from under Michael's, but he pushes harder.

"Keep going," Michael says.

The next snowbank is massive. She turns the wheel to avoid it as Michael tromps hard on her foot. They careen towards the ditch. She cranks the wheel back, and they're airborne.

Glass splinters. Metal groans and squeals. The spinning stops as the storm rushes in.

6 2

WHEN I WALK INTO MBP, Dave's on his phone, pacing and waving his baseball cap. "You damn well better find them." He ends the call.

"What's wrong?" I ask.

He looks like he's going to throw up. "Cami's skates are missing."

"What?"

Dave paces while he explains. He sent a half dozen pairs, including Cami's, to a local sport store for "flat bottom hollow sharpening." No time for him to look after all our blades, which took a beating from last night's seven periods of hockey. This morning, a hockey parent came into the store and picked up Cami's skates by accident. The store staff and most of the Huskies Game Day personnel have been combing Saskatoon's rinks ever since.

"I'd rip my hair out if I thought it would help," Dave says. "And I've still got skates to do. Will you wait here and see if anyone shows up with Cami's? Basil's watching the main entrance."

"Sure. Does Cami know about this?"

"Not yet," he says. "I'm hoping I don't have to tell her."

No kidding. Cami's not just our captain. She's our points leader.

"Is she here yet?" I ask.

He nods. "She's getting a massage. There're tables set up in the concourse. I think every student-trainer on campus is up there." Dave walks away, muttering to himself.

Tightness creeps into my shoulders, back, and calves. A massage would feel so good, but I promised him I'd wait here.

I check my phone. No messages.

I call Dad to see if he's in Saskatoon yet but get his voicemail. Then I text Courtney to see how ice fishing went. No reply. I could text Mom, but I just had lunch with her. I text Liam and tell him about Cami's skates.

He texts right back.

Isn't there another pair at the sports store?

Even *he* doesn't get it.

I root in my knapsack for my sociology notes and sit on the floor with my back against the wall. Might as well make use of the time.

Cooker, a fourth-year, walks in. I can tell she's favouring her left shoulder. She hurt it last night when she dumped the puck down the ice and got hit into the boards on a line change. Just one of several playoff casualties.

"What'd the doctor say?" I ask.

"Slight separation," Cooker says. "The kind I can play with. Thank goodness for drugs and freezing." She disappears into the dressing room.

Next, Diane, our team manager, bustles by with an armload of black jerseys. "Honour the streak!" she calls over her shoulder.

"That's why I'm wearing the sports bra from Game One!" I call back.

Superstitions and streaks are inseparable. Our team decided to wear the black uniforms for playoffs, and we haven't lost in them yet. Two times we had to wear our white uniforms because it was our opponent's home game and both times we lost.

A while later, there's a commotion at the end of the hallway. Dave skips towards me, holding a pair of skates above his head like he's hoisting the Stanley Cup.

"We got 'em!" he shouts before he makes a sharp left into our dressing room.

At last! I can get ready.

I text Liam to tell him the good news, but he doesn't reply.

Doesn't he care I'm about to play in a Canada West final?

63

METAL CREAKS. ICE CRYSTALS POKE her eyelids. She smells gasoline. Snow gusts through the wound where the windshield used to be. Is she dead or dreaming? Panic squeezes her chest. Blood pulses in her ears. Where the hell is she? *Who* is she?

Something drips from her chin to her forehead. Her arms dangle. She's hanging from her seatbelt, and she has to get down. Now!

She takes a deep breath. Her right arm fights gravity and finds the latch. Will she land on broken glass? She cradles her head and neck with her left arm and releases.

Click.

She drops in an awkward mass on the truck roof. She squirms to get her body and legs under her and avoid the steering wheel.

A moan.

She peers around the driver's seat. Two bodies sway in the back. Shane and Reid.

"Are you okay?" Courtney's voice rasps in her ears.

Reid stirs, arms bending at the elbows. He shakes his head. His toque is gone. He looks weird with his reddish blonde hair hanging like that.

"How are you?" she asks.

"I've been better." His voice calms her.

Reid releases his own latch and rearranges his long limbs in the confined space. The side windows are still intact, but the snow hurled through the windshield gathers in the cracks and crevices.

"I'll get Shane down," Reid says.

Courtney's hands are cold. Where are her mittens? Was she wearing them when they rolled?

"I don't suppose Michael's up there with you," Reid says.

She shoves the panic down. "He must have been thrown out when we rolled. Josh too."

Are they even alive?

Shane comes to—as if awaking violently. He flings his arms and screams.

"It's okay, buddy." Kneeling, Reid grabs him around the waist. "Courtney and I are here. We'll get you down."

Click.

"I got you," Reid says as Shane slumps into his arms.

While he eases Shane into a sitting position, Courtney lies down so she can look outside. She sees only snow.

"Have you got your phone?" Reid asks. "I was holding mine when we rolled. No idea where it went."

"Mine's gone too," Shane says mournfully.

Courtney unzips her pocket and pulls hers out. "No service."

"Damn," Reid says.

She peers out the side window. "We have to find the others. How much daylight do you think we have left?"

Shane sobs softly.

"We should stay here," Reid says. "That's what makes sense."

"Nothing makes sense." Courtney looks around. "The roof is only slightly buckled, and most of the windows weren't knocked out. Maybe we didn't roll that many times." She tucks her hands into her sleeves and uses her elbows to commando crawl out the gap in the front.

"Where are you going?" Reid demands.

"Just to have a look," she says over her shoulder.

She wriggles from under the hood and stands, using the frame for support. The truck's headlights are still on, but there's no sound except for the wind. Her hair whips her face, and her clothing snaps.

"Josh!" she calls. "Michael!"

She circles the truck, still calling their names. The snowy curtain parts, and a figure limps towards her.

"Josh!" she shouts. "Over here!"

She hurries to help him, slipping an arm around his waist. "Are you all right?"

He laughs then groans. "I think one of my ribs is broken, and my ankle's kinda wobbly."

How drunk is he still?

"You're lucky if that's all you hurt," Courtney says. "Did you see Michael?"

"Nope."

Reid climbs out from under the truck.

"Did anyone call 911?" Josh asks.

"No service," Reid says.

"There's a farm up the road," Courtney says. "It's not far."

"We should stay here," Reid says.

"We'll freeze to death. And Michael's out there somewhere. We need help." Courtney closes her eyes, visualizing the road to the lake. "There was barbed wire on either side of the road and power poles to the south. If I can find the road, I can walk to the farm."

She can no longer feel her feet or the tips of her fingers as she releases Josh and turns in a slow circle. No landmarks. No buildings. Nothing but stones and dead grass poking through the snow-sculpted prairie. The wind holds its breath, and thin shapes emerge.

Power poles.

"Over there!" she shouts, pointing. "The road's that way!"

"Are you sure?" Josh asks.

"Positive!" she says. "Once I get to the road, as long as I keep the poles on my right, I'll find that farm."

"No," Reid says.

"I have to do it, and you know it," she says.

She doesn't wait for him to talk her out of it. She snugs up the strings of her hood and starts walking. Fixes her gaze on the horizon. Closes her eyes—one then the other—as her tears freeze. She nearly trips on something. It's a side mirror from the truck. She comes upon more twisted debris. Fishing tackle. Pieces of the cooler. Something dark cartwheels across the snow.

A jacket.

"Michael!" she calls.

When she stoops to grab the jacket, a wind gust threatens to blow it away.

"Michael!" she calls again.

Another dark shape sprawls on the ground to her left.

"Michael!" she shouts.

She battles the wind and kneels beside him. He's splayed like a rag doll. She puts a hand on his back and is relieved when it rises and falls. She bends over and lays her cheek against his cold ear.

"Michael, can you hear me?" She sits back and watches his face.

His lips move. She places her hand on his forehead, but her own flesh is so chilled, she can't find the warmth in his.

"The others are going to be okay, Michael. And you are too. We're going to help you."

She senses rather than hears movement behind her. Josh and Reid drop beside her.

"What—"

"Carson, you young bugger!" Josh announces joyfully. "How's it going, man?"

"We followed you," Reid says. "To get you to come back. How'd you find him?"

Courtney shivers. "I saw pieces of the truck and some other stuff."

"Should we take him back to the truck?" Josh wonders, patting Michael's head.

"What if we hurt his neck?" Courtney swats Josh's hand away. "We could paralyze him."

"Well, he'll freeze to death out here," Reid reasons. "At least we can keep him out of the wind. We'll drag him over the snow once we get him on his back."

The lesser of two evils.

"Okay," Courtney says. "I'll hold Michael's head, and Josh, you hold his legs, while you two flip him over." Courtney cups her frozen hands over Michael's ears. "We can zip him inside his jacket." Once the jacket is in place, she says, "Ready, Josh? Do exactly what we tell you."

"Okay," Josh says.

"We'll turn him towards Josh on three," Reid says. "You count it, Courtney."

"One. Two. Three. Lift," she says.

When they turn him, Michael screams and faints. Courtney prays they aren't doing more damage as they zip him, arms at his sides, inside his jacket.

"We'll take turns dragging him." Reid reaches inside Michael's jacket to grip his shirt collar. "I'll go first."

The truck is a hunk of metal in the middle of the pasture. Josh grabs Reid's belt to guide his backwards steps. It seems to take forever—with Josh and

Courtney each taking Reid's place for a stint—before they get Michael under the truck and out of the wind.

"You found him!" Shane, huddled in the cab, sounds more like himself.

"Yep," Josh says.

"I'm going to try this again," Courtney says to Reid. She looks for and finds the power poles. "I'll be back with help. Soon."

Her sneakers break through the shin deep crust. Why did she wear ankle socks today? Why didn't she put on winter boots? A toque? Thank goodness she's got a parka.

She sidesteps the debris a second time then stumbles and nearly falls across a boulder. She finally reaches three humming strands of barbed wire, and the wind snatches her shout of victory. She steps on the bottom strand, hunches, stretches the middle one up, and pivots between. Her sleeve snags on a barb, but she tears the fabric free. She loses her footing on the steep decline of the ditch, flounders in the snow, and ascends the opposite side. Exultant, she tops the grid. The road will take her from here. She takes a few strides then kicks it up. Hurdles a drift. Settles into a run.

6 4

Sunday, March 2nd
Canada West Final (Game 3/Best of Three)
University of Saskatchewan vs. University of Regina Cougars
Merlis Belsher Place, Saskatoon

THE MUSIC IS LOUD, AND A CHEER erupts each time a hero video plays on the MBP jumbotron. The fans are rocking already. I can't find Mom and Dad in the stands, which isn't a surprise, considering how full this place is.

I'm still feeling the pain of yesterday's one hundred forty minutes of lung-sucking, leg-grinding hockey. I'm hoping our warm-up will be short.

"People were lined up an hour and a half before the game," Kathy says when I position myself behind her for the next drill. She gestures broadly. "Did you ever dream MBP would be *this* full?"

"Nope. But you know half these people are cheering for the Cougars," I point out.

"Don't get me started," Kathy says.

When we leave the ice for the flood, Coach is talking to Liam outside our dressing room. Their faces are grim, and I know right away something's wrong.

"Liam's got some news, Jessie," Coach says.

Fear squeezes my chest.

"You need to call your mom," Liam says. "Courtney's okay, but she was in a rollover."

What in the hell?

"But I had lunch with Mom this afternoon. And Dad's driving up from—"

Liam's hands rest on my shoulders. "They're on their way to Estevan."

My knees turn to water. "My phone," I say weakly.

"Use mine," Liam says.

Coach gives me a quick hug. "Don't worry about the game. If you need to go, go." He steps into our dressing room.

My eyes blur as I stare at Liam's screen.

"I'll dial," he says.

I wipe my nose. "How did you find out?"

"Your mom called me. She wanted to wait until she saw Courtney before she got you worked up, but she was afraid you'd hear about it through social media. Here she is."

"Mom?"

"Oh, Jessie, I'm so glad you called." Mom's voice trembles. "Did Liam tell you?"

"Yes. What happened?"

Mom's explanation makes no sense. Drinking underage. Courtney driving with no licence. Making life and death decisions in a Saskatchewan blizzard.

"Michael's hurt the worst," Mom says. "He was thrown from the truck, and he's in ICU in Regina. Josh was thrown too, but his injuries are minor. Courtney has a few stitches on her forehead and some frostbite. Shane has a concussion. Reid doesn't have a scratch."

"Sounds like they got off lucky—except for Michael. Where's Courtney now?"

"St. Joe's. We just talked to Dr. Bilku. He'll release her when we get there. Will you please call your sister? She wants to hear from you."

"Of course."

"Don't forget to tell her what Courtney did," I hear Dad say.

Mom takes a deep breath. "Jessie, your sister ran to a neighbouring farm to get help. How she had the presence of mind to even *find* it in that storm, I'll never know. Word got out quickly and local people showed up to lead the paramedics to the kids. STARS flew Michael to Regina. He wouldn't still be alive otherwise." She pauses. "I'm sorry we'll miss your game."

"Mom, stop. You need to be with Courtney. I'll call her right away."

"Thanks. We love you, Jessie."

"Love you too."

Courtney picks up on the second ring. "Hello, Jessie." She sounds exhausted.

"Mom told me about the accident, so you don't have to explain anything," I say.

She sighs.

Beeping and a voice on the PA fill the silence.

"Jessie?"

"Yeah, sis."

"I feel so guilty. For months I've wished he'd disappear. And now—" Her voice catches.

"Don't beat yourself up. Everyone's alive. That's the important thing," I assure her.

"But I only found him by *accident*. What if—"

"Don't think about that. You're all alive right now. Focus on that."

She blows her nose. "I'm sorry to dump this on you. You have a big game tonight."

"It's okay. You're the only person that matters right now."

"But what's going to happen? I shouldn't have been driving. The truck is wrecked, and Michael's parents hate me. What if they sue Mom and Dad?" Her voice rises with each word.

It takes me a while to talk her down from that ledge. "You can't worry about that now," I conclude.

She blows her nose again. "Thanks, Jessie. I should go now. Reid's mom is here."

"I'll talk to you in the morning," I say.

"I love you, Jessie."

"Love you too, little sis."

I press End and hand the phone to Liam. A sob shakes me as I cling to him. That rollover could have torn a hole that time would never fill.

"Tissue?" Liam asks.

I wipe my eyes and blow my nose.

"Do you want me to drive you back to Estevan?" he asks.

The dressing room door opens. Faces radiate concern as my teammates troop past. Coach must have told them. Robbie and Dan each give me a shoulder squeeze. Kathy and Darian stop to throw their arms around me.

"Little Mac okay?" Kathy whispers.

"She's fine," I whisper back.

"You do what you need to do," Darian says.

As they move on, the MBP announcer intones, "The University of Regina Cougars!"

A train horn bellows, and the Cougar fans respond. I visualize our opponents hitting the ice, and my hockey heart quickens.

"And your University of Saskatchewan—"

A second horn roars.

"Didn't know we had one!" I shout at Liam while the crowd lifts the roof off MBP.

"I hear Gresch's dad bought it!" he shouts back.

I stare down the causeway that leads to our players box.

Liam puts an arm around my shoulders. His lips hover by my ear. "This is your call, Jessie."

Melinda's sweet voice rises with our anthem, and the crowd joins in. Liam steps back as I take off my helmet. I shift from skate to skate and stretch the muscles in my neck. Tonight, the female Huskies could win their first ever Canada West title. How can I not be *here*? Melinda lets her crowd take over, and robust voices carry the song to its conclusion.

I wipe my eyes, put on my helmet, and fasten the snaps of my visor.

Liam places his forehead against mine. "I'll be here to watch you. Every second. Play your heart out, and when this is over, I'll drive you home."

"I might be a while," I tell him.

"Even better," he says.

As I walk to the exit, I pass Dave. He tips his baseball cap, and I salute him with my stick. The crowd roars as I step out of the image of Courtney lost in a blizzard and into the pride, passion, and purpose of Game Three. Nerves and fears dissipate.

Tonight, I'll leave it all on the ice.

6 5

THEY'RE ON THEIR WAY OUT of St. Joseph's Hospital when Dad's phone rings.

"Is it Jessie?" Mom asks. "I never even thought to check on the game."

Courtney's exhausted. Every muscle aches. Her bones feel displaced. She can't bear the thought of anything standing between her and her bed.

Dad tucks the phone under his chin as he fumbles in his jacket pocket for his keys. "This is not a good time." He opens the driver's door.

Who's he talking to?

"It's late," Dad continues after a few seconds. "She's been through a lot today. I know you have too. How is he?"

Could be Josh's mom. Or Clint. Or Abby. Maybe Mrs. Bonokoski?

Courtney climbs into their SUV and tries not to think about the twisted roof and hood of Reid's truck.

Dad hands the phone to Mom. "Put him on speaker."

"I wanted to thank you for what you did for Michael. For all the boys." Mr. Carson's voice cracks. "Courtney, I don't know to repay you."

Is he drunk?

"I do," Mom says. "Your son has serious issues—beyond the injuries he sustained in this accident. I really hope he makes it, and when he does, he needs professional help."

Ragged sob.

"You need to straighten him out before he gets behind the wheel of a car," Mom says. "Won't he be getting his learner's licence this year?"

Mom's back, Courtney thinks. *This* is Mom.

"I have to go," Mr. Carson says. "But I'll think about what you said."

He hangs up.

"Well, that was totally unexpected," Dad says.

Will Michael's dad remember Mom's warning tomorrow? Or will he find a way to rationalize Michael's behaviour? Will Michael even *live?*

The phone rings again.

"Now that's Jessie." Mom answers the call and presses Speaker again.

"We won!" Jessie shrieks. "We won!"

66

"DO YOU HAVE ANY IDEA what a *frustrating* season this was?" Coach holds up his big hands and paces off the left side of my iPhone screen. "We had seventeen one-goal games. *Seventeen*," I hear him say. "And we win the title with a 2-1 win in double OT?"

"At least we stuck to the pattern." I recognize Darian's voice. She's sitting next to Kathy.

Where I should be sitting.

Instead, I'm rocketing down Highway 11 with Liam in his truck while Kathy FaceTimes me from our dressing room. For the first time in the history of our program, the female Huskies are Canada West champs. I'd love to still be there.

After Willo scored the OT winner, I spilled over the boards. I cried and hugged my teammates. I trembled during the medal ceremony and posed for the team photo with our Canada West banner.

On my way out of the rink, I passed Cami, still wearing her gear and Canada West medal as she cooled down on a stationary bike. She saluted me with a beer. "Thanks for keeping an eye out for my skates!"

Liam and his truck, engine running, waited for me outside the rear entrance.

Erv's voice brings me back to the present. "I don't know about you, ladies, but I'm not taking off this medal. *Ever!*"

"Me neither." I hold up my own.

"There's blood on mine," Cassidy says. "Got a nosebleed during the celebration."

Liam reaches over and squeezes my knee.

"Blood, sweat, and tears, ladies," Robbie says off screen. "That's what it's about."

"Speaking of blood."

Kathy bobbles her phone but manages to find Gresch.

"Near the end, I block a shot, blow up my finger, and I'm getting stitches. Again." Gresch points to the other set, a souvenir from Game Two, on her chin. "I hear a horn and screaming, but I don't know *whose* horn or *whose* fans. How brutal is that?"

In the background, Coach rambles about the mental, emotional, and physical strain of our low-scoring, high stakes series with the Cougars. So many team leaders stepping up. So many individuals contributing in small ways for big success.

"Power play sucked tonight." Dan's dark hair is wild. "And thanks, Chun, for that unsportsmanlike thirty seconds into OT so we could play four-on-four. So appreciated."

"You're welcome," Chun says.

"Still." Dan folds his arms over his chest. "This weekend you ladies played seventeen *incredible* periods. You showed complete and utter persistence. You were fearless."

Izzie sobs.

"Keep it together girl," Paige says.

I'm having the same problem. I dig in the console for a napkin and blow my nose.

"This is something you'll never forget," Dan continues. "And neither will I. Thanks for letting me be a part of it. Now have some fun. You earned it." He pumps his fist and walks off screen while my team erupts.

Ceiling. Floor. Faces. Did Kathy toss her phone in the air?

Finally, Kathy's back, and her blue eyes are red. "Mac, don't you love it when a hockey heart melts?"

"I do."

"Can you feel your legs yet, Jessie?" Darian asks.

I remember the sensation of them being too weak to lift me onto the bench. "Not really. They'll hurt tomorrow."

"Doesn't matter," Darian says. "We're going to *Nationals*."

I can see both my linemates now, and they are the most beautiful young women in the world.

"Three more games, Mac," Kathy says. "Two pool. One final. We're gonna bring home hardware from Fredericton. You wait and see."

"I can't think about it yet." Concern for my sister and exhaustion wash over me. "I'm going now, ladies."

"Sleep well, champ," Darian says.

"Give Little Mac a hug from me," Kathy says.

I press End.

"What a game." Liam shakes his head. "I'm proud of you, hockey girl. And I wouldn't have missed it for the world."

"Me neither." I cushion my head with my Huskie jacket and close my eyes.

Three more games. Three games. Three . . .

67

March 7
Estevan Moose vs. Weyburn Co-op Wings (Game 3/Best of Three)
Tom Zandee Sports Arena, Weyburn

JOSH'S STEPDAD HUGS COURTNEY the minute she enters the rink lobby. Then Josh's mom nearly smothers her. "Thank you. Thank you so much. You have no idea." She sobs and shudders.

"What you did was absolutely heroic," Austin's mom says. "We're so proud of you."

The rest of the Moose parents line up to congratulate her too. Courtney searches amongst them for Reid or his mom or his sister. She hasn't seen Reid or even talked to him since the accident, and she hasn't had the nerve to reach out first. After all that's happened, he probably wants nothing to do with her.

A man who looks vaguely familiar shoulders his way to the front of the crowd, and Mom steps up to block him.

Who is *he*?

"Mrs. McIntyre, I'm from the *Mercury*. I've left a few messages, but no one has gotten back to me. I'd like permission to interview Courtney."

"That's up to her," Mom says.

He's the same reporter who took her picture when she shaved her teammates' moustaches. He drove to Weyburn to talk to her?

When Josh's mom finally releases her, Courtney dumps her hockey bag at her feet so no one else can get close. "I have a playoff game, and I don't know where my dressing room is."

Abby appears like a vision. "I do. Come with me, sweet girl."

"Maybe we could talk later?" The reporter steps around Mom. "What you did is a big story, Courtney. A *really* big story."

Maybe to him it is. To her, it's a stream of What Ifs that shock her wide awake in the middle of the night. What if she hadn't found Michael? What if Josh had been hurt just as bad? What if—

"In the meantime, can I please get a picture?" He holds up his camera. "With the ice surface in the background. Kind of fitting."

Fitting would be snow-crusted fields. Stinging cold. Ragged breath. A farmyard looming.

Muttered prayers.

Someone be home. Someone please be home. Please God.

Click.

"Thanks so much," the reporter says.

"You're sure you're okay to play?" Josh's mom asks.

"She's fine." Dr. Bilku says. "These McIntyre girls are tough."

"Michael's injuries are staggering. I hope he recovers," Austin's dad says as Courtney drags her hockey bag through her crowd of admirers. Hands reach out to pat her arm or shoulder. Murmurs of approval.

Her equipment bumps against her calves—a bump for each of Michael's injuries.

Two collapsed lungs.

All but two ribs broken.

Broken femur.

Two broken shoulder blades.

Broken left shoulder joint.

Broken nose and forehead.

Several spinal fractures—fortunately not serious.

Small brain bleed.

Lacerated liver and spleen.

"This is it." Abby stops in front of a door and gives Courtney a hug. "That's from Clint." She squeezes tighter. "This one's from me. You have no idea how glad I am you were there."

Unable to speak, Courtney pushes open the door.

Behind her, Josh calls. "Wait up!"

He limps towards them, hockey bag slung from one shoulder.

"Josh, you're not playing today," Abby says.

"Try to stop me," he says.

"What about your ankle? And your ribs?" Abby argues.

"That's what tape is for." When he reaches them, he puts his weight on his right foot.

"This is not a good decision," Abby says.

"I've made worse." Josh leans on his stick. "Courtney, I've got news. Did you hear Michael's off the ventilator?"

"Thank God," Abby says.

Courtney blinks to stop the tears.

Josh puts an arm around her shoulders and tugs her against his side. "He's gonna be okay."

Courtney has a full head of steam as she charges up the right wing. At Weyburn's blue line, Josh fires her the puck. When it hits her blade, it springs into the air, and her eyes track it. Something crushes the side of her head. Lights explode, the world tilts, and she's flying. Her belly smacks the ice and expels air from her lungs. Pain radiates through her jaw. She can't breathe. Stars and flashes blind her.

Blades scrape. Someone roars. Socks and skates. F-bombs. More skates. She wants to cover her head, but her arms feel so far away. Whistles blow.

Jutin's face hovers near hers. "Are you okay?"

Courtney sucks air. "No." Her voice rasps in her ears.

Boots appear, running and sliding.

"There's a stretcher coming, Courtney. Don't move," Clint says.

She has no intention of moving. "What happened?" she croaks.

"Elbow to the head," Abby says.

"That jerk blindsided you, Courtney," Austin says.

How many injuries has she had this year? It hurts her brain to think.

Clint shifts away and yells, "Guys! Enough!"

She closes her eyes. More swearing. Grunts.

"Straight to the dressing room," Clint says.

Scraping.

She opens her eyes.

Josh takes a knee across from Abby. His cheeks are red and blotchy. His lower lip leaks blood.

"Where's your helmet?" Courtney asks.

"Are you okay?" he demands.

"Sure she is. Get out of here," Abby says. When he's gone, she leans close and whispers in Courtney's ear, "If he tells you later he wasn't defending your honour, he's lying. Here's the stretcher, sweet girl. Do whatever they tell you."

6 8

As soon as the Fasten Seatbelt sign goes out, Coach slips into the empty seat next to me. "Mac, I heard you've got video of that U15 brawl."

"Yup." I dig for my phone.

"Josh's mom shot it," Kathy explains. "It's epic."

"Your sister's okay though, right?" Dean, one of our goalie coaches, peers over the seat ahead of us.

"Yeah. She was in St. Joe's overnight, but our doctor sent her home." I scroll, set up the footage, and hand my phone to Coach.

I know the video by heart. I can tell exactly what's happening by watching Coach's face.

Courtney's open. Josh throws the puck up to her before she hits the Weyburn blue line. The puck flips in the air, and Courtney looks up as 8 elbows her in the head. She goes down—in Dan's words—like "a sack of spuds." The fact that Courtney's okay makes the collision easier to watch.

But the rest is the stuff of legends.

Josh tackles 8 from behind and knocks him down while Jutin and Austin huddle protectively over Courtney. Josh throws haymakers as Weyburn 16 and 14 pull him off their teammate. When the ref intervenes, Josh swings at him.

Then Shane and Brandon join the brawl, and Josh punches them too.

"He's out of control," Coach says.

"Possessed," Kathy says.

Now comes the part when the camera pans to show the Weyburn goalie leaning on his crossbar. He raises his mask and reaches for his water bottle as Toby barrels in from the right side of the screen and takes him—and the net— into the boards. That's when Josh's mom drops her phone.

"Wow," Coach says.

He restarts the video. Pauses and plays.

"8 lined her up," Kathy says.

"Totally," Coach says. "Can I show this to Robbie and Dan?"

"They've already seen it," Kathy says.

Coach hands me my phone. "Hospitals are a habit for your sister, aren't they? How'd the game finish up?"

"It took half an hour for the ref to sort the penalties, and he handed out a schwack. The player who hit Courtney was ejected, as well as Josh and a bunch of other knuckleheads. The Moose ended up with four skaters and no goalie. They lost 16-3." I tuck my phone in my pocket. "U15 season is officially over."

"In a blaze of glory," Coach says. "But not ours. Right, ladies?"

A chorus of cheering erupts.

"Fredericton here we come!" Kathy shouts.

March 13
National Championship Pool Game 1
University of Saskatchewan vs. University of Montreal Carabins
Grant-Harvey Centre, Fredericton
Huskies 3-0 Loss

March 14
National Championship Pool Game 2
University of Saskatchewan vs. St. Thomas Tommies
Grant-Harvey Centre, Fredericton
Huskies 3-2 Win

March 16
National Championship Bronze Medal Game
University of Saskatchewan vs. Laurier Golden Hawks
Grant-Harvey Centre, Fredericton

"Wish we had another shot at the Carabins," I say to Kathy as we step off the ice after our warm-up.

Nerves and penalties got to us in our first pool game against the University of Montreal. And that loss put us out of gold medal contention.

"But we didn't come all this way to go home empty-handed, right?" Kathy says. "Better bronze than fourth."

"No doubt." I turn to look for my dad in the stands. I find him, sitting with Darian's girlfriend Melinda and Walter Myers, and I wave.

Courtney couldn't fly with her concussion, and Mom stayed home with her. I wish with all my heart that they were here, and Liam too.

In the hall between the ice surface and our dressing room, we pass Pete, who's giving our goalies a final pep talk.

"Still keeping an eye on the ladies, Pete?" I tease.

Pete waves a hand. "What happens in Montreal stays in Montreal."

Our team arrived in Fredericton ahead of a snowstorm that created havoc with subsequent flights. Many Huskie fans, including my dad, arrived without their luggage.

Some of our female personnel—namely Vanessa, Diane, and Trina the Trainer—were storm stayed in Montreal. Coach called Pete, whose own flight had been delayed, to ask him to keep an eye on them. Pete ended up taking them for lunch—accidentally—at a bar that featured exotic dancers. He was mortified, but the women thought it was hilarious.

As we assemble in our dressing room and make adjustments to our equipment, Coach reviews our game plan.

"Stick to it, and push hard," he concludes. "This is a big stage. Don't let it get to you."

"Don't let it get to *you*, Coach of the Year," Darian quips.

Coach, who took top honours at the U Sports banquet on Wednesday night, looks pleased and embarrassed. "Couldn't have done it without you ladies. Robbie, any words of inspiration?"

Robbie bites her lip and wipes her eyes.

Honestly, we're all going to start crying if she's not careful.

"I want you ladies to know that nothing you do today could disappoint us," she says. "Be brave. You deserve to be here."

"Willo for sure does," Erv says. "We've got the top rookie in the nation. Who's going to stop us?"

Willo smiles. "Shucks, Erv."

Dan clears his throat, and we turn to him. His dark hair is neatly combed, but it's sure to come unleashed as the game ahead of us unfolds. "You show everyone that Canada West is the toughest division in this country, and that the Huskies are the toughest breed."

Kathy howls, and we join in. We bark and yip as we leave the dressing room. I calm my butterflies through the pre-game rituals and the anthem. I focus on the flag and resist the urge to crowd surf. I already know who's here. The tournament organizers are blown away by the large contingent of Huskie fans. So far, I've managed to avoid Izzie's brother Scott. The anthem ends, and the starters from both teams square off. The puck drops, and the bronze medal match is underway.

As our first two lines clash with the Hawks' best players, the pace is fast with action at both ends of the ice. When the Hawks score on a rebound, Dan sends Kathy, Darian, and me to neutralize their speedy first line. We're gasping when we finish our shift. The Hawks take a penalty at the midway point, and our first power play unit boxes them in. Hanna passes to Flinton, who blasts a shot from the point.

Scores!

Gresch's dad fires up the train horn. Kathy and I grin at each other while we pound the boards with our gloves. The horn got storm-stayed in Montreal, and when it finally arrived, the Huskie dads drove past our hotel in a rental car, train horn blaring, to make sure we knew.

"Did you hear some McGill parents offered him $2500 for it?" Kathy yells as Flinton and the others run our bench. "He wouldn't sell! What a guy!"

At the end of the first period, we're tied 1-1 and outshooting the Hawks 11-9.

"Keep pressuring them," Coach says in the dressing room.

The Hawks set us on our heels in the second. I'm battling in the corner for the puck when Kathy forces a Hawk to take a hooking penalty.

"Guess we'll find out if our power play units have done their homework," Kathy says as we return to the bench.

Cami, Willo, and Erv pen the Hawks in, and Flinton scores again from the point.

We're up by a goal!

The Hawks forecheck hard. They outshoot us. We take penalties defending, but our PK has been perfect.

In the corner, I tussle for the puck with a Hawk D. She punches me, I punch her back, and we're issued coincidental roughing minors. The Hawks put one past Cassidy, and we're tied up.

Damn.

I return, head down, to our bench.

"Let it go, Mac. Shit's gonna happen when you play with intensity," Dan says to me.

A heartbeat later, the Hawks take two minutes for holding. Our power play units hem them in, and Flinton scores her third goal.

Hat trick!

Dave hurls his baseball cap onto the ice. More hats follow, and the officials scoop them up.

When the second period ends, we lead the Hawks 3-2.

"Our power play's killing 'em. You're making me eat my words, ladies," Dan says in the dressing room.

The Hawks score short-handed less than a minute into the third, and our power play unit returns to the bench, tails dragging.

Dan jerks his head at Kathy, Darian, and me. We scramble to shut down the Hawks' top line. We're trapped in our end, but we force them wide, and we don't give them scoring chances.

On a power play, Gresch wheels past the Hawks' D and scores on a backdoor rebound. A few minutes later, the puck pops loose in the slot, and she fires it in again.

"I can almost taste that bronze medal," Kathy says as we skate to centre ice for the faceoff.

I smack her arm. "Don't say that. You know how fast the ice can tilt in their favour."

We keep battling. The Hawks are outshooting us, but they're not outplaying us.

"We can do this," Darian says to me as we line up for a faceoff. "They're running out of time."

We battle to win our shifts. Give our top lines a chance to rest.

As the clock ticks down, the Hawks' coach pulls the goaltender, and Erv seals the deal with an empty netter.

The buzzer sounds, and we spill onto the ice, shrieking.

"We're bringing home the hardware!" Kathy shouts.

We hug and cry and congratulate each other. We've won the last game of the season.

We won't need any ice packs today.

69

"YOU ARE GOING DOWN THIS TIME," Christina says.

"Not a chance." Courtney adjusts her grip on the remote.

"Hurry up," Aiden says. "I get to play the winner, remember?"

They're playing "Avengers" on Xbox. Courtney knows she can beat Christina. She usually spots her a few rounds to build her confidence, but Aiden is unbeatable.

Aiden came down from Regina last night to spend the weekend. Yesterday was the first time Courtney saw her since last November. Aiden got a funky haircut, and her long, razored bangs are dyed blue.

"Courtney, you've got some visitors," Mom calls from the top of the basement stairs. "Are you up to it? There's quite a few."

Courtney puts down the Xbox remote. "Sure!"

Mom steps aside, and the Moose thunder down the stairs. Is it the whole team?

"Hey, how are ya?" Toby asks.

"Good," Courtney says.

"Hello, Shane," Christina says.

"Hi, Christina," Shane says. His cheeks are flaming.

Are *they* going out?

Brandon stares at the ground.

"Courtney, introduce us to your friend," Jutin says.

"This is Aiden," Courtney says. "She played with the Regina Buffaloes."

"Hey, Aiden." Shane gives her a little wave. "Nice to see you."

The other boys shift uncomfortably, clear their throats, and look everywhere except at Aiden.

"Aiden's been kicking our butts on Xbox all morning," Courtney says.

"She is ruthless," Christina says.

"Nice," Shane says.

"Maybe Christina and I should go upstairs," Aiden offers. "This looks like a team meeting."

"Thanks," Courtney says. "It won't take long."

Aiden, head high, glides through the pack. Christina walks past Brandon without acknowledging him, but her hand brushes Shane's. Courtney can't see Christina's face, but she can see Shane is beaming.

Well. Well. Well.

She realizes that the team is staring at her.

"What are you waiting for?" she asks. "Make yourselves at home."

Austin and Jutin wrestle over the recliner. Toby and Shane pile onto the sectional next to Courtney. Josh lingers at the bottom of the stairs, and Brandon leans against the wall. Austin wins the recliner battle. Jutin and the rest park themselves on the floor.

When they're finally settled, Courtney asks, "What's up?"

Toby grins. "Just wanted you to know we're thinking about ya."

"As if the texts and snaps aren't proof enough," she replies.

"We heard you're going back to girls hockey next year," Austin blurts.

"Yeah, I might," she says.

"But you can't," Toby protests. "You're a Moose."

"Correction. I *was* a Moose," Courtney points out. "Season's over, and Josh made sure no one forgets it."

Josh digs his hands deeper in his pockets.

"Funny you got nothing to say, Thompson," Toby observes.

"I appreciate your concern for my welfare, Josh," Courtney says, "but promise me you'll never take on an entire team, the officials, and your own teammates again."

Josh shrugs, but he moves closer to the sectional.

"You know that isn't gonna happen," Brandon says.

"How's your head, Courtney?" Jutin asks.

"Okay. My neck's still sore though."

"And you're still going with Bonokoski?" Shane asks.

"I have no idea." Courtney folds her hands in her lap. "But I hope I am."

She wishes she had the guts to call Reid.

"So, you're going to Notre Dame then," Austin concludes, looking at the others. "Didn't I say this would happen?"

"You're going to Notre Dame because of some *guy?*" Brandon accuses.

"Does your mother know?" Jutin asks.

"Look, if I go, it won't be because of Reid," Courtney says. "But I like the idea of playing AAA—if I can make a team somewhere."

"Like your *sister*," Shane says.

"You need to live your own life," Brandon asserts.

They look so serious.

Courtney shakes her head. "I'm tired of looking after you guys."

"McIntyre, you're the closest thing we had to a team leader this year," Josh says.

Wow.

"Not a captain," he adds. "You got a bit to learn about the game. But in terms of here—" He points to his heart—"you taught us a lot." He taps his temple. "And this. Man, Courtney, you give new meaning to the phrase 'mental toughness.'"

Tears sting her eyes.

"Even though you clearly have trust issues," Austin interjects. "You need to work on that."

"Shut up, Austin," Jutin says.

"What Josh means—is we want you to play U18 next year," Toby says.

"But it won't be the same," Courtney contends. "We'll end up on different teams. Some of you might even play AA."

"Yeah, that's true," Toby admits. "But if any one of us was on *your* team, we'd be honoured."

Courtney flicks away a tear. "Thanks."

"There's one more reason we came over." Shane leans closer. "Some of us are going to St. Joe's to see Michael."

"He's back in Estevan?" she asks.

"As of today," Josh says. "Will you come?"

"I don't think that's a good idea." Courtney picks at a piece of lint on her leggings. "I'll wait till he's out of the hospital."

"He wants to see you," Brandon says. "He asked me to ask you."

Her head swims.

Josh moves closer. "In the meantime, we should let you get back to your jam. See ya, McIntyre." He reaches out a hand.

She stands to shake it, then realizes all the boys want her to do the same. She shakes Shane's hand last and realizes she's looking him in the eye.

"How'd you get to be so tall?" she asks.

"Testosteroni," he says.

7 0

OUR CHARTERED CITY BUS PULLS up in front of MBP for the last time.

"This is it, ladies," Coach says. "It's been a great ride."

My limbs are heavy as I grab my stuff and follow my teammates off the bus. Most of us still wear our bronze medals. Diane, our team manager, wears hers as she sleeps near the front. She's got dark patches under her eyes. I reach out to wake her, but Vanessa, one of our goalie coaches, stops me.

"Let her catch a few more zzs," she whispers. "She's had quite a week. The week of her life."

"Of all our lives," I whisper back.

"Anyone up for green beer? It's St. Paddy's Day," Kathy says as I step off the bus.

Groans. Everyone's still recovering from a night on the town in Moncton, where we stayed before catching the red-eye home. It's been a long day of airports and airplanes.

I grab my equipment from under the bus.

"All in all, it was a great season," Dave says as he hands me my suitcase. "Kicked some ass. Took some names. Finished third in the nation—though we were never ranked higher than eighth. And you, Mac, played that bronze medal game like it was your last."

A March gust rips off his ball cap, and Dave chases it.

"Welcome to Saskatchewan!" Darian calls.

"Looks like your ride is here, Mac," Kathy says.

Liam waves at me from beside his truck.

"Anybody else need a ride?" I ask.

"Nah, you better give McArthur your full attention." Kathy hugs me. "It's been a blast playing with you, sista."

"Same." I nearly choke on the word.

Darian hugs me too. I have no words for her, and she has none for me. Come to think of it, we don't need any.

Liam tosses my suitcase and hockey bag in the back of his truck. "For a bronze medalist, you look worn out."

"I need to get to bed," I groan. "But thanks for calling me that."

He opens his door and I climb across the seat. The truck is toasty warm, and the glare of the sun on snow is blinding. I buckle up and close my eyes. All those highs and lows, ending in a high. I'm so tired. . . .

"Jessie."

"Hmm?"

"We're here."

I blink and try to focus on the unfamiliar, residential street. I must have fallen asleep—again. "Where are we?"

"I got a new place," Liam says. "No more crummy basement suite. Come on. I'll show it to you."

I'm too exhausted to care, but I unbuckle and crawl to Liam's side. I slip on the icy pavement, and he steadies me.

The house is hidden behind a huge spruce and cedars wrapped in burlap. There are more spruce in the backyard and large empty plant pots.

"This must be beautiful in the summer. Too bad you won't be here then," I say as he unlocks the back door.

He ushers me inside. "Who says I won't?"

The sunken living room overlooks the backyard. The kitchen and dining room are lit by the south sun. There are three bedrooms down the hall. One of them, the one also overlooking the backyard, has been converted to an office.

"How did you get this place?" I ask.

"The owners moved into assisted living. They rented it to me for six months—with an option to rent for another twelve if things work out," he explains.

"But how can you afford it?" I ask.

"Well, a few things have happened lately."

"Okay." I stifle a yawn.

"First off, I got a job at VIDO for the summer."

"Wow. Vaccine and Infectious Diseases."

His gap-toothed smile is wide. "And I picked up a couple of scholarships."

The shoe drops. "You got into vet med."

His smile widens.

I squeeze him hard. "Oh, Liam. That's fantastic."

"What would you think about us moving in together next year?"

His question takes me by surprise. I take a deep breath. I'm swirling in a tidal wave of emotions already, and he wants me to think about *this?*

"You don't need to decide right now," he says. "Take all the time you need."

I can hardly hear him above the hum of white noise. I walk into the bedroom across from the office, close the door, and collapse on the bed.

What a great ride it was.

And it's over.

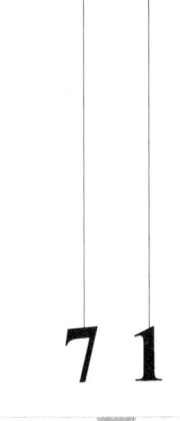

71

MICHAEL'S MOM OPENS HER FRONT door. She looks like she hasn't slept in weeks. Her jaw drops when she sees Rufus.

"Is it all right I brought him?" Courtney asks. "Michael likes him."

Mrs. Carson nods and leads them into the den. The blinds are drawn. The floor and coffee table are littered with textbooks, video games, and takeout containers. Michael, arm shielding his eyes, lies on the couch.

"Mikey, some of your teammates are here," his mother announces. "Can I get the rest of you anything? Coke? Apple juice? Water?"

"Water would be nice," Shane says.

"Coke for me," Josh says.

"Diet Coke," Toby says.

Courtney looks at him.

"Pam says I could drop a few pounds," he explains.

"I'm fine," Courtney says.

Mrs. Carson disappears into the kitchen.

"Hey, Michael, how are ya?" Toby asks.

"You shouldn't have come," Michael says.

He looks young, helpless, and damaged. Courtney surveys the cast on his leg.

The injuries to his face. The bruises. The bandages. How is he even comfortable? He must be on a ton of painkillers.

"We got a bit of a history," Josh says.

"We had to see the Miracle Kid for ourselves," Shane says. "The last time we saw you—"

"I don't want to talk about it," Michael mumbles.

"Maybe I should go." Rufus licks Courtney's neck.

"No, *we* should." Josh disappears into the kitchen. "But we won't be far away."

Toby follows him. Shane gives Courtney a little push and points to the chair beside the couch before he steps out of the room.

Why does *she* have to talk to Michael alone? After all he's done to her?

Courtney perches on the edge of the chair. When Rufus whines, Michael reaches out a hand. Rufus licks it. Courtney sets Rufus on the couch, and the little dog curls up beside him. She hates the way Rufus responds to Michael, but maybe the dog knows more about him than she does.

"I read the article about you in the newspaper," Michael says. "The reporter wanted to interview me too. But I never." He strokes Rufus' ears. "You didn't tell him or the cops what I did. How come?"

Courtney sighs. "I thought it would make things worse. And things were bad enough. When I talked to the cops, I didn't know if you were going to live or die."

"Did you tell Reid about the laxative I gave him?" he asks.

She shakes her head. "Not yet. Again—what would be the point?" She wonders if Michael's dad told him what Mom said about getting professional help.

"I've done some lousy things to you," Michael says. "I can't count how many."

"Would you like me to tell you?" she asks.

"Not really." He shifts his body a little and winces.

Rufus puts his head on Michael's stomach.

"Do you need something?" she asks.

"Yes. I need to say something." Michael's voice breaks. "I need to say I'm sorry. I don't know why I cared so much about making you quit. It seems so stupid now."

"Yeah, it was stupid. What you did was not okay," she says. "But I forgive you."

He sucks in his breath and lets it out slowly. Rufus snuggles closer.

The other boys come back into the living room with their drinks.

Michael holds out his hand, and she stares at it. She's said she's forgiven him, but she's not sure she means it. Not after all he's done to her. Does she really have to *touch* him?

Josh tries to stifle a belch, but it finds an alternate route. The fart is long and loud and squeaks at the end.

"Thanks for sharing that," Toby says.

"Anytime," Josh says.

Saved by a fart.

"Nice that you've forgiven Michael," Reid says. "But if he doesn't treat you any better when he comes back to school, you should go to the police. He could be playing you again."

Courtney shifts her phone to her left ear. "I don't think he is. He seemed sincere."

"Time will tell," Reid says. "Courney, I'm sorry I didn't call till now. How often does a guy shit himself into oblivion in front of the girl he's hoping to impress? I was humiliated."

What a relief.

"That's understandable," she says. "I'm sorry about your dad's truck. Was it totalled?"

"Pretty much, but it didn't kill any of us. That's the main thing."

Awkward silence.

"So, are we a thing?" she asks.

"A thing?"

"Yeah. Are we going out? Are we friends? You seem interested. But you've never . . . you know."

"I've never what?"

His tone is playful. Why is he making *her* say this?

"You've never made a move or anything." She heaves a sigh. "I'm making a fool of myself."

"No. You're not." He clears his throat. "I don't know what we are either. And as for making the first move, I was waiting on you."

"Me?"

"You're Estevan's poster girl for gender equity. Why should I have to do it?"

If he was here right now, she totally would.

The doorbell rings. Of all the rotten timing.

"Look, I gotta go. Somebody's here, and Mom and Dad are in the backyard." She gets off the couch and walks to the front door.

"Who is it?" Reid asks.

"No idea." She opens the door.

Reid stands on her porch, back turned, phone tucked between right ear and shoulder.

"You!"

Reid tucks his phone in his back pocket and, turning to face her, spreads his palms. "Let's see what you got, Crash."

7 2

"BURGER OR HOT DOG?" Dad asks. "Cheese or no cheese?"

While we place our orders, Dad loads up the barbecue.

Reid walks into the backyard. Good deal.

It's my birthday. Mom and Dad wanted me to invite a bunch of friends, but Liam and I are headed to a street dance in Lampman tonight. We have a lot to pack in on the weekends he comes home from Saskatoon.

"Jessie, I can't believe you're twenty already," Mom says. "Where did the time go?"

I know exactly where. To practice and dryland. Faceoffs and power plays. Penalties and breakaways. Wins and losses. Banter and laughter. Hugs and tears.

"When are you going to tell everyone?" Liam whispers.

"Pretty quick," I say.

My phone bings.

It's a snapchat of Ethel—the Ethel Cartwright Trophy—at a country music concert. All summer, the Canada West trophy will be making the rounds to the hometowns of the Huskies. Ethel even has her own Twitter account.

Reid rolls up his sleeves and helps Dad man the barbecue. Dad and Reid have gotten along since the day Reid helped take down the backyard rink. Fair to say, my parents think Courtney could do worse.

"Jessie, what time's your slow-pitch game tomorrow?" Courtney asks.

"11:00. Why?"

"Can I come with you? Jade's playing against the Lampman boys team."

"By herself?" Dad asks.

Ever the comedian.

"No, Dad," Courtney says patiently. "She's playing with the Redvers boys. She's supposed to be as good at baseball as she is at hockey." She pauses. "I think I'd like to try baseball next year."

"Oh no. Here we go."

I must have said it out loud because Courtney's brown eyes blaze at me.

"Easy now," Liam breathes.

"Can we talk about that later, Courtney?" I say before she gets wound up. "Mom. Dad. There's something I need to tell you."

Drum roll.

Mom's eyes dart to Dad, who balances a cooked burger on the end of his flipper.

"I'm quitting the Huskies."

Mom lets out her breath. Dad drops the burger, and Rufus darts from under Mom's chair and chows down. I bend down to pick up the dog, but it's too late. That burger is toast.

Instead, I rub my hands on my shorts. "I can't do it anymore. I love playing too much."

"Jessie, that makes absolutely no sense," Courtney says.

"Actually, it does," Reid says.

"Nothing in my life will ever come close to what that playoff run felt like," I say.

Dad looks crushed. "When did you decide?"

"Months ago."

I made the decision when I saw Cami's skates on Dave's sharpener and realized what it takes to be a fifth-year. I knew I would give it all this season, but I also knew I would hang up my own skates at the end.

"Hockey has always been there for me when I needed it, but I don't need it anymore," I say.

"Have you told your coaches?" Mom asks.

"After I wrote my last exam," I explain. "Robbie and Dan were ticked. Coach tried to talk me out of it for ten minutes. It was thrilling he tried."

"What did he say?" Courtney asks.

Liam nudges me. "Tell them."

"He said I'm a phenomenal utility player." I stare at the patio block under my feet. "He said all he needed was to point me in a direction, and I'd do whatever it took." I raise my head and lock eyes with Mom. "Well, I'm pointed in a new direction now."

I tell my family about my notion of doing quantitative analysis for Indigenous Affairs after I graduate. A career like that would merge what I've learned in my mathematics, history, and psych classes.

"Jessie, I'm so proud," Mom says.

"It might mean a postgraduate degree," I add. "I could go to school my whole life and still not cover everything."

"Let's try to avoid that." Dad wipes his eyes. "Your mother and I would like to retire before we're eighty."

"And you know what else?" Courtney says. "I'm going to be a doctor one day."

My parents' mouths dangle. I'm pretty shocked myself.

"Makes sense," Reid says. "You spend a lot of time in the hospital."

Mom and Dad fawn over her, buzzing. She'll need to excel in her sciences in high school. U of S has a great program. Aim high. Stay focused. Anything is possible if you try really hard. I suddenly feel insignificant.

"What do you think?" Liam whispers.

"About what?"

"About your baby sister being a doctor."

I shrug. I can't put my feelings into words.

"What if she plays AAA for the next three years?" Liam asks. "What if she turns out to be good enough to play U Sports—and gets into medicine? How will you deal with that?"

Now I know the feeling, and it's not jealousy. It's competition. It's in our McIntyre DNA, and if we tap into it, it'll take us as far as we can dream.

Acknowledgments

Truth time.

I have been wanting to write a fourth book in the Jessie Mac Hockey Series since 2014. Julia, I'm sorry it took a global pandemic to force me to knit a story together. I hope I've done justice to you and your teammates.

I have taken some liberties with the history of the University of Saskatchewan Women's Huskies. They did not in fact win the Canada West title in Merlis Belsher Place. They won it in good old Rutherford Rink in 2013-14. I apologize to the real-life Huskies who were shoved to the side to make room for my fictional players. Chelsey Sundby, Paige Anakaer, and Cassy Jorgenson were the *real* muckers and grinders on the third line. Reaching Nationals was a momentous achievement for the Huskie women. If you haven't already done so, please check out a women's university team in your province or state. You'll be glad you did.

As for Courtney's story, a friend remarked to me long ago, "You need to write about hazing. It's a part of hockey culture that some people can't let go of." I'm heartened to see the approach that SHA and Hockey Canada have adopted. On a lighter note, my daughter Robin's experiences playing (and coaching) boys hockey inspired a few scenes, and I might have also tapped some memories of Estevan Junior High band trips.

It takes a village to write a book, and that's a good thing. These folks helped me hone and authenticate Courtney and Jessie's experiences: Blaire Ulrich (my sharpest critic and most fervent cheerleader), Robin Ulrich, Randy Ulrich, my enthusiastic Estevan Writers Group, Jeanne Martinson (my eagle-eyed publisher), Sharon Plumb, Marie Powell, MaryAnne Veroba, Tim Hubic, Mathias F, Kasenya E, Sherlene R, Kruz S, Kody Scholpp, Steve Kook, Basil Hughton, Julia Flinton, Juanita McArthur Big Eagle, Drumlin Cape, Sunny Houssain, the Jasmins, Dr. Amanda River, and Doug Casler. Many, many thanks.

Maureen Ulrich – Author

Maureen Ulrich was born in Saskatoon, Saskatchewan but grew up in Edmonton and Calgary, Alberta. She started writing horse stories when she was eleven and historical fiction during her high school years. In 1976, Maureen returned to Saskatoon to attend university and graduated in 1980 with an education degree. Her first teaching assignment was Lampman, Saskatchewan and she has pretty much lived there ever since.

She has been writing plays for young people since 1997. Two titles *Sam Spud: Private Eye* (2007) and *The Banes of Darkwood* (2010) are available through www.samuelfrench.com. Maureen has also written and produced several professional adult productions: *Snowbirds* (2015), *Diamond Girls* (2016-2018), and *Lords of Sceptre* (2018-2019). Souris Valley Theatre in Estevan, Saskatchewan produced her full-length musical *Pirate Heart* (2018), scored by the incomparable Ben Redant.

Maureen's poem "Ode to Penelope" was recently published in the Saskatchewan Writers' Guild anthology, *Apart: A Year of Pandemic Poetry and Prose*.

In her free time—of which there is not a great deal—Maureen loves to read, travel, knit, golf, ski, ride her motorcycle, and hang out at rinks, football stadiums and ball diamonds. Please visit her on Facebook, Twitter, Instagram, or maureenulrich.ca.

Book Club Questions

1. Allusion is an indirect or passing reference to something. Courtney and Christina read *The Wonderful Wizard of Oz* by L. Frank Baum for their Grade Nine English Language Arts class. Can you find allusions to events, characters, or themes from this famous book throughout *Shootout?*

2. A motif is a dominant or reoccurring idea in an artistic or literary work. Look for evidence of a dog motif in *Shootout.*

3. How do Jessie and Courtney positively influence their hockey teams? How do their teams influence each of them?

4. Can you find instances of shootouts—challenging confrontations between characters—that occur *off* the ice in *Shootout?*

5. Who is your favourite character in *Shootout?* Why? Who is your least favourite?

6. What event would you say is the climax of Courtney's storyline? Of Jessie's? Why?

7. Foreshadowing occurs when authors give hints or clues of what is to come. Did you foresee the ending of *Shootout?* What hints or clues were provided along the way?

Did you miss the first three books in the *Jessie Mac Hockey Series*?

Jessie McIntyre, 14, is new to Estevan, and she's having trouble fitting in. By signing her up with the local girls hockey team, her parents hope to give her a fresh start and help her make new friends. But bullies can be found everywhere—even in the dressing room. Will Jessie be able to find a way to protect herself and find acceptance?

Jessie McIntyre, 15, has it made. She's got the world's best boyfriend, great teammates, and a hockey coach she really looks up to. But a bad decision at a party changes everything. Worse, some of the guys at school seem determined not to let her, or anyone else, forget it.

Jessie McIntyre, 17, starts her last year of minor hockey—and high school—with loads on her mind. Her AAA team is short a head coach, her future plans are unclear, and some of her teammates aren't impressed with her new role as team captain. On top of it all, her little sister is making some lousy decisions while Jessie's parents seem unaware. But, hey, should Jessie be critical? She's made some pretty bad ones herself—especially when it comes to guys.

Julia Flinton – The Player

The five years I spent playing hockey at University of Saskatchewan were some of the best years of my life. The memories I have from that time spring up at random moments, making me laugh or cry. Some of the most memorable moments were the Canada West Championship, Nationals in Fredericton, bus rides, one-on-ones with Robbie, and of course all the girls.

After my five years at the U of S, I moved back to BC to my hometown of Williams Lake. I worked as a Wildland Fire Fighter for seven years before I had my daughter Eilidh with my partner Anthony. We both now work in Williams Lake and help with the family ranches, hoping to one day have a ranch of our own.

The Jessie Mac Dictionary

Assist – a point awarded to up to two players who have successively touched the puck immediately before a teammate scores a goal

Backcheck – return to the offensive zone and check attacking opponents

Backhand – a pass or shot made by striking the puck with the back of the stick's blade

Bag skate – when a coach tries to tire out a team by using skating drills in practice, usually for punishment

Beauty (or beautician) – slang for a talented player or, more often, a player who is fun to be around; the highest praise

Bench penalty (or bench minor) – a penalty given to the team as a whole and served by a single player, usually because the coach was "mouthing off" at officials

Bench Run – a celebration where the players on the ice for a goal skate past their own box and tap their teammates' gloves; the line is generally led by the goal scorer

Biscuit – slang for puck

Blocker – a glove fitted with a rectangular pad; a goaltender wears a blocker to protect the hand holding the stick

Blue line – one of two lines between the centre red line and the goal

Blueliner – a player who plays defence

Boarding – a penalty issued for bodychecking a player into the boards with excessive force

Body contact – a penalty issued in women's hockey or in non-contact hockey for giving a bodycheck

Bodycheck – using one's body to separate a player from the puck

Boxed – slang for a female player being hit by a puck, stick, or skate in the genital area

Breakaway – a long rush towards the goal after passing all the defenders

Breakdown – a collapse or mistake made by the opposing team

Breakout – a strategy used when opposing players are near or behind the net; the defence attempts to quickly move the puck up the boards to a winger or the centre

Bucket – slang for helmet

Bye-weekend – no games scheduled for that weekend

Canada West – division of U Sports which includes university teams from British Columbia, Alberta, Manitoba, and Saskatchewan

Celly – slang for goal celebration

Centre – the middle player, usually highly skilled, on a forward line

Centre ice – the central area of a rink; the spot where faceoffs take place at the start of each period and after each goal

Charging – a penalty issued for a forward attack of more than two steps against a member of the opposing team for the purpose of taking him or her out of the play

Checking-from-behind – a bodycheck in the middle of the back that sends an opposing player, sometimes headfirst, into the boards; the offending player is ejected from the game

Cheese (or cheddar) – slang for a puck shot into the net's top corner, or "top shelf"

Cheese Wagon – a school bus used for transporting hockey players

Cherry picker – a player who hangs out at the opposing team's blueline, out of the play, waiting for a breakaway pass; definitely not a compliment to be called one

Chicklets – slang for teeth

Chirp – slang for backtalk

Circuit Training – using weights and machines to build muscle and strength

Clearing (the puck) – moving the puck past a team's own blue line

Crease – a semi-circular area, usually in blue, in front of a hockey net into which the puck must proceed the player

Crossbar – the horizontal bar between two upright bars on a hockey net

Cross-check – a penalty given when a player holds a stick horizontally in both hands and thrusts it at an opposing player's body

D – slang for a player on defence

Defence – one of two players assigned to protect the goal from attack, also defender

Deke (or dangling) – a fake movement or shot to draw a defensive player or goaltender out of position, thereby creating a scoring opportunity

Dirty (or filthy) – an adjective of high praise, (for example, a "filthy" goal is a nice one)

Drop Pass – when a player passes the puck backwards, sometimes through his or her skates

Dub – slang for the WHL or Western Hockey League

Dump-and-chase – a strategy in which a player shoots the puck into the opposing team's end and then chases after it

Dryland – off-ice training

Faceoff – the action of an official starting or restarting play by dropping the puck between two opposing players' sticks

Faceoff dot – each of the nine circles where faceoffs may be taken, including one at centre ice and four in each end, situated to the left and right of the net

Fan (on a shot) – missing the puck entirely with the stick blade

Five-hole – slang for the gap between a goaltender's parted legs through which a puck can pass

Flamingo – when a player lifts his or her leg to avoid blocking a shot; this practice is frowned upon by teammates

Flow – slang for hockey hair; generally long and free; a compliment

Forecheck – an aggressive style of defence; checking opposing players before they can organize an attack

Forward – an attacking player positioned near the front of the team

Goal judge – a volunteer who sits behind the goal and turns on a red light if the puck goes into the net

Goalpost – either of two upright bars on a hockey net

Goalie pads – a pair of thick rectangular pads worn on the legs of a goaltender; sometimes referred to as "pillows"

Goaltender – a player stationed to protect the goal

Goose Egg – a zero; no goals scored

Greasy (or garbage) goal – a loose puck or rebound shot into the net

Hash mark – one of four short lines on the edge of each faceoff circle

Hat Trick – when a player scores three goals in one game; in a "true" hat trick, the three goals are scored consecutively

Haymaker – the mother of all punches

Healthy Scratch – an uninjured player who doesn't dress for a game; depending on the league, only a certain number of players can dress.

Hooking – a penalty given for an illegal check where a player attempts to hold back or hinder an opposing player by tugging with the stick blade

House hockey – a level of minor hockey open to any child or youth who signs up; the SHA encourages these coaches to give equal ice-time to all players

Ice (the puck) – shooting the puck from one's own half of the rink to the far end or other half, which is permitted only while killing a penalty

Ice-time – the amount of playing time a player logs during a game; great players play thirty minutes out of sixty; for those players (and parents) who are deadly serious about hockey, there's no such thing as too much ice-time

Icing – an infraction for shooting the puck to the other half of the ice, in which case the referee stops the play and a faceoff is held in the offending team's end

Interference – the illegal blocking or hindering of an opposing player

Jill – clothing worn by female players to protect the genital area

Left wing (left winger) – a forward whose position is to the left of the centre

Lettuce – slang for hair (for example, a moustache might be termed "lip lettuce")

Linemate – one of three players who plays on the same forward line as another

Linesperson/linesman – an on-ice official whose role is to make offside or icing calls and break up fights

Major Junior – the highest level of men's amateur hockey in Canada which includes the Western Hockey League (WHL), Ontario Hockey League (OHL), and Quebec Hockey League (QMJHL)

NCAA – National Collegiate Athletic Association; the US equivalent to U Sports

Neutral Zone – the area at centre ice between the two blue lines

Offence – the act of attacking in order to score goals

Offside – an infraction where an opposing player crosses the blue line ahead of the puck in which case a faceoff is called outside the blue line

One-timer – receiving a pass and striking the puck with the stick blade at the same time

Passing lane – any open space on the ice through which a player can move the puck to his or her teammate

Pipes – slang for goalposts

Penalty – a punishment for breaking a rule in which case a player is temporarily removed from the game and his or her team is forced to resume play with one less player; the length of a penalty is generally two minutes, but may go as high as four, five, or ten minutes, or in extreme cases, can result in the player's removal from the game

Penalty box – an area of seating near the timekeeper's booth for players who have been temporarily withdrawn from play because of a penalty

Penalty Kill – when a team must play with one or, in some cases, two less players because of a penalty; also called PK

Penalty killer – a player, usually highly skilled, who plays while his or her team is reduced in strength due to a penalty

Penalty shot – a breakaway shot by an offensive player on the goaltender, allowed as the result of a penalty

PIM – Penalties in Minutes; a statistic often tracked besides goals and assists

PK – slang for penalty kill

Penalty shot – a breakaway shot by an offensive player on the goaltender, allowed as the result of a penalty

Plus-Minus – a statistic indicating a player's effectiveness on both offence and defence, adjusted every time an even-strength goal is scored while the player is on the ice, with one added to the cumulative score if the player's own team scores and one subtracted if the opponent scores; ideally a player's plus-minus should be a high positive integer (for example, +30)

Point (a shot from the point) – either of two areas to the right or left of the net, just inside the blue line where it meets the boards

Poke-check – pushing the puck off an opposing player's stick with one's own blade

Power play – when a team has a one or two player advantage over the opposing team because the latter is killing a penalty; having a power play greatly increases the opportunity to score

Red line – the centre line on the ice surface midway between the two blue lines

Referee – an official, authorized to issue penalties, who supervises the game to make sure the players obey the rules; wears a black and white striped jacket with a red arm band

Regulation Win/Loss – when a team wins or loses within sixty minutes of "regular" time

Right wing (right winger) – a forward whose position is to the right of the centre

Ringette – a game resembling hockey, often played by girls and women, with a straight stick and a rubber ring

Rink rat – a small child, often unsupervised, who runs amuck in the rink lobby; usually found in packs

Roughing – a penalty given for unnecessary or excessive use of force

Rubbing out – using body position along the boards to separate an opposing player from the puck; generally allowed in women's hockey

Rushing (the puck) – bringing the puck up the ice, often without passing to another player

SaskFirst – an SHA program designed to provide better understanding of the game as well as promote the development of quality players, coaches, trainers, officials, and administrators.

SHA – Saskatchewan Hockey Association

Saucer – shooting or passing a puck so that it passes overtop the sticks of opposing players, also known as "chuckin' sauce"

SFU18AAAHL – Saskatchewan Female Under 18 AAA Hockey League; made up of teams from Regina, Saskatoon, Prince Albert, The Battlefords, Weyburn, Athol Murray College (Notre Dame), and Swift Current; until 2019, Melville Prairie Fire participated in this league

Shift – a relay of players on a team; usually two defence and three forwards

Shinny – informal or "pick-up" hockey; usually played without full equipment on a neighbourhood rink

Shootout – a method of deciding the outcome of a game, which would otherwise end in a tie; each team takes a specified number of penalty shots; the team that scores the most wins the shootout and the game; a shootout occurs after a sudden death overtime

Shorten (the bench) – when a coach puts the best players on the ice; the opposite of "rolling lines"

Short-handed – slang for penalty killing; not having the usual number of players on the ice

Short-handed goal – when a team scores a goal while playing with fewer players, especially while killing a penalty

Shutout – when the opposition doesn't score a single goal in a game; winning goaltenders love a shutout

Sin bin – slang for penalty box

SJHL – Saskatchewan Junior Hockey League

Slashing – a penalty given for striking or swinging at an opposing player with one's stick

Slapshot (clapper) – a hard shot taken by raising the stick blade at or above waist height before striking the puck

Slew foot – to trip an opposing player by using one's own skates

Slot – an unmarked area in front of the net which is considered an excellent scoring position for an offensive player; low slot is closer to the net than high slot

Snipe – a skillful goal, usually top shelf, performed by a "sniper"

Soft hands – slang for the ability to take and give passes with finesse

Special teams – a combination of players that are trained for penalty killing or the power play

Split the D – when an offensive player maneuvers between the two defensive players

Stop time – when the game clock is stopped between plays

Straight time – when the game clock is not stopped between plays; often used for younger players or if the score is very one-sided

Sudden death – an extra period (overtime) to decide a tied game, in which the first team to score wins

Sweep – winning a series without any losses, for example winning three games out of three; rather demoralizing for the losing team

Taco-in-a-Bag – a rink delicacy consisting of a bag of Nachos filled with taco meat, shredded cheddar, lettuce, tomatoes, sour cream, and salsa; usually eaten with a fork while sitting in the stands or talking about a magnificent goal after a game

Time out – a stoppage of play called by the coach so that the team can consider or discuss strategy or attend to an injured player

Toe drag (toey) – an evasive move where the puck carrier drags the puck along the ice with the toe of the blade faced down then pulls back to cause a defender to lunge forward while the dragger or "dangler" skates past

Top Shelf – the highest part of the net, just beneath the crossbar

Toque – a close-fitting knitted hat, sometimes with a tassel or pom-pom on the crown; standard attire for hockey players

U13 – a team with 11 and 12-year-old players (under 13 years old)

U15 – a team with 13 and 14-year-old players (under 15 years old)

U18 – a team with 15, 16, and 17-year-old players (under 18 years old)

U Sports – the organization of Canadian university sports, formerly CIS (Canadian Intercollegiate Sports)

Unsportsmanlike – a penalty given for unprofessional or unseemly conduct (for example, pulling the hair of an opponent or swearing at an official)

Wheeling – 1. stickhandling through opposing players. 2. trying to impress or get the attention of an individual you're interested in (off-ice)

World Junior Hockey Championships – an annual, international U20 male hockey tournament which begins on Boxing Day and ends in early January; players for each nation are generally selected from Major Junior and NCAA teams; many of these individuals have already been scouted for the National Hockey League

Wraparound – when a player attempts to score by coming from behind the net

Wrist shot – a shot taken by sweeping the puck along the ice with a fluid motion before releasing it

Zamboni – a tractor-like machine used to shave snow off the rink and replace it with a fresh flood of water to create a smooth skating surface